C000297726

MEMOIRS OF
JOSEPH GRIMALDI

CHARLES DICKENS

MEMOIRS OF JOSEPH GRIMALDI

PUSHKIN PRESS
LONDON

For Max

First published in 1838 as
Memoirs of Joseph Grimaldi

This edition first published in 2008 by
Pushkin Press
12 Chester Terrace
London NW1 4ND

ISBN 978 1 901285 94 9

The Afterword is an edited version of Appendix B to
Memoirs of Joseph Grimaldi edited by Richard Findlater
© MacGibbon & Kee Ltd 1968

Cover: *Joseph Grimaldi* John Cawse 1807
© National Portrait Gallery London

Frontispiece: Charles Dickens courtesy of
The Library of Congress Prints and Photographs Division

Set in 9.5 on 12 Monotype Baskerville
and printed in Great Britain
by TJ International

MEMOIRS OF
JOSEPH GRIMALDI

CHAPTER ONE

THE PATERNAL GRANDFATHER of Joseph Grimaldi was well known both to the French and Italian public as an eminent dancer, possessing a most extraordinary degree of strength and agility—qualities which, being brought into full play by the constant exercise of his frame in his professional duties, acquired for him the distinguishing appellation of 'Iron Legs'. Thomas Dibdin, in his *History of the Stage*, relates several anecdotes of his prowess in these respects, many of which are current elsewhere, though the authority on which they rest would appear from his grandson's testimony to be somewhat doubtful. The best known of these, however, is perfectly true. Jumping extremely high one night in some performance on the stage, possibly in a fit of enthusiasm occasioned by the august presence of the Turkish Ambassador, who, with his suite, occupied the stage-box, Grimaldi actually broke one of the chandeliers which hung above the stage doors; and one of the glass drops was struck with some violence against the eye or countenance of the Turkish Ambassador aforesaid. The dignity of this great personage being much affronted, a formal complaint was made to the Court of France, who gravely commanded 'Iron Legs' to apologise, which 'Iron Legs' did in due form, to the great amusement of himself, and the Court, and the public; and, in short, of everybody else but the exalted gentleman whose person had been grievously outraged. The mighty affair terminated in the appearance of a squib, which has been thus translated:

Hail, Iron Legs! immortal pair,
Agile, firm knit, and peerless,
That skim the earth, or vault in air,
Aspiring high and fearless.
Glory of Paris! outdoing compeers,
Brave pair! may nothing hurt ye;
Scatter at will our chandeliers,
And tweak the nose of Turkey.
And should a too presumptuous foe
But dare these shores to land on,
His well-kicked men shall quickly know
We've Iron Legs to stand on.

This circumstance occurred on the French stage.

The first Grimaldi who appeared in England was the father of the subject of these memoirs and the son of 'Iron Legs'. Holding the appointment of dentist to Queen Charlotte, he came to England in that capacity in 1760; he was a native of Genoa, and long before his arrival in this country had attained considerable distinction in his profession. We have not many instances of the union of the two professions of dentist and dancing-master: but Grimaldi, possessing a taste for both pursuits and a much higher relish for the latter than the former, obtained leave to resign his situation about the Queen soon after his arrival in this country, and commenced giving lessons in dancing and fencing, occasionally giving his pupils a taste of his quality in his old capacity. In those days of minuets and cotillions private dancing was a much more laborious and serious affair than it is at present; and the younger branches of the nobility and gentry kept Mr Grimaldi in pretty constant occupation. In many scattered notices of *our* Grimaldi's life it has been stated that the father lost his situation at court in consequence of the rudeness of his behaviour, and some disrespect which he had shown the King, an accusation which his son always took very much to heart, and which the continual patronage of the King and Queen bestowed upon him publicly, on all possible occasions, sufficiently proves to be unfounded.

His new career being highly successful, Mr Grimaldi was appointed ballet-master of old Drury Lane Theatre and Sadler's Wells, with which he coupled the situation of *primo buffo*; in this double capacity he became a very great favourite with the public and Their Majesties, who were nearly every week accustomed to command some pantomime of which Grimaldi was the hero. He bore the reputation of being a very honest man, and a very charitable one, never turning a deaf ear to the entreaties of the distressed, but always willing, by every means in his power, to relieve the numerous reduced and wretched persons who applied to him for assistance. It may be added—and his son always mentioned it with just pride—that he was never known to be inebriated: a rather scarce virtue among players of later times, and one which men of far higher rank in their profession would do well to profit by.

Grimaldi's father appears to have been a very singular and eccentric man. He purchased a small quantity of ground at Lambeth once, part of which was laid out as a garden; he entered into possession of it in the very depth of a most inclement winter, but he was so impatient to ascertain how this garden would look in full bloom, that, finding it quite impossible to wait till the coming of spring and summer gradually developed its beauties, he had it at once decorated with an immense quantity of artificial flowers, and the branches of all the trees bent beneath the weight of the most luxuriant foliage, and the most abundant crops of fruit, all, it is needless to say, artificial also.

A singular trait in Mr Grimaldi's character was a vague and profound dread of the fourteenth day of the month. At its approach he was always nervous, disquieted, and anxious: directly it had passed he was another man again, and invariably exclaimed, in his broken English, "Ah! now I am safe for anoder month." If this circumstance were unaccompanied by any singular coincidence it would be scarcely worth mentioning; but it is remarkable that he actually died on the fourteenth day of March (in fact, the sixteenth); and that he was born, christened, and married on the fourteenth of the month.

These are not the only odd characteristics of the man. He was a most morbidly sensitive and melancholy being, and entertained a horror of death almost indescribable. He was in the habit of wandering about churchyards and burying-places for hours together, and would speculate on the diseases of which the persons had died; figure their death-beds, and wonder how many of them had been buried alive in a fit or a trance; a possibility which he shuddered to think of, and which haunted him both through life and at its close. Such an effect had this fear upon his mind, that he left express directions in his will that, before his coffin should be fastened down, his head should be severed from his body, and the operation was actually performed in the presence of several persons. It is a curious circumstance that death, which always filled the older Grimaldi's mind with the most gloomy and horrible reflections, and which in his unoccupied moments can hardly be said to have been ever absent from his thoughts, should have been chosen by him as the subject of one of his most popular scenes in the pantomimes of the time. Among many others of the same nature, he invented the well-known skeleton scene for the clown, which was very popular in those days, and is still occasionally represented. Whether it be true, that the hypochondriac is most prone to laugh at the things which most annoy and terrify him in private, as a man who believes in the appearance of spirits upon earth is always the foremost to express his unbelief; or whether these gloomy ideas haunted the unfortunate man's mind so much, that even his merriment assumed a ghastly hue, and his comicality sought for grotesque objects in the grave and the charnel-house; the fact is equally remarkable.

This was the same man who, in the time of Lord George Gordon's riots (in 1780), when people, for the purpose of protecting their houses from the fury of the mob, inscribed upon their doors the words '*No Popery*'—actually, with the view of keeping in the right with all parties, and preventing the possibility of offending any by his form of worship, wrote up *No religion at all*; which announcement appeared in large characters in front of his house, in Little Russell Street. The idea was perfectly successful; but whether from the humour of the description, or because the rioters did not happen to go down that particular street, we are unable to determine.

On 18th December 1779, the year in which Garrick died, Joseph Grimaldi, 'Old Joe', was born, in Stanhope Street, Clare-Market; a part of the town then, as now, much frequented by theatrical people, in consequence of its vicinity to the theatres. At the period of his birth, his eccentric father was over sixty years old, and twenty five months afterwards another son was born to him—Joseph's only brother. The child did not remain very long in a state of helpless and unprofitable infancy, for at the age of one year and eleven months he was brought out by his father on the boards of Old Drury, where he made his first bow and his first tumble. The piece in which his precocious powers were displayed was the well-known pantomime of *Robinson Crusoe*, in which the father sustained the part of the Shipwrecked Mariner, and the son performed that of the Little Clown. The child's success was complete; he was instantly placed on the establishment, accorded a magnificent weekly salary of fifteen shillings, and every succeeding year was brought forward in some new and prominent part. He became a favourite behind the curtain as well as before it, being henceforth distinguished in the green-room as 'Clever little Joe'; and Joe he was called to the last day of his life.

In 1782, Grimaldi first appeared at Sadler's Wells, in the arduous character of a monkey; and here he was fortunate enough to excite as much approbation as he had previously elicited in the part of clown at Drury Lane. He immediately became a member of the regular company at this theatre, as he had done at the other; and here he remained (one season only excepted) until the termination of his professional life, years afterwards. Now that he had made, or rather that his father had made for him, two engagements, by which he was bound to appear at two theatres on the same evening and at very nearly the same time, his labours began in earnest. They would have been arduous for a man, much more so for a child; and it will be obvious that if at any one portion of his life his gains were

14

very great, the actual toil both of mind and body by which they were purchased was at least equally so.

We have already remarked that the father of Grimaldi was an eccentric man; he appears to have been peculiarly eccentric, and rather unpleasantly so, in the correction of his son. The child being bred up to play all kinds of fantastic tricks, was as much a clown, a monkey, or anything else that was droll and ridiculous, off the stage, as on it; and being incited thereto by the occupants of the green-room, used to skip and tumble, about as much for their diversion as that of the public. All this was carefully concealed from the father, who, whenever he did happen to observe any of the child's pranks, always administered the same punishment—a sound thrashing; terminating in his being lifted up by the hair of the head and stuck in a corner, whence his father, with a severe countenance and awful voice, would tell him "to venture to move at his peril". Venture to move, however, he did, for no sooner would the father disappear than all the cries and tears of the boy would disappear too; and with many of those winks and grins which afterwards became so popular, he would recommence his pantomime with greater vigour than ever; indeed, nothing could ever stop him but the cry of "Joe! Joe! Here's your father!" upon which the boy would dart back into the old corner, and begin crying again as if he had never left off.

This became quite a regular amusement in course of time, and whether the father was coming or not, the caution used to be given for the mere pleasure of seeing Joe run back to his corner; this Joe very soon discovered, and often confounding the warning with the joke, received more severe beatings than before from him whom he very properly describes in his manuscript as his "severe but excellent parent". On one of these occasions, when Joe was dressed for his favourite part of the Little Clown in *Robinson Crusoe*, with his face painted in exact imitation of his father's, which appears to have been part of the fun of the scene, the old gentleman brought him into the green-room, and placing him in his usual solitary corner, gave him strict directions not to stir an inch on pain of being thrashed.

The Earl of Derby, who was at that time in the constant habit of frequenting the green-room, happened to walk in at the moment, and seeing a lonesome-looking little boy dressed and painted after a manner very inconsistent with his solitary air, good-naturedly called him towards him.

"Hollo! here, my boy, come here!" said the Earl.

Joe made a wonderful and astonishing face, but remained where he was. The Earl laughed heartily, and looked round for an explanation.

"He dare not move!" explained Miss Farren, to whom his lordship was then much attached, and whom he afterwards married. "His father will beat him if he does."

"Indeed!" said his lordship. At which Joe, by way of confirmation, made another face more extraordinary than his former contortions.

"I think," said his lordship, laughing again, "the boy is not quite so much afraid of his father as you suppose. Come here, sir!"

With this, he held up half a crown, and the child, perfectly well knowing the value of money, darted from his corner, seized it with pantomimic suddenness, and was darting back again, when the Earl caught him by the arm.

"Here, Joe!" said the Earl, "take off your wig and throw it in the fire, and here's another half-crown for you."

No sooner said than done. Off came the wig—into the fire it went; a roar of laughter arose; the child capered about with a half-crown in each hand; the Earl, alarmed for the consequences to the boy, busied himself to extricate the wig with the tongs and poker; and the father, in full dress for the Shipwrecked Mariner, rushed into the room at the same moment. It was lucky for 'Little Joe' that Lord Derby promptly and humanely interfered, or it is exceedingly probable that his father would have prevented any chance of *his* being buried alive at all events, by killing him outright.

As it was, the matter could not be compromised without the boy receiving a smart beating, which made him cry very bitterly; and the tears running down his face, which was painted 'an inch thick', came to the 'complexion at last', in parts, and made him look as much like a little clown as like a little human being, to neither of which characters he bore the most distant resemblance. He was 'called' almost immediately afterwards, and the father being in a violent rage, had not noticed the circumstance until the little object came on the stage, when a general roar of laughter directed his attention to his grotesque countenance. Becoming more violent than before, old Grimaldi fell upon his son at once, and beat him severely, and the child roared vociferously. This was all taken by the audience as a most capital joke; shouts of laughter and peals of applause shook the house; and the newspapers next morning declared that it was perfectly wonderful to see a mere child perform so naturally, and highly creditable to his father's talents as a teacher!

This is no bad illustration of some of the miseries of a poor actor's life. The jest on the lip and the tear in the eye, the merriment on the mouth and the aching of the heart, have called down the same shouts of laughter and peals of applause a hundred times. Characters in a state of starvation are almost invariably laughed at upon the stage; the audience have had their dinner.

The bitterest portion of the boy's punishment was the being deprived of the five shillings, which the excellent parent put into his own pocket, possibly because he received the child's salary also, and in order that everything might be, as Goldsmith's Bear-leader has it, "in a concatenation accordingly". The Earl gave him half a crown every time he saw him afterwards, though, and the child had good cause for regret when his lordship married Miss Farren and left the green-room.

At Sadler's Wells Grimaldi became a favourite almost as speedily as at Drury Lane. King, the comedian who was principal proprietor of the former theatre and acting manager of the latter, took a great deal of notice of him, and occasionally gave the child a guinea to buy a rocking-horse or a cart, or some toy that struck his fancy. During the run of the first piece in which Grimaldi played at Sadler's Wells, he produced his first serious effect, which, but for the good fortune which seems to have attended him in such cases, might have prevented his subsequent appearance on any stage. He played a monkey, and had to accompany the clown (his father) throughout the piece. In one of the scenes, the clown used to lead him on by a chain attached to his waist, and with this chain he would swing Joe round and round, at arm's length, with the utmost velocity. One evening, when this feat was in the act of performance, the chain broke, and he was hurled a considerable distance into the pit, fortunately without sustaining the slightest injury; for he was flung by a miracle into the very arms of an old gentleman, who was sitting gazing at the stage with intense interest.

Among the many persons who in this early stage of Joe's career behaved with great kindness were the famous rope-dancers, Mr and Mrs Redigé, then called *Le Petit Diable* and *La Belle Espagnole*, who often gave him a guinea to buy some childish luxury. His father invariably took the coin away and deposited it in a box, with his name written outside, which he would lock very carefully, and then, giving the boy the key, say, "Mind, Joe, ven I die, dat is your vortune." Eventually he lost both the box and the fortune, as will hereafter appear.

As Grimaldi had now nearly four months vacant out of every twelve, the run of the Christmas pantomime at Drury Lane seldom exceeding a month and Sadler's Wells not opening until Easter, he was sent for that period of the year to a boarding-school at Putney, kept by a Mr Ford, of whose kindness and goodness of heart to him on a later occasion of his life he spoke, when an old man, with the deepest gratitude. Grimaldi fell in here with many schoolfellows who afterwards became connected one way or another with dramatic pursuits, among whom was Mr Henry Harris, of Covent Garden Theatre. We do not find that any of these schoolfellows afterwards became pantomime actors; but recollecting the humour and vivacity of the boy, the wonder to us is that they were not all clowns when they grew up.

In the Christmas of 1782, Grimaldi appeared in his second character at Drury Lane, called *Harlequin Junior*, *The Magic Cestus*, in which he represented a demon, sent by some opposing magician to counteract the power of the Harlequin. In this, as in his preceding part, he was fortunate enough to meet with great applause; and from this period his reputation was made, although it naturally increased with his years, strength, and improvement. In Christmas 1783, he once more appeared at Drury Lane, in a pantomime called *Hurly Burly*. In this piece Grimaldi had to represent not only the old part of the monkey but that of a cat besides; and in sustaining the latter character he met with an accident, his speedy recovery from which would almost induce one to believe that he had so completely identified himself with the character as to have eight additional chances for his life. The dress he wore was so clumsily contrived that when it was sewn upon him he could not see before him; consequently, as he was running about the stage, he fell down a trap-door which had been left open to represent a well and tumbled down a distance of forty feet, thereby breaking his collarbone and inflicting several contusions upon his body. He was immediately conveyed home and placed under the care of a surgeon, but he did not recover soon enough to appear any more that season at Drury Lane, although at Easter he performed at Sadler's Wells as usual.

In the summer of this year Joe used to be allowed as a mark of high and special favour to spend every alternate Sunday at the house of his mother's father, "who," says Grimaldi himself, "resided in Newton Street, Holborn, and was a carcase butcher, doing a prodigious business; besides which, he kept the Bloomsbury slaughter-house, and, at the time of his death, had done so for more than sixty years." With this grandfather, Joe was a great favourite; and as he was very much indulged and petted when he went to see him, he used to look forward to every visit with great anxiety. His father, upon his part, was most anxious that Joe should support the credit of the family upon these occasions, and, after great deliberation, and much consultation with tailors, the 'Little Clown' was attired for one of these Sunday excursions in the following style. On his back he wore a green coat, embroidered with almost as many artificial flowers as his father had put in the garden at Lambeth; beneath this there shone a satin waistcoat of dazzling whiteness; and beneath that again were a pair of green cloth breeches, richly embroidered. His legs were fitted into white silk stockings, and his feet into shoes with brilliant paste buckles, of which he also wore another resplendent pair at his knees: he had a laced shirt, cravat, and ruffles; a cocked-hat upon his head; a small watch set with diamonds—theatrical, we suppose—in his fob; and a little cane in his hand, which he switched to and fro as our Clowns may do now.

Being thus thoroughly equipped for starting, Joe was taken in for his father's inspection: the old gentleman was pleased to signify his entire approbation with his appearance, and, after kissing him in the moment of his gratification, demanded the key of the 'fortune-box'. The key being got with some difficulty out of one of the pockets of the green smalls, the bottom of which might be somewhere near the buckles, the old gentleman took a guinea out of the box, and, putting it into the boy's pocket, said, "Dere now, you are a gentleman, and something more—you have got a guinea in your pocket." The box having been carefully locked, and the key returned to the owner of the 'fortune', off he started, receiving strict injunctions to be home by eight o'clock. The father would not allow anybody to attend him, on the ground that he was a gentleman, and consequently perfectly able to take care of himself; so away he went, to walk all the way from Little Russell Street, Drury Lane, to Newton Street, Holborn.

The child's appearance in the street excited considerable curiosity, as the appearance of any other child, alone, in such a costume, might very probably have done; but he was a public character besides, and the astonishment was proportionate. "Hollo!" cried the boy, "here's 'Little Joe!'" "Get along," said another, "it's the monkey." A third thought it was the "bear dressed for a dance", and the fourth suggested "it might be the cat going out to a party", while the more sedate passengers could not help laughing heartily, and saying how ridiculous it was to trust such a child in the streets alone. However, he walked on, with various singular grimaces, until he stopped to look at a female of miserable appearance, who was reclining on the pavement, and whose diseased and destitute aspect had already collected a crowd. The boy stopped, like others, and hearing her tale of distress, became so touched that he thrust his hand into his pocket, and having at last found the bottom of it, pulled out his guinea, which was the only coin he had, and slipped it into her hand; then away he walked again with a greater air than before.

The sight of the embroidered coat, and breeches, and the paste buckles, and the satin waistcoat and cocked-hat, had astonished the crowd not a little in the outset; but directly it was understood that the small owner of these articles had given the woman a guinea, a great number of people collected around him, and began shouting and staring by turns most earnestly. The boy, not at all abashed, headed the crowd, and walked on very deliberately, with a train a street or two long behind him, until he fortunately encountered a friend of his father's, who no sooner saw the concourse that attended him than he took him in his arms and carried him, despite a few kicks and struggles, in all his brilliant attire, to his grandfather's house, where he spent the day, very much to the satisfaction of all parties concerned.

When Joe got safely home at night his father referred to his watch, and finding that his son had returned home punctual to the appointed time, kissed him, extolled him for paying such strict attention to his instructions, examined his dress, discovered satisfactorily that no injury had been done to his clothes, and concluded by asking for the key of the 'fortune-box' and the guinea. The boy, at first, quite forgot the morning adventure; but, after rummaging his pockets for the guinea, and not finding it, he recollected what had occurred, and, falling upon the knees of the knee-smalls, confessed it all and implored forgiveness. The father was puzzled; he was always giving away money in charity himself, and he could scarcely reprimand the child for doing the same. He looked at him for some seconds with a perplexed countenance, and then, contenting himself with simply saying, "I'll beat you," sent him to bed.

Among the eccentricities of the old gentleman, one—certainly not his most amiable one—was that whatever he promised he performed; and that when, as in this case, he promised to thrash the boy, he would very coolly let the matter stand over for months, but never forget it in the end. This was ingenious, inasmuch as it doubled, or trebled, or quadrupled the punishment, giving the unhappy little victim all the additional pain of anticipating it for a long time, with the certainty of enduring it in the end. Four or five months after this occurrence, and when the child had not given his father any new cause of offence, old Grimaldi suddenly called him one day, and communicated the intelligence that he was going to beat him forthwith. Hereupon the boy began to cry most piteously, and faltered for the enquiry, "Oh! Father, what for?"—"Remember the guinea!" said the father. And he gave Joe a caning which he remembered to the last day of his life.

The family consisted at this time of the father, mother, Joe, his only brother John Baptist, three or four female servants, and a man of colour who acted as footman, and was dignified with the appellation of 'Black Sam'. The father was extremely hospitable, and fond of company; he rarely dined alone, and on certain gala days, of which Christmas Eve was one, had a very large party, upon which occasions his really splendid service of plate, together with various costly articles of bijouterie, were laid out for the admiration of the guests. Upon one Christmas Eve, when the dining-parlour was decorated and prepared with all due gorgeousness and splendour, the two boys, accompanied by Black Sam, stole into it, and began to pass various encomiums on its beautiful appearance.

"Ah!" said Sam, in reply to some remark of the brothers, "and when old Massa die, all dese fine things vill be yours."

Both the boys were much struck with this remark, and especially John, the younger, who, being extremely young, probably thought much less about death than his father, and accordingly exclaimed, without the least reserve or delicacy, that he should be exceedingly glad if all these fine things were his.

Nothing more was said upon the subject. Black Sam went to his work, the boys commenced a game of play, and nobody thought any more of the matter except the father himself, who, passing the door of the room at the moment the remarks were made, distinctly heard them. He pondered over the matter for some days, and at length, with the view of ascertaining the dispositions of his two sons, formed a singular resolution, still connected with the topic ever upwards in his mind, and determined to feign himself dead. He caused himself to be laid out in the drawing-room, covered with a sheet, and had the room darkened, the windows closed, and all the usual ceremonies which accompany death, performed. All this being done, and the servants duly instructed, the two boys were cautiously informed that their father had died suddenly, and were at once hurried into the room where he lay, in order that he might hear them give vent to their real feelings.

When Joe was brought into the dark room on so short a notice, his sensations were rather complicated, but they speedily resolved themselves into a firm persuasion that his father was not dead. A variety of causes led him to this conclusion, among which the most prominent were, his having very recently seen his father in the best health; and, besides several half-suppressed winks and blinks from Black Sam, his observing, by looking closely at the sheet, that his deceased parent still breathed. With very little hesitation the boy perceived what line of conduct he ought to adopt, and at once bursting into a roar of the most distracted grief, flung himself upon the floor and rolled about in a seeming transport of anguish.

John, not having seen so much of public life as his brother, was not so cunning, and perceiving in his father's death nothing but a relief from flogging and books (for both of which he had a great dislike), and the immediate possession of all the plate in the dining-room, skipped about the room, indulging in various snatches of song, and, snapping his fingers, declared that he was glad to hear it.

"Oh! you cruel boy," said Joe, in a passion of tears, "hadn't you any love for your dear father? Oh! what would I give to see him alive again!"

"Oh! never mind," replied the brother; "don't be such a fool as to cry; we can have the cuckoo-clock all to ourselves now."

This was more than the deceased could bear. He jumped from the bier, opened the shutters, threw off the sheet, and attacked his younger son most unmercifully; while Joe, not knowing what might be his own fate, ran and hid himself in the coal-cellar, where he was discovered fast asleep some four hours afterwards by Black Sam, who carried him to his father, who had been anxiously in search of him, and by whom he was received with every demonstration of affection, as the son who truly and sincerely loved him.

CHAPTER TWO

GRIMALDI'S FATHER expired of dropsy on the sixteenth of March 1788 at the age of seventy-eight and was interred in the burial-ground attached to Exmouth Street Chapel. He left a will by which he directed all his effects and jewels to be sold by public auction, and the proceeds to be added to his funded property, which exceeded fifteen thousand pounds; the whole of the gross amount, he directed, should be divided equally between the two brothers as they respectively attained their majority. Mr King, to whom allusion has already been made, was appointed co-executor with a Mr Joseph Hopwood, a lace manufacturer in Long Acre, at that time supposed to possess not only an excellent business but independent property to a considerable amount besides. Shortly after they entered upon their office, in consequence of Mr King declining to act, the whole of the estate fell to the management of Mr Hopwood, who, employing the whole of the brothers' capital in his trade, became a bankrupt within a year, fled from England, and was never heard of afterwards. By this unfortunate and unforeseen event, the brothers lost the whole of their fortune, and were thrown upon their own resources and exertions for the means of subsistence.

It is very creditable to all parties, and while it speaks highly for the kind feeling of the friends of the widow, and her two sons, it bears high testimony to their conduct and behaviour that no sooner was the failure of the executor known than offers of assistance were heaped upon them from all quarters.

Mr Ford, the Putney schoolmaster, offered at once to receive Joseph into his school and to adopt him as his own son; this offer was declined by his mother. Mr Sheridan, who was then proprietor of Drury Lane, raised the boy's salary, unasked, to one pound per week, and permitted his mother, who was and had been from her infancy a dancer at that establishment, to accept a similar engagement at Sadler's Wells. This was, in fact, equivalent to a double salary, both theatres being open together for a considerable period of the year.

At Sadler's Wells, where Joseph appeared as usual in 1788, shortly after his father's death, they were not so liberal, nor was the aspect of things so pleasing, his salary of fifteen shillings a week being very unceremoniously cut down to three. His mother was politely informed, upon her remonstrating, that if the alteration did not suit her he was at perfect liberty to transfer his valuable services to any other house. Small as the pittance was, they could not afford to refuse it; and at that salary Grimaldi remained at Sadler's Wells for three years, occasionally superintending the property-room, sometimes assisting in the carpenter's and sometimes in the painter's, and, in fact, lending a hand wherever it was most needed.

When the defalcation of the executor took place, the family were compelled to give up their comfortable establishment and to seek for lodgings of an inferior description. Joe's mother knowing a Mr and Mrs Bailey, who then resided in Great Wild Street and who let lodgings, applied to them, and there the Grimaldis lived, in three rooms on the first floor, for several years. His brother John could not be prevailed upon to accept any regular engagement, for he thought and dreamt of nothing but going to sea, and evinced the utmost detestation of the stage. Sometimes when boys were wanted in the play at Drury Lane, John was sent for, and attended, for which he received a shilling per night; but so great was his unwillingness and evident dissatisfaction on such occasions, that Mr Wroughton, the comedian, who by purchasing the property of Mr King, became about this period proprietor of Sadler's Wells, stepped forward in the boy's behalf and obtained for him a situation on board an East Indiaman which then lay in the river and was about to sail almost immediately. John was delighted when the prospect of realising his ardent wishes opened upon him so suddenly; but his raptures were diminished by the discovery that an outfit was indispensable, and that it would cost upwards of fifty pounds: a sum which, it is scarcely necessary to say, his friends, in their reduced position, could not command. But the same kind-hearted gentleman removed this obstacle, and with a generosity and readiness which enhanced the value of the gift a hundredfold, advanced, without security or obligation, the whole sum required, merely saying, "Mind, John, when you come to be a captain you must pay it me back again."

There is no difficulty in providing the necessaries for a voyage to any part of the world when you have provided the first and most important—money. In two days John took his leave of his mother and brother, and with his outfit, or kit, was safely deposited on board the vessel in which a berth had been procured for him; but the boy, who was of a rash, hasty, and inconsiderate temper, finding that a delay of ten days would take place before the ship sailed, and that a king's ship, which lay near her, was just then preparing to drop down to Gravesend with the tide, actually swam from his own ship to the other. He entered himself as a seaman or cabin-boy on board the latter in some feigned name—what it was, his friends never heard—and so sailed immediately, leaving every article of his outfit, down to the commonest necessary of wearing apparel, on board the East Indiaman. He disappeared in 1789, and he was not heard of, or from, or seen, for fourteen years afterwards.

At this period of his life, Joseph was far from idle; he had to walk from Drury Lane to Sadler's Wells every morning to attend rehearsals, which then began at ten o'clock; to be back at Drury Lane to dinner by two, or go without it; to be back again at Sadler's Wells in the evening, in time for the commencement of the performance at six o'clock; to go through uninterrupted labour from that time until eleven o'clock, or later; and then to walk home again, repeatedly after having changed his dress twenty times in the course of the night. Occasionally, when the performances at Sadler's Wells were prolonged so that the curtain fell very nearly at the same time as the concluding piece at Drury Lane began, he was so pressed for time as to be compelled to dart out of the former theatre at his utmost speed, and never to stop until he reached his dressing-room at the latter. That he could use his legs to pretty good advantage at this period of his life, two anecdotes will sufficiently show.

On one occasion, when by unforeseen circumstances Joe was detained at Sadler's Wells beyond the usual time, he and Mr Fairbrother (the father of the well-known theatrical printer), who, like himself, was engaged at both theatres, and had agreed to accompany him that evening, started hand-in-hand from Sadler's Wells and ran to the stage door of Drury Lane in eight minutes by the stopwatches which they carried. Grimaldi adds that this was considered a great feat at the time: and we should think it was. Another night, when the Drury Lane company were playing at the Italian Opera House in the Haymarket in consequence of the old theatre being pulled down and a new one built, Mr Fairbrother and Grimaldi, again put to their utmost speed by lack of time, ran from Sadler's Wells to the Opera House in fourteen minutes, meeting with no other interruption by the way than one which occurred at the corner of Lincoln's Inn Fields, where they unfortunately ran against and overturned an infirm old lady, without having time enough to pick her up again. After Grimaldi's business at the Opera House was over (he had merely to walk in the procession in *Cymon*), he ran back alone to Sadler's Wells in thirteen minutes, and arrived just in time to dress for Clown in the concluding pantomime.

For some years Grimaldi's life went on quietly enough, possessing very little of anecdote or interest beyond his steady and certain rise in his profession and in the estimation of the public, which, although very important to him from the money he afterwards gained by it, and to the public from the amusement which his peculiar excellence yielded them for so many years, offers no material for our present purpose. This gradual progress in the good opinion of the town exercised a material influence on Grimaldi's receipts; for, in 1794, his salary at Drury Lane was trebled, while his salary at Sadler's Wells had risen from three shillings per week to four pounds. He lodged in Great Wild Street with his mother all this time: their landlord had died, and the widow's daughter, from accompanying Mrs Grimaldi to Sadler's Wells, had formed an acquaintance with, and married Mr Robert Fairbrother, of that establishment and Drury Lane, upon which Mrs Bailey, the widow, took Mr Fairbrother into partnership as a furrier, in which pursuit, by industry and perseverance, he became eminently successful.

This circumstance would be scarcely worth mentioning, but that it shows the industry and perseverance of Grimaldi, and the ease with which, by the exercise of those qualities, a very young person may overcome all the disadvantages and temptations incidental to the most precarious walk of a precarious pursuit, and become a useful and respectable member of society. He earned many a guinea from Mr Fairbrother by working at his trade and availing himself of his instruction in his leisure hours; and when he could do nothing in that way he would go to Newton Street, and assist his uncle and cousin, the carcase butchers, for nothing; such was his unconquerable antipathy to being idle. He does not inform us whether it required a practical knowledge of trade to display that skill and address with which, in his subsequent prosperity, he would diminish the joints of his customers as a baker, or increase the weight of their meat as a butcher; but we hope, for the credit of trade, that his morals in this respect were wholly imaginary.

These were moments of occupation, but Grimaldi contrived to find moments of amusement besides, which were devoted to the breeding of pigeons and collecting of insects. This latter amusement he pursued with such success as to form a cabinet containing no fewer than four thousand specimens of butterflies, "collected," he says, "at the expense of a great deal of time, a great deal of money, and a great deal of vast and actual labour"—for all of which, no doubt, the entomologist will deem him sufficiently rewarded. He appears in old age to have entertained a peculiar relish for the recollection of these pursuits, and calls to mind a part of Surrey where there was a very famous fly; one of these was called the Camberwell Beauty (which he adds was very ugly), and another the Dartford Blue, by which he seems to have set great store; and which were pursued and caught in the manner following, in June 1794, when they regularly make their first appearance for the season.

Being engaged nightly at Sadler's Wells, Grimaldi was obliged to wait till he had finished his business upon the stage: then he returned home, had supper, and shortly after midnight started off to walk to Dartford, fifteen miles from town. Here he arrived about five o'clock in the morning, and calling upon a friend of the name of Brooks, who lived in the neighbourhood and who was already stirring, he rested, breakfasted, and sallied forth into the fields. His search was not very profitable, however, for after some hours he only succeeded in bagging, or bottling, one Dartford Blue, with which he returned to his friend perfectly satisfied. At one o'clock he bade Brooks goodbye, walked back to town, reached London by five, washed, took tea, and hurried to Sadler's Wells. No time was to be lost—the fact of the appearance of the Dartford Blues having been thoroughly established—in securing more specimens; so on the same night, directly the pantomime was over and supper over, too, off he walked to Dartford again, and resumed his search again. Meeting with better sport, and capturing no fewer than four dozen Dartford Blues, he hurried back to the friend's, set them—an important process, which consists in placing the insects in the position in which their natural beauty can be best displayed—started off with the Blues in his pocket for London once more, reached home by four o'clock in the afternoon, washed, took a hasty meal, and then went to the theatre for the evening's performance.

As not half the necessary number of Blues had been taken, Grimaldi had decided upon another visit to Dartford that same night, and was consequently much pleased to find that, from some unforeseen circumstance, the pantomime was to be played first. By this means he was enabled to leave London at nine o'clock, to reach Dartford at one, to find a bed and supper ready, to meet a kind reception from his friend, and finally to turn into bed, a little tired with the two days' exertions. The next day was Sunday, so that he could indulge himself without being obliged to return to town, and in the morning he caught more flies than he wanted; so the rest of the day was devoted to quiet sociality. He went to bed at ten o'clock, rose early next morning, walked comfortably to town, and at noon was perfect in his part at the rehearsal.

It is probable that by such means as these, united to temperance and sobriety, Grimaldi acquired many important bodily requisites for the perfection which he afterwards attained. But his love of entomology, or exercise, was not the only inducement in the case of the Dartford Blues; he had, he says, another strong motive, and this was, that he had promised a little collection of insects to "one of the most charming women of her age"—the lamented Mrs Jordan, at that time a member of the Drury Lane company.

Upon one occasion Joe had held under his arm, during a morning rehearsal, a box containing some specimens of flies: Mrs Jordan was much interested to know what could possibly be in the box that Grimaldi carried about with him with so much care and would not lose sight of for an instant, and in reply to her enquiry whether it contained anything pretty, he replied by exhibiting the flies. He does not say whether these particular flies which Mrs Jordan admired were Dartford Blues, or not; but he gives us to understand that his skill in preserving and arranging insects was really very great; that all this trouble and fatigue were undertaken in a spirit of respectful gallantry to the most winning person of her time; and that, having requested permission previously, he presented two frames of insects to Mrs Jordan on the first day of the new season, immediately after she had finished the rehearsal of Rosalind in *As You Like It*; that Mrs Jordan was delighted; that he was at least equally so; that she took the frames away in her carriage; and that she warmed his heart by telling him that his Royal Highness the Duke of Clarence considered the flies equal, if not superior, to any of the kind he had ever seen.

Joe's only other companion in these trips besides his Dartford friend, was Robert Gomery, or 'friend Bob', as he was called by his intimates, at that time an actor at Sadler's Wells, and for many years afterwards a public favourite at the various minor theatres of the metropolis; who is now, or was lately, enjoying a handsome independence at Bath. With this friend Grimaldi had a little adventure, which it was his habit to relate with great glee. One day, he had been fly-hunting with Gomery from early morning until night, thinking of nothing but flies, until, at length, their thoughts naturally turning to something more substantial, they halted for refreshment.

"Bob," said Grimaldi, "I am very hungry."

"So am I," said Bob.

"There is a public house," said Grimaldi.

"It is *just* the very thing," observed the other.

It was a very neat public house and would have answered the purpose admirably, but Grimaldi having no money, and very much doubting whether his friend had either, did not respond to the sentiment quite so cordially as he might have done.

"We had better go in," said Bob. "It is getting late—*you* pay."

"No, no! You."

"I would in a minute," said Joe's friend, "but I have not got any money."

Grimaldi thrust his hand into his right pocket with one of his queerest faces, then into his left, then into his coat pockets, then into his waistcoat, and finally took off his hat and looked into that; but there was no money anywhere. They still walked on towards the public house, meditating with rueful countenances, when Grimaldi, spying something lying at the foot of a tree, picked it up, and suddenly exclaimed, with a variety of winks and nods, "Here's a sixpence."

The hungry friend's eyes brightened, but they quickly resumed their gloomy expression as he rejoined, "It's a piece of tin!"

Grimaldi winked again, rubbed the sixpence or the piece of tin very hard, and declared, putting it between his teeth by way of test, that it was as good a sixpence as he would wish to see.

"I don't think it," said Bob, shaking his head.

"I'll tell you what," said Grimaldi, "we'll go to the public house, and ask the landlord whether it's a good one, or not. They always know."

To this Bob assented, and they hurried on, disputing all the way whether it was really a sixpence or not; a discovery which could not be made at that time, when the currency was defaced and worn nearly plain, with the ease with which it could be made at present.

The publican, a fat jolly fellow, was standing at his door, talking to a friend, and the house looked so uncommonly comfortable, that Gomery whispered as they approached, that perhaps it might be best to have some bread and cheese first, and ask about the sixpence afterwards. Grimaldi nodded his entire assent, and they went in and ordered some bread and cheese and beer. Having taken the edge off their hunger, they tossed up a farthing which Grimaldi happened to find in the corner of some theretofore undiscovered pocket, to determine who should present the 'sixpence'. The chance falling on himself, he walked up to the bar, and with a very lofty air, and laying the questionable metal down with a dignity quite his own, requested the landlord to take the bill out of that.

"Just right, sir," said the landlord, looking at the strange face that his customer assumed, and not at the sixpence.

"It's right, sir, is it?" asked Grimaldi, sternly.

"Quite," answered the landlord. "Thank ye, gentlemen." And with this he slipped the—whatever it was—into his pocket. Gomery looked at Grimaldi; and Grimaldi, with a look and air which baffled all description, walked out of the house, followed by his friend.

"I never knew anything so lucky," Grimaldi said, as they walked home to supper. "It was quite a Providence—that sixpence."

"A piece of tin, you mean," said Gomery.

Which of the two it was, is uncertain, but Grimaldi often patronised the same house afterwards, and as he never heard anything more about the matter, he felt quite convinced that it was a real good sixpence.

In the early part of 1794, the Grimaldis quitted their lodgings in Great Wild Street, and took a six-roomed house in Penton Place, Pentonville, with a garden attached; a part of this they let off to a Mr and Mrs William Lewis, who then belonged to Sadler's Wells; and in this manner they lived for three years, during the whole of which period Grimaldi's salaries steadily rose in amount, and he began to consider himself quite independent. At Easter, Sadler's Wells opened as usual, and making a great hit in a new part, his fame rapidly increased. At this time he found a new acquaintance, which exercised a material influence upon his comfort and happiness for many years. The intimacy commenced thus.

When there was a rehearsal at Sadler's Wells, his mother, who was engaged there as well as himself, was in the habit of remaining at the theatre all day, taking her meals in her dressing-room and occupying herself with needlework. This she had done to avoid the long walk in the middle of the day from Sadler's Wells to Great Wild Street, and back again almost directly. It became a habit; and when they had removed to Penton Place, and consequently were so much nearer the theatre that it was no longer necessary, it still continued. Mr Hughes, who had now become principal proprietor of the theatre, and who lived in the house attached to it, had several children, the eldest of whom was Miss Maria Hughes, a young lady of considerable accomplishments. She had always been much attached to Grimaldi's mother, and embraced every opportunity of being in her society. Knowing the hours at which Mrs Brooker was in the dressing-room during the day, Miss Hughes was in the habit of taking her work and sitting with her from three or four o'clock until six, when, the other female performers beginning to arrive, she retired. Grimaldi was generally at the theatre between four and five, always taking tea with his mother at the last-named hour and sitting with her until the arrival of the ladies broke up the little party. In this way an intimacy arose between Miss Hughes and himself, which ultimately ripened into feelings of a warmer nature.

The day after he made his great hit in the new piece, he went as usual to tea in the dressing-room, where Mrs Lewis, their lodger, who was the wardrobe-keeper of the theatre, happening to be present, overwhelmed him with compliments on his great success. Miss Hughes was there too, but she said nothing for a long time, and Grimaldi, who would rather have heard her speak for a minute than Mrs Lewis for an hour, listened as patiently as he could to the encomiums which the good woman lavished upon him. At length she stopped, as the best talkers must now and then to take breath, and then Miss Hughes, looking up, said with some hesitation that she thought Mr Grimaldi had played the part uncommonly well; so well that she was certain there was no one who could have done it at all like him.

Now, before he went into the room, he had turned the matter over in his mind, and had come to the conclusion that if Miss Hughes praised his acting he would reply by some neatly turned compliment to her, which might afford some hint of the state of his feelings; and with this view he had considered of a good many very smart ones, but somehow or other the young lady no sooner opened her lips in speech than Grimaldi opened his in admiration, and out flew all the compliments in empty breath, without producing the slightest sound. He turned very red, looked very funny, and felt very foolish. At length he made an awkward bow, and turned to leave the room.

It was six o'clock, and the lady performers just then came in. As he was always somewhat of a favourite among them, a few of the more volatile and giddy—for there are a few such in almost all companies, theatrical or otherwise—began to praise his acting, and then to rally him upon another subject.

"Now Joe has become such a favourite," said one, "he ought to look out for a sweetheart."

Here Joe just glanced at Miss Hughes, and turned a deeper red than ever.

"Certainly he ought," said another. "Will any of us do, Joe?"

Upon this Joe exhibited fresh symptoms of being uncomfortable, which were hailed by a general burst of laughter.

"I'll tell you what, ladies," said Mrs Lewis. "If I'm not greatly mistaken, Joe has got a sweetheart already."

Another lady said that to her certain knowledge he had two, and another that he had three, and so on: he standing among them the whole time, with his eyes fixed upon the ground, vexed to death to think that Miss Hughes should hear these libels, and frightened out of his wits lest she should be disposed to believe them.

At length he made his escape, and being induced, by the conversation which had just passed, to ponder upon the matter, he was soon led to the conclusion that the fair daughter of Mr Hughes had made an impression on his heart, and that unless he could marry her he would marry nobody and must be for ever miserable, with other like deductions which young men are in the habit of making from similar premises. The discovery was not unattended by many misgivings. The great difference of station then existing between them appeared to interpose an almost insurmountable obstacle in the way of their marriage; and, further, he had no reason to suppose that the young lady entertained for him any other sentiments than those with which she might be naturally disposed to regard the son of a friend whom she had known so long. These considerations rendered him as unhappy as the most passionate lover could desire to be;

he ate little, drank little, slept less, lost his spirits; and, in short, exhibited a great variety of symptoms sufficiently dangerous in any case, but particularly so in one, where the patient had mainly to depend upon the preservation of his powers of fun and comicality for a distant chance of the fulfilment of his hopes.

It is scarcely to be supposed that such a sudden and complete change in the merry genius of the theatre could escape the observation of those around him, far less of his mother, who, as he had been her constant and affectionate companion, observed him with anxious solicitude. Various hints and soundings and indirect enquiries were the consequence but they were far from eliciting the truth; he was ill, fatigued by constant exertion in difficult parts, and that was all that his friends could gather from him. There was another circumstance which puzzled Joe's mother more than all. This was, that he never visited the dressing-room, whither he had been accustomed regularly to resort; and that he either took tea before he went to the theatre, or not at all. The truth was that he was quite unable to endure the facetiousness of the ladies in the presence of Miss Hughes; the more so, because he fancied that his annoyance seemed to afford that young lady considerable amusement; and rather than find this the case, he determined to relinquish the pleasure of her society.

So matters stood for some weeks, when one night, having occasion during the performances to repair to the wardrobe for some articles of dress, Grimaldi hastily entered, and instead of discovering his old friend, Mrs Lewis, found himself confronted and alone with Mr Hughes's daughter. In these cases, if the lady exhibits emotion, the gentleman gains courage; but Miss Hughes exhibited no emotion, merely saying:

41

"Why, Joe, I have not seen you for a fortnight; where *have* you been hiding! How is it that I never see you at tea now?"

The tone of kindness in which this was said somewhat reassured the lover, so he made an effort to speak, and got as far as, "I'm not well."

"Not well!" said the young lady. And she said it so kindly that all poor Joe's emotion returned; and being really ill and weak, and very sensitive withal, he made an effort or two to look cheerful, and burst into tears.

The young lady looked at him for a moment or two quite surprised, and then said, in a tone of earnest commiseration, "I see that you are not well, and that you are very much changed: what is the matter with you? Pray tell me."

At this enquiry, the young man, who seems to have inherited all the sensitiveness of his father's character without its worst points, threw himself into a chair and cried like a child, vainly endeavouring to stammer out a few words, which were wholly unintelligible. Miss Hughes gently endeavoured to soothe him, and at that moment Mrs Lewis, suddenly entering the room, surprised them in this very sentimental situation; upon which Grimaldi, thinking he must have made himself very ridiculous, jumped up and ran away.

Mrs Lewis being older in years, and in such matters too, than either Miss Hughes or her devoted admirer, kept her own counsel, thought over what she had seen, and discreetly presented herself before Grimaldi next day, when, after a sleepless night, he was sauntering moodily about the garden, aggravating all the doubts and diminishing all the hopes that involved themselves with the object nearest his heart.

"Dear me, Joe!" exclaimed the old lady. "How wretched you do look! Why, what is the matter?"

He tried an excuse or two, but reposing great trust in the sagacity and sincerity of his questioner, and sadly wanting a confidante, he first solemnly bound her to secrecy and then told his tale. Mrs Lewis at once took upon herself the office of a go-between; undertook to sound Miss Hughes without delay; and counselled Grimaldi to prepare a letter containing a full statement of his feelings, which, if the conversation between herself and Miss Hughes on that very evening were propitious, should be delivered on the following.

Accordingly, he devoted all his leisure time that day to the composition of various epistles, and the spoiling of many sheets of paper, with the view to setting down his feelings in the very best and appropriate terms he could possibly employ. One complete letter was finished at last, although even that was not half powerful enough; and going to the theatre, and carefully avoiding the old dressing-room, he went through his part with greater éclat than before. Having hastily changed his dress, he hurried to Mrs Lewis's room, where that good lady at once detailed all the circumstances that had occurred since the morning, which she thought conclusive, but which the lover feared were not.

It seems that Mrs Lewis had embraced the first opportunity of being left alone with Miss Hughes to return to the old subject of Joe's looking very ill; to which Miss Hughes replied that he certainly did, and said it, too, according to the matured opinion of Mrs Lewis, as if she had been longing to introduce the subject without exactly knowing how.

"What can be the matter with him?" said Miss Hughes.

"I have found it out, Miss," said Mrs Lewis. "Joe is in love."

"In love!" said Miss Hughes.

"Over head and ears," replied Mrs Lewis. "I never saw any poor dear young man in such a state."

"Who is the lady?" asked Miss Hughes, inspecting some object that lay near her with every appearance of unconcern.

"That's a secret," said Mrs Lewis. "I know her name; she does not know he is in love with her yet; but I am going to give her a letter tomorrow night, telling her all about it."

"I should like to know her name," said Miss Hughes.

"Why," returned Mrs Lewis, "you see I promised Joe not to tell; but as you are so very anxious to know, I can let you into the secret without breaking my word: you shall see the direction of the letter."

Miss Hughes was quite delighted with the idea, and left the room, after making an appointment for the ensuing evening for that purpose.

Such was Mrs Lewis's tale in brief; after hearing which, Grimaldi, who, not being so well acquainted with the subject, was not so sanguine, went home to bed, but not to sleep: his thoughts wavering between his friend's communication and the love letter, of which he could not help thinking that he could still polish up a sentence or two with considerable advantage.

The next morning was one of great agitation, and when Mrs Lewis posted off to the theatre with the important epistle in her pocket, the lover fell into such a tremor of anxiety and suspense that he was quite unconscious how the day passed: he could stay away from the theatre no longer than five o'clock, at which time he hurried down to ascertain the fate of his letter.

"I have not been able to give it yet," said Mrs Lewis, softly, "but do you just go to the dressing-room; she is there—only look at her, and guess whether she cares for you or not."

He went, and saw Miss Hughes looking very pale, with traces of tears on her face. Six o'clock soon came, and the young lady, hurrying to the room of the confidante, eagerly enquired whether she had got Joe's letter.

"I have," said Mrs Lewis, looking very sly.

"Oh! pray let me see it," said Miss Hughes. "I am so anxious to know who the lady is, and so desirous that Joe should be happy."

"Why, upon my word," said Mrs Lewis, "I think I should be doing wrong if I showed it to you, unless Joe said I might."

"Wrong!" echoed the young lady; "oh! if you only knew how much I have suffered since last night!" Here she paused for some moments, and added, with some violence of tone and manner, that if that suspense lasted much longer, she should go mad.

"Hey-day! Miss Maria," exclaimed Mrs Lewis. "Mad! Why surely you cannot have been so imprudent as to have formed an attachment to Joe yourself? But you shall see the letter, as you wish it; there is only one thing you must promise, and that is, to plead Joe's cause with the lady herself."

Miss Hughes hesitated, faltered, and at length said she would try. At this point of the discourse, Mrs Lewis produced the laboured composition and placed it in her hand. Miss Hughes raised the letter, glanced at the direction, saw her own name written as plainly as the nervous fingers of its agitated writer would permit, let it fall to the ground, and sank into the arms of Mrs Lewis.

While this scene was acting in a private room, Grimaldi was acting upon the public stage; and conscious that his hopes depended upon his exertions, he did not suffer his anxieties, great as they were, to interfere with his performance. Towards the conclusion of the first piece he heard somebody enter Mr Hughes's box—and there sat the object of all his anxiety.

"She has got the letter," thought the trembling actor. "She must have decided by this time."

He would have given all he possessed to have known what had passed—when the business of the stage calling him to the front, exactly facing the box in which she sat, their eyes met, and she nodded and smiled. This was not the first time that Miss Hughes had nodded and smiled to Joseph Grimaldi, but it threw him into a state of confusion and agitation which at once deprived him of all consciousness of what he was about. He never heard that he did not finish the scene in which he was engaged at the moment, and he always supposed, in consequence, that he did so: but how, or in what manner, he never could imagine, not having the slightest recollection of anything that passed.

It is singular enough that throughout the whole of Grimaldi's existence, which was a chequered one enough, even at those years when other children are kept in the cradle or the nursery, there always seemed some odd connection between his good and bad fortune; no great pleasure appeared to come to him unaccompanied by some accident or mischance: he mentions the fact more than once, and lays great stress upon it. On this very night, a heavy platform, on which ten men were standing, broke down, and fell upon him as he stood underneath; a severe contusion of the shoulder was the consequence, and he was carried home immediately. Remedies were applied without loss of time, but he suffered intense pain all night. It gradually abated towards morning, in consequence of the inestimable virtues of a certain embrocation, which he always kept ready in case of such accidents, and which was prepared from a recipe left him by his father, having performed a great many cures. (He afterwards gave to one Mr Chamberlaine, a surgeon of Clerkenwell, who christened it, in acknowledgement, *Grimaldi's Embrocation*, and used it in his general practice some years with perfect success.) Before Joe was carried from the theatre, however, he had had the presence of mind to beg Mrs Lewis to be called to him, and to request her to communicate the nature of the accident to Miss Hughes (who had quitted the box before it occurred) as cautiously as she could. This, Mrs Lewis, who appears to have been admirably qualified for the task in which she was engaged, and to have possessed quite a diplomatic relish for negotiation, undertook and performed.

There is no need to lengthen this part of Grimaldi's history. However interesting, and most honourably so, to the old man himself, who in the last days of his life looked back with undiminished interest and affection to the time when he first became acquainted with the excellence of a lady to whom he was tenderly attached and whose affection he never forgot or trifled with, the story would possess but few attractions for the general reader. The main result is quickly told: he was lying on a sofa next day, with his arm in a sling, when Miss Hughes visited him, and did not affect to disguise her solicitude for his recovery; and, in short, by returning his affection, made him the happiest man, or rather boy (for he was not yet quite sixteen) in the world.

There was only one thing that damped his joy, and this was Miss Hughes's firm and steadfast refusal to continue any correspondence or communication with him unknown to her parents. Nor is it unnatural that this announcement should have occasioned him some uneasiness, when their relative situations in life are taken into consideration: Mr Hughes being a man of considerable property, and Grimaldi entirely dependent on his own exertions for support. He made use of every persuasion in his power to induce the young lady to alter her determination; he failed to effect anything beyond the compromise that for the present she would only mention their attachment to her mother, upon whose kindness and secrecy she was certain she could rely. This was done, and Mrs Hughes, finding that her daughter's happiness depended on her decision, offered no opposition, merely remarking that their extreme youth forbade all idea of marriage at that time. Three years elapsed before Mr Hughes was made acquainted with the secret.

After this, Joe's time passed away happily enough; he saw Miss Hughes every evening in his mother's presence, and every Sunday she spent with them. All this time his reputation was rapidly increasing; almost every new part he played rendered him a greater favourite than before, and altogether his lot in life was a cheerful and contented one.

CHAPTER THREE

At this period the only inhabitants of the house in Penton Place were Grimaldi and his mother, and Mr and Mrs Lewis. There was no servant, a girl that had lived with them some time having gone into the country to see her friends, and no other having been engaged in her absence. One night in the middle of August a 'night rehearsal' was called at Sadler's Wells: this takes place after the other performances of the evening are over, and the public have left the house. Being an inconvenient and fatiguing ceremony, it is never resorted to but when some very heavy piece (that is, one on a very extensive scale) is to be produced on a short notice. In this instance a new piece was to be played on the following Monday, of which the performers knew very little, and there being no time to lose, a 'night rehearsal' was called, the natural consequence of which would be the detention of the company at the theatre until four o'clock in the morning, at least. Mr Lewis, having notice of the rehearsal in common with the other performers, locked up their dwelling-house, being the last person who left it; brought the street-door key with him; and handed it over to Grimaldi.

But after the performances were over, when the curtain was raised, and the performers, assembling on the stage, prepared to commence the rehearsal, the stage manager addressed the company in the following unexpected and very agreeable terms:

"Ladies and gentlemen, as the new drama will not be produced, as was originally intended, on Monday next, but is deferred until that night week, we shall not be compelled to trouble you with a rehearsal tonight."

This notification occasioned a very quick dispersion of the performers, who, very unexpectedly released from an onerous attendance, hurried home. Grimaldi, having something to do at the theatre which would occupy him about ten minutes, sent his mother and his friend Mrs Lewis to prepare supper, and followed them shortly afterwards, accompanied by Mr Lewis and two other performers attached to the theatre.

When the females reached home they found to their great surprise that the garden gate was open.

"Dear me!" said Mrs Grimaldi (Mrs Brooker). "How careless this is of Mr Lewis!"

It was, undoubtedly; for at that time a most notorious gang of thieves infested that suburb of London. Several of the boldest had been hanged, and others transported, but these punishments had no effect upon their more lucky companions, who committed their depredations with, if possible, increased hardihood and daring.

They were not a little surprised, after crossing the garden, to find that not only was the garden-gate open, but that the street door was unlocked; and pushing it gently open, they observed the reflection of a light at the end of the passage, upon which of course they both cried "Thieves!" and screamed for help. A man who was employed at Sadler's Wells happened to be passing at the time, and tendered his assistance.

"Do you wait here with Mrs Lewis a minute," said Grimaldi's mother, "and I will go into the house. Don't mind me unless you hear me scream; then come to my assistance." So saying, she courageously entered the passage, descended the stairs, entered the kitchen, hastily struck a light, and on lighting a candle and looking around, discovered that the place had been plundered of almost everything it contained. She was running upstairs to communicate their loss, when Grimaldi and his friends arrived. Hearing what had occurred, they entered the house in a body and proceeded to search it narrowly, thinking it probable that some of the thieves, surprised upon the premises, might be still lurking there. In they rushed, the party augmented by the arrival of two watchmen—chosen, as the majority of that fine body of men invariably were, with a specific view to their old age and infirmities—and began their inspection: the women screaming and crying, and the men all shouting together.

The house was in a state of great disorder and confusion, but no thieves were to be seen; the cupboards were forced, the drawers had been broken open, and every article they contained had been removed, with the solitary exception of a small net shawl, which had been worked by Miss Hughes, and given by her to her chosen mother-in-law. Leaving the others to search the house, and the females to bewail their loss, which was really a very severe one, Grimaldi beckoned a Mr King, one of the persons who had accompanied him home from the theatre, and suggested in a whisper that they should search the garden together. King readily complied, and he having armed himself with a heavy stick, and Grimaldi with an old broadsword which he had hastily snatched from its peg on the first alarm, they crept cautiously into the back garden, which was separated from those of the houses on either side by a wall from three to four feet high, and from a very extensive piece of pasture land beyond it at the bottom, by another wall two or three feet higher.

It was a dark night, and they groped about the garden for some time, but found nobody. Grimaldi sprang upon the higher wall, and looking over the lower one descried a man in the act of jumping from the wall of the next garden. Upon seeing another figure, the robber paused, and taking it for that of his comrade in the darkness of the night, cried softly, "Hush! hush! Is that you?"

"Yes!" replied Grimaldi, getting as near as he could. Seeing that the man, recognising the voice as a strange one, was about to jump down, he dealt him a heavy blow with the broadsword. The man yelled out loudly, and stopping for an instant, as if in extreme pain, dropped to the ground, limped off a few paces, and was lost in the darkness.

Grimaldi shouted to his friend to follow him through the back gate, but seeing, from his station on the wall, that he and the thief took directly opposite courses, he leapt into the field, and set off at full speed. He was stopped in the very outset of his career by tumbling over a cow, which was lying on the ground, in which involuntary pantomimic feat he would most probably have cut his own head off with the weapon he carried, if his theatrical practice as a fencer had not taught him to carry edged tools with caution. The companion, having taken a little run by himself, soon returned out of breath to say he had seen nobody, and they re-entered the house, where by the light of the candle it was seen that the sword was covered with blood.

The constable of the night had arrived by this time; and a couple of watchmen bearing large lanterns, to show the thieves they were coming, issued forth into the field, in hopes of taking the offenders alive or dead—they would have preferred the latter—and of recovering any of the stolen property that might be scattered about. The direction which the wounded man had taken having been pointed out, they began to explore, by very slow degrees.

Bustling about, striving to raise the spirits of the party, and beginning to stow away in their proper places such articles as the thieves had condescended to leave, one of the first things Grimaldi chanced to light upon was Miss Hughes's shawl.

"Maria's gift, at all events," he said, taking it up and giving it a slight wave in his hand; when out fell a lozenge-box upon the floor, much more heavily than a box with any ordinary lozenges inside would do.

Upon this his mother clapped her hands, and set up a louder scream than she had given vent to when she found the house robbed.

"My money! My money!" she screamed.

"It can't be helped, my dear madam," said everybody. "Think of poor Mrs Lewis; she is quite as badly off."

"Oh, I don't mean that," was the reply. "Oh! thank Heaven, they didn't find my money." So with many half-frantic exclamations, she picked up the lozenge-box, and there, sure enough, were thirty-seven guineas (it was completely full), which had lain securely concealed beneath the shawl!

They sat down to supper; but although Mrs Brooker now cheered up wonderfully, and quite rallied her friend upon her low spirits, poor Mrs Lewis, who had found no lozenge-box, was quite unable to overcome her loss. Supper over, and some hot potations, which the fright had rendered absolutely necessary, dispatched, the friends departed, and the usual inmates of the house were left alone to make such preparations for passing the night as they deemed fitting.

They were ludicrous enough: upon comparing notes, it was found that nobody could sleep alone, upon which they came to the conclusion that they had better all sleep in the same room. For this purpose a mattress was dragged into the front parlour, upon which the two females bestowed themselves without undressing; Lewis sat in an easy chair; and Grimaldi, having loaded two pistols, wiped the sanguinary stains from the broadsword, laid it by his side, drew another easy chair near the door, and there mounted guard.

All had been quiet for some time, and they were falling asleep, when they were startled by a long loud knocking at the back door, which led into the garden. They all started up and gazed upon each other, with looks of considerable dismay. The females would have screamed, only they were too frightened; and the men would have laughed it off, but they were quite unable from the same cause to muster the faintest smile. Grimaldi was the first to recover the sudden shock, which the supposed return of the robbers had communicated to the party, and turning to Lewis, said, with one of his oddest looks, "You had better go to the back door, old boy, and see who it is." Mr Lewis did not appear quite satisfied upon the point. He reflected for a short time, and looking with a very blank face at his wife, said he was much obliged to Mr Grimaldi, but he would rather not. In this dilemma, it was arranged that Lewis should wait in the passage, and that Grimaldi should creep softly upstairs, and reconnoitre the enemy from the window above—a plan which Lewis thought much more feasible, and which was at once put in execution.

While these deliberations were going forward, the knocking had continued without cessation, and it now began to assume a subdued and confidential tone, which, instead of subduing their alarm, rather tended to increase it. Armed with the two pistols and the broadsword, and looking much more like Robinson Crusoe than either the Shipwrecked Mariner or the Little Clown, Grimaldi thrust his head out of the window and hailed the people below, in a voice which, between agitation and a desire to communicate to the neighbours the full benefit of the discussion, was something akin to that in which his well-known cry of "Here we are!" afterwards acquired so much popularity.

It was between two and three o'clock in the morning—the day was breaking, and the light increasing fast. He could descry two men at the door heavily laden with something, but with what he could not discern. All he could see was, that it was not firearms, and that was a comfort.

"Hollo! Hollo!" Joe shouted out of the window, displaying the brace of pistols and the broadsword to the best advantage. "What's the matter there?" Here he coughed very fiercely, and again demanded what was the matter.

"Why, sir," replied one of the men, looking up, and holding on his hat as he did so, "we thought we should never wake ye."

"And what did you want to wake me for?" was the natural enquiry.

"Why, the property!" replied both the men at the same time.

"The what?" enquired the master of the house, taking in the broadsword, and putting the pistols on the window sill.

"The property!" replied the two men, pettishly. "Here we have been a-looking over the field all this time, and have found the property."

No further conversation was necessary. The door was opened, and the watchmen entered bearing two large sacks,

which they had stumbled on in the field, and the females, falling
on their knees before them, began dragging forth their contents
in an agony of impatience. After a lengthy examination it was
found that the sacks contained every article that had been
taken away; that not one, however trifling, was missing; and
that they had come into possession, besides, of a complete and
extensive assortment of house-breaking tools, including centre-
bit, picklock, keys, screws, dark lanterns, a file, and a crowbar.
The watchmen were dismissed with ten shillings and as many
thousand thanks, and the party breakfasted in a much more
comfortable manner than that in which they had supped on the
previous night.

The conversation naturally turned upon the robbery, and
various conjectures and surmises were hazarded relative to the
persons by whom it had been committed. It appeared perfectly
evident that the thieves, whoever they were, must have obtained
information of the expected night rehearsal at Sadler's Wells;
it was equally clear that if the rehearsal had not been most
fortunately postponed, the Lewises and Grimaldis would not
only have lost everything they possessed, but the thieves would
have got clear off with the booty into the bargain. It was worthy
of remark that the house had never been attempted when the
servant girl was at home, and the females were half inclined to
attach suspicion to her; but on reflection it seemed unlikely that
she was implicated in the transaction, for she was the daughter
of very respectable parents; her uncle had held the situation of
master-tailor to the theatre for forty years; and her aunt had
served the family in the same capacity as the girl herself. In
addition to these considerations, she had been well brought
up, had always appeared strictly honest, and had already lived

in the house for nearly four years. Upon these grounds it was resolved that the girl could not be a party to the attempt.

But whoever committed the burglary, it was necessary that the house should be well secured, with which view a carpenter was sent for, and a great supply of extra bolts and bars were placed upon the different doors. Notwithstanding these precautions, however, and the additional security which they necessarily afforded, the females were very nervous for a long time, and the falling of a plate, or slamming of a door, or a loud ringing at the bell, or above all, the twopenny postman after dark, was sufficient to throw them into the extremity of terror. Being determined not to leave the house in future without somebody to take care of it while the family were at the theatre, they resolved, after many pros and cons, to engage for the purpose a very trustworthy man, who was employed as a watchman to the theatre, but was not required to attend until eleven o'clock at night, by which time, at all events, some of the family would be able to reach home. The man was hired, and commenced his watch, on the night after the robbery; and there he continued to remain every evening, until the return of the servant girl from the country released him from further attendance.

The agitation and surprise of this girl were very great, when she was informed of what had occurred, but they did not appear to be the emotions of a guilty person. All agreed that there was no good ground of suspicion against her. She was asked if she would be afraid to be left alone in the house after what had taken place, when she declared that she was not afraid of any thieves and that she would willingly sit up alone, as she had been accustomed to do; merely stipulating that she should be allowed to light a fire in the Lewis's sitting room, for the purpose of inducing robbers to suppose that the family were at home, and that she should be provided with a large rattle, with which to alarm the neighbours at any appearance of danger. Both requests were complied with; and as an additional precaution the street watchman, whose box was within a few yards of the door, was fee'd to be on the alert, to keep a sharp eye upon the house and to attend to any summons from within, whenever it might be made.

The thieves, whoever they were, were very wanton fellows, and added outrage to plunder, for with the most heartless cruelty, and an absence of all taste for scientific pursuits which would stigmatise them at once as occupying a very low grade in their profession, had broken open a closet in Grimaldi's room, containing his chosen cabinet of insects, including Dartford Blues, which, either because it was not portable, or because they thought it of no value, attaching no importance to flies, they most recklessly and barbarously destroyed. With the exception of one small box, they utterly annihilated the whole collection, including even his models, drawings, and colours: it would have taken years to replace them, if the collector had been most indefatigable; and it would have cost at least two hundred pounds to have replaced them by purchase. This unforeseen calamity put a total stop to the fly-catching; so, collecting together his nets and cases, and the only box which was not destroyed, Grimaldi gave them all away next day to an acquaintance who had a taste for such things, and never more employed himself in a similar manner.

After a lapse of a short time, the arrangements and pre-cautions infused renewed confidence into the inmates of the house, and they began to feel more secure than they had yet done since the robbery; a fortnight had now passed over, and they strengthened themselves with the reflection that the thieves having met with so disagreeable a reception, one of them at least having been severely wounded, were very unlikely to renew the attempt. But well founded as these conjectures might seem, they reckoned without their host.

On the third night—the previous two having passed in perfect quiet and security—the servant girl was at work in the kitchen, when she fancied she heard a sound as if some person were attempting to force open the garden door. She thought it merely the effect of fancy at first, but the noise continuing, she went softly up stairs into the passage, and on looking towards the door, saw that the latch was moved up and down several times by a hand outside, while some person pushed violently against the door itself. The poor girl being very much frightened, her first impulse was to scream violently; but so far were her cries from deterring the persons outside from persisting in their attempt, that they only seemed to press it with redoubled vigour. Indeed, so violent were their exertions, as if irritated by the noise the girl made, that the door was very nearly forced from its position. If it had not been proof against the attacks of the thieves the girl would assuredly have been murdered. Recovering her presence of mind, however, on finding that they could not force an entrance, she ran to the street door, flung it open, and had immediate recourse to the rattle, which she wielded with such hearty good will that the watchman and half the neighbourhood were quickly on the spot. Immediate search was made for the robbers in the rear of the house, but they had thought it prudent to escape quietly.

Upon the return of the family, all their old apprehensions were revived and increased tenfold by the bold and daring nature of this second attempt. Watch was kept all night, the watchers starting at the slightest sound; rest was out of the question, and nothing but dismay and confusion prevailed. The next morning it was resolved that the house should be fortified with additional strength, and that when these precautions had been taken, Grimaldi should repair to the police office of the district, state his case to the sitting magistrate, and claim the assistance of the constituted authorities. Having had bars of iron, and plates of iron, and patent locks, and a variety of ingenious defences affixed to the interior of the garden door, which, when fastened with all these appurtenances, appeared nearly impregnable, Grimaldi accordingly walked down to Hatton Garden, with the view of backing the locks and bolts with the aid of the executive.

There was at that time a very shrewd, knowing officer attached to that establishment, whose name was Trott. He was occasionally employed to assist the regular constables at the theatre, when they expected a great house; and Grimaldi no sooner stepped into the passage, than, walking up to him, Trott accosted him with:

"How do, master?"

"How do *you* do?"

"Pretty well, thankee, master; I was just going to call up at your place."

"Ah!" said the other, "you've heard of it, then?"

"Yes, I have heard of it," said Mr Trott, with a grin, "and heard a great deal more about it than you know on, master."

"You don't surely mean to say that you have apprehended the burglars?"

"No, no, I don't mean that; I wish I did: they have been one

60

too many for me as yet. Why, when they first started in business there worn't fewer than twenty men in that gang. Sixteen or seventeen on 'em have been hung or transported, and the rest is them that has been at your house. They have got a hiding-place somewhere in Pentonville. I'll tell you what, master," said Trott, taking the other by the button, and speaking in a hoarse whisper, "they are the worst of the lot; up to everything they are; and take my word for it, Mr Grimaldi, they'll stick at nothing."

Grimaldi looked anything but pleased at this intelligence, and Trott, observing his disturbed countenance, added:

"Don't you be alarmed, master; what they want is, their revenge for their former disappointment. That's what it is," said Trott, nodding his head sagaciously.

"It appears very extraordinary," said Grimaldi. "This is a very distressing situation to be placed in."

"Why, so it is," said the officer, after a little consideration. "So it is, when you consider that they never talk without doing. But don't be afraid, Mr Grimaldi."

"Oh, no I'm not," replied the other; adding, in as cool a manner as he could assume, "they came again last night."

"I know that," said the officer. "I'll let you into another secret, master. They are coming again tonight."

"Again, tonight!" exclaimed Grimaldi.

"As sure as fate," replied the officer, nodding to a friend who was passing down the street on the other side of the way. "And if your establishment ain't large enough, and powerful enough to resist 'em … "

"Large and powerful enough!" exclaimed the other. "Why, there are only three women and one other male person besides myself in the house."

"Ah!" said Mr Trott, "that isn't near enough."

"Enough! No!" rejoined Grimaldi. "And it would kill my mother."

"I dare say it would," acquiesced the officer. "My mother was killed in a similar manner."

This, like the rest of the officer's discourse, was far from consolatory, and Grimaldi looked anxiously in his face for something like a ray of hope.

Mr Trott meditated for some short time, and then, looking up with his head on one side, said, "I think I see a way now, master."

"What is it? What do you propose? I'm agreeable to anything," said Grimaldi, in a most accommodating manner.

"Never mind that," said the officer. "You put yourself into my hands, and I'll be the saving of your property, and the taking of them."

Grimaldi burst into many expressions of admiration and gratitude, and put his hand into Mr Trott's hands, as an earnest of his readiness to deposit himself there.

"Only rid us," said Grimaldi, "of these dreadful visitors, who really keep us in a state of perpetual misery, and anything you think proper to accept shall be cheerfully paid you."

The officer replied with many moral observations on the duties of police officers, their incorruptible honesty, their zeal, and rigid discharge of the functions reposed in them. If Mr Grimaldi would do his duty to his country, and prosecute them to conviction, that was all he required. To this, Grimaldi, not having any precise idea of the expense of a prosecution, readily assented, and the officer declared he should be sufficiently repaid by the pleasing consciousness of having done his duty.

He did not consider it necessary to add that a reward had been offered for the apprehension of the same offenders, payable on their conviction.

They walked back to the house together, and the officer having inspected it with the practised eye of an experienced person, declared himself thoroughly satisfied, and stated that if his injunctions were strictly attended to, he had no doubt his final operations would be completely successful.

"It will be necessary," said Trott, speaking with great pomp and grandeur, as the inmates assembled round him to hear his oration, "it will be necessary to take every portable article out of the back kitchen, the parlour, and the bedroom, and to give me up the entire possession of this house for one night; at least until such time as I shall have laid my hand upon these here gentlemen."

It is needless to say that this proposition was agreed to, and that the females at once went about clearing the rooms as the officer had directed. At five o'clock in the afternoon he returned, and the keys of the house were delivered up to him. These arrangements having been made, the family departed to the theatre as usual, leaving Mr Trott alone in the house; for the servant girl had been sent away to a neighbour's by his desire, whether from any feeling of delicacy on the part of Mr Trott (who was a married man), or from any apprehension that she might impede his operations, we are not informed.

The officer remained alone in the house, taking care not to go near any of the windows until it was dark, when two of his colleagues, coming by appointment to the garden door, were stealthily admitted into the house. Having carefully scrutinised the whole place, they disposed themselves in the following order. One man locked and bolted in the front kitchen, another locked and bolted himself in the sitting-room above stairs, and Mr Trott, the presiding genius, in the front parlour towards the street; the last-named gentleman having, before he retired into ambuscade, bolted and barred the back door, and only locked the front one. Here they remained for some time, solitary enough, no doubt, for there was not a light in the house, and each man being fastened in a room by himself was as much alone as if there had been no one else in the place. The time seemed unusually long; they listened intently, and were occasionally deceived for an instant by some noise in the street, but it soon subsided again, and all was silent as before.

At length, some time after nightfall, a low knock came to the street door. No attention being paid to it, the knock was repeated, and this time it was rather louder. It echoed through the house, but no one stirred. After a short interval, as if the person outside had been listening and had satisfied himself, a slight rattling was heard at the keyhole, and, the lock being picked, the footsteps of two men were heard in the passage. They quietly bolted the door after them, and pulling from beneath their coats a couple of dark lanterns, walked softly upstairs. Finding the door of the front room locked, they came down again, and tried the front parlour, which was also locked, whereat, Mr Trott, who was listening with his ear close to the handle, laughed immoderately, but without noise. Unsuccessful in these two attempts, they went downstairs, and with some surprise found one of the kitchens locked, and the other open. Only stopping just to peep into the open one, they once more ascended to the passage.

"Well," said one of the men, as he came up the kitchen stairs, "we have got it all to ourselves tonight, anyway, so we had better not lose any time. Hollo!"

"What's the matter?" said the other, looking back.

"Look here!" rejoined his comrade, pointing to the garden door, with the bolts, and iron plates, and patent locks, "here's protection, here's security for a friend. These have been put on since we were here afore; we might have tried to get in for everlasting."

"We had better stick it open," said the other man, "and then if there's any game in front, we can get off as we did t'other night."

"Easily said. How do you do it?" said the first speaker, "it will take no end of time, and make no end of noise, to undo all these things. We had better look sharp. There's no rehearsal tonight, remember."

At this, they both laughed, and determining to take the front parlour first, picked the lock without more ado. This done, they pushed against the door to open it, but were unable to do so by reason of the bolts inside, which Mr Trott had taken good care to thrust into the staples as far as they would possibly go.

"This is a rum game!" said one of the fellows, giving the door a kick, "it won't open!"

"Never mind, let it be," said the other man. "There's a spring or something. The back kitchen's open; we had better begin there; we know there's some property here, because we took it away before. Show yourself smart, and bring the bag."

As the speaker stopped to trim his lantern, the other man joined him, and said, with an oath and a chuckle:

"Shouldn't you like to know who it was as struck you with the sword, Tom?"

"I wish I did," growled the other. "I'd put a knife in him before many days was over. Come on."

They went downstairs, and Trott, softly gliding from his hiding-place, double-locked the street door, and put the key in his pocket. He then stationed himself at the top of the kitchen stairs, where he listened with great glee to the exclamations of surprise and astonishment which escaped the robbers, as they opened drawer after drawer, and found them all empty.

"Everything taken away!" said one of the men. "What the devil does this mean?"

The officer, by way of reply, fired a pistol charged only with blank powder, down the stairs, and retreated expeditiously to his parlour. This being the signal, the sound was instantly followed by the noise of the other two officers unlocking and unbolting the doors of their hiding-places. The thieves, scrambling upstairs, rushed quickly to the street door, but, in consequence of its being locked, they were unable to escape; were easily made prisoners, handcuffed, and borne away in triumph.

The affair was all over, and the house restored to order, when the family came home. The officer who had been dispatched to bring the servant home, and left behind to bear her company in case any of the companions of the thieves should pay the house a visit, took his departure as soon as they appeared, bearing with him a large sack left behind by the robbers, which contained as extensive an assortment of the implements of their trade, as had been so fortunately captured on their first appearance. Grimaldi appeared at Hatton Garden the next morning, and was introduced to the prisoners for the first time. His testimony having been taken, and the evidence of Mr Trott and his men received, by which the identity of the criminals was clearly proved, they were fully committed for trial, and Grimaldi was bound over to prosecute. They were tried at the ensuing Sessions, the jury at once found them guilty, and they were transported for life.

This anecdote, which is narrated in every particular precisely as the circumstances occurred, affords a striking and curious picture of the state of society in and about London, in this respect, at the very close of the last century. The bold and daring highwaymen who took the air at Hounslow, Bagshot, Finchley, and a hundred other places of quite fashionable resort, had ceased to canter their blood-horses over heath and road in search of plunder, but there still existed in the capital and its environs, common and poorer gangs of thieves, whose depredations were conducted with a daring and disregard of consequences which to the citizens of this age is wholly extraordinary. One attempt at robbery similar to that which has just been described, committed nowadays (1838) in such a spot, would fill the public papers for a month; but three such attempts on the same house and by the same men would set all London, and all the country for thirty miles round to boot, in a ferment of wonder and indignation.

It was proved, on the examination of these men at the police-office, that they were the only remaining members of a band of thieves called the 'Pentonville Robbers', and the prosecutor and his family congratulated themselves not a little upon the fact, inasmuch as it relieved them from the apprehension that there were any more of their companions left behind who might feel disposed to revenge their fate. This was Grimaldi's first visit to a police-office. His next appearance on the same scene was under very different circumstances. But of this anon.

CHAPTER FOUR

T HE FEARS OF THE GRIMALDI FAMILY had been so thoroughly roused, and their dreams were haunted by such constant visions of the Pentonville Robbers, that the house in Penton Place grew irksome and distressing, especially to the females. Moreover, Grimaldi now began to think it high time that his marriage should take place; and, as now that he had gained the mother's approval he did not so entirely despair of succeeding with the father, he resolved to take a larger house, and to furnish and fit it up handsomely on a scale proportionate to his increased means. He naturally trusted that Mr Hughes would be more disposed to entrust his daughter's happiness to his charge when he found that her suitor was enabled to provide her with a comfortable, if not an elegant home, and to support her in a sphere of life not very distantly removed from that in which her father's fortune and possessions entitled her to be placed.

Accordingly, he gave notice to the landlord of the ill-fated house in Penton Place that he should quit it in the following March; and accompanied by Miss Hughes, to whom, as he very properly says, *of course* he referred everything, they wandered about the whole neighbourhood in search of some house that would be more suitable to them. Penton Street was the St James's of Pentonville, the Regent's Park of the City Road, in those days, and here he was fortunate enough to secure the house at number thirty-seven, which was forthwith furnished and fitted up agreeably to the taste and direction of Miss Hughes herself.

Grimaldi had plenty of time to devote to the contemplation of his expected happiness and the complete preparation of his new residence, for Sadler's Wells was then closed, and as he was never wanted at Drury Lane until Christmas, and not much then unless they produced a pantomime, his theatrical avocations were not of a very heavy or burdensome description.

This year, too, the proprietors of Drury Lane, in pursuance of a custom to which they had adhered for some years, produced an expensive pageant instead of a pantomime; an alteration which was, in Grimaldi's opinion, very little for the better, if not positively for the worse. It having been the established custom for many years to produce a pantomime at Christmas, the public naturally looked for it; and although such pieces as *Blue Beard*, *Feudal Times*, *Lodoiska* and others of the same class undoubtedly drew money to the house, still it is questionable whether they were so profitable to the treasury as the pantomimes at Covent Garden. If we may judge from the result, they certainly were not, for after several years' trial, during the whole of which time pantomimes were annually produced at Covent Garden, they were again brought forward at Drury Lane, to the exclusion of spectacle. Grimaldi played in all these pieces; yet his parts, being of a trifling description, occupied no time in the getting up, and as he infinitely preferred the company of Miss Hughes to that of a theatrical audience, he was well pleased.

By the end of February, the whitewashers, carpenters, upholsterers, even the painters, had left the Penton Street mansion, and there being no pantomime, it seemed a very eligible period for being married at once. Grimaldi told Miss Hughes that he thought so: Miss Hughes replied that he had only to gain her father's consent in the first instance, and then the day should be fixed without more ado. This was precisely what the lover was most anxious to avoid, for two reasons: firstly, because it involved the very probable postponement of his happiness; and secondly, because obtaining this consent was an awkward process. At last he recollected that in consequence of Mr Hughes being out of town, it was quite impossible to ask him.

"Very good," said Miss Hughes. "Everything happens for the best. I am sure you would never venture to speak to him on the subject, so you had far better write. He will not keep you long in suspense, I know, for he is quite certain to answer your letter by return of post."

Mr Hughes was then at Exeter; and as it certainly did appear to his destined son-in-law a much better course to write than to speak, even if he had been in London, he sat down without delay, and, after various trials, produced such a letter as he thought would be most likely to find its way to the father's heart. Miss Hughes approving of the contents, it was re-read, copied, punctuated, folded, and posted. Next day the lady was obliged to leave town, to spend a short time with some friends at Gravesend; and the lover, very much to his annoyance and regret, was fain to stay behind and console himself as he best could, in his mistress's absence and the absence of a reply from her father, to which he naturally looked forward with considerable impatience and anxiety.

Five days passed away, and still no letter came; and poor Grimaldi, being left to his own fears and apprehension, was reduced to the most desperate and dismal forebodings. Having no employment at the theatre, and nothing to do but to think of his mistress and his letter, he was almost beside himself with anxiety and suspense. It was with no small pleasure, then, that he received a note from Miss Hughes, entreating him to take a trip down to Gravesend in one of the sailing-boats on the following Sunday, as he could return by the same conveyance the same night. Of course, he was not slow to avail himself of the invitation; so he took shipping at the Tower on the morning of the day appointed, and reached the place of his destination in pretty good time. He found Miss Hughes waiting for him at the landing-place, and getting into a 'tide-coach', they proceeded to Chatham, Miss Hughes informing him that she had made a confidant of her brother, who was stationed there, and that they purposed spending the day together.

"And now, Joe," said Miss Hughes, when he had expressed the pleasure which this arrangement afforded him, "tell me everything that has happened. What does my father say?"

"My dear," replied Grimaldi, "he says nothing at all; he has not answered my letter."

"Not answered your letter!" said the lady. "His punctuality is proverbial."

"So I have always heard," replied Grimaldi. "But so it is; I have not heard a syllable."

"Then you must write again, Joe," said Miss Hughes, "immediately, without the least delay. Let me see, you cannot very well write today, but tomorrow you must not fail; I cannot account for his silence."

"Nor I," said Grimaldi.

"Unless, indeed," said Miss Hughes, "some extraordinary business has driven your letter from his memory."

As people always endeavour to believe what they hope, they were not long in determining that it must be so. Dismissing the subject from their minds, they spent the day happily in company with young Mr Hughes, and returning to Gravesend in the evening by another tide-coach, Grimaldi was on board the sailing-boat shortly before eleven o'clock; it being arranged that Miss Hughes was to follow on the next Saturday.

In the cabin of the boat he found Mr De Cleve, at that time treasurer of Sadler's Wells. There are jealousies in theatres, as there are in courts, ballrooms, and boarding-schools; and this Mr De Cleve was jealous of Grimaldi—not because he stood in *his* way, for he had no touch of comedy in his composition, but because he had eclipsed, and indeed altogether outshone, one Mr Hartland, "a very clever and worthy man", says Grimaldi, who was at that time also engaged as a pantomimic and melodramatic actor at Sadler's Wells. Mr De Cleve, thinking for his friends as well as himself, hated Grimaldi most cordially, and the meeting was consequently by no means an agreeable one to him; for if he had chanced to set eyes upon Miss Hughes, great mischief-making and turmoil would be the inevitable consequence.

"In the name of wonder, Grimaldi," said this agreeable character, "what are you doing here?"

"Going back to London," replied Grimaldi, "as I suppose most of us are."

"That is not what I meant," said De Cleve. "What I meant was, to ask you what business might have taken you to Gravesend?"

"Oh! no business at all," replied the other. "Directly I landed I went off by the tide-coach to Chatham."

"Indeed!" said the other.

"Yes," said Grimaldi.

The treasurer looked rather puzzled at this, sufficiently showing by his manner that he had been hunting about Gravesend all day in search of the young man. He remained silent a short time, and then said, "I only asked because I thought you might have had a dinner engagement at Gravesend, perhaps with a young lady even. Who knows?"

This little sarcasm on the part of the worthy treasurer convinced Grimaldi that having somewhere picked up the information that Miss Hughes was at Gravesend, and having heard afterwards from Mrs Lewis or somebody at the theatre that Grimaldi was going to the same place, he had followed him thither with the amiable intention of playing the spy and watching the proceedings. If he had observed the young people together his mischievous intentions would have been completely successful; but the tide-coach had balked him, and Mr De Cleve's good-natured arrangements were futile.

Grimaldi laughed in his sleeve as the real state of the case presented itself to his mind; and feeling well pleased that he had not seen them together, in the absence of any reply from Mr De Cleve he ascended to the deck and left the treasurer to his meditations. Upon the deck, on a green bench, with a back to it and arms besides, there sat a neighbour, and a neighbour's wife, and the neighbour's wife's sister, and a very pretty girl, who was the neighbour's wife's sister's friend. There was just room for one more on the bench, and they insisted upon Mr Grimaldi occupying the vacant seat, which he readily did, for they were remaining on deck to avoid the closeness of the cabin, and he preferred the cold air of the night to the cold heart of Mr De Cleve.

So down he sat next to the pretty friend; and the pretty friend being wrapped in a very large seaman's coat, it was suggested by the neighbour, who was a wag in his way, that she ought to lend a bit of it to Mr Grimaldi, who looked very cold. After a great deal of blushing and giggling, the young lady put her left arm through the left arm of the coat, and Grimaldi put his right arm through the left arm of the coat, to the great admiration of the whole party, and after the manner in which they show the giants' coats at the fairs. They sat in this way during the whole voyage, and Grimaldi always declared that it was a very comfortable way of travelling, as no doubt it is.

"Laugh away!" he said, as the party gave vent to their delight in bursts of merriment. "If we had only something here to warm us internally as well as the greatcoat does externally, we would laugh all night."

"What would you recommend for that purpose?" asked the neighbour.

"Brandy," said the friend.

"Then," rejoined the neighbour, "if you were a Harlequin instead of a Clown, you could not have conjured it up quicker." And with these words, the neighbour, who was a plump, red-faced, merry fellow, held up with both hands a large heavy stone bottle, with an inverted drinking-horn resting on the bung; and having laughed very much at his own forethought, he set the stone bottle down, and sat himself on the top of it.

It was the only thing wanting to complete the mirth of the party, and very merry they were. It was a fine moonlight night, cold, but healthy and fresh, and it passed pleasantly and quickly away. The day had broken before they reached Billingsgate Stairs; the stone bottle was empty, the neighbour asleep, Grimaldi and the young lady buttoned up in the greatcoat, and the wife and daughter very jocose and good-humoured.

Here they parted: the neighbour's family went home in a

hackney-coach, and Grimaldi, bidding them goodbye, walked away to Gracechurch Street, not forgetting to thank the young lady for her humanity and compassion. He had occasion to call at a coach-office, but finding that it was not yet open (for it was very early), and not feeling at all fatigued by his journey, he determined to walk about the city for a couple of hours or so, and then return to the coach-office. By doing so, he would pass away the time till the office opened, gain an opportunity of looking about him in that part of London, to which he was quite a stranger, and avoid disturbing the family at home until a more seasonable hour. So he made up his mind to walk the two hours away, and turned back for that purpose.

It was now broad day. The sun had risen, and was shedding a fine mild light over the quiet streets. The crowd so soon to be let loose upon them was not yet stirring, and the only people visible were the passengers who had landed from the boats, or who had just entered London by other early conveyances. Although Grimaldi had lived in London all his life, he knew far less about it than many country people who have visited it once or twice; and so unacquainted was he with the particular quarter of the city in which he found himself, that he had never even seen the Tower of London. He walked down to look at that; and then he stared at the buildings round about, and the churches, and a thousand objects which no one but a loiterer ever bestows a glance upon; and so was walking on pleasantly enough, when all at once he struck his foot against something which was lying on the pavement. Looking down to see what it was, he perceived, to his great surprise, a richly-ornamented net purse of a very large size, filled with gold coin.

Grimaldi was perfectly paralysed by the sight. He looked

at it again and again without daring to touch it. Then by a sudden impulse, he glanced cautiously round, and seeing that he was wholly unobserved, and that there was not a solitary being within sight, he picked up the purse and thrust it into his pocket. As he stooped for this purpose, he observed, lying on the ground on very nearly the same spot, a small bundle of papers tied round with a piece of string. He picked them up too, mechanically. What was his astonishment, on examining this last discovery more narrowly, to find that the bundle was composed exclusively of bank-notes!

There was still nobody to be seen: there were no passers-by, no sound of footsteps in the adjacent streets. He lingered about the spot for more than an hour, eagerly scrutinising the faces of the people, who now began passing to and fro, with looks which themselves almost seemed to enquire whether they had lost anything. No! There was no enquiry, no searching; no person ran distractedly past him, or groped among the mud by the pavement's side. It was evidently of no use waiting there; and, quite tired of doing so, Grimaldi turned and walked slowly back to the coach-office in Gracechurch Street. He met or overtook no person on the road who appeared to have lost anything, far less the immense sum of money (for such it appeared to him) that he had found.

All this time, and for hours afterwards, he was in a state of turmoil and agitation almost inconceivable. He felt as if he had committed some dreadful theft, and feared discovery, and the shameful punishment which must follow it. His legs trembled beneath him so that he could scarcely walk, his heart beat violently and the perspiration started on his face. The more Grimaldi reflected upon the precise nature of his situation, the more distressed and apprehensive he became. Suppose the money were to be found upon him by the loser, who would believe him, when he declared that he picked it up in the street? Would it not appear much more probable that he had stolen it? And if such a charge were brought against him, by what evidence could he rebut it? As these thoughts, and twenty such, passed through his mind, he was more than once tempted to draw the money from his pocket, fling it on the pavement, and take to his heels; which he was only restrained from doing by reflecting, that if he were observed and questioned, his answers might at once lead him to be accused of a charge of robbery, in which case he would be as badly off as if he were in the grasp of the real loser. It would appear at first sight a very lucky thing to find such a purse; but Grimaldi thought himself far from fortunate as these torturing thoughts filled his mind.

When he got to Gracechurch Street, he found the coach-office still closely shut, and turning towards home through Coleman Street and Finsbury Square, he passed into the City Road, which then, with the exception of a few houses in the immediate neighbourhood of the Angel at Islington, was entirely lined on both sides with the grounds of market-gardeners. This was a favourable place to count the treasure; so, sitting down upon a bank in a retired spot, just where the Eagle Tavern now stands, he examined his prize. The gold in the purse was all in guineas. The whole contents of the bundle were in bank-notes, varying in their amounts from five to fifty pounds each. And this was all there was; no memorandum, no card, no scrap of paper, no document of any kind whatever, afforded the slightest clue to the name or residence of the owner. Besides the money, there was nothing but the piece of string which kept the notes together, and the handsome silk net purse before mentioned, which held the gold. Grimaldi could not count the money then, for his fingers trembled so that he could scarcely separate the notes, and he was confused and bewildered that he could not reckon the gold. He counted it shortly after he reached home, though, and found that there were three hundred and eighty guineas and two hundred pounds in notes, making in the whole the sum of five hundred and ninety-nine pounds. He reached home between seven and eight o'clock, where, going instantly to bed, he remained sound asleep for several hours. There was no news respecting the money, which he longed to appropriate to his own use; so he put it carefully by, determining of course to abstain rigidly from doing so, and to use all possible means to discover the owner.

Grimaldi did not forget the advice of Miss Hughes in the hurry and excitement consequent upon his morning's adventure, but wrote another epistle to the father, recapitulating the substance of a former letter, and begged to be favoured with a reply. Having dispatched this to the post office, he devoted the remainder of the day to a serious consideration of the line of action it would be most proper to adopt with regard to the five hundred and ninety-nine pounds so suddenly acquired. Eventually, he resolved to consult an old and esteemed friend of his father's, upon whose judgement he knew he might depend, and whose best advice he felt satisfied he could command. This determination Grimaldi carried into execution that same evening; and after a long conversation with the gentleman in question, during which he met all the young man's natural and probably apparent inclination to apply the money to his own occasions and views with arguments and remarks which were wholly unanswerable, Joe submitted to be guided by him, and acted accordingly.

For a whole week the two friends carefully examined every paper which was published in London, if not in the hope, at least in the expectation, of seeing the loss advertised; but, strange as it may seem, nothing of the kind appeared. At the end of the period named an advertisement, of which the following is a copy, their joint production, appeared in the daily papers.

Found by a gentleman in the streets of London, some money, which will be restored to the owner upon his giving a satisfactory account of the manner of its loss, its amount, the numbers of the notes, etc.

To this was appended a full and particular address: but, notwithstanding all these precautions, notwithstanding the publicity that was given to the advertisement, and notwithstanding that the announcement was frequently repeated, from that hour to the very last moment of his life Grimaldi never heard one word or syllable regarding the treasure he had so singularly acquired, nor was he ever troubled with any one application relative to the notice.

Four anxious days (he had both money and a wife at stake) passed heavily away, but on the fifth, Saturday, a reply arrived from Mr Hughes, which, being probably one of the shortest epistles ever received through the hands of the general postman, is subjoined verbatim.

Dear Joe, Expect to see me in a few days. Yours truly, R Hughes

If there was nothing decidedly favourable to be drawn from this brief morceau, there was at least nothing very appalling to his hopes: it was evident that Mr Hughes was not greatly offended at his presumption, and probable that he might be eventually induced to give his consent to Grimaldi's marriage with his daughter. This conclusion, to which he speedily came, tended greatly to elevate his spirits; nor did they meet with any check from the sudden appearance of Miss Hughes from Gravesend. The meeting was a joyful one on both sides. As soon as their mutual greetings were over, he showed her her father's letter, of which she appeared to take but little notice.

"Why, Maria!" he exclaimed, with some surprise, "you scarcely look upon this letter, and seem to care little or nothing about it!"

"To tell you the truth, Joe," answered Miss Hughes, smiling, "my father has already arrived in town: I found him at home when I got there two or three hours back, and he desired me to tell you that he wishes to see you on Monday morning, if you will call at the theatre."

Upon hearing this, all the old nervous symptoms returned, and Joe felt as though he were about to receive a final death-blow to his hopes.

"You may venture to take courage, I think," said Miss Hughes. "I have very little fear or doubt upon the subject."

Her admirer had a good deal of both; but he was somewhat reassured by the young lady's manner, and her conviction that her father, who had always treated her most kindly and indulgently, would not desert her then. Comforted by discussing the probabilities of success, and all the happiness that was to follow it, they spent the remainder of the day happily enough, and looked forward as calmly as they could to the Monday which was to decide their fate. Concealing his inward agitation as best he might, Joe walked to the theatre, on Monday morning, and there in the treasury found Mr Hughes. He was received very kindly, but, after some trivial conversation, was much astonished by Mr Hughes saying, "So you are going to leave Sadler's Wells, and all your old friends, merely because you can get a trifle more elsewhere, eh Joe?"

Grimaldi was so amazed at this, he could scarcely speak, but quickly recovering, said, "I can assure you, sir, that no such idea ever entered my head; in fact, even if I wished such a thing, which, Heaven knows, is furthest from my thoughts, I could not do so, being under articles to you."

"You forget," replied Mr Hughes, somewhat sternly, "your articles have expired here."

And so they had, and so he had forgotten, and so he was constrained to confess.

"It is rather odd," continued Mr Hughes, "that so important a circumstance should have escaped your memory: but tell me, do you know Mr Cross?"

Mr Cross was manager of the Circus, now the Surrey Theatre, and had repeatedly made Grimaldi offers to leave Sadler's Wells, and join his company. He had done so, indeed, only a few days before this conversation, offering to allow Grimaldi to name his own terms. But these and other similar invitations Grimaldi had firmly declined, being unwilling for many reasons to leave the theatre to which he had been accustomed all his life. From this observation of Mr Hughes, and the manner in which it was made, it was obvious to Grimaldi that someone had endeavoured to injure him in that gentleman's opinion; and fortunately chancing to have in his pocket-book the letters he had received from Mr Cross, and copies of his own replies, he lost no time in clearing himself of the charge.

"My dear sir," Grimaldi said, "I do not know Mr Cross

personally, but very well as a correspondent, inasmuch as he has repeatedly written, offering engagements to me, all of which I have declined"—and he placed the papers before Mr Hughes.

The perusal of these letters seemed to satisfy Mr Hughes, who returned them, and said smilingly, "Well then, we'll talk about a fresh engagement here, as you prefer old quarters. Let me see: your salary is now four pounds per week: well, I will engage you for three seasons, and the terms shall be these: for the first season, six pounds per week: for the second, seven: and for the third, eight. Will that do?"

Grimaldi readily agreed to a proposition which, handsome in itself, greatly exceeded anything he had anticipated. As Mr Hughes seemed anxious to have the affair settled, and Grimaldi was perfectly content that it should be, two witnesses were sent for, and the articles were drawn up and signed upon the spot. Then again they were left alone, and after a few moments more of desultory conversation, Mr Hughes rose, saying, "I shall see you, I suppose, in the evening, as I am going to Drury Lane to see *Blue Beard*." He advanced towards the door as he spoke, and then suddenly turning round, added, "Have you anything else to say to me?"

Now was the time, or never. Screwing his courage to the sticking-place, Grimaldi proceeded to place before Mr Hughes his hopes and prospects, strongly urging that his own happiness and that of his daughter depended upon his consent being given to their marriage. Mr Hughes had thought over the subject well, and displayed by no means that displeasure which the young man's anxious fears had prophesied; he urged the youth of both parties as an argument against acceding to their wishes, but finally gave his consent, and by doing so transported the lover with joy. Mr Hughes advanced to the door of the room, and throwing it open as he went out, said to his daughter, who chanced to be sitting in the next room, "Maria, Joe is here: you had better come and welcome him." Miss Hughes came like a dutiful daughter, and *did* welcome her faithful admirer, as he well deserved for his true-hearted and constant affection. In the happiness of the moment, the fact that the door of the room was standing wide open quite escaped the notice of both, who never once recollected the possibility of any third person being an unseen witness to the interview.

This was a red-letter day in Grimaldi's calendar; he had nothing to do in the evening at Drury Lane until the last scene but one of *Blue Beard*, so went shopping with his future wife, buying divers articles of plate and such other small wares as young housekeepers require. On hurrying to the theatre at night, he found Mr Hughes anxiously regarding the machinery of the last scene in *Blue Beard*, which he was about getting up at the Exeter theatre.

"This machinery is very intricate, Joe," said the father-in-law-to-be upon seeing him.

"You are right, sir," replied Joe; "and, what is more, it works very badly."

"So I should expect," was the reply, "and as I am afraid we shall not manage this very well in the country, I wish I could improve it."

Among the numerous modes of employing any spare time to which Grimaldi resorted for the improvement of a vacant hour, the invention of model transformations and pantomime tricks held a foremost place at that time, and did, though in a limited degree, to the close of his life. At the time of his death he had many excellent models of this description, besides several which he sold to Mr Bunn so recently as a few months prior to December 1836, all of which were used in the pantomime of *Harlequin and Gammer Gurton*, produced at Drury Lane. He rarely allowed any machinery which came under his notice, especially if a little peculiar, to pass without modelling it upon a small scale. He had a complete model of the skeleton 'business' in *Blue Beard*; and not merely that, but an improvement of his own besides, by which the intricate nature of the change might be avoided, and many useless flaps dispensed with.

Nervously anxious to elevate himself as much as possible to the opinion of Mr Hughes at this particular juncture, Grimaldi eagerly explained to him the nature of his alterations, as far as the models were concerned, and plainly perceived that the manager was agreeably surprised at the communication. He begged his acceptance of models, both of the original mechanism, and of his own improved version of it; and Mr Hughes, in reply, invited him to breakfast on the following morning, and requested him to bring both models with him. This Joe failed not to do. It happened that a rather ludicrous scene awaited him.

Grimaldi had one or two enemies connected at that time with Sadler's Wells, who allowed their professional envy to impel them to divers acts of small malignity. One of these persons, having been told of Joe's saluting Miss Hughes by a servant-girl with whom he chanced to be acquainted, and who had witnessed the action, sought and obtained an interview that evening with the father upon his return from Drury Lane, and stated the circumstances to him, enlarging and embellishing the details with divers comments upon the ingratitude of Grimaldi in seducing the affections of a young lady so much above him, and making various wise and touching reflections most in vogue on such occasions. Mr Hughes heard all this with a calmness which first of all astonished the speaker, but which he eventually attributed to concentrated rage. After he had finished his speech, the former quietly said, "Will you favour me by coming here at nine o'clock tomorrow morning, sir?"

"Most certainly," was the reply.

"Allow me, however, at once," continued Mr Hughes, "to express my thanks for your kindness in informing me of that which so nearly concerns my domestic happiness. Will you take a glass of Madeira?"

"I thank you, sir," answered the other.

The wine was brought and drunk, and the friend departed, congratulating himself, as he walked away, upon having "settled Joe's business"; which indeed he had, but not after the fashion he expected or intended.

As to Grimaldi, he was up with the lark, arranging the machinery and making it look and work to the best advantage. Having succeeded to his heart's content, he put the models he had promised Mr Hughes into his pocket, and walked down to his house to breakfast, agreeable to the arrangement of the night before. Upon his arrival he was told that breakfast was not quite ready, and likewise that Mr Hughes wished to see him immediately in the treasury, where he was then awaiting his arrival. There was something in the manner of the servant-girl (the same, by-the-by, who had told of the kissing), as she said this, which induced him involuntarily to fear some ill, and, without knowing exactly why, he began to apprehend those thousand and one impossible, or at least improbable, evils, the dread of which torments the man nervously afraid of losing some treasure upon the possession of which his happiness depends.

"Is Mr Hughes alone?" Joe asked.

"No, sir," answered the girl, "there is a gentleman with him," and then she mentioned a name which increased Joe's apprehensions. However, plucking up all his courage, he advanced to the appointed chamber, and in two minutes found himself in the presence of Mr Hughes and his accuser. The former received him coldly; the latter turned away when he saw him without vouchsafing a word.

"Come in, sir," said Mr Hughes, "and close the door after you." Joe did as he was told; never, either before or afterwards, feeling so strangely like a criminal.

"Mr Grimaldi," continued Mr Hughes, with a mingled formality and solemnity which appalled him, "I have something very important to communicate to you—in fact, I have had a charge preferred against you of a most serious description, sir."

"Indeed, sir!"

"Yes, indeed, sir!" said the enemy, with a look very like one of triumph.

"It is true," replied Mr Hughes, "and I fear you will not be able to clear yourself from it: however, in justice to you, the charge shall be fully stated in your own presence. Repeat, sir, if you please," he continued, addressing the accuser, "what you told me last night."

And repeat it he did, in a speech replete with malignity, and not destitute of oratorical merit: in which he dwelt upon the serpentlike duplicity with which young Grimaldi had stolen into the bosom of a happy and hospitable family for the purpose of robbing a father and mother of their beloved daughter, and dragging down from her own respectable sphere a young and inexperienced girl, to visit her with all the sorrows consequent upon limited means and the needy home of a struggling actor.

It was with inexpressible astonishment that Grimaldi heard all this; but still greater was his astonishment at witnessing the demeanour of Mr Hughes, who heard this lengthened oration with a settled frown of attention, as though what he heard alike excited his profound consideration and anger; occasionally, too, vouchsafing an encouraging nod to the speaker, which was anything but encouraging to the other party.

"You are quite right," said Mr Hughes, at length; on hearing which, Grimaldi felt quite wrong. "You are *quite* right—nothing can justify such actions, except one thing, and that is … "

"Mr Hughes," interrupted the *friend*, "I know your kind heart well—so well, that I can perceive your charitable feelings are even now striving to discover some excuse or palliation for this offence; but permit me, as a disinterested observer, to tell you that nothing can justify a man in winning the affections of a young girl infinitely above him, and, at the same time, the daughter of one to whom he is so greatly indebted."

"Will you listen to me for half a minute?" enquired Mr Hughes, in a peculiarly calm tone.

"Certainly, sir," answered the other.

"Well, then, I was going to observe, at the moment when you somewhat rudely interrupted me, that I quite agreed with you, and that nothing can justify a man in acting in the manner you have described, unless, indeed, he has obtained the sanction of the young lady's parents; in which case, he is, of course, at liberty to win her affections as soon as he likes, and she likes to let him."

"Assuredly, sir," responded the other; "but in the present instance … "

"But in the present instance," interrupted Mr Hughes, "that happens to be the case. My daughter Maria has my full permission to marry Mr Grimaldi; and I have no doubt she will avail herself of that permission in the course of a very few weeks."

The accuser was dumbfounded, and Grimaldi was delighted— now, for the first time, perceiving that Mr Hughes had been amusing himself at the expense of the mischief-maker.

"Nevertheless," said Mr Hughes, turning to his accepted son-in-law with a grave face, but through all the gravity of which he could perceive a struggling smile. "Nevertheless, you acted very wrong, Mr Grimaldi, in kissing my daughter so publicly; and I beg that whenever, for the future, you and she deem it essential to indulge in such amusements, it may be done in private. This is rendered necessary by the laws which at present govern society, and I am certain will be far more consonant to the feelings and delicacy of the young lady in question."

With these words Mr Hughes made a low bow to the officious and disinterested individual who had made the speech, and, opening the door, called to the servants "to show the gentleman out". Then turning to Grimaldi, he took him by the arm, and walked towards the breakfast-room, declaring that the meal had been waiting half-an-hour or more, that the coffee would be cold, and Maria quite tired of waiting for him.

From this moment the course of true love ran smooth for once: and Mr Hughes, in all his subsequent behaviour to Grimaldi, sufficiently evinced his high sense of the innate worth of a young man, who, under very adverse circumstances and with many temptations to contend against, had behaved with so much honesty and candour. On the Saturday after this pleasant termination of a scene which threatened to be attended with very different results, the house in Penton Street was taken possession of, and next Easter Sunday the young couple were asked in church for the first time.

CHAPTER FIVE

SADLER'S WELLS OPENED as usual on Easter Monday, 1798, and Grimaldi appeared in a new part, a more prominent one than he had yet had, and one which increased his reputation considerably. At this time, in consequence of his great exertions in this character, after four or five months of comparative rest, he began to feel some of those wastings of strength and prostrations of energy to which this class of performers are more peculiarly exposed, and which leave them, if they attain old age as they left Grimaldi himself, in a state of great bodily infirmity and suffering. He was cheered throughout the play; but the applause of the audience only spirited him to increased exertions, and at the close of the performances he was so exhausted and worn out that he could scarcely stand. It was with great difficulty that he reached his home, although the distance was so very slight; and immediately on doing so, he was obliged to be put to bed. (He was wont in after-life frequently to remark, that if at one period of his career his gains were great, his labours were at least equally so, and deserved the return. He spoke from sad experience of their effects at that time, and he spoke the truth. It must be a very high salary, indeed, that could ever repay a man—and especially a feeling, sensitive man, as Grimaldi really was—for premature old age and early decay.)

Grimaldi awoke at eleven o'clock next day invigorated and refreshed; this long rest was an extraordinary indulgence for him to take, for it was his constant habit to be up and dressed by seven o'clock or earlier, either attending to his pigeons, practising the violin, occupying himself in constructing models, or employing himself in some way. Idleness wearied him more than labour; he never could understand the gratification which many people seem to derive from having nothing to do.

It is customary on the morning after a new piece to 'call' it upon the stage with a view to condensing it where it will admit of condensation, and making such improvements as the experience of one night may have suggested. All the performers engaged in the piece of course attend these 'calls', as any alterations will necessarily affect the dialogue of their parts, or some portions of the stage business connected with them. Grimaldi being one of the principal actors in the new drama, it was indispensably necessary that he should attend, and accordingly, much mortified at finding it so late, he dressed with all possible dispatch, and set forth towards the theatre.

At this time all the ground upon which Claremont, Myddleton, Lloyd and Wilmington Squares have since been built, together with the numberless streets which diverge from them in all directions, was then pasture land or garden ground, bearing the name of Sadler's Wells Fields. Across these fields it was of course necessary that Grimaldi should pass and repass in going to and from the theatre. Upon this particular morning a mob was engaged here in hunting an over-driven ox, a diversion then in very high repute among the lower orders of the metropolis, but which is now, happily for the lives and limbs of the more peaceable part of the community, falling into desuetude: there not being quite so many open spaces or waste grounds to chase oxen in, as there used to be a quarter of a century ago. The mob was a very dense one, comprised of the worst characters; and perceiving that it would be a task of some difficulty to clear a passage through it, Grimaldi paused for a minute or two, deliberating whether he had not better turn back at once and take the longer but less obstructed route by the Angel at Islington, when a young gentleman whom he had never seen before, after eyeing him with some curiosity, walked up and said:

"Is not your name Grimaldi, sir?"

"Yes, sir, it is," replied the other. "Pray, may I enquire why you ask the question?"

"Because," answered the stranger, pointing to a man who stood among a little group of people hard by, "because I just now heard that gentleman mention it to a companion."

The person whom the young man pointed out was a very well-known character about Clerkenwell and its vicinity, being an object of detestation with the whole of the neighbourhood. 'Old Lucas' was his familiar appellation, and he filled the imposing office of parish constable. Parish constables are seldom very popular in their own districts, but Old Lucas was more unpopular than any man of the same class: and if the stories which are current of him be correct, with very good reason. In short, he was a desperate villain. It was very generally understood of him, that where no real accusation existed against a man, his course of proceeding was to invent a false one and to bolster it up with the most unblushing perjury and an ingenious system of false evidence, which he had never any difficulty in obtaining, for the purpose of pocketing certain small sums which, under the title of 'expenses', were paid upon the conviction of the culprit. Being well acquainted with Lucas's reputation, Grimaldi was much astonished, and not at all pleasantly so, by the information he had just received; and he enquired with considerable anxiety and apprehension whether the young man was quite certain that it was *his* name which the constable had mentioned.

"Quite certain," was the reply. "I can't have made any mistake upon the subject, because he wrote it down in his book."

"Wrote it down in his book!" exclaimed Grimaldi. "What on earth can he want with me? Well, sir, at all events I have to thank you for your kindness in informing me, although I am not much wiser on the point than I was before."

Exchanging bows with the stranger, they separated; the young man mixing with the crowd, and Grimaldi turning back, and going to the theatre by the longest road, with the double object of avoiding Old Lucas and keeping out of the way of the mad ox.

Having to attend to his business immediately on his arrival at the theatre, the circumstance escaped Joe's memory, nor did it occur to him again until he returned thither in the evening, shortly before the performances commenced. Being reminded of it by some accidental occurrence, he related the morning's conversation to some of his more immediate associates, among whom were Dubois, a celebrated comic actor, another per-former of the name of Davis, and Richer, a very renowned rope-dancer. Grimaldi's communication, however, elicited no more sympathetic reception than a general burst of laughter, which having subsided they fell to bantering the unfortunate object of Old Lucas's machinations.

"That fellow Lucas," said Dubois, assuming a grave face, "is a most confirmed scoundrel; he would stick at nothing, not even at Joe's life, to gain a few pounds, or perhaps even a few shillings."

Joe looked none the happier for this observation, and another friend took up the subject.

"Lucas, Lucas," said Richer. "That is the old man who wears spectacles, isn't it?"

"That's the man," replied Dubois, "the constable, you know. He hasn't written your name down in his book for nothing, Joe, take my word for that."

"Precisely my opinion," said Davis. "He means to make a regular property out of him. Don't be frightened, Joe, that's all."

These prophetic warnings had a very serious effect upon the spirits of the party principally interested—which his companions perceiving, hastened to carry on the joke, by giving vent to sundry other terrible surmises upon the particular crime with which the officer meant to charge him; one suggesting that it was murder, another that he thought it was forgery (which made no great difference in the end, the offence being punished with the same penalty), and a third good-naturedly remarking that perhaps it might not be quite so bad, after all, although certainly Lucas did possess such weight with the magistrates, that it was invariably two to one against the unfortunate person whom he charged with any offence.

Although he was at no loss to discern and appreciate the raillery of his friends, Grimaldi could not divest himself of some nervous apprehensions connected with the adventure of the morning: when, just as he was revolving in his mind all the improbabilities of the officer's entertaining any designs against him, one of the messengers of the theatre abruptly entered the room in which they were all seated, and announced that Mr Grimaldi was wanted directly at the stage door.

"Who wants me?" enquired Grimaldi, turning rather pale.

"It's a person in spectacles!" replied the messenger, looking at the rest of the company, and hesitating.

"A person in spectacles!" echoed the other, more agitated than before. "Did he give you his name, or do you know who he is?"

"Oh yes, I know who he is," answered the messenger, with something between a smile and a gasp. "It's Old Lucas."

Upon this, there arose a roar of laughter, in which the messenger joined. Grimaldi was quite petrified and stood rooted to the spot, looking from one to another with a face in which dismay and fear were visibly depicted. Having exhausted themselves with laughing, his companions, regarding his unhappy face, began to grow serious, and Dubois said:

"Joe, my boy, a joke's a joke, you know. We have had one with you, and that was all fair enough, and it's all over; but if there is anything really serious in this matter, we will prove ourselves your friends, and support you against this old rascal in any way in our power."

All the others said something of the same sort, for which Grimaldi thanked them very heartily, being really in a state of great discomfort, and entertaining many dismal forebodings. It was then proposed that everybody present should accompany him in a body to the stage door, and be witnesses to anything that the thief-taker had to say or do; it being determined beforehand that in the event of his being insolent, he should be summarily put into the New River. Accordingly, they went down in a body, bearing Joe in the centre; and sure enough at the door stood Old Lucas *in propria persona*.

"Now then, what's the matter?" said the leader of the guard; upon which Grimaldi summoned up courage, and echoing the enquiry, said, "What's the matter?" too.

"You must come with me to Hatton Garden," said the constable, in a gruff voice. "Come, I can't afford to lose any more time."

Here arose a great outcry, mingled with various exclamations of, "Where's your warrant?" and many consignments of Mr Lucas to the warmest of all known regions.

"Where's your warrant?" cried Davis, when the noise had in some measure subsided.

The officer deigned no direct reply to this enquiry, but, looking at Grimaldi, demanded whether he was ready; in answer to which question the whole party shouted "No!" with tremendous emphasis.

"Look here, Lucas," said Dubois, stepping forward. "You are an old scoundrel!—no one knows that better, or perhaps could prove it easier than I. Now, so far as concerns Mr Grimaldi, all we have got to say is, either show us a warrant which authorises you to take him into custody, or take yourself into custody and take yourself off under penalty of a ducking."

This speech was received with a shout of applause, not only by the speaker's companions, but by several idlers who had gathered round.

"I'm not a-talking to you, Mr Dubois," said Lucas, as soon as he could make himself heard. "Mr Grimaldi's my man. Now, sir, will you come along with me?"

"Not without a warrant," said the rope-dancer.

"Not without a warrant," added Davis.

"Not upon any consideration whatever," said Dubois.

"Don't attempt to touch him without a warrant; or … "

"Or what?" enquired Lucas. "Or what, Mr Dubois? Eh sir!"

The answer was lost in a general chorus of "The River!"

This intimation, pronounced in a very determined manner, had a visible effect upon the officer, who at once assuming a more subdued tone, said:

"Fact is, that I've not got a warrant (*a shout of derision*); fact is, it's not often that I'm asked for warrants, because people generally knows that I'm in authority, and thinks that's sufficient. (*Another shout*). However, if Mr Grimaldi and his friends press the objection, I shall not urge upon his going with me now, provided he promises and they promises on his behalf to attend at Hatton Garden Office, afore Mr Blamire, at eleven o'clock, tomorrow morning."

This compromise was at once acceded to, and Old Lucas turned to go away; but he did not entirely escape even upon this occasion, for while the above conversation was going forward at the door, the muster of people collected around had increased to a pretty large concourse. The greater part of them knew by sight both Grimaldi and the constable; and as the latter was about to depart, the lookers-on pressed round him, and a voice from the crowd cried out, "What's the matter, Joe?"

"The matter is this, gentlemen," said Dubois, returning to the top of the steps, and speaking with great vehemence and gesticulation. "This rascal, gentlemen," pointing to the constable, "wants to drag Joe Grimaldi to prison, gentlemen."

"What for? What for?" cried the crowd.

"For doing nothing at all, gentlemen," replied the orator, who had reserved the loudest key of his voice for the concluding point.

This announcement was at once received with a general yell, which caused the constable to quicken his pace very considerably. The mob quickened theirs also, and in a few seconds the whole area of Sadler's Wells yard rang with whoops and yells almost as loud as those which had assailed the ox in the morning; and Mr Lucas made the best of his way to his dwelling, amidst a shower of mud, rotten apples, and other such missiles. The performances in the theatre went off as usual. After all was over, Grimaldi returned home to supper, having been previously assured by his friends that they would one and all accompany him to the police-office in the morning, and having previously arranged so as to secure as a witness the young gentleman who had given the first information regarding the views and intentions of the worthy thief-taker.

At the appointed hour, Grimaldi and his friends repaired to the police-office, and were duly presented to Mr Blamire, the sitting magistrate, who, having received them with much politeness, requested Old Lucas to state his case, which he forthwith proceeded to do. He deposed, with great steadiness of nerve, that Joseph Grimaldi had been guilty of hunting, and inciting and inducing other persons to hunt, an over-driven ox, in the fields of Pentonville, much to the hazard and danger of his majesty's subjects, much to the worry and irritation of the animal, and greatly to the hazard of its being lashed into a state of furious insanity. Mr Lucas deposed to having seen with his own eyes the offence committed, and in corroboration of his eyesight produced his companions of the morning, who confirmed his evidence in every particular. This, Mr Lucas said, was his case.

The accused, being called upon for his defence, stated the circumstances as they had actually occurred, and produced his young acquaintance, who, as it appeared, was the son of a most respectable gentleman in the neighbourhood. The young gentleman confirmed the account of the affair which had been given last; deposed to the accused not having been in the field more than two or three minutes altogether; to his never having been near the ox-hunters; and to his having gone to the theatre by a route much longer than his ordinary one, for the express purpose of avoiding the ox and his hunters, Mr Lucas and his companions.

The magistrate heard all this conflicting evidence upon an apparently very unimportant question, with a great deal more patience and coolness than some of his successors have been in the habit of displaying; and after hearing it, and various audible and unreserved expressions of opinions from Mr Dubois and others touching the respectability and probity of Lucas, turned to the accused, and said:

"Mr Grimaldi, I entirely believe your version of the affair to be the correct and true one; but I am bound to act upon the deposition of this constable and his witnesses, and accordingly I must, however unwillingly, convict you in some penalty. I shall take care, though, that your punishment is one which shall neither be heavy to you nor serviceable to the complainant. I hereby order you to pay a fine of five shillings, and to be discharged. As to you, Lucas, I would recommend you to be careful how you conduct yourself in future, and more especially to be careful as to the facts which you state upon oath."

After this decision, which his friends and himself looked upon as a complete triumph, they bowed to the magistrate and quitted the police-office, Grimaldi previously paying the five shillings which he had been fined, and an additional shilling for his discharge. It was then proposed and unanimously agreed that the party should adjourn to a tavern called The King of Prussia (now bearing the sign of The Clown), opposite Sadler's Wells for the purpose of having some lunch; and thither they proceeded, and made themselves very merry with the mortified looks of Old Lucas, mingling with their mirth some dry and abstruse speculations upon the nature of the laws which compelled a magistrate to accept the oath of a reputed perjurer, and to convict upon it a person whom he conscientiously believed to be innocent of the offence laid to his charge.

While they were thus engaged, some person came running into the room, and, looking hastily round, cried, "Joe! Joe! Here's Old Lucas again." The friends began to laugh, and Grimaldi joined them, thinking that this was but a jest; but he was greatly mistaken, for in less than a minute Lucas entered the room.

"Why, Mister Constable!" exclaimed Dubois, rising angrily. "How dare you come here?"

"Because I have business," surlily replied Lucas. "Mr Grimaldi has been very properly convicted of an offence at the police-office, and sentenced to pay a fine of five shillings, besides one shilling more for his discharge: neither of these sums has he paid, so he is still my prisoner."

"Not paid?" exclaimed the accused. "Why, I paid the six shillings before I left the office."

This statement was corroborated by the friends, and the mute but eloquent testimony of his purse, which contained precisely that sum less than it had done an hour previously.

"It's no use," said Lucas, grinning. "Pay the money, or come on with me."

"I have already paid all that was required, and I will neither give you another farthing, nor allow myself to be made prisoner," was the reply.

"We'll see that," responded the constable, advancing.

"Take care," said Grimaldi, warningly. "Venture to touch me, and to the ground you go!"

Not a bit daunted, Old Lucas darted upon him, dragged him from his seat, and attempted to force him towards the door; in doing which he managed to tear his waistcoat and shirt-collar literally to ribbons. Until then Grimaldi had remained quite cool, merely acting upon the defensive; but now he gave way to his rage, and fulfilled his threat to the letter by giving Lucas a blow which felled him to the ground, and caused his nose to bleed in a manner neither sentimental nor picturesque. Lucas, however, immediately rose again, and producing his staff, was about, thus strengthened, to renew the combat, when a gentleman who chanced to be sitting in the room, a stranger to the party, rose, and drawing from his pocket a silver staff, shook it at Lucas, and said, "I will have no more of this violence! Let all parties adjourn to the police-office; and if Mr Grimaldi's tale be true, and your purpose be merely that of endeavouring to extort money, as I have no doubt it is, I will take care that things be laid properly before the magistrate."

Lucas, who appeared to succumb before the vision of the silver staff, surlily assented, and they all presented themselves for the second time that day before Mr Blamire, who was greatly astonished at their reappearance, and greatly surprised at the altered appearance of Old Lucas's face. The magistrate, moreover, seemed to know the silver-staffed gentleman very well, and greeted him cordially.

"Well," said Mr Blamire, after the bustle of entrance had ceased, "what's the matter, now? Speak, you Lucas!"

"Your worship," said the person called upon, "Mr Grimaldi was fined five shillings just now, and had to pay one for his discharge, all of which he left the office without doing."

"Indeed!—is that true?" enquired the magistrate of the clerk, in an undertone.

"No, sir," replied the latter, with a slight but meaning smile.

"Go on, sir," said Mr Blamire, addressing Lucas.

Lucas was a little abashed at the 'aside' confab between the magistrate and his clerk; but, affecting not to hear it, he continued, "Of course, therefore, he still remained my prisoner; and I followed him and insisted upon his paying the money. This he refused: I therefore collared him for the purpose of making him return here, and in so doing I tore his shirt and waistcoat. The moment he perceived I had done so, he … "

Lucas paused for an instant, and Mr Blamire filled up the sentence by saying:

"He gave you a blow on the nose?"

"Exactly so, sir," said Lucas, eagerly.

"And very well you merited it," added the magistrate, in a tone which caused a general roar of laughter. "Well, Mr Grimaldi, let us hear what *you* have to say."

Grimaldi briefly recounted the circumstances; and when he had finished, the unknown with the silver staff advanced and corroborated the statement, making several severe remarks upon the private intentions and violent manner of Lucas.

"Who," says Grimaldi, with profound respect and an air of great mystery, "who this gentleman was, I never could ascertain; but that he was a person possessing a somewhat high degree of authority was evident to me from the great respect paid to him at the police-office. Someone afterwards told me he was a city marshal, possessing power to exercise his authority without the city; but I know not whether he was so or not."

After this disguised potentate had given his testimony, which rendered the matter conclusive, Mr Blamire said, "Place Lucas at the bar," which being done, the magistrate proceeded to mulct him in a penalty of five pounds, the money to go to the poor of the parish, and likewise ordered him to make Grimaldi every necessary reparation and amendment for the results of his violence.

On this sentence being pronounced, Old Lucas foamed at the mouth in a manner not unlike the over-driven ox, the original cause of the disaster, and protested, with many disrespectful oaths and other ebullitions of anger, that he would not pay one farthing. The magistrate, nothing daunted, commanded him to be locked up forthwith, which was done to the great delight and admiration not only of the friends and other spectators but of the officers also, who, besides being in duty bound to express their admiration of all the magistrate did, participated in the general dislike of Old Lucas, as the persons best acquainted with his perjury and villainy.

The friends once again bade the magistrate good morning, and soon afterwards dispersed to their several homes. They heard next day that Old Lucas, after having been under lock and key for six hours, the whole of which time he devoted to howls and imprecations, paid the fine. A few hours after he was set at liberty he wrote a very penitent letter to Grimaldi, expressing his great regret for what had occurred and his readiness to pay for the spoiled shirt and waistcoat, upon being made acquainted with the amount of damage done. Grimaldi thought it better to let the matter remain where it did, thinking that, setting the broken nose against the torn shirt and waistcoat, Lucas was already sufficiently punished. After this, 'Old Lucas' never did anything more terrible, connected with the Sadler's Wells company, at least; and, there is reason to believe, he shortly afterwards lost his situation.

CHAPTER SIX

FROM THIS TIME FORWARD, for several months, all went merry as a marriage bell. On the eleventh of May following the little adventure just recorded, the marriage bell went too, for Grimaldi was married to Miss Maria Hughes at St George's, Hanover Square, with the full consent and approbation of the young lady's parents, and to the unbounded joy of his own mother, by whom she had been, from her earliest youth, beloved as her daughter.

Five days after the wedding, the young couple paid their first visit to Mr and Mrs Hughes. After sitting a short time, Grimaldi left his wife there and went to the theatre, where a rehearsal in which he was wanted had been called for that morning. Upon entering the yard of Sadler's Wells, in which the different members of the company were strolling about until the rehearsal commenced, he was accosted by Richer, with, "Joe, may I enquire the name of the lady with whom I saw you walking just now?"

"Nay, you need not ask him," cried Dubois. "I can tell you. It was Miss Maria Hughes."

"I beg your pardon," interrupted Grimaldi. "That is not the lady's name."

"No!" exclaimed Dubois. "Why, I could have sworn it was Miss Hughes."

"You would have sworn wrong, then," replied he. "The lady's name *was* Hughes once, I grant; but on Friday last I changed it to Grimaldi."

His friends were greatly surprised at this intelligence; but they lost no time in disseminating it throughout the theatre. Congratulations poured in upon him; and so great was the excitement occasioned by the fact of "Joe Grimaldi's marriage" becoming known, that the manager, after vainly endeavouring to proceed with the rehearsal, gave up the task and dismissed the company for that morning. In the evening they had a supper at the theatre to commemorate the event; and on the following Sunday Joe gave a dinner to the carpenters for the same purpose. In the long run all the members of the establishment, from the highest to the lowest, participated in the long-expected happiness of their single-hearted and good-natured comrade.

In the summer of this year, Grimaldi lost a guinea wager in a somewhat ludicrous manner—in a manner sufficiently ludicrous to justify in this place the narration of the joke which gave rise to it. He was acquainted at that time with a very clever and popular writer, who happened to have occasion to pass through Gravesend on the same day as Joe had to go there; and, as they met shortly before, they agreed to travel in a post-chaise and share the expense between them. They arranged to start early in the morning, as Grimaldi had to play at Sadler's Wells at night.

The journey was very pleasant, and the hours passed quickly away. Grimaldi's companion, who was a witty and humorous fellow, was in great force upon the occasion, and, exerting all his powers, kept Joe laughing without intermission. About three miles on the London side of Dartford the friend, whose buoyant and restless spirits prevented his sitting in any one position for a minute, began incessantly poking his head out of one or other of the chaise windows, and making various remarks on the landscape, the persons and the vehicles passing to and fro.

While thus engaged, he happened to catch sight of a man on horseback about a quarter-of-a-mile behind, who was travelling in the same direction with themselves, and was coming up after the chaise at a rapid pace.

"Look, Joe!" he said. "See that fellow behind! Well mounted, is he not?"

Grimaldi looked back, and saw the man coming along at a fast trot. He was a stout, hearty fellow, dressed like a small farmer, as he very probably was, and was riding a strong horse of superior make, good pace, and altogether an excellent roadster.

"Yes, I see him," was his reply. "He's well enough, but I see nothing particular about him or the horse either."

"Nor is there anything particular about either of them that I am aware of," answered his companion. "But wouldn't you think, judging from the appearance of his nag, and the rate at which he is riding, that he would pass our chaise in a very short time?"

"Most unquestionably; he will pass us in a few seconds."

"I'll tell you what, Joe, I'll bet you a guinea he does not," said the friend.

"Nonsense!"

"Well, will you take it?"

"No, no; it would be robbing you."

"Oh, leave me to judge about that," said the friend. I shall not consider it a robbery: and, so far from that, I'm willing to make the bet more in your favour. Come, I'll bet you a guinea, Joe, that the man don't pass our chaise between this and Dartford."

"Done!" said Grimaldi, well knowing that, unless some sudden and most unaccountable change took place in the pace

at which the man was riding, he must pass in a minute or two—
"Done!"

"Very good," said the other. "Stop—I forgot: remember that
if you laugh or smile, so that he can see you, between this and
Dartford, you will have lost. Is that agreed?"

"Oh, certainly," replied Grimaldi, very much interested to
know by what mode his friend proposed to win the wager.

He did not remain very long in expectation: the horseman
drew nearer and nearer, and the noise of his horse's feet was
heard close behind the chaise, when the friend, pulling a pistol
from his pocket, suddenly thrust his head and shoulders out
of the window and presented the pistol full at the face of the
unconscious countryman, assuming at the same time a ferocious
countenance and menacing air which were perfectly alarming.
Grimaldi was looking through the little window at the back of
the chaise, and was like to die with laughter when he witnessed
the effect produced by this singular apparition.

The countryman was coming along at the same hard trot,
with a very serious and business-like countenance, when, all of
a sudden, half a man and the whole of a pistol were presented
from the chaise window; which he no sooner beheld, than all
at once he pulled up with a jerk which almost brought him
into a ditch, and threw the horse upon his haunches. His red
face grew very pale, but he had the presence of mind to pat
his beast on the neck and soothe him in various ways, keeping
his eyes fixed on the chaise all the time and looking greatly
astonished. After a minute or so, he recovered himself, and,
giving his horse the spur and a smart cut in the flank with his
riding-whip, dashed across the road, with the view of passing
the chaise on the opposite side. The probability of this attempt

had been foreseen, however, by the other party, for with great agility he transferred himself to the other window, and, thrusting out the pistol with the same fierce and sanguinary countenance as before, again encountered the farmer's gaze; upon which the rider pulled up, with the same puzzled and frightened expression of countenance, and stared till his eyes seemed double their natural size.

The scene became intensely droll. The countryman's horse stood stock still; but as the chaise rolled on, he gradually suffered him to fall into a gentle trot, and, with an appearance of deep perplexity, was evidently taking council with himself how to act. Grimaldi had laughed in a corner till he was quite exhausted, and seeing his guinea was fairly lost, determined to aid the joke. With this view, he looked out of the vacant window, and, assuming an authoritative look, nodded confidentially to the horseman, and waved his hand as if warning him not to come too near. This caution the countryman received with much apparent earnestness, frequently nodding and waving his hand after the same manner, accompanying the pantomime with divers significant winks, to intimate that he understood the gentleman was insane and that he had accidentally obtained possession of the dangerous weapon. Grimaldi humoured the notion of his being the keeper, occasionally withdrawing his head from the window to indulge in peals of laughter. The friend, bating not an inch of his fierceness, kept the pistol pointed at the countryman; and the countryman followed on behind at an easy pace on the opposite side of the road, continuing to exchange most expressive pantomime with one of its best professors, and to reciprocate, as nearly as he could, all the nods and winks and shrugs with which Grimaldi affected to deplore the situation of his unhappy friend. And so they went into Dartford. When they reached the town, the friend resumed his seat, and Grimaldi paid the guinea. The instant the pistol barrel was withdrawn, the countryman set spurs to his horse and scoured through the town, to the great astonishment of its inhabitants, at full gallop.

The success of this guinea wager put the friend upon telling a story of a wager of Sheridan's which was much talked of at the time, and ran thus: George the Fourth, when Prince of Wales, used occasionally to spend certain hours of the day in gazing from the windows of a club-house in St James's Street: of course he was always surrounded by some of his chosen companions, and among these Sheridan, who was then the Drury Lane lessee, was ever first and foremost. The Prince and Sheridan in these idle moments had frequently remarked among the passers backwards and forwards a young woman who regularly every day carried through the street a heavy load of crockery-ware, and who, the Prince frequently remarked, must be possessed of very great strength and dexterity to be able to bear so heavy a burden with so much apparent ease, and to carry it in the midst of such a crowd of passengers without ever stumbling.

One morning, as usual, she made her appearance in the street from Piccadilly, and Sheridan called the Prince's attention to the circumstance.

"Here she is," said Sheridan.

"Who?" inquired the Prince.

"The crockery-girl," replied Sheridan. "And more heavily laden than ever."

"Not more so than usual, I think," said the Prince.

"Pardon me, your Highness, I think I'm right. Oh dear me, yes! It's decidedly a larger basket, a much larger basket," replied Sheridan. "Good God, she staggers under it! Ah! she has recovered herself. Poor girl, poor girl!"

The Prince had watched the girl very closely, but the symptoms of exhaustion which Sheridan had so feelingly deplored were nevertheless quite invisible to him.

"She will certainly fall," continued Sheridan, in a low abstracted tone. "That girl will fall down before she reaches this house."

"Pooh, pooh!" said the Prince. "*She* fall!—nonsense, she is too well used to it."

"She will," said Sheridan.

"I'll bet you a cool hundred she does not," replied the Prince.

"Done!" cried Sheridan.

"Done!" repeated his Royal Highness.

The point of the story is, that the girl *did fall down just before she reached the club-house.* It was very likely an accident, in as much as people seldom fall down on purpose, especially when they carry crockery; but still there were not wanting some malicious persons who pretended to trace the tumble to another source. At all events, it was a curious coincidence, and a strong proof of the accuracy of Sheridan's judgement in such matters.

Grimaldi's friend told this story while they were changing horses, laughing very much when he had finished; and, as if it had only whetted his appetite for fun, at once looking out for another object on whom to exercise his turn for practical joking. The chaise, after moving very slowly for some yards, came to a dead stop behind some heavy wagons which obstructed the road. This stoppage chanced to occur directly opposite the principal inn, from one of the coffee-room windows of which, on the first floor, a gentleman was gazing into the street. He was a particularly tall, big man, wearing a military frock and immense mustachios, and eyeing the people below with an air of much dignity and grandeur. The jester's eyes no sooner fell upon this personage than he practised a variety of devices to attract his attention, such as coughing violently, sneezing, raising the window of the chaise and letting it fall again with a great noise, and tapping loudly at the door. At length he clapped his hands and accompanied the action with a shrill scream; upon which the big man looked down from his elevation with a glare of profound scorn, mingled with some surprise. Their eyes no sooner met, than the man in the chaise assumed a most savage and unearthly expression of countenance, which gave him all the appearance of an infuriated maniac. After grimacing in a manner sufficiently uncouth to attract the sole and undivided attention of the big man, he suddenly produced the pistol from his pocket, and, pretending to take a most accurate aim at the warrior's person, cocked it and placed his hand upon the trigger. The big man's face grew instantly blanched; he put his hands to his head, made a step or rather stagger back, and instantly disappeared, having either fallen or thrown himself upon the floor. The friend put his pistol in his pocket without the most remote approach to a smile or the slightest change of countenance, and Grimaldi sank down to the bottom of the chaise nearly suffocated with laughter.

At Gravesend they parted, the friend going on in the same chaise to Dover, and Grimaldi, after transacting the business which brought him from town, returning to play at the theatre at night; all recollection even of the Dartford Blues fading as he passed through the town on his way home, before the exploits of his merry friend, which afforded him matter for diversion until he reached London.

The summer passed pleasantly away, the whole of Grimaldi's spare time being devoted to the society of his wife and her parents, until the departure of the latter from London for Weymouth, of which theatre Mr Hughes was the proprietor.

Drury Lane opened for the season on the fifteenth of September, and Sadler's Wells closed ten days afterwards: but while the latter circumstance released Grimaldi from his arduous labours at one theatre, the former one did not tend to increase them at the other, for pantomime was again eschewed at Drury Lane, and *Blue Beard*, *Feudal Times* and *Lodoiska* reigned paramount. At the commencement of the season he met Mr Sheridan, when the following colloquy ensued:

"Well, Joe, still living—eh?"

"Yes, sir; and what's more, married as well."

"Oho! Pretty young woman, Joe?"

"Very pretty, sir."

"That's right! You must lead a domestic life, Joe: nothing like a domestic life for happiness, Joe: I lead a domestic life myself." And then came one of those twinkling glances which no one who ever saw them can forget the humour of.

"I mean to do so, sir."

"Right. But Joe, what will your poor little wife do while you are at the theatre of an evening? Very bad thing, Joe, to let a pretty young wife be alone of a night. I'll manage it for you, Joe: I'll put her name down upon the free list; herself and friend.

115

But, mind, it's a female friend, that's all, Joe; any other might be dangerous—eh, Joe?" And away he went without pausing for a moment to listen to Grimaldi's expressions of gratitude for his thoughtful kindness. However, Sheridan did not omit performing his friendly offer, and Grimaldi's wife, availing herself of it, went to the theatre almost every night he played, sat in the front of the house until he had finished, and then they went home together.

In this pleasant and quiet manner the autumn and winter passed rapidly away. In the following year, 1799 (1800) it became apparent that his young wife would shortly make him a father; and while this prospect increased the happiness and attention of her husband and parents, it added little to their slight stock of cares and troubles, for they were too happy and contented to entertain any other but cheerful anticipations of the result.

There is little to induce one to dwell upon a sad and melancholy chapter in the homely life of every-day. After many months of hope, and some of fear, and many lingering changes from better to worse, and back and back again, his dear wife, whom he had loved from a boy with so much truth and feeling, and whose excellences were the old man's fondest theme to the last moment of his life, many years afterwards, died.

"Poor Joe! Oh Richard, be kind to poor Joe!" were the last words she uttered. They were addressed to her brother, A few minutes afterwards, he sat beside a corpse.

They found in her pocket-book a few pencilled lines, beneath which she had written her wish that when she died they might be inscribed above her grave:

Earth walks on Earth like glittering gold;
Earth says to Earth, We are but mould:

Earth builds on Earth castles and towers;
Earth says to Earth, All shall be ours.

They were placed upon the tablet erected to her memory. She was buried in the family vault of Mr Hughes at St James's, Clerkenwell.

In the first passion of his grief the widower went distracted. Nothing but the constant attention and vigilance of his friends, who never left him alone, would have prevented Grimaldi from laying violent hands upon his life. There were none to console him, except with sympathy, for his friends were hers, and all mourned no common loss. Mr Richard Hughes, the brother, never forgot his sister's dying words, but proved himself under all circumstances and at all times Grimaldi's firm and steady friend. The poor fellow haunted the scenes of his old hopes and happiness for two months, and was then summoned to the theatre to set the audience in a roar; and chalking over the seams which mental agony had worn in his face, was hailed with boisterous applause in the merry Christmas pantomime!

The title of this pantomime, which was produced at Drury Lane, was *Harlequin Amulet*, or *The Magic of Mona*; it was written by Mr Powell, and produced under the superintendence of Mr James Byrne, the ballet-master. It was highly successful, running without intermission from the night of its production until Easter, 1800 (1801). This harlequinade was distinguished by several unusual features besides its great success; foremost among them was an entire change both in the conception of the character of Harlequin and in the costume. Before that time it had been customary to attire the Harlequin in a loose jacket and trousers, and it had been considered indispensable that he should be perpetually attitudinizing in five positions, and doing nothing else but passing instantaneously from one to the other, and never pausing without being in one of the five. All these conventional notions were abolished by Byrne, who this year made his first appearance as Harlequin, and also made Harlequin a very original person to the play-going public, His attitude and jumps were all new, and his dress was infinitely improved: the latter consisted of a white silk patches fitting without a wrinkle, and into this the variegated silk patches were woven, the whole being profusely covered with spangles and presenting a very sparkling appearance. The innovation was not resisted: the applause was enthusiastic; "nor," says Grimaldi, "was it undeserved; for, in my judgement, Mr James Byrne was at that time the best Harlequin on the boards, and never has been excelled, even if equalled, since that period." The alteration soon became general, and has proved a lasting one, Harlequin having been ever since attired as upon this memorable occasion.

Grimaldi's part in this production was a singularly arduous and wearying one: he had to perform Punch, and to change afterwards to Clown. He was so exceedingly successful in the first-mentioned part, that Mr Sheridan wished him to preserve the character throughout—a suggestion which he was compelled resolutely to oppose. His reason for doing so will not be considered extraordinary when we inform the present generation that his personal decorations consisted of a large and heavy hump on his chest, and a ditto, ditto, on his back; a high sugar-loaf cap, a long-nosed mask, and heavy wooden shoes; the weight of the whole dress, and of the humps, nose, and shoes especially, being exceedingly great. Having to exercise all his strength in this costume, and to perform a vast quantity of comic business, Grimaldi was compelled by fatigue at the end of the sixth scene to assume the Clown's dress, and so relieve himself from the immense weight which he had previously endured. "The part of Columbine," he tells us, "was supported by Miss Menage; and admirably she sustained it. I thought at the time that, taking them together, I never saw so good a Harlequin and Columbine; and I still entertain the same opinion."

Harlequin Amulet being played every night until Easter, Grimaldi had plenty to do: but although his body was fatigued, his mind was relieved by constant employment, and he had little time in the short intervals between exertion and repose to brood over the heavy misfortune which had befallen him. Immediately after his wife's death, he had removed from the scene of his loss to a house in Baynes' Row, and he gradually became more cheerful and composed. In this new habitat Grimaldi devoted his leisure hours to the breeding of pigeons, and for this purpose he had a room, which fanciers termed a *dormer*, constructed at the top of his house, where he used to sit for hours together, watching the birds as they disported in the air above him. At one time he had upwards of sixty pigeons, all of the very first order and beauty, and many of them highly valuable: in proof of which he notes down with great pride a bet concerning one pigeon of peculiar talents, made with Mr Lambert, himself a pigeon-fancier.

This Mr Lambert being, as Grimaldi says, "like myself, a pigeon-fancier, but, unlike myself, a confirmed boaster," took it into his head to declare and pronounce his birds superior in all respects to those in any other collection. This comprehensive declaration immediately brought all the neighbouring pigeon-breeders up in arms; and Grimaldi, taking up the gauntlet on behalf of the inmates of the 'dormer', accepted a bet offered by Lambert, that there was no pigeon in his flight capable of accomplishing twenty miles in twenty minutes. The sum at stake was twenty pounds. The money was posted, the bird exhibited, the day on which the match should come off named, and the road over which the bird was to fly agreed upon—the course being from the twentieth milestone on the Great North Road to Grimaldi's house. At six o'clock in the morning, the bird was consigned to the care of a friend, with instructions to throw it up precisely as the clock struck twelve, at the appointed milestone near St Albans; and the friend and the pigeon, accompanied by a gentleman on behalf of the opposite party, started off, all parties concerned first setting their watches by Clerkenwell Church. It was a very dismal day, the snow being very deep on the ground, and a heavy sleet falling, very much increasing the odds against the bird—the weather, of course, having great effect, and the snow frequently blinding it. There was no stipulation made, however, for fine weather; so at twelve o'clock the two parties, accompanied by several friends, took up their station in the dormer. In exactly nineteen minutes afterwards the pigeon alighted on the roof of the house. An offer of twenty pounds was immediately made for the bird, but it was declined.

The pigeons, however, did not always keep such good hours, or rather minutes; for sometimes they remained away so long on their aerial excursions that their owner gave them up in despair. On one occasion they were absent upwards of four hours. As Grimaldi was sitting disconsolately, concluding they were gone for ever, his attention was attracted by the apparently unaccountable behaviour of three birds who had been left behind, and who, with their heads elevated in the air, were all gazing with intense earnestness at one portion of the horizon. After straining his eyes for a length of time without avail, their master began to fancy that he discerned a small black speck a great height above him. He was not mistaken, for by and by the black speck turned out, to his infinite joy, to be the lost flight of pigeons returning home, after a journey probably of several hundred miles.

When the pantomime had ceased to run, Grimaldi had but little to do at Drury Lane, his duties being limited to a combat or some such business, in *Lodoiska*, *Feudal Times* and other spectacles, for which he could well manage to reach the theatre in time, after the performances at Sadler's Wells were over. Drury Lane closed in June and reopened in September, ten days after the season at Sadler's Wells had terminated; but as Grimaldi did not expect to be called into active service until December, he played out of town, for the first time in his life, in the month of November, 1801.

There was at that time among the Sadler's Wells company a clever man named Lund, who in the vacation time usually joined Mrs Baker's company on the Rochester circuit. His benefit was fixed to take place at Rochester and he waited on Grimaldi and entreated him to play for him on the occasion. Whenever it was in his power to accede to such a request it was Grimaldi's invariable custom not to refuse; he therefore willingly returned an answer in the affirmative. He reached Rochester about noon on the day fixed for the benefit, rehearsed half-a-dozen pantomime scenes, and having dined, went to the theatre, every portion of which was crammed before six o'clock. On his appearance he was received with a tremendous shout of welcome; his two comic songs were each encored three times, and the whole performance went off with great éclat. Mrs Baker, the manageress, at once offered Grimaldi an engagement for the two following nights, the receipts of the house to be divided between them. Grimaldi's acceptance of this proposal delighted the old lady so much, that the arrangement was no sooner concluded than she straightway walked upon the stage, dressed in the bonnet and shawl in which she had been taking the money and giving the checks, and in an audible voice announced the entertainments herself, to the immense delight of the audience, who shouted vociferously.

This old lady appears to have been a very droll personage. She managed all her affairs herself, and her pecuniary matters were conducted on a principle quite her own. She never put her money out at interest, or employed it in any speculative or profitable manner, but kept it in six or eight large punch-bowls, which always stood upon the top shelf of a bureau, except when she was disposed to make herself particularly happy, and then she would take them down singly, and after treating herself with a sly look at their contents, would put them up again.

Mrs Baker had a factotum to whom was attached the elegant sobriquet of 'Bony Long'. At a supper after the play, at which the guests were Lund, Grimaldi, Henry and William Dowton (sons of the celebrated actor of that name), the manageress, and 'Bony', it was arranged that Grimaldi should perform Scaramouch in *Don Juan* on the following night. A slight difficulty occurred, in consequence of his having brought from London no other dress than a Clown's; but Mrs Baker provided against it by sending for one Mr Palmer, then a respectable draper and tailor at Rochester. Having received the actor's instructions, he manufactured for Grimaldi the best Scaramouch dress he ever wore. The assurances which were given Mr Palmer at the time that his abilities lay in the theatrical way were not without good foundation, for two years afterwards he left Rochester, came to London, and became principal Master Tailor at Covent Garden. He later removed to Drury Lane and filled the same office, which he still continues to hold.

On the second night the house was filled in every part, and a great number of persons were turned away. On the following evening, on which Grimaldi made his last appearance, the orchestra was turned into boxes, seats were fitted up on every inch of available room behind the scenes, and the receipts exceeded those of any former occasion. At another supper that night with Mrs Baker, Grimaldi made an arrangement to join her company for a night or two at Maidstone in the following March, provided his London engagements would admit of his doing so. They were not at all behindhand with the money; for, at eight o'clock next morning, Bony Long repaired to his lodgings, taking with him an account of the two nights' receipts. Grimaldi's share came to one hundred and sixty pounds, which was at once paid over to him, down upon the nail, all in three-shilling pieces. This was an addition to his baggage which he had not expected, and he was rather at a loss how to convey his loose silver up to town, when he was relieved by a tavern-keeper, who being as glad to take the silver as Grimaldi was to get notes, very soon made the exchange, to the satisfaction of all parties. Having had this satisfactory settlement with the old lady, Grimaldi took his leave and returned to town, not at all displeased with the success which had attended his first professional excursion from London.

At Christmas *Harlequin Amulet* was revived at Drury Lane in place of a new pantomime, and ran without interruption till the end of January, drawing as much money as it had in the previous year. It was about this time that Grimaldi's old friend Jew Davis made his first appearance at Drury Lane. This is the man whose eccentricity gave rise to a ludicrous anecdote of John Kemble, of which the following is a correct version:

Kemble was once 'starring' in the north of England, and paid a visit to the provincial theatre in which Jew Davis was engaged, where he was announced for Hamlet. Every member of the little company was necessarily called into requisition, and Davis was cast to play the first grave-digger. All went well until the first scene of the fifth act, being the identical one in which Davis was called upon to appear: and here the equanimity and good temper of Kemble were considerably shaken, the grave-digger's representative having contracted a habit of grimacing which, however, valuable in burlesque or farce, was far from being desirable in tragedy, and least of all in that philosophical tragedy of which Hamlet is the hero. But if the actor had contracted a habit of grimacing upon his part, the audience upon its part had contracted an equally constant habit of laughing at him: so the great tragedian, moralizing over the skull of Yorick, was frequently interrupted by the loud roars of laughter attendant upon the grave-digger's strangely comical and increasing grins.

This greatly excited the wrath of Kemble, and after the play was finished he remonstrated somewhat angrily with Davis upon the subject, requesting that such "senseless buffoonery" might not be repeated in the event of their sustaining the same parts on any subsequent occasion. All this was far from answering the end proposed: the peculiarities of temper belonging to Jew Davis were aroused, and he somewhat tartly replied that he did not wish to be taught his profession by Mr Kemble. The latter took no further notice of the subject, but pursued the even tenor of his way with so beneficial an effect upon the treasury that his engagement was renewed for "a few nights more", and on the last of these "few nights" *Hamlet* was again the play performed.

As before, all went well till the grave-diggers' scene commenced: when Kemble, while waiting for his 'cue' to go on, listened bodingly to the roars of laughter which greeted the colloquy of Davis and his companion. At length he entered, and at the same moment Davis, having manufactured a grotesque visage, was received with a shout of laughter, which greatly tended to excite the anger of 'King John'. His first words were spoken, but failed to make any impression: and upon turning towards Davis, he discovered that worthy standing in the grave, displaying a series of highly unsuitable although richly comic grimaces. In an instant all Kemble's good temper vanished, and stamping furiously upon the stage, he expressed his anger and indignation in a muttered exclamation, closely resembling an oath. This ebullition of momentary excitement produced an odd and unexpected effect. No sooner did Davis hear the exclamation and the loud stamping of the angry actor than he instantly raised his hands above his head in mock terror, and, clasping them together as if he were horrified by some dreadful spectacle, threw into his face an expression of intense terror, and uttered a frightful cry, half-shout and half-scream, which electrified his hearers. Having done this, he very coolly laid himself flat down in the grave (of course disappearing from the view of the audience), nor could any entreaties prevail upon him to emerge from it or to repeat one word more. The scene was done as well as it could be without a grave-digger, and the audience, while it was proceeding, loudly expressed their apprehension from time to time "that some accident had happened to Mr Davis".

Some months after this, Sheridan happening to see Davis act in the provinces, and being struck with his talents (he was considered the best stage Jew upon the boards) engaged him for Drury Lane; and, in that theatre, on the first day of the ensuing season, he was not immediately recognised, although Kemble evidently remembered having seen him somewhere; but, after a time, plainly devoted to consideration, he said:

"Oh, ah, ah! I recollect now. You, sir, you are the gentleman who suddenly went into the grave, and forgot to come out again, I think?"

Davis admitted the fact without equivocation, and hastened to apologise for his ill-timed jesting. The affair was related to Sheridan, to whom, it is needless to say, it afforded the most unbounded delight, and all three joining in a hearty laugh, dismissed the subject.

When *Harlequin Amulet* was withdrawn, there was very little for Grimaldi to do during the rest of the season. On the fourth of March, therefore, in pursuance of his previous arrangement, he joined Mrs Baker at Maidstone, and was announced for Scaramouch. The announcement of his name excited an unwonted sensation in this quiet little town. As early as half-past four in the afternoon, the street in front of the theatre was rendered quite impassable by the vast crowd of persons that surrounded the doors. Mrs Baker, who had never beheld such a scene in her lifetime, became at first very much delighted, and then very much frightened. After some consideration, she dispatched a messenger for an extra quantity of constables, and upon their arrival, threw the doors open at once, previously placing herself in the pay-box, according to custom, to take the money.

"Now then, pit or box, pit or gallery, box or pit?" was her constant and uninterrupted cry.

"Pit, pit!" from half a dozen voices, the owners clinging to the little desk to prevent themselves from being carried away by the crowd before they had paid.

"Then pay two shillings—pass on, Tom-fool!" such was the old lady's invariable address to everybody on busy nights, without the slightest reference to their quality or condition.

On this occasion of the doors being opened at five o'clock, when the house was quite full she locked up the box in which the money was deposited, and going round to the stage, ordered the performance to be commenced immediately, remarking with a force of reasoning which it was impossible to controvert that "the house could be but full, and being full to the ceiling now, they might just as well begin at once, and have it over so much the sooner". The performance accordingly began without delay, to the great satisfaction of the audience, and terminated shortly after nine o'clock.

Grimaldi was very much caressed by the townspeople, and received several invitations to dinner next day from gentlemen residing in the neighbourhood; all of which he declined, however, being already engaged to the eccentric manageress, who would hardly allow him out of her sight. Happening to walk about the town in the course of the morning, he was recognised and saluted by the boys, in the same way as when he walked the streets of London. On the night of his second appearance the house was again crowded, the door-keepers having managed, indeed, by some ingenious contrivance, to squeeze three pounds more into it than on the previous night. The first evening produced one hundred and fifty-four pounds, and the second one hundred and fifty-seven pounds. Of the gross sum, his share was one hundred and fifty-five pounds, seventeen shillings, which was promptly paid to him after supper, on the second and last night.

Mrs Baker had no sooner handed it over through the ever-useful Bony than she proposed to Grimaldi to go on with them to Canterbury, and to act there for the next two nights upon similar terms. He no sooner signified his willingness to do so, than she directed bills for distribution to be made out and sent to the printer's instantly. They were composed and printed by four o'clock in the morning. No sooner did they arrive wet from the press than men on horseback were immediately dispatched with them to Canterbury, about which city the whole impression was circulated and posted before nine o'clock. The old lady had theatres at Rochester and Maidstone and Canterbury, besides many other towns in the circuit, and the size of the whole being very nearly the same, the scenery which was suitable to one fitted them all. Early in the morning the whole company left Maidstone for Canterbury, whither Grimaldi followed in a post-chaise at his leisure. When he arrived there about one o'clock, everything was ready; no rehearsal was necessary, for there were the same performers, the same musicians, scene-shifters, and lamp-lighters. Having inspected the box-book, which notified that every takeable seat in the house was taken, he retired to Mrs Baker's sitting-room, which was the very model of the one at Maidstone and at Rochester too, and found a good dinner awaiting his arrival. Here he was, and here they all were, in the city of Canterbury, about twenty miles from Maidstone, at one o'clock in the day, with the same scenery, dresses, decorations, and transformations as had been in use at the latter theatre late over-night, surrounded by the same actors, male and female, and playing in the same pieces which had been represented by the same men and women, and the same adjuncts, fourteen hours before at Maidstone. He played here two nights, as had been agreed upon, to very nearly the same houses as at Maidstone. Early the next morning he returned to London with three hundred and eleven pounds, six shillings and sixpence in his pocket, the profits he had acquired during an absence of only four days.

Shortly after Grimaldi's return to town, and about a week before Easter, he saw with great astonishment that it was announced or, to use the theatrical term, 'underlined', in the Drury Lane bills, that *Harlequin Amulet* would be revived at Easter, and that Mr Grimaldi would sustain his original character. This announcement being in direct violation of his articles of agreement at Drury Lane, and wholly inconsistent with the terms of his engagement at Sadler's Wells, he had no alternative but at once to wait upon Mr Kemble, the stage manager of the Lane, and explain to him the exact nature of his position.

He found Kemble at the theatre, who received him with all the grandeur and authority of demeanour which it was his habit to assume when he was about to insist upon something which he knew would be resisted. Grimaldi bowed, and Kemble formally and gravely touched his hat.

"Joe," said Kemble, with great dignity, "what is the matter?"

In reply, Grimaldi briefly stated his case, pointing out that he was engaged by his articles at Drury Lane to play in last pieces at and after Easter, but not in pantomime; that at Sadler's Wells he was bound to perform in the first piece; that these distinct engagements had never before been interfered with by the management of either theatre in the most remote manner upon any one occasion; and that, however much he regretted the inconvenience to which the refusal might give rise, he could not possibly perform the part for which he had been announced at Drury Lane. Kemble listened to these representations with a grave and unmoved countenance; and when Grimaldi had finished, after waiting a moment, as if to make certain that he had really concluded, rose from his seat, and said in a solemn tone, "Joe, one word here, sir, is as good as a thousand—you *must* come!"

Joe felt excessively indignant at this, not merely because *must* is a disagreeable word in itself, but because he conceived that the tone in which it was uttered rendered it additionally disagreeable; so, saying at once what the feeling of the moment prompted, he replied, "Very good, sir. In reply to *must*, there is only one thing that can very well be said—I will *not* come, sir."

"Will not, Joe, eh?" said Kemble.

"I will not, sir," replied Grimaldi.

"Not!" said Kemble again, with great emphasis.

Grimaldi repeated the monosyllable with equal vehemence.

"Then, Joe," said Kemble, taking off his hat, and bowing in a ghost-like manner, "I wish you a very good morning!"

130

Grimaldi took off his hat, made another low bow, and wished Mr Kemble good morning; and so they parted. Next day his name was taken from the bills, and that of some other performer, quite unknown to the London stage, was inserted instead; which performer, when he did come out, went in again—for he failed so signally that the pantomime was not played after the Monday night.

In the short interval between this interview and the Easter holidays, Grimaldi was engaged in the study of a new part for Sadler's Wells, which was a very prominent character in a piece bearing the sonorous and attractive title of *The Great Devil*. He entertained very strong hopes that both the part and the piece would be very successful. It came out on Easter Monday, and its success entailed upon Grimaldi no inconsiderable degree of trouble and fatigue. He played two parts in it, and, to say nothing of such slight exertions as acting and fighting, had to change his dress no fewer than nineteen times. It made a great noise, and ran the whole season through.

As we had occasion to notice the ease with which Grimaldi acquired a large sum of money by his professional exertions, and as we may have to describe other large gains hereafter, it may not be amiss to show in this place how much of fatigue and harassing duty those exertions involved, and how much bodily toil and fatigue he had to endure before those gains could be counted. At Sadler's Wells Grimaldi commenced the labour of the evening by playing a long and arduous part in *The Great Devil*; after this he played in some little burletta which immediately succeeded it; upon conclusion of that he was clown to the rope-dancer; and, as a wind-up to the entertainments, he appeared as Clown in the pantomime, always singing two comic songs, both of which were regularly encored. He had then to change his dress with all possible speed, and take a hurried walk, and often a rapid run, to Drury Lane to perform in the last piece. This immense fatigue, undergone six days out of every seven, left Grimaldi at the conclusion of the week completely worn out and thoroughly exhausted, and, beyond all doubt, by taking his bodily energies far beyond their natural powers, sowed the first seeds of that extreme debility and utter prostration of strength from which, in the latter years of his life, he suffered so much. The old man had a good right to say that, if his gains had been occasionally great, they were won by labour more than proportionate.

His attention to his duties and invariable punctuality were always remarkable. To his possession in an eminent degree of these qualities may be attributed the fact that during the whole of his dramatic career, long and arduous as it was, Grimaldi never once disappointed the public, or failed in his attendance at the theatre to perform any part for which he was cast.

CHAPTER SEVEN

G RIMALDI CONTINUED to his duties as a member of the Drury Lane company for three months without finding that any violent consequences arose from his interview with John Kemble. The only perceptible difference was, that when they met, Kemble, instead of accosting him familiarly, as he had before been accustomed to do, would pull off his hat and make him a formal bow, which Grimaldi would return in precisely the same manner; so that their occasional meetings were characterized by something about half-way between politeness and absurdity. All this pleased Grimaldi very much, but rather surprised him too, for he had confidently expected that some rupture would have followed the announcement of his determination not to act. He was not very long, however, in finding that his original apprehensions were correct, for on the twenty-sixth of June he received the following epistle:

"Sir,

"I am requested by the proprietors to inform you that your services will be dispensed with for the next ensuing season."

This notice was signed by Powell, the prompter, and its contents considerably annoyed and irritated Grimaldi. To command him in the first place to perform what was out of his engagement and out of his power, and to punish him in the next by dispensing with his services, which involved his dispensing with his salary, seemed exceedingly harsh and unjust treatment. For a time Grimaldi even contemplated bringing

133

an action against Sheridan, against whom, under the terms
of his agreement, he would in all probability have obtained a
verdict; but he ultimately gave up all idea of seeking this mode
of redress, and determined to consult his staunch and sincere
friend Mr Hughes, by whose advice he was always guided. To
that gentleman's house Grimaldi repaired, and showing him the
notice he had received, inquired what in Mr Hughes's opinion
he had best do.

"Burn the letter," said Hughes, "and don't waste a minute
in thinking about it. You shall go with me to Exeter as soon
as the Sadler's Wells season is over, and stop there until it
recommences. You shall have four pounds a week all the time,
and a clear benefit. It will be strange if this does not turn out
better for you than your present engagement at Drury Lane."

Grimaldi accepted the terms so kindly offered without a
moment's hesitation, and, determining to be guided by the
advice of Mr Hughes, thought no more about the matter.

At Sadler's Wells the summer season went on very briskly
until August, when a circumstance occurred which impeded
the course of his success for some time, and might have been
attended with much more dangerous consequences. Grimaldi
played the first lieutenant of a band of robbers in *The Great Devil*,
and in one scene had a pistol secreted in his boot, which, at a
certain point of interest, he drew forth, presented at some of
the characters on the stage, and fired off, thus producing what
is technically termed an effect; in producing it on the fourteenth
of August, he very unintentionally presented another effect, the
consequences of which confined him to his bed for upwards of
a month. While Grimaldi was in the act of drawing out the
pistol, the trigger by some accident caught in the loop of his

boot, into which (the muzzle being downwards) its contents were immediately discharged. The boot itself puffed out to a great size, presenting a very laughter-moving appearance to everybody but the individual in it, who was suffering the most excruciating agony. Determined not to mar the effect of the scene, however, by leaving the stage before it was finished, Joe remained on until its conclusion; and then, when by the assistance of several persons the boot was got off, it was found that the explosion had set fire to the stocking, which had been burning slowly all the time he had remained upon the stage; besides which, the wadding was still alight and resting upon the foot. He was taken home and placed under medical care; but the accident confined him to the house for more than a month. At length, after a tedious, and, as it appeared to him *then*, almost an interminable confinement, Grimaldi resumed his duties at Sadler's Wells, and the part also. But the effect was never more produced; for from that time forth the pistol was worn in his belt, in compliance with the established usage of robber-chieftains upon the stage, who, at minor theatres especially, would be quite incomplete and out of character without a very broad black belt, with a huge buckle, and at least two brace of pistols stuck into it.

During this illness Grimaldi received great attention and kindness from Miss Bristow, one of the actresses at Drury Lane. She attended upon him every morning to assist in dressing the wound, and enlivened the hours which would otherwise have been very weary, by her company and conversation. In gratitude for her kindness Grimaldi married her on the following Christmas Eve, and it may be as well to state in this place that with her he lived very happily for more than thirty years; when she died.

Drury Lane opened on the thirtieth of September with *As You Like It* and *Blue Beard*. Grimaldi's chief part in this piece was a combat in the last scene but one; which, being very effective, had always been regularly and vociferously applauded. It was not originally in the piece, but had been 'invented', and arranged with appropriate music for the purpose of keeping the attention of the house engaged, while the last scene, which was a very heavy one, was being 'set up'. Now, if any fresh combatant had been ready in Grimaldi's place, very probably the piece might have gone off as well as it had theretofore, but Kemble totally forgetting the reason of the combat's introduction, omitted to provide any substitute. The omission was pointed out at rehearsal, and then he gave direction that it should be altogether dispensed with. The effect of this order was very unsatisfactory both to himself and the public. There was a very full house at night and the play went off as well as it could, and so did the afterpiece up to the time when the last scene should have been displayed; but there the stage manager discovered his mistake too late. The last scene was not ready, it being quite impossible to prepare it in time, and the consequence was that the audience, instead of looking at the combat, were left to look at each other or at the empty stage, as they thought fit. Upon this, there gradually arose many hisses and other expressions of disapprobation, and at last some playgoer in the pit, who all at once remembered the combat, shouted out very loudly for it. The cry was instantly taken up and became universal: some demanded the combat, others required an apology for the omission of the combat, a few called upon Kemble to fight the combat himself, and a scene of great commotion ensued. The exhibition of the last scene, instead of allaying the tumult, only increased it, and when the curtain fell, it was in the midst of a storm of hisses and disapprobation.

It so happened that Sheridan had been sitting in his own private box with a party of friends all the evening, frequently congratulating himself on the crowded state of the house, and repeatedly expatiating upon the admirable manner in which both pieces went off. He was consequently not a little annoyed at the sudden change in the temper of the audience; and not only that, but, as he knew nothing at all about the unlucky combat, very much confounded and amazed into the bargain. The moment the curtain was down, he rushed on to the stage, where the characters had formed a picture, and in a loud and alarming voice exclaimed: "Let no one stir!"

Nobody did stir; and Sheridan walking to the middle of the proscenium, and standing with his back to the curtain, said in the most solemn manner, "In this affair I am determined to be satisfied, and I call upon somebody here to answer me one question. What is the cause of this infernal clamour?"

This question was put in such an all-important way, that no one ventured to reply until some seconds had elapsed, when Barrymore, who played Blue Beard, stepped forward and said, that the fact was, there had formerly been a combat between Mr Roffey and Joe and the audience was dissatisfied at its not being done.

"And why was it not done, sir? Why was it not done? Where is Joe, sir?"

"Really, sir," replied Barrymore, "it is impossible for me to say where he may be. Our old friend Joe was dismissed at the close of the last season by the stage manager."

At this speech Sheridan fell into a great rage, said a great many things, and made a great many profoundly important statements, to the effect that he would be master of his own house, and that nobody should manage for him, and so forth; all of which was said in a manner more or less polite. He concluded by directing the 'call' porter of the theatre to go immediately to Joe's house, and to request him to be upon the stage at twelve precisely next day. He then took off his hat with a great flourish, made a polite bow to the actors and actresses on the stage, and walked very solemnly away. He received Grimaldi very kindly next day, and reinstated him in the situation he had previously held, adding unasked a pound a week to his former salary, "in order," as he expressed himself, "that matters might be arranged in a manner profoundly satisfactory." On the day after, *Harlequin Amulet* flourished in the bills in large letters for the following Monday; a rehearsal was called, and during its progress Kemble took an opportunity of encountering Grimaldi, and said, with great good humour, that he was very glad to see him there again and that he hoped it would be very long before they parted company. In this expression of feeling Grimaldi very heartily concurred; and so ended his discharge from Drury Lane, entailing upon him no more unpleasant consequences than the easily-borne infliction of an increased salary. So ended, also, the Exeter scheme, which was abandoned at once by Mr Hughes, whose only object had been to serve his son-in-law.

"About this time," says Grimaldi, "I used frequently to see the late Mr M G Lewis, commonly called Monk Lewis, on account of his being the author of a well-known novel, better known from its dramatic power than from its strait-laced propriety or morality of purpose. He was an effeminate looking man, almost constantly lounging about the green-room of Drury Lane, and entering into conversation with the ladies and gentlemen, but in a manner so peculiar, so namby-pamby (I cannot think at this moment of a more appropriate term), that it was far from pleasing a majority of those thus addressed. His writings prove him to have been a clever man; a consummation which his conversation would most certainly have failed signally in producing. I have often thought that Sheridan used to laugh in his sleeve at this gentleman; and I have, indeed, very good reason for believing that Lewis, upon many more occasions than one, was the undisguised butt of our manager. Be that as it may, Monk Lewis's play of *The Castle Spectre* was most undoubtedly a great card for Drury Lane; it drew immense houses, and almost invariably went off with loud applause. I have heard the following anecdote related, which, if true, clearly proves that Sheridan by no means thought so highly of this drama as did the public at large. One evening it chanced that these two companions were sitting at some tavern in the neighbourhood discussing the merits of a disputed question and a divided bottle; when Lewis, warming to his subject, offered to back his opinion with a bet.

'What will you wager?' inquired Sheridan, who began to doubt whether his was not the wrong side of the argument.

'I'll bet you one night's receipts of *The Castle Spectre*!' exclaimed the author.

'No,' replied the manager. 'That would be too heavy a wager for so trifling a matter. I'll tell you what I'll do—I'll bet you its intrinsic worth as a literary production!'

"Lewis received these little sallies from his lively acquaintance with the most perfect equanimity of temper, never manifesting annoyance by action further than by passing his hand though his light-coloured hair, or by word further than a murmured interjection of 'Hum!' or 'Hah!'"

There is another little anecdote in this place which we will also leave Grimaldi to tell in his own way:

"In the winter of the year (1801?) I frequently had the honour of seeing the late Majesty George the Fourth, then Prince of Wales, who used to be much behind the scenes of Drury Lane, delighting everybody with his affability, his gentlemanly manners and his witty remarks. On Twelfth Night, 1802, we all assembled in the green-room as usual on that anniversary at Drury Lane, to eat cake given by the late Mr Baddeley, who by his will left three guineas to be spent in the purchase of a Twelfth-cake for the company of that theatre. In the midst of our merriment, Sheridan, accompanied by the Prince, entered the apartment, and the former looking at the cake, and noticing a large crown with which it was surmounted, playfully said, 'It is not right that a crown should be the property of a *cake:* What say you, George?' The Prince merely laughed: and Sheridan, taking up the crown, offered it to him, adding:

'Will you deign to accept this trifle?'

'Not so,' replied his highness. 'However it may be doubted, it is nevertheless true that I prefer the cake to the crown, after all.' And so, declining the crown, he partook of the feast with hilarity and condescension."

There was no pantomime at Drury Lane, either in 1801 or 1802, nor was any great novelty produced at Sadler's Wells in the latter year. The year 1802, indeed, seems to have been productive of no melodramatic wonder whatever; the most important circumstance it brought to Grimaldi being the birth of a son on the twenty-first of November; an event which afforded him much joy and happiness.

But if 1802 brought nothing with it, its successor did, for it was ushered in with an occurrence of a rather serious nature, the consequences of which were not very soon recovered. Whether it was ill-fortune or want of caution, or want of knowledge of worldly matters it did so happen that whenever Grimaldi succeeded in scraping together a little money, so surely did he lose it afterwards in some strange and unfortunate manner. He had at that period been for some time acquainted with a very respected merchant of the City of London, named Charles Newland (not Abraham) who was supposed to have an immense capital embarked in business, who lived in very good style, keeping up a great appearance and who was considered to be, in short, a very rich man. He called at Grimaldi's house one morning in February, and requesting a few minutes private conversation, said hastily:

"I dare say you will be surprised, Joe, when you hear what business I have come upon; but although I am possessed of a great deal of wealth, it is all embarked in business, and I am at this moment very short of ready money; so I want you to lend me a few hundred pounds, if it is quite convenient." All this was said with a brisk and careless air, as if such slight trifles as 'a few hundred pounds' were scarcely deserving of being named.

Grimaldi had never touched the five hundred and odd pounds which he had picked up on Tower Hill, but had added enough to make six hundred in all. This sum he hastened to place before his friend, assuring him, with great sincerity, that if he had possessed double or treble the amount, he would have been happy to have lent it him with the greatest readiness. The merchant expressed the gratification he derived from his friendship, and giving him a bill for the money at three months' date, shook his hand warmly, and left him. The bill was dishonoured: the merchant became bankrupt, left England for America, and died upon the passage out. And thus the contents of the net purse and the bundle of notes were lost as easily as they were gained, with the addition of some small savings besides. (The 'savings' amounted to one pound!)

One evening in the second week of November 1803, Grimaldi, then playing at Drury Lane, had been called by the prompter and was passing from the green-room to the stage when a messenger informed him that two gentlemen were waiting to see him at the stage door. Afraid of keeping the stage waiting, he enjoined the messenger to tell the gentlemen that he was engaged at the moment, but that he would come down to them directly he left the stage.

As soon as he could get away Joe hurried downstairs, and, inquiring who wanted him, was introduced to two strangers, who were patiently awaiting his arrival. They were young men of gentlemanly appearance, and upon hearing the words, "Here's Mr Grimaldi—who wants him?" one of them turned hastily round, and warmly accosted him. He looked about Grimaldi's own age, and had evidently been accustomed to a much warmer climate than that of England. He wore the fashionable evening-dress of the day—that is to say, a blue body-coat with gilt buttons, a white waistcoat, and tight pantaloons—and carried in his hand a small goldheaded cane.

"Joe, my lad!" exclaimed this person, holding out his hand, in some agitation, "how goes it with you now, old fellow?"

Grimaldi was not a little surprised at this familiar address from a person whom he was not conscious of ever having seen in his life, and, after a moment's pause, replied that he really had not the pleasure of the stranger's acquaintance.

"Not the pleasure of my acquaintance!" repeated the stranger, with a loud laugh. "Well, Joe, that seems funny, anyhow!" He appealed to his companion, who concurred in the opinion, and they both laughed heartily. This was all very funny to the strangers, but not at all so to Grimaldi: he had a vague idea that they were rather laughing at than with him, and as much offended as surprised, was turning away, when the person who had spoken first said, in rather a tremulous voice:

"Joe, don't you know me now?"

Grimaldi turned, and gazed at the stranger again. He had opened his shirt, and was pointing to a scar upon his breast, the sight of which at once assured Grimaldi that it was no other than his brother John who stood before him. They were naturally much affected by this meeting, especially the elder brother, who had been so suddenly summoned into the presence of the near relative whom long ago he had given up for lost. They embraced again and again, and gave vent to their feelings in tears.

"Come upstairs," said Grimaldi, as soon as the first surprise was over. "Mr Wroughton is there—Mr Wroughton, who was the means of your going to sea—he'll be delighted to see you."

The brothers were hurrying away, when the friend, whose presence they had quite forgotten in their emotion, said:

"Well, John, then I'll wish you good night!"

"Good night! good night!" said the other shaking his hand. "I shall see you in the morning."

"Yes," replied the friend, "at ten, mind!"

"At ten precisely: I shall not forget," answered John.

The friend, to whom he had not introduced his brother in any way, departed; and they went upon the stage together, where Grimaldi introduced his brother to Powell, Bannister, Wroughton, and many others in the green-room, who, attracted by the singularity of John's return under such circumstances, had collected round them.

Having his stage business to attend to, Grimaldi had very little time for conversation; but of course he availed himself of every moment that he could spare off the stage, and in answer to his inquiries, his brother assured Grimaldi that his trip had been eminently successful.

"At this moment," he said, slapping his breast-pocket, "I have six hundred pounds here."

"Why, John," said his brother, "it's very dangerous to carry so much money about with you!"

"Dangerous!" replied John, smiling. "We sailors know nothing about danger. But, my lad, even if all this were gone, I should not be penniless." And he gave a knowing wink, which induced his brother to believe that he had indeed "made a good trip of it".

At this moment Grimaldi was again called upon the stage; and Mr Wroughton, taking that opportunity of talking to his brother, made many kind inquiries of him relative to his success and the state of his finances. In reply to these questions John made in effect the same statements as he had already communicated to Joseph, and exhibited as evidence of the truth of his declarations a coarse canvas bag, stuffed full of various coins, which he carefully replaced in his pocket again.

As soon as the comedy was ended, Grimaldi joined John; and Mr Wroughton having congratulated his brother on his return, and the fortunate issue of his adventures, bade them good night; when Grimaldi took occasion to ask how long the sailor had been in town. He replied, two or three hours back; and he had merely tarried to get some dinner, and had come straight to the theatre. In answer to inquiries about what he intended doing, John said he had not bestowed a thought upon the matter, and that the only topic which had occupied his mind was his anxiety to see his mother and brother. A long and affectionate conversation ensued, in the course of which it was proposed by Joseph, that as his mother lived with himself and his wife and they had a larger house than they required, John should join them, and they should all live together. To this the brother most gladly and joyfully assented, and, adding that he must see his mother that night, or his anxiety would not suffer him to sleep, asked where she lived. Grimaldi gave him the address directly; but, as he did not play in the afterpiece, said, that he had done for the night, and that if John would wait while he changed his costume, he would go with him. His brother was, of course, glad to hear there was no necessity for them to separate, and Grimaldi hurried away to his dressing-room, leaving him on the stage.

The agitation of his feelings, the suddenness of his brother's return, the good fortune which had attended John in his absence, the gentility of his appearance, and his possession of so much money, all together confused Grimaldi so, that he could scarcely use his hands. He stood still every now and then quite lost in wonder, and then suddenly recollecting that his brother was waiting, looked over the room again and again for articles of dress that were lying before him. At length, after having occupied a much longer time than usual in changing his dress, he was ready, and ran down to the stage. On his way he met Powell, who heartily congratulated him on the return of his relative, making about the thirtieth who had been kind enough to do so already. Grimaldi asked him, more from nervousness than for information, if he had seen John lately.

"Not a minute ago," was the reply. "He is waiting for you upon the stage. I won't detain you, for he complains that you have been longer away now, than you said you would be."

Grimaldi hurried downstairs to the spot where he had left his brother. He was not there.

"Who are you looking for, Joe?" inquired Bannister, as he saw him looking eagerly about.

"For my brother," he answered. "I left him here a little while back."

"Well, and I saw and spoke to him not a minute ago," said Bannister. "When he left me, he went in that direction" (pointing towards the passage that led towards the stage door). "I should think he had left the theatre."

Grimaldi ran to the stage door, and asked the porter if his brother had passed. The man said he had, not a minute back; he could not have got out of the street by that time. Joe ran out at the door, and then up and down the street several times, but saw nothing of him. Where could John be gone to? Possibly, finding Grimaldi longer gone that he had anticipated, he might have stepped out to call upon one of his old friends close by, whom he had not seen for so many years, with the intention of returning to the theatre. This was not unlikely; for in the immediate neighbourhood there lived a Mr Bowley, who had been his bosom friend when they were boys. The idea no sooner struck Grimaldi than he ran to the house and knocked hastily at the door. The man himself answered the knock, and was evidently greatly surprised.

"I have indeed seen your brother," he said, in reply to Grimaldi's question. "Good God! I was never so amazed in all my life."

"Is he here now?" was the anxious inquiry.

"No; but he has not been gone a minute; he cannot have gone many yards."

"Which way?"

"That way—towards Duke Street."

"He must have gone," thought Grimaldi, "to call on Mr Bailey, our old landlord." He hurried away to the house in Great Wild Street, and knocked long and loudly at the door. The people were asleep. He knocked again and rang violently being in a state of great excitement; at length a servant-girl thrust her head out of an upper window and said, both sulkily and sleepily:

"I tell you again, he is not at home."

"What are you talking about? Who is not at home?"

"Why, Mr Bailey: I told you so before. What do you keep on knocking for, at this time of night?"

Joe could not understand a word of all this, but hurriedly told his name and requested the girl to come down directly, for he wished to speak to her. The head was directly withdrawn, the window closed, and in a minute or two afterwards the girl appeared at the street door.

"I'm sure I beg your pardon, sir," she said, after pouring forth a volume of apologies. "But there was a gentleman here knocking and ringing very violently not a minute before you came. I told him Mr Bailey was not at home; and when I heard you at the door, I thought it was him, and that he would not go away."

Grimaldi was breathless with the speed he had made, and trembling with vague apprehensions of he knew not what. He asked if she had seen the gentleman's face. The girl, surprised at his emotion, replied that she had not; she had only answered him from the window, being afraid to open the door to a stranger so long after dark, when all the family were out. The only thing she had noticed was that he had got a white waistcoat on; for she had thought at the time, seeing him dressed, that perhaps he might have called to take her master to a party. He must have gone back to the theatre.

Grimaldi left the surprised girl standing at the door, and ran to Drury Lane Here, again, he was disappointed; his brother had not been seen. He ran from place to place, and from house to house, wherever he thought it possible his brother could have called, but nobody had heard of or seen him. Many of the persons to whom Joe appealed openly expressed their doubts to each other of his sanity of mind; which were really not without a shadow of probability, seeing that he knocked them out of their beds, and, with every appearance of agitation and wildness, demanded if they had seen his brother, whom nobody had heard of for fourteen years, and whom most of them considered dead.

It was so late now, that the theatre was just shutting up; but Grimaldi ran back once more, and again inquired if his brother had been there. Hearing that he had not, Joe concluded that, recollecting the address he had mentioned, John had gone straight to his mother's home. This seemed probable; and yet Joe felt a degree of dismay and alarm which he had never before experienced, even when there were good grounds for such feelings. The more he thought of this, however, the more probable it seemed, and he blamed himself as he walked quickly homewards for not having thought of it sooner. He remembered the anxiety his brother had expressed to see their mother, the plan they had discussed for their all living together, and the many little schemes of future happiness which they had talked over in their hurried interview, and in all of which she was comprised. He reached home, and, composing himself as well as he could, entered the little room in which they usually supped after the play. His brother was not there, but his mother was, and, as she looked much paler than usual, he thought she had seen John.

"Well, mother," he said, "has anything strange occurred here tonight?"

"No; nothing that I have heard of."

"What! no stranger arrived!—no long-lost relative recovered!" exclaimed Grimaldi, all his former apprehension returning.

"What do you mean?"

"Mean! Why, that John is come home safe and well, and with money enough to make all our fortunes."

His mother screamed wildly at this intelligence and fainted; she recovered after a time, and Grimaldi recounted to her and his wife the events of the evening, precisely as they are here narrated. They were greatly amazed at the recital. The mother held that John would be sure to come before the night was over; that he had probably met with some of his old friends, and would be there after he had left them. She insisted that Grimaldi, who was tired, should go to bed, while she sat up and waited for her son. He did so, and the mother remained the long night anxiously expecting his arrival.

This may appear a long story, but its conclusion invests it with a degree of interest which warrants the detail. The running away to sea of a young man, and his return after a lapse of years, is, and ever has been, no novelty in this island. This is not the burden of the tale. It possessed an awful interest to those whom it immediately concerned, and cannot fail to have some for the most indifferent reader. From that night in November 1803, to this month of January 1838, the missing man was never seen again; nor was any intelligence, or any clue of the faintest or most remote description, ever obtained by his friends respecting him. Next morning, and many mornings afterwards, the mother still anxiously and hopelessly expected the arrival of her son. Again and again did she question Grimaldi about him—his appearance, his manner, what he said, and all the details of his disappearance; again and again was every minute fact recalled, and every possible conjecture hazarded relative to his fate. Grimaldi could scarcely persuade himself but that the events of the preceding night were a delusion of his brain, until the inquiries after his brother, which were made by those who had seen him on the previous night, placed them beyond all doubt. He communicated to his friends the strange history of the last few hours, with all the circumstances of John's sudden appearance and of his equally sudden disappearance. He was advised to wait a little while before he made the circumstance public, in the hope that John might have been induced to spend the night with some shipmates, and might speedily return.

But after a week passed away, further silence would have been criminal, and Grimaldi proceeded to set on foot every inquiry which his own mind could suggest, or the kindness of his friends prompted them to advise. A powerful nobleman who at that time used to frequent Drury Lane, and who had on many occasions expressed his favourable opinion of Grimaldi, interested himself greatly in the matter and set on foot a series of inquiries at the Admiralty: every source of information possessed by that establishment that was deemed at all likely to throw any light upon the subject was resorted to, but in vain; the newspapers were searched to ascertain what ships had came, what crews they carried, what passengers they had; the police-officers were paid to search all London through, and endeavour to gain some information, if it were only of the lost man's death. Everything was tried by the family, and by many very powerful friends whom the distressing nature of the inquiry raised up about them, to trace the object of their regret and labour, but all in vain. The sailor was seen no more.

Various surmises were afloat at the time regarding the real nature of this mysterious transaction; many of them, of course, were absurd enough, but the two most probable conjectures appear to have been hazarded many years afterwards, and when all chance of John being alive were apparently at an end—the one by the noble lord who had pursued the investigation at the Admiralty, and the other by a shrewd long-headed police-officer who had been employed to set various inquiries on foot in the neighbourhood of the theatre.

The former suggested that a press-gang, to whom the person

of Grimaldi's brother was known, might possibly have pounced upon him in some by-street, and have carried him off; in which case, as John had previously assumed a false name, the fact of his friends receiving no intelligence of him was easily accounted for; while, as nothing could be more probable than that he was slain in one of the naval engagements so rife about that time, his never appearing again was easily explained. This solution of the mystery, however, was by no means satisfactory to Grimaldi's friends, as it was liable to many very obvious doubts and objections. Upon the whole, they felt inclined to give far more credence to the still more tragical, but, it is to be feared, more probable explanation which the experience of the police-officer suggested. This man was of opinion that the unfortunate subject of their doubts had been lured into some low infamous den, by persons who had either previously known or suspected that he had a large sum of money in his possession; that here he was plundered, and afterwards either murdered in cold blood or slain in some desperate struggle to recover his gold. This conjecture was encouraged by but too many corroboratory circumstances: John Grimaldi was of a temper easily persuaded: he had all the recklessness and hardihood of a sea-faring man, only increased by the possession of prize-money and the release from hard work: he had a very large sum of money about him, the greater part *in specie* and not in notes or any security which it would be difficult or dangerous to exchange: all this was known to his brother and to Mr Wroughton, both eyewitnesses of the fact.

One other circumstance deserves a word. It was, both at the time and for a long period afterwards, a source of bitter, although of most groundless self-reproach to Grimaldi, that he could not sufficiently recollect the appearance of the man who accompanied his brother John to the stage door of the theatre, to describe his person. If he could have been traced out, some intelligence respecting the poor fellow might perhaps have been discovered: but Grimaldi was so much moved by the unexpected recognition of his brother, that he scarcely bestowed a thought or look upon his companion: nor, after taxing his memory for many years, could he ever recollect more than that he was dressed in precisely the same attire as John, even down to the white waistcoat; a circumstance which had not only been noticed by himself, but was well remembered by the door-keeper, and others who had passed in and out of the theatre during the time the two young men were standing in the lobby.

Recollecting the intimate terms upon which the two appeared to be, and the appointment which was made between them for the following morning, "at ten precisely", there is little reason to doubt that if the sailor had disappeared without the knowledge or privity of his companion, the latter would infallibly have applied to Grimaldi to know where his brother was. Coupling the fact of his never doing so, and never being seen or heard of again, with the circumstance of the lost man never having evinced the least inclination to take him home with him, to retain him when he was in Joe's company, or even to introduce him in the slightest manner (from all of which it would seem that he was some bad or doubtful character), the family arrived at the conclusion—if it should ever be an unjust one, it will be forgiven—that this man was cognizant of, if indeed he was not chiefly instrumental in bringing about, the untimely fate of the murdered man, for such they always supposed him. Whether they were right or wrong in this conclusion will probably ever remain unknown.

CHAPTER EIGHT

SIGNOR BOLOGNA, better known to his intimates by the less euphonious title of Jack Bologna, was a countryman of Grimaldi's father, having been, like him, born at Genoa; he had been well acquainted with him, indeed, previously to his coming to England. He arrived in this country in 1787, with his wife, two sons, and a daughter. The signor was a posture-master, and his wife a slack-wire dancer; John, the eldest son (afterwards the well-known Harlequin), Louis, his second son, and Barbara, the youngest child, were all dancers. They were first engaged at Sadler's Wells, and here an intimacy commenced between Bologna and Grimaldi, which lasted during the remainder of their lives; they were children when it commenced, playing about the street in the morning and at the theatre at night.

The signor and his family remained at Sadler's Wells until 1793, when Mr Harris engaged him and his children (his wife had died before this time) at Covent Garden, where they remained for several years. (Jack) Bologna played during the summer months at the Surrey Circus, as Grimaldi used to act at Sadler's Wells. In 1801 he left Covent Garden, and in 1803 the Circus; upon the conclusion of the latter engagement, he was immediately secured for the ensuing season at Sadler's Wells, where he reappeared on Easter Monday in 1804. During the many years which had passed away since Jack closed his first engagement at Sadler's Wells, he and Grimaldi had been necessarily prevented by their different occupations from seeing much of each other; but being now once more engaged at the same theatre, their old intimacy was renewed. They met with a droll adventure in company, which may as well be related in this place.

Drury Lane closed in June and reopened on the fourth of October; but, as usual, Grimaldi's services were not required until Christmas. He had been in great request at Sadler's Wells, for the season was one of the heaviest the performers had ever known. The two friends were speaking of this one evening, and complaining of their great fatigue, when Bologna recalled to mind that he had a friend residing in Kent who had repeatedly invited him down to his house for a few days' shooting, and to take a friend with him; he proposed, therefore, that he and Grimaldi should go down by way of relaxation. On the sixth of November, accordingly, the friend having been previously apprized of their intention, and having again returned a most pressing invitation, they left town in a gig hired for the purpose.

On the road, Bologna told Grimaldi that the gentleman whom they were going down to visit was an individual of the name of Mackintosh; that he was understood to be wholly unconnected with any business or profession, that he was a large landed proprietor, and that he had most splendid preserves. The intelligence pleased Grimaldi very much, as he looked forward to a very stylish visit, and felt quite elated with the idea of cultivating the acquaintance of so great a man.

"I have never seen his place myself," said Bologna, "but when he is in London, he is always about the theatres, and he has often asked me to come down and have some shooting."

They were talking thus, when they arrived at Bromley, which

156

was about two miles and a half from the place to which they were bound. Here they met a man in a fustian jacket, driving a tax-cart drawn by a very lame little horse, who suddenly pulled up, hailed the party with a loud "Hallo!" and a "Well, Joe, here you are!"

Grimaldi was rather surprised at this intimate salutation from a stranger; and he was a little more so when Bologna, after shaking hands very heartily with the man in fustian, introduced him as the identical Mr Mackintosh whom they were going down to visit.

"I'm glad to see you, Joe," said Mr Mackintosh with an air of patronage. "I thought I'd meet you here and show you the way."

Grimaldi made some suitable acknowledgement for this politeness, and the tax-cart and the gig went on together.

"I am sorry you have hit upon a bad day for coming down here, so far as the shooting goes," said Mackintosh, "for tomorrow is a general fast. At any rate you can walk about and look at the country; and the next day—the next day—won't we astonish the natives!"

"Are there plenty of birds this year?" inquired Bologna.

"Lots—lots," replied the other man, whose manner and appearance scarce bore out Grimaldi's preconceived notion of the gentleman they were going to visit. If he were already surprised, however, he had much greater cause to be so eventually.

After travelling upwards of two miles, Bologna inquired if they were not near their place of destination.

"Certainly," answered Mackintosh. "That is my house."

Looking in the direction pointed out, their eyes were greeted with the appearance of a small roadside public house, in front of which hung a signboard, bearing the words '*Good Entertainment for Man and Beast*' painted on it, and beneath the name of *Mackintosh*. Bologna looked at Grimaldi, and then at the public house, and then at the man in the fustian jacket; but he was far too much engaged in contemplating with evident satisfaction the diminutive dwelling they were approaching, to regard the surprise of his companions. "Yes," he said, "that house contains the best of wines, ales, beds, tobacco, stabling, skittle-grounds, and every other luxury."

"I beg your pardon," interposed Bologna, who was evidently mortified, while Grimaldi had a strong and almost irresistible inclination to laugh, "but I thought you were not connected with business at all?"

"No more I am," said Mackintosh, with a wink, "The business belongs to mother!"

Bologna looked inexpressibly annoyed, and Grimaldi laughed outright, at which Mr Mackintosh seemed rather pleased than otherwise, taking it to all appearance as quite complimentary. "Yes," he said, "I may be said to be a gentleman at large, for I do nothing but ride about in my carriage here," pointing to the tax-cart, "or stroll out with my gun or my fishing-rod. Mother's quite a woman of business; but as I am an only child, I suppose I shall have to look after it myself some day or other."

He remained silent a moment, and then said, touching Bologna smartly with his whip, "I suppose, old fellow, you didn't think you were coming to a public house, eh?"

"Indeed I did not," was the sulky reply.

"Ah. I thought you'd be surprised," said Mackintosh, with a hearty laugh. "I never let my London friends know who or what

I am, except they're very particular friends, like you and Joe, for instance. I just lead them to guess I'm a great man, and there I leave 'em. What does it matter what other ideas strangers have about one?—But here we are, so get out of your gig; and rest assured you shall have as hearty a welcome as you'll ever get at a nobleman's house."

There was something hearty and pleasant in the man's manner, despite his coarseness; so, finding that Bologna was not inclined to speak, Grimaldi said something civil himself; which was extremely well received by their host, who shook his hand warmly, and led them into the house, where, being introduced to Mrs Mackintosh by her son as particular friends of his, they were received with great hospitality, and shortly afterwards sat down in the little bar to a capital plain dinner, which, in conjunction with some sparkling ale, rather tended to soothe the wounded spirit of Bologna.

After dinner they walked about the neighbourhood, which was all very pleasant, and returning to supper, were treated with great hospitality. On retiring to rest, Bologna acknowledged that "matters might have been worse", but before pronouncing a final opinion, prudently waited to ascertain how the preserves would turn out. On the following day they divided their time pretty equally between eating, drinking, chatting with the chance customers of the house, their host and his mother, and, though last, not least, preparing their guns for the havoc which they purposed making the next morning in Mr Mackintosh's preserves, of which he still continued to speak in terms of the highest praise.

Accordingly, they met at the breakfast-table a full hour earlier than on the previous day, and having dispatched a hearty meal, sallied forth accompanied by Mr Mackintosh, who declined carrying a gun and contented himself with showing the way. Having walked some little distance they came to a stile, which they climbed over, and after traversing a plot of pasture-land arrived at a gate, beyond which was a field of fine buckwheat. Here the guide called a halt.

"Wait a minute!—wait a minute!" cried he. "You are not so much accustomed to sporting as I."

They stopped. He advanced to the gate, looked over, and hastily returned.

"Now's the time!" he cried eagerly. "There's lots of birds in that field!" They crept very cautiously onwards: but when they reached the gate and saw beyond it, were amazed to discern nothing but an immense quantity of pigeons feeding in the field.

"There's a covey!" said Mackintosh, admiringly.

"A covey!" exclaimed Grimaldi. "Where? I see nothing but pigeons!"

"Nothing but pigeons!" exclaimed Mackintosh, contemptuously.

"What did you expect to find? Nothing but pigeons!—Well!"

"I expected to find pheasants and partridges," answered both sportsmen together. Bologna, upon whom the sulks were again beginning to fall, gave a grunt of disapprobation; but Mackintosh either was, or pretended to be, greatly surprised.

"Pheasants and partridges!" he exclaimed, with a ludicrous expression of amazement. "Oh dear, quite out of the question! I invited you down here to shoot birds—and pigeons are birds; and there are the pigeons—shoot away, if you like. I have performed my part of the agreement. Pheasants and partridges!" he repeated, "most extraordinary!"

"The fellow's a humbug!" whispered Bologna. "Kill as many of his pigeons as you can."

With this understanding, Bologna fired at random into the nearest cluster of pigeons and Grimaldi fired upon them as they rose frightened from the ground. The slaughter was very great: they picked up twenty in that field, five in the one beyond, and saw besides several fall which they could not find. This great success, and the agreeable employment of picking up the birds, restored their equanimity of temper, and all went well for some time, until Mackintosh said inquiringly:

"I think you have them all now?"

"I suppose we have," replied Bologna. "At least, all except those which we saw fall among the trees yonder."

"Those you will not be able to get," said Mackintosh.

"Very good; such being the case, we have 'em all," replied Bologna.

"Very well," said Mackintosh, quietly, "and now, if you will take my advice, you will cut away at once."

"Cut away!" said Bologna.

"Cut away!" exclaimed Grimaldi.

"Cut away is the word!" repeated Mr Mackintosh.

"And why, pray?" asked Bologna.

"Why?" said Mr Mackintosh. "Isn't the reason obvious? Because you've killed the pigeons."

"But what has our killing these pigeons to do with cutting away?"

"Bless us!" cried Mackintosh, "You are not very bright today! Don't you see that when the squire comes to hear of it, he'll be very angry. Now, what can be plainer, if he is very angry, as I know he will be, then if you are here, he'll put you in prison?

161

Don't you 'stand that. No, no: what I say is cut away at once and don't stop for him to catch you."

"Pooh!" said Bologna, with a contemptuous air. "I see you know nothing of the law. There's not a squire in all England who has power to put us in prison, merely because we have killed your pigeons, although we may not have taken out certificates."

"*My* pigeons!" exclaimed Mackintosh. "Lord help you! they're none o' mine!—they belong to the squire, and very fond of them he is, and precious savage he'll be when he finds out how you have been peppering them. So there I come back again to what I set out with. If you two lads will take my advice, now you've got your pigeons, you'll cut away with them."

The remarkable disclosure contained in this little speech fairly overwhelmed them; they stared at each other in stupid surprise, which shortly gave way first to anger and then to fear.

They were greatly awed at contemplating the risk which they had incurred of being "sent to prison"; and after a few words of angry remonstrance addressed to Mr Mackintosh, which that gentleman heard with a degree of composure and philosophy quite curious to behold, they concluded that they had better act upon his advice, and "cut away" at once. They lost no time in returning to the inn; and here, while they were engaged in packing up the "birds", the singular host got a nice luncheon ready, of which they did not fail to partake, and then mounting their gig, they bade farewell to him and his mother, the former of whom at parting appeared so much delighted and vented so many knowing winks that for the very life they could not help laughing outright.

On the following morning, Bologna and Grimaldi encountered

each other by chance in Covent Garden. Grimaldi had been to Drury Lane to see if he were wanted, and Bologna had been into the Strand, in which he had an exhibition during the winter months, when he was not engaged at any theatre. They laughed heartily at meeting, as the recollection of the day previous and its adventures came upon them, and finally adjourned to the Garrick's Head in Bow Street to have a glass of sherry and a biscuit, and once more talk the matter over. The house was then kept by a man of the name of Spencer, who had formerly been Harlequin at Drury Lane, but who, having left the profession, had turned Boniface instead. He was standing at the door when they arrived, and all three being upon intimate terms, was invited to join in a glass of wine; to this he readily assented, and they adjourned to his private room, where the Kentish adventures were related, to his great amusement and pleasure.

"By the by, though," he said, when the merriment was pretty well over, "I wish you had happened to mention to me that you wanted a few days' shooting, for I could have procured that for you with the greatest ease. I was born at Hayes, and all my relatives live in Kent; in fact, when in town they invariably come to this house, and would have been delighted to have obliged any friend of mine."

"Ah!" said Bologna, "and in that case we should have had birds to shoot at, and not pigeons."

Here Mr Spencer indulged in a laugh which was interrupted by the entrance of a young man. Though unknown to Bologna and Grimaldi, he appeared well acquainted with the landlord, who, after shaking him warmly by the hand and bidding him be seated, said, "But, Joseph, what has brought you so suddenly to town?"

"Oh, drat it!" exclaimed the new-comer, "very disagreeable business indeed. There were two vagabonds down in our parts yesterday from London, and they killed and stole fifty or sixty of Master's pigeons. I've come up here to find them out and apprehend them: I've got a constable drinking in the tap."

This information rather flustered them, and Bologna turned as pale as death; but the host, after indulging in two winks, and one fit of reflection, quietly said:

"Well, but Joseph, how can you find them out, think you? London's a large place, Joseph."

"Why, I'll tell you," replied the gamekeeper, for such, as they afterwards discovered, he was. "I found out, that the rascals had been staying at Mrs Mackintosh's house, and were friends of her son, so I went to him last night, and asked him where the fellows were. 'Oh,' says he, 'I know what you've come about; they've cut away with them pigeons!' 'Yes,' says I, 'and unless you tell me where they've cut away to, I shall make you answerable.' 'Oh,' says he again, 'I know nothing about 'em; they're no friends of mine,' he says, 'they're only play-actors: one's a Clown and t'other a Harlequin at one of the London theatres.' And this was all I could get from him; so up I came this morning, and knowing that you were acquainted with theatrical people, I thought I'd come and ask you which of the Clowns and which of the Harlequins it was most likely to be."

"Is the squire very angry?" asked Spencer.

"Oh, very," responded Joseph, with a shake of the head. "He's determined to pursue them to the very extremity of the law."

Upon hearing this, Grimaldi was much troubled in mind; not that he thought Spencer was a man likely to betray his friends, but fearing that by some inadvertence he might disclose what he felt certain his will would prompt him to conceal. As to Bologna, his agitation alone was sufficient to announce the real state of the fact; for, in addition to a ghastly paleness which overspread his face, he trembled so much, that in an attempt to convey some wine to his lips he deposited it upon his knees and left it there, staring all the while at the gamekeeper with a most crestfallen visage.

"There's one thing the squire appears to have forgotten," said Spencer, "and that is simply this—that before he can pursue these fellows to the extremity of the law, he has got to find them."

"True," answered Joseph, "and unless you assist me, I'm afraid I shan't be able to do that. I suppose, now, there are a good many Clowns and Harlequins in London, eh?"

"A great many," replied Spencer. "I am one, for instance."

"Oh!" smiled the gamekeeper, "but it isn't you."

"That's true," said the host, composedly. "But I'll tell you what; it is two particular friends of mine, though, who did it!"

Joseph exclaimed, "Indeed!" and Bologna gave Grimaldi a look which clearly evidenced his conviction, firstly, that it was all up, and secondly, that it was impossible to "cut away."

"Friends of yours, hey?" said Joseph, ruminating. "Then I expect you won't assist me in finding them out?"

"Not a bit of it," answered Spencer, "so you may go and look among the Harlequins and Clowns yourself, and Heaven help you! for the jokes they will play and the tricks they will serve you will be enough to wear your heart out."

Joseph looked greatly mortified at this compassionate speech, and, after a moment's pause, stammered out something about "that being Mr Spencer's friends it made a great difference".

165

"I'll tell you what it is, Joseph," said the landlord. "Say no more about this affair, and my two friends will pay a reasonable sum for the pigeons, and stand a rump-steak dinner and a bottle of wine this very day. What say you?"

Joseph's countenance brightened up. "Oh!" said he, "as to the pigeons, of course, I could manage. If the gentlemen are friends of yours, consider the matter settled—I'll talk the squire over about the matter. And as to the steak and wine, why I don't mind partaking of them; and, in return, they shall come down into Kent some day next week, and *I'll* give them a morning's shooting."

"Then," said Spencer, rising formally, "these are the gentlemen. Gentlemen, this is Mr Joseph Clarke."

All was satisfactorily settled: the rump steak and wine were ordered, duly eaten and drunk; and they spent the afternoon together very jovially, accepting Mr Clarke's invitation for another "day's shooting" with great alacrity. Nor did they omit keeping the appointment; but, on the day fixed, went once more into Kent, when, under the able guidance of their new acquaintance, they succeeded in killing and bagging four hares and five brace of pheasants in less than two hours. They returned to town without seeing anything more of their friend Mr Mackintosh, but being upon the very best terms with Mr Joseph Clarke, who—but for his really keeping his word and giving them a day's sport—might be not unreasonably suspected of having been in league with the landlord to use the sportsmen for their joint amusement, and to extract a good dinner from them besides.

At Drury Lane no novelty was brought out until the holidays. John Kemble had left the theatre on the termination of the previous season, and had become a proprietor of the other house (Covent Garden) by purchasing the share in the establishment which had previously belonged to Mr W. Lewis. He became acting manager at once; Mr Wroughton succeeding to his old situation at Drury Lane.

CHAPTER NINE

S ADLER'S WELLS REOPENED in 1805, as usual, at Easter; Grimaldi and Bologna were again engaged, and the season was a very profitable one. When Drury Lane's pantomime had ceased running, he did not play there above half-a-dozen times during the rest of the season. The theatre closed in June, and reopened again on the twenty-first of September with *Othello* and *Lodoiska*, in which latter piece Grimaldi, his wife, and mother all appeared. On the conclusion of the night's amusements, he had an interview with the acting manager (Wroughton), which, although at first both pleasing and profitable, led in less than six weeks to his departure from the theatre at which he had originally appeared and in which he had constantly played with all possible success for nearly four-and-twenty years.

The manager of Drury Lane had advertised Tobin's comedy of *The Honey Moon* as the play for the second night of the season; not recollecting, until it was too late to alter the bills, that in consequence of the secession of Mr Byrne, who had been ballet-master, and the non-engagement of any other person in his place, there was no one to arrange the dance incidental to the piece. In this dilemma, Grimaldi, who had been accustomed to arrange the dances at Sadler's Wells, was sent for. Mr Wroughton, after stating that he was in a very unexpected dilemma and that unless Grimaldi would assist him he would have to change the piece for the ensuing night— which it was exceedingly desirable to avoid doing, if possible—

169

briefly narrated the circumstances in which the theatre was placed, and concluded by offering him two pounds per week in addition to his regular salary, if he would arrange the dance in question, and assist in getting up any other little dances and processions that might be required. This offer Grimaldi readily accepted, merely stipulating that the increased salary should be understood to extend over the whole season, and not merely until another ballet-master was engaged. Mr Wroughton observed that nothing could be fairer, that this was what he meant, and that Grimaldi had his instructions to engage as many male dancers as he might deem necessary. Grimaldi at once entered upon his new office, immediately engaged as many hands (or legs) as he required, arranged the dance during the night, called a rehearsal of it at ten in the morning, got it into a perfect state by twelve, rehearsed it again in its proper place in the comedy, and at night had the satisfaction of hearing it encored with great applause.

At the end of the week, Grimaldi received his increased salary from Mr Peake, the treasurer, a gentleman well known and highly respected by all connected with the stage or theatrical literature, who shook Grimaldi by the hand, congratulated him on this new improvement of his income, and cordially wished him success. Before Grimaldi accepted the money, he said, "My dear sir, to prevent any future difference it is thoroughly understood, is it, that this increase is for the season?"

"Undoubtedly," replied Mr Peake "I will show you, if you like, Mr Graham's written order to me to that effect." This he did, and Grimaldi of course was perfectly satisfied. Mr Graham, who was then a magistrate at Bow Street, was at the head of affairs at Drury Lane.

All went on well for some little time. Mr James D'Egville was engaged as ballet-master shortly afterwards; but this made no alteration in the footing upon which Grimaldi was placed. There was no difference of opinion between the ballet-master and himself, for he continued to arrange the minor dances and processions, and his arrangements were repeatedly very warmly commended by Mr D'Egville. A new grand ballet, called *Terpsichore*, was produced by the latter gentleman immediately after his joining the company, in which Grimaldi performed Pan, which he always considered a capital character, and one of the best he ever had to play. The ballet was got up to bring forward Madame Parisot, who was engaged for the season for one thousand guineas. It was thoroughly rehearsed at least fourteen times before the night of performance, was very favourably received, and had a good run.

Grimaldi was not a little surprised, on Saturday the twenty-sixth of October, when he went as usual to the treasury to draw his salary, to hear that henceforth the extra two pounds would not be paid. Mr Peake admitted that he was also very much surprised and annoyed, again producing Mr Graham's letter, and candidly acknowledging that in his opinion this uncalled-for attempt to rescind the contract, which was none of Grimaldi's seeking, was very paltry. Grimaldi immediately waited upon Mr Wroughton and mentioned the circumstance, at which he too appeared greatly vexed, although it was not in his power to order the additional sum to be paid. Grimaldi then told his wife, dwelling upon it with great irritation; but she, observing that it was of no consequence, for they could do very well without the money, proposed that, having nothing to do at Drury Lane that night, they should go for an hour or two to Covent Garden.

To this proposition Grimaldi made no objection; so, as he passed down Bow Street, he called in upon Mr T Dibdin for an order, and the conversation happening naturally enough to turn upon theatrical affairs, mentioned what had just occurred at Drury Lane. Mr Dibdin immediately expressed himself in very strong terms upon the subject, and counselled Grimaldi to withdraw from the theatre and to accept an engagement at Covent Garden. The advice generated a long conversation between them which terminated in Grimaldi saying, Mr Dibdin might, if he pleased, mention the subject to Mr Harris, and say, if the management were willing to engage him, he was willing to enter into articles for the following season.

In the course of the evening, Grimaldi received a note begging his attendance at Covent Garden on Monday, at twelve, and keeping the appointment, was ushered into a room in which were Mr Harris and John Kemble. The latter greeted him in a very friendly manner, and said:

"Well, Joe, I see you are determined to follow me."

"Yes, sir," replied Grimaldi, who had been thinking of something polite. "You are a living magnet of attraction, Mr Kemble."

At this Mr Harris laughed and congratulated the tragedian on receiving so handsome a compliment. Kemble inquired of Grimaldi whether he knew Mr Harris, and receiving a reply in the negative, introduced him to that gentleman as Joe Grimaldi, whose father he had known well, who was a true chip of the old block, and the first low comedian in the country. Mr Harris said a great many fine things in reply to these commendations, and, rising, requested Grimaldi to follow him into an adjoining apartment. Joe did so, and in less than a quarter-of-an-hour had signed articles for five seasons; the terms being, for the first season, six pounds per week; for the second and third seven pounds; and for the fourth and fifth, eight pounds. Independent of these emoluments, Grimaldi had several privileges reserved to him, among which was the very important one of permission to play at Sadler's Wells, as he had theretofore done at Drury Lane. These arrangements being concluded, he took his leave, greatly satisfied with the improved position in which he stood, as up to that time he had only received four pounds per week at Drury Lane.

In the evening, Grimaldi had to play Pan in the ballet at Drury. When he had dressed for the part he entered the green-room, which was pretty full of ladies and gentlemen, among whom was Mr Graham, who, the moment he saw him, inquired if a report that had reached him of Joe's going to Covent Garden for the following season were correct. Grimaldi replied in the affirmative, adding that he was engaged for the four ensuing seasons. Mr Graham started up in a state of considerable excitement on hearing this, and addressed the performers present at considerable length, expatiating in strong language upon what he termed "Grimaldi's ingratitude" in leaving the theatre. Grimaldi waited patiently until he had concluded, and then, addressing himself to the same auditors, made a counter-statement in which he recapitulated the whole of the circumstances as they had actually occurred. When he came to mention Mr Graham's letter to Mr Peake, the treasurer, the former hastily interrupted him by demanding what letter he referred to.

"The letter," replied Grimaldi, "in which you empowered Mr Peake to pay the increased salary for the whole of the season."

"If Mr Peake showed you that letter," replied Mr Graham, in a great passion, "Mr Peake is a fool for his pains."

"Mr Peake," rejoined Grimaldi, "is a gentleman, sir, and a man of honour, and, I am quite certain, disdains being made a party to any such unworthy conduct as you have pursued towards me."

A rather stormy scene followed, from which Grimaldi came off victorious; Barrymore and others taking up his cause so vigorously that Mr Graham at length postponed any further discussion and walked away. Enough having taken place, however, to enable Grimaldi to foresee that his longer stay at Drury Lane would only be productive of constant discomfort to himself, he gave notice to Mr Graham on the following morning of his intention to leave the theatre on the ensuing Saturday week. This resolve gave rise to another battle between Mr Graham and himself, in the course of which Mr Graham was pleased to say that he could not play the ballet without Grimaldi, and, consequently, that if he left, Mr Graham would bring an action against him for loss incurred by its not being performed. Grimaldi, however, firmly adhered to his original resolution: acting therein upon the advice of Mr Hughes, who strenuously counselled him by no means to depart from it.

Considering himself now at perfect liberty until Easter, Grimaldi entered into an engagement to perform at Astley's theatre in Dublin, which had just been taken for a short period by Messrs Charles and Thomas Dibdin. These gentlemen had engaged the greater part of the Sadler's Wells company, including Bologna and his wife (who had been engaged by Mr Harris for the next season at Covent Garden on the same day as Grimaldi himself), and they offered Grimaldi fourteen guineas a week for himself, and two for his wife, half a clear benefit at the end of the season, and all his travelling expenses both by land and sea.

On the ninth of November Grimaldi closed his engagement at Drury Lane, performing Pan in the ballet of *Terpsichore*. He started for Dublin on the following morning, accompanied by his wife, leaving his little son, who was in very weak health, at home. They had a very tedious journey to Holyhead, and a very stormy one thence to Dublin; experiencing the usual troubles from cold, sickness, fatigue, and otherwise, by the way. Mr and Mrs Charles Dibdin, who had arrived first, received them with much cordiality and kindness; and they took lodgings at the house of a Mr Davis, in Peter Street. On Monday, November the eighteenth, the theatre opened, and their career was for some time eminently successful, as long, indeed, as the fine weather lasted; but no sooner did the rainy weather set in than the manager discovered to his horror and surprise that the roof of the theatre, being in a dilapidated condition, was not waterproof. At length, one night towards the end of December, a very heavy rain coming down during the performance actually drove the audience out of the house. The water descended in torrents into the pit and boxes: some people who were greatly interested in the performances put up their umbrellas, and others put on great-coats and shawls; but at length it came down so heavily upon the stage that the performers themselves were obliged to disappear. In a few minutes the stage was covered, the scenery soaked through, the pit little better than a well, and the boxes and gallery streaming with water. This unforeseen occurrence threw both literally and figuratively a damp upon the performances from which there was no recovering. From that time, with the single exception of one evening, the theatre was deserted. Tarpaulins and all kinds of cheap remedies were tried, but they all failed in producing their intended effect. They never kept the water out, or drew the company in. As to any thorough repair of the roof it was wholly out of the question; for the Dibdins only held the theatre until March, and the necessary repairs under his head alone would have cost at the very least two hundred pounds.

In this state of things, Mr Charles Dibdin was compelled to write to London for remittances wherewith to pay his company. Knowing exactly how he was situated, Grimaldi volunteered his services in the only way in which he could render them, and offered not to send to the treasury for his salary, but to leave it to be paid whenever the manager might appoint after their return to London. This offer, it is almost unnecessary to add, was gratefully accepted.

About the middle of January Mr Jones, the manager of the Crow Street Theatre, hearing how badly the Astley's people were doing and yet finding that, bad as their business was, it injured his, made an offer to Mr Dibdin to take his company off his hands at the terms upon which he had originally engaged them, and for the remainder of the time specified in their articles; and, further, to make some pecuniary compensation to Mr Dibdin himself. The manager assembled the company on the stage, after they had the mortification of playing to an empty house, on Tuesday, the twenty-eighth of January, and communicated this offer to them, and earnestly urged upon them the acceptance of the proposal, as the only means by which himself and his brother could hope to recover any portion of the losses they had already sustained. Grimaldi at once expressed his readiness to accede to the proposition, and used his utmost influence with the other members of the company to induce them to do the like. He succeeded, except in the case of two of the performers, who preferred returning at once to England.

When this was arranged to the satisfaction of all parties, Mr Dibdin announced his intention to close the theatre on the next Saturday, the first of February. Grimaldi took the opportunity of inquiring what was to become of his half-benefit, which had been agreed upon. The manager replied, with a melancholy smile, that he might give him anything he liked for *his* half—twenty pounds would do, and he should have the entire house next Saturday. Grimaldi immediately paid the twenty pounds, and on the following morning commenced making preparations for his benefit, having barely four days in which to announce the performance and sell his tickets. He had borne an introductory letter to Captain Trench, whose unvarying kindness to him on every possible occasion he most gratefully acknowledged, and to this gentleman he first mentioned his intention of taking a benefit. He also mentioned it to his landlord. Their replies were characteristic.

"Let me have a hundred box-tickets," said Captain Trench. "Keep the two centre boxes for me. If I want any more tickets I'll send for them; but here's the money for the hundred."

"Give me a hundred pit-tickets," said the landlord. "If I can sell more, I will; but here is the money for them."

Grimaldi had his bills printed and well circulated, but did no more business until the Saturday morning, which made him uneasy; though the fact simply was that the people were waiting to see how the weather would turn out; very well knowing that if

177

it were a wet night, the theatre would be the very worst place in which to encounter the rain. Fortune, however, was propitious; the day was cloudless, fair and beautiful; and the result was that although at nine o'clock in the morning not one place was taken except the two boxes bespoken by Captain Trench, at one o'clock in the afternoon not a single place remained unlet. At one time, when there was no doubt of the weather remaining dry, there were no fewer than sixteen carriages standing before Grimaldi's door, the owners of which were all anxious to obtain places and all of whom he was reluctantly compelled to disappoint. The receipts of the house amounted to one hundred and ninety-seven pounds and nineteen shillings, not to mention a variety of presents, including a magnificent gold snuff-box from Captain Trench which was worth, in weight alone, more than thirty pounds sterling. This purchase of Dibdin's half of the benefit for twenty pounds was not only a very fortunate thing for Grimaldi, but was, on the other hand, in some degree serviceable to Dibdin also, inasmuch as it enabled Grimaldi to oblige him with a loan of one hundred pounds, of which at that moment, in consequence of his undeserved misfortunes, he stood much in need. This advance, together with salary due and other matters, left Mr Dibdin indebted to Grimaldi in the sum of one hundred and ninety-six pounds, the whole of which was honourably repaid a few months afterwards. This benefit closed the season of the 'wet' Theatre in Peter Street and on the following Monday Grimaldi and the greater part of the London company appeared at the Crow Street Theatre, where they acted until the twenty-ninth of March.

On Sunday, the thirtieth of March, they packed up, and at ten o'clock in the evening of Monday went on board the packet, in which they had taken their berths to Holyhead, after receiving the warmest and kindest hospitality from every person they had encountered in Dublin. With only one letter of introduction Grimaldi had found himself in the course of a few days surrounded by friends whose hospitality and cordiality, not only of profession but of action, were beyond all bounds: one would invite him to dinner, and be personally affronted by his not dining with him every day; another who wished to pay him a similar attention, but whose dinner-hour would have interfered with the rehearsal, only gave up his claim upon the condition that his wife and himself should dine with him every Sunday; a third placed a jaunting-car at his disposal, and sent it to his door at eleven every morning; and a fourth expected him to meet a small party at supper regularly every night. Grimaldi had heard and read a great deal of Irish hospitality, but had formed no conception of its extent and heartiness until he experienced its effects in his own person.

He was much struck, as most Englishmen are, by the enormous consumption of whisky-punch, and the facility with which the good folks of Dublin swallow tumbler after tumbler of it, without any visible symptoms of intoxication. He entertained a theory that some beverage of equal strength, to which they were unaccustomed, would be as trying to them as their whisky-punch was to him (for he was always afraid of a second tumbler of toddy) and, with a view of putting it to the proof, gave a little party at his lodgings on Twelfth Night, and compounded some good strong English rumpunch with rather more than a dash of brandy in it. Grimaldi considered that the experiment was eminently successful, asserting that one-fourth of the quantity, which the guests would have drunk

179

with complete impunity had it been their ordinary beverage, quite overset them; and states with great glee that Mr Davis, his landlord, who could drink his seven tumblers of whisky-punch and go to bed afterwards rather dull from excessive sobriety, was carried upstairs after one tumbler of the new composition, decidedly drunk. We are inclined to think, however, that Mr Davis had been taking a few tumblers of whisky-punch in his own parlour before he went upstairs to qualify himself for the party, and that the success of the experiment is not sufficiently well established to justify us in impressing it on the public mind without the addition of this trifling qualification.

They were six days getting back to London, the weather being very inclement and the travelling very indifferent. Through a mistake of the booking-office keeper, Grimaldi had to travel the earlier portion of the road from Holyhead outside the coach. The cold was so intense and the frost so severe that he actually got frozen to his seat; and when the coach arrived at Red Landford it was with some difficulty that he was lifted off, and conveyed into an inn in a complete state of exhaustion and helplessness. His feet were bathed in brandy, and various other powerful stimulants applied with the view of restoring suspended circulation, but several hours elapsed before he recovered, and it was not until the following morning that he was enabled to resume his journey towards London, where he at length arrived without further hindrance or accident.

Grimaldi had no sooner returned to town than an unpleasant circumstance occurred, as if in especial illustration of his often-urged remark that he never had a sum of money but some unforeseen demand was made upon him, or some extraordinary exigency arose. He had been one morning to the City on business, and was somewhat amazed on his return to find a broker and his assistant in the best parlour, engaged in coolly taking an inventory of his goods and chattels.

"What on earth is the meaning of this?" he inquired.

"Only an execution for rent," replied the broker, continuing his instructions to his amanuensis. "Mirror in gilt frame, Villiam."

The tenant replied that it was quite impossible, and searching among his papers, found and produced the receipt for his rent. The broker looked it over with a cheerful smile, and then, with many legal phrases, proceeded to apprize him that the landlord himself was but a lessee, and that, in consequence of his not having paid his rent, the head landlord had determined to seize upon whatever property was found upon the premises.

Greatly annoyed at this information, Grimaldi hurried to Mr Hughes, his constant adviser in all difficulties, to consult with him. Having narrated the affair, Mr Hughes asked what was the amount claimed.

"Eighty-four pounds."

"Well then, Joe," said he, "you must pay it, or lose your furniture."

Accordingly Grimaldi returned home very indignant, and handed over the specified sum to the broker, who said nothing could be more satisfactory, and walked away accompanied by his assistant. The next morning the landlord came, and being ushered in, expressed much trouble in his countenance, and said that he was very glad to see Mr Grimaldi and such a fine morning together.

"But I beg your pardon," he added. "I don't think you know me."

Grimaldi replied, that unless he was the gentleman who had imposed upon him the necessity of paying his rent twice over, he had not the pleasure of his acquaintance. At which remark the landlord assumed a very penitent and disconsolate visage, declared his sorrow for what had occurred, and, as some light reparation for the loss and wrong, proposed to assign the lease to him. Grimaldi under all the circumstances was extremely glad to accede to the proposal, and cheerfully paid all the legal expenses contingent upon the transfer. The upshot of the matter was that a very short time afterwards he received another communication from the same landlord, in which he imparted the very unexpected fact that either party to the lease had a discretionary power of cancelling it at that period if he thought proper, and that he intended to avail himself of that clause, unless indeed Mr Grimaldi would prefer retaining the house at an advanced rent, which he was at liberty to do if he pleased. An inspection of the deed proved but too clearly that this statement was correct; so the eighty-four pounds were lost, together with the legal charges for the assignment of the lease and the costs of the execution; and the burden of an increased rent was imposed upon the unlucky tenant into the bargain.

His old articles at Sadler's Wells expiring this year, Grimaldi entered into a fresh engagement under which he bound himself to that theatre for three years, at a weekly salary of twelve pounds and two clear benefits. The pantomime produced at Easter was entitled *Harlequin and the Forty Virgins* and proved remarkably successful, running indeed through the whole of the season. In this piece he sang a song called *Me and my Neddy*, which afterwards became highly popular, and was in everybody's mouth. Several presents were made to him by admirers of his performance, and, among others, a very handsome watch, the face of which was so contrived as to represent a portrait of himself in the act of singing the romantic ditty just mentioned.

All this season the pantomime was played first, which arrangement released him at half-past eight, thus affording Grimaldi an opportunity, which he enjoyed for the first time in his life, of being abroad in the evening in the spring and summer. During the greater portion of his life in those seasons, he had entered Sadler's Wells every night at six o'clock and remained there until twelve. The novelty of being at liberty before it was yet dark was so great that he scarcely knew what to do with himself, sometimes strolling about the streets in perfect astonishment at finding himself there, and then turning home in pure lack of employment.

On the opening of Covent Garden Theatre in October, he became first acquainted with Mr Farley, between whom and himself a very warm and sincere friendship ever after existed. This gentleman inquired in what character Grimaldi would wish to make his first appearance. He mentioned Scaramouch in *Don Juan*, which had been one of his most successful parts at the other house; but Mr Farley suggested Orson, in *Valentine and Orson*, urging that the drama, which had not been acted for several years, had been very popular with the town, and that Orson was a character well suited to his abilities, in which it was very probable he would make a great hit. Grimaldi at once consented to play the part, merely requesting that Mr Farley would be good enough to give him some instruction in it, as he had never seen any portion of the piece, and was at some loss how to study the character. Mr Farley readily agreed to do so, and faithfully kept his word. It has been sometimes said, and indeed stated in print, that Grimaldi was a pupil and copyist of Dubois. No greater mistake can be made: if he can be said to have been the pupil of anybody, Mr Farley was certainly his master, as he not only took infinite pains to instruct Grimaldi in the character of Orson, but afterwards gave him very valuable advice and great assistance in getting up many other parts, in which he was also highly successful.

Grimaldi was very anxious about his first appearance at Covent Garden, and studied Orson with great assiduity and application for some time. He made his first appearance in the character on the tenth of October 1806, Farley playing Valentine. The piece, which was received with most decided success, was acted nearly every night until the production of the pantomime at Christmas rendered its withdrawal imperative. The part of Orson was in Grimaldi's opinion the most difficult he ever had to play; the multitude of passions requiring to be portrayed, and the rapid succession in which it was necessary to present them before the spectators, involving an unusual share of both mental and physical exertion upon the part of the performer. He played this character both in town and country on many occasions, but the effect produced upon him by the exertions of the last scene of the first act was always the same. As soon as the act-drop fell, he would stagger off the stage into a small room behind the prompter's box, and there sinking into an armchair, he would give full vent to the emotions which he found it impossible to suppress. He would sob and cry aloud, and suffer so much from violent and agonizing spasms, that those about him, accustomed as they at length became to the distressing scene, were very often in doubt, up to the very moment of his being 'called', whether he would be able to go upon the stage for the second act. He never failed, however; extraordinary as his sufferings were, his fear of not being ready as the time for his call approached, and the exertions he made to conquer those painful feelings, invariably enabled him to rally at the necessary time—a curious instance of the power of habit in enabling him to struggle successfully with the weaknesses which no length of habit, and no repetition of the same part, however frequent, were sufficient to banish. The effect produced on the audience by Grimaldi's personation of this character was intense: it enhanced his reputation greatly, bringing him before the public in quite a new line. The compliments and congratulations which he received from persons ranking high in his own profession, in literature, and in the fine arts, bore high testimony to the merit and striking character of this singular performance.

Preparations now began to be made for the production of *Mother Goose*, destined to acquire a degree of popularity quite unprecedented in the history of pantomime, and to occupy a place in the choicest recollections of the play-goers of the time. At Drury Lane the management, well-knowing that great preparations were being made at Covent Garden for the production of a new harlequinade on the twenty-sixth of December, and dreading the advantage they had gained in securing Grimaldi, hurried on the preparations for their own pantomime. Engaging Montgomery, who had acquired some celebrity at the Circus, at a high salary to play Clown, they produced their pantomime on the twenty-third, thus gaining an advantage of three days over the other house. The Drury Lane piece, however, partook infinitely more of the character of a spectacle than a pantomime—the scenery and tricks were good, but the 'business' was so wretched that the audience began to hiss before it was half-over, and eventually grew so clamorous that it was deemed prudent to drop the curtain long before the intended conclusion of the piece. Grimaldi and his friend Bologna were present, and were very far from regretting this failure. Up to that time Drury Lane had always been more successful in pantomime than Covent Garden; and there is little doubt that the production of this unsuccessful but very splendid piece, three days before the usual time, was intended not merely to crush the pantomime in preparation at Covent Garden, but Grimaldi too, if possible.

They had a night rehearsal of *Mother Goose* at Covent Garden on the ensuing evening, and the performers were in a state of great anxiety and uncertainty as to its fate. It had always been the custom to render a pantomime the vehicle for the display of gorgeous scenery and splendid dresses; on the last scene especially, the energies of every person in the theatre connected with the decoration of the stage were profusely lavished, the great question with the majority of the town being which pantomime had the finest conclusion. *Mother Goose* had none of these accessories; it had neither splendid scenery nor showy dresses. There was not even a spangle used in the piece, with the exception of those which decked the Harlequin's jacket, and even they would have been dispensed with but for Grimaldi's advice. The last scene, too, was as plain as possible, and the apprehensions of the performers were proportionately rueful. But all these doubts were speedily set at rest; for on the production of the pantomime on the twenty-sixth of December, 1806, it was received with the most deafening shouts of applause, and played for ninety-two nights, being the whole remainder of the season. The houses it drew were immense: the doors were no sooner open than the theatre was filled; and every time it was played the applause seemed more uproarious than before—another instance of the bad judgement of actors in matters appertaining to their craft. *She Stoops to Conquer* was doomed by the actors to inevitable failure up to the very moment when the performances commenced (although in this case many eminent literary men and critics of the time held the same opinion); and *The Honey Moon* lay neglected on the manager's shelf for many years, it being considered impossible that an audience would be found to sit out its representation.

Grimaldi's opinion of *Mother Goose*—it may or may not be *another* instance of the bad judgement of actors—always remained pretty much the same, notwithstanding its great success. He considered the pantomime, as a whole, a very indifferent one, and always declared his own part to be one of the worst he ever played; nor was there a trick or situation in the piece to which he had not been well accustomed for many years before. However this may be, there is little doubt that the exertions of Bologna and himself, as Harlequin and Clown, contributed in a very important degree to the success of the piece; it being worthy of remark, that whenever the pantomime had been played without the original Harlequin and Clown, it has invariably gone off flatly and generally failed to draw.

During the run of this pantomime, Grimaldi fell curiously into a new and mysterious circle of acquaintance. The mystery which overhung them, the manner of his introduction, their style of living, and his subsequent discovery of their rank and title are not a little curious. On the sixth of January 1807, a gentleman called at his house in Baynes' Row, and was shown into the parlour. Grimaldi was surprised to recognise his quondam friend Mackintosh, who owned the preserves. He apologised for calling, entered into conversation with great ease, and trusted that the little trick he had played in mere thoughtlessness might be completely forgiven. Being courteously requested not to trouble himself by referring to it, Mr Mackintosh went on to say that his mother had sold her inn and had retired to a distant part of the country; while he himself, having attached himself to business, had come to reside permanently in London, and had taken a house and offices in Throgmorton Street.

Mr Mackintosh's appearance was extremely smart, his manners were greatly improved, and altogether he had acquired much polish and refinement since the days of the chaise-cart and the fustian jacket. As, notwithstanding the absurd scrape into which he had led his guests, he had treated them very hospitably, Grimaldi invited him to dine on the following Sunday. He came in due course; his conversation was jocose and amusing, and, becoming a favourite at the house, he frequently dined or supped there: Grimaldi and his wife occasionally doing the same with him in Throgmorton Street, where he had a very business-looking establishment, plainly but genteelly furnished.

About a month after his first calling, Mackintosh waited upon Grimaldi one morning and said that some friends of his residing in Charlotte Street, Fitzroy Square, were very anxious to make his acquaintance, and wished much for his company at supper one evening after he had finished at the theatre. Grimaldi, who if he had accepted all the invitations he received at this period would have had very little time for his profession, parried the request for some time, alleging that he was a very domestic person, and that he preferred adhering to his old custom of supping at home with his wife after the play. Mackintosh, however, urged that his friends were very wealthy people, that Grimaldi would find them very useful and profitable acquaintances, and by these and a thousand other persuasions overcame his disinclination to go. Grimaldi consented, and an evening was fixed for the visit.

On the appointed night, as soon as he had finished at the theatre, Grimaldi called a coach and directed the driver to set him down at the address which Mackintosh had given him. The coach stopped before a very large house, apparently handsomely furnished, and brilliantly lighted up. Not having any idea that the man could possess friends who lived in such style, Grimaldi at first supposed that the driver had made a mistake; but while they were discussing the point, Mackintosh, elegantly dressed, darted out of the passage, and, taking his arm, conducted him into a brilliant supper-room. If the outside of the house had given Joe cause for astonishment, its internal appearance redoubled his surprise. Everything was on a scale of the most costly splendour: the spacious rooms were elegantly papered and gilded, elegant chandeliers depended from the ceilings, the richest carpets covered the floors, and the other furniture, too, was of the most expensive description. The supper comprised a choice variety of luxuries, and was splendidly served; the costliest wines of various kinds and vintages sparkled upon the table.

There were just twelve persons in the supper room besides Mackintosh and himself—to wit, six ladies and six gentlemen, who were all introduced as married people. The first couple to whom Grimaldi was introduced were, of course, the host and hostess, Mr and Mrs Farmer, who welcomed him with enchanting urbanity and condescension. Every member of the party was beautifully dressed: the ladies wore jewellery of the most brilliant description, the numerous attendants were in handsome liveries, and the whole scene was so totally different from anything Grimaldi had anticipated that he was thoroughly bewildered, and actually began to doubt the reality of what he saw. The politeness of the gentlemen and the graceful ease of the ladies, however, soon restored his self-possession; while the delicious flavour of the wines and dishes convinced him that with respect to that part of the business, at all events, he was labouring under no delusion. In eating, drinking, singing and story-telling the night wore on till past five o'clock, when Grimaldi was at length suffered to return home. A recital of all the circumstances astonished his wife not a little; and he was quite as much amazed at recollecting what he had seen, as she at hearing of it.

A few days afterwards, Mackintosh called again; hoped Grimaldi had enjoyed himself, was delighted to hear he had, and bore an invitation for the next night. To this Grimaldi urged all the objections he had before mentioned, and added to them an expression of his unwillingness to leave his wife at home. Mr Mackintosh, with great forethought, had mentioned this in Charlotte Street; he was commissioned to invite her, Mrs Farmer trusting she would come in a friendly way and excuse the formality of her calling. Well, there was no resisting this; so Grimaldi and his wife went to Charlotte Street next night, and there were the rooms, and the six ladies, and the six gentlemen, and the chandeliers, and the wax-lights, and the liveries, and, what was more to the purpose than all, the supper, all over again. There were several other parties after this; and then the six ladies and the six gentlemen *would* come and see Mr Grimaldi at his own house—whereat Mrs Grimaldi was rather vexed, inasmuch as they had not one quarter so many spoons as the Charlotte Street people, and no chandeliers at all. However, they were polite enough to say that they had never spent a more delightful evening; and as they talked and laughed very much, and were very friendly and kind, the visit passed off to the admiration of all parties.

There was some mystery about these great friends, which the worthy couple were quite unable to solve. It did not appear that they were connected by any other ties than those of friendship, and yet they were always together and never had a stranger among them; there were always the same six ladies and the same six gentlemen, the only change being in their dresses, which varied in make and colour but never in quality. Then they did not seem to be in any business, and there was a something in the politeness of the gentlemen and the jocoseness of the ladies which struck the Grimaldis as rather peculiar, although they could never tell what it was. Joe saw they were not like the noblemen and gentlemen he was in the habit of meeting in the green-rooms of the theatres; and yet, notwithstanding that he pondered upon the matter a great deal, he could not for the life of him discover in what the difference consisted. His wife was in just the same state of perplexity; but although they talked the matter over very often, they never arrived at any tangible conclusion. While they were thinking about it the parties kept going on, and January and February passed away.

On the thirteenth of March Grimaldi had promised to act, in conjunction with Messrs Bartley, Simmons, Chapman, and Louis Bologna, at the Woolwich theatre, for the benefit of Mr Lund. Chancing to mention the circumstance at one of the Charlotte Street parties a few days before the time, Mr Farmer immediately proposed that he and the other five gentlemen should accompany their excellent friend; that they should all sup together at Woolwich after the theatre was over, and return to town next day. This was immediately agreed to by all the party except one gentleman, with the uncommon name of Jones, who had an appointment with a nobleman, which it was impossible to postpone.

The five gentlemen were punctual, and they, Mackintosh, and Grimaldi started together. They dined at Woolwich and afterwards adjourned to the theatre, where the five gentlemen and Mackintosh went into the boxes and Grimaldi went upon the stage. The five gentlemen talked very loud and applauded very much; and their magnificent appearance created quite a sensation, not only among the audience but the actors also. They supped together at the hotel at which they had dined, slept there, and returned to town next day. Mr Farmer and the four gentlemen came home in a barouche; Mackintosh, Grimaldi, and some other professional persons preferred to walk, for the benefit of the exercise. Upon the way, Grimaldi sounded Mackintosh about the professions, connexions, and prospects of his friends; but he evaded making any reply, further than observing, with an air of great respect, that they were very wealthy people. Grimaldi dined at Throgmorton Street a few days afterwards, and again tried to penetrate the mystery, as did his wife, who accompanied him. Mr Mackintosh threw no light upon it, but it was destined to be shortly revealed.

About three weeks had elapsed since the last dinner in Throgmorton Street, during the whole of which time nothing had been seen or heard either of the six ladies or of the six gentlemen, when, as Grimaldi was sitting reading in his parlour in Islington, a strange gentleman was shown into the room. As he was accustomed to be waited upon by many people of whom he knew nothing, he requested the gentleman to take a chair, and after a few commonplace remarks upon the weather and the papers, begged to ask his business with him.

"Why, my business with you, Mr Grimaldi," said the stranger, putting down his hat, as if he had come to stop a long time, "is of a very peculiar nature. Perhaps I had better commence by telling you who I am. My name is Harmer."

"Harmer?" said Grimaldi, running over in his mind all the theatrical names he had ever heard.

"Mr James Harmer, of Hatton Garden. The reason of my waiting upon you is this—I wish to speak to you upon a very disagreeable affair."

There was a peculiar solemnity in the visitor's manner, although it was very gentlemanly and quiet, which at once threw Grimaldi into a state of great nervous excitement. He entreated him, with a very disturbed countenance, to be kind enough to explain the nature of the communication he had to make, as explicitly as he could.

"To come, then, at once to the point," said Mr Harmer, "do you not know a person of the name of Mackintosh?"

"Yes, certainly," replied Grimaldi, his thoughts flying off at a tangent, first to Throgmorton Street, and then to the ladies and gentlemen in Charlotte Street. "Oh yes, I know him."

"He is now," said Mr Harmer, solemnly, "in great danger of losing his life."

Grimaldi at once supposed his visitor was a doctor, said he was sorry to hear it, asked how long he had been ill, and begged to know what was the matter with him.

"His bodily health is good enough," replied Mr Harmer, with a half-smile. "In the course of my professional career, Mr Grimaldi, I have known many men in imminent danger of losing their lives, who have been in most robust health."

Grimaldi bowed his head, and presumed that his visitor referred to cases in which the patient had gone off suddenly. Mr Harmer said that he certainly did, and that he had strong reasons to fear Mr Mackintosh would go off one morning very suddenly indeed.

"I greatly regret to hear it," said Grimaldi. "But pray tell me his condition without reserve: you may safely be communicative to me. What is the nature of the disorder? What is it called?"

"Burglary," answered Mr Harmer, quaintly.

"Burglary!" exclaimed Grimaldi, trembling from head to foot.

"Nothing less," replied Mr Harmer. "The state of the case, Mr Grimaldi, is simply this: Mackintosh is accused of having committed a burglary at Congleton, in Cheshire. I am a solicitor, and am engaged on his behalf; the evidence against him is very strong, and if he be found guilty, which I must say appears to me extremely likely, he will most infallibly be hanged."

This intelligence so amazed Grimaldi that he fell into a chair as if he had been shot, and it was some little time before he was sufficiently recovered to resume the conversation. The moment he could do so, he hastened to explain that he had never supposed Mackintosh to be other than an honest man, or he would carefully have shunned all acquaintance with him.

"He has been anything but an honest man for a long time past," said Mr Harmer. "Still, I may say that he is anxious to reform; and at all events, I am certain that this particular robbery was not committed by him."

"Good God! and he still likely to be hanged for it!"

"Certain," said Mr Harmer, "unless we can prove an alibi. There is only one man who has it in his power to do so; and that man, Mr Grimaldi, is yourself."

"Then," said Mr Grimaldi, "you may command me."

In a long and, to Grimaldi, very interesting conversation which ensued he learned that the robbery had been committed on the thirteenth of March, on the very night on which he had played for Lund's benefit at Woolwich, and afterwards supped with Mackintosh and his friends. This accidental circumstance was of course of the last importance to Mr Harmer's client, and that gentleman receiving a promise from Grimaldi that he would make an affidavit of the fact, if required, wished him a good morning and left him.

Mackintosh, being admitted to bail a few days afterwards, called upon Grimaldi to express his gratitude for the readiness with which he had consented to give his important evidence. The insight into the man's character which Mr Harmer had given him rendered Grimaldi of course desirous to be as little in his company as possible; but as his kind nature would not allow him to wound Mackintosh's feelings more than was absolutely necessary in this interview (quite voluntary on his part), immediately after the exposure, and as he was moreover very desirous to put a few questions to Mackintosh concerning the twelve ladies and gentlemen, Grimaldi dissembled his dislike, and placed some refreshment before Mackintosh. He then said:

195

"Mr Mackintosh, I cannot suppose you to be guilty of any act of this kind, for you have so many circumstances in your favour. Putting myself out of the question—I am merely an actor, working for my subsistence—you can call, to prove your alibi, gentlemen of station and undoubted respectability. Mr Farmer and his friends, for instance, could not fail to have great weight with the court."

A very perceptible change overspread the countenance of Mr Mackintosh when he heard these words. He shook his head with great vehemence, and looked strongly disposed to laugh. Grimaldi, who was one of the simplest creatures in all worldly matters that ever breathed, paused for a reply, but finding his acquaintance said nothing, added:

"Besides—the ladies. Dear me, Mr Mackintosh, the appearance of those gentlemen's wives would be almost enough to acquit you at once!"

"Mr Grimaldi," said Mackintosh, with a slight tremor in his voice which, despite his serious situation, arose from an incipient tendency to laughter, "Mr Grimaldi, none of those women are married."

Grimaldi stared incredulously.

"Not one," said Mackintosh. "They only pass for married people—they are not really so."

"Then how," said Grimaldi, waxing very angry, "how dared you to invite my wife among them, and induce me to take her there!"

"I'm very sorry, sir," said the man, humbly.

"I'll tell you what, sir," interposed Grimaldi. "I'll be put off no longer: this is not the time for secrecy and falsehood, nor is it in your interest to tell me anything but the truth. Now, I demand to know at once the real characters of these people, and why you shook your head when I mentioned your bringing them forward as witnesses."

"Mr Grimaldi," replied the man, with great apparent humility, "they would not come if they were sent for; and besides, if they did, it would injure, not assist me, for they are all marked men."

"Marked men!" exclaimed Grimaldi.

"Too true, sir," said Mackintosh. "Desperate characters every one."

"What! Farmer?"

"He was sentenced to death at the Old Bailey, and got a reprieve while standing on the drop beneath the gallows."

"And Williams?"

"Williams is a forger of notes."

"And Jesson?"

"He and Barber are both burglars."

"And the Jewish-looking man—I forget the rascal's name—the man who sings Kelly's songs; what is he?"

"Oh, he helps to pass the forged notes, and has been three times in the pillory."

"There is one other man whom I have not named—that fellow Jones. What is he—a murderer?"

"No sir, only a burglar," answered Mackintosh. "Don't you recollect, Mr Grimaldi, that he would not join the party to Woolwich?"

"Perfectly well."

"Well, sir, the truth is, he left town for Cheshire the same day as the party was proposed, and he is the man who actually committed the deed I am charged with. He did the robbery. I found it out only today; but, though I know it, I can't prove it now: and all those people in Charlotte Street are doing their best to get me found guilty, and save the real man, who is better liked among them than I am."

The enumeration of all these crimes, the reflection of having been intimately associated with such wretches, and the fear of having his innocence confounded with their guilt quite overwhelmed their unfortunate victim. He was thoroughly stupefied for some minutes, and then, starting up with uncontrollable fury, seized Mackintosh by the throat, and demanded how he durst take him among such a horde of villains, under pretence of being his friend. Mackintosh, alarmed at this unexpected ebullition of resentment, fell on his knees before Grimaldi in the most abject manner, and poured forth many entreaties for mercy and protestations of regret.

"Answer me one question," said Grimaldi, releasing his hold. "Give me a plain and straightforward answer, for it's only by telling me the truth now, that you can hope for any leniency at my hands. What was your motive for taking me into the company of these men and women, and why did they want to have me among them?"

"I'll tell you the truth, by God!" replied Mackintosh, "and without the smallest attempt at disguise. They thought you must be very good company, and hearing me say that I knew you, gave me no rest until I consented to take you to the house in Charlotte Street; which I at last agreed to do, stipulating, upon my soul, that no harm should ever be done you, and that their real characters should be carefully concealed. You turned out as they expected; they were very much delighted with your songs and stories, and I was obliged to promise to bring you again. And that's the truth."

Although this explanation relieved Grimaldi from some very terrible fears relative to the motives of these persons in seeking his companionship, it was a very galling reflection to have been playing the jester to a gang of robbers and vagabonds; and as it presented itself to his mind, it drove him almost mad with rage. Never accustomed to give way to his passions, the fit of fury into which he had worked himself was such that it was many hours before he recovered from its effects. Mr Mackintosh, with much wisdom, took himself off the moment his confession was concluded.

About a week after this agreeable visit, Grimaldi was sitting at breakfast one morning when his servant announced a lady, and in walked—as he sat paralysed with surprise—no less a person than Mrs Farmer, who, sitting down with great composure and freedom, said, when the servant had left the room:

"Well, Grim, here's Jack Mackintosh has got himself into a pretty hobble, hasn't he?"

"He has indeed," said Grim, all abroad with amazement, "and I am very sorry for it."

"Lord! you don't mean that!" returned the lady. "I'm sure it's more than I am. Of course, it's everybody's turn on time; and Jack's had a very long string."

It being now thoroughly evident that the party, deeming longer concealment hopeless, wished to treat Grimaldi as one of themselves, and to imply that he had been acquainted with their real characters all along, he resolved to act decidedly; so, the moment the lady had finished speaking, said:

"By some extraordinary mistake and blindness I have been

led into the society of yourself and your associates, Ma'am. I regret this bitterly for many reasons, but for two especially: first, that I should ever have had acquaintance with such characters; and secondly, that it compels me to act with apparent harshness to a woman. As I have no other course to pursue, however, I beg you will have the goodness to tell the ladies and gentlemen whom I have had the unhappiness to meet in Charlotte Street, that I request them never to show their faces here; and that I wish never to see, and certainly shall never speak to any of them again."

The servant entering the room at this point, in reply to the summons he had previously given, he continued:

"As soon as this person has rested herself after her walk, show her to the door; and take care that you never admit her, or any of the people who have been in the habit of coming here with her, into the house again." With these words Grimaldi quitted the room, as did the 'lady' immediately afterwards; and well pleased he was to be rid of her society.

In the July of this year a very extraordinary circumstance occurred at Sadler's Wells, which was the great topic of conversation in the neighbourhood for some time afterwards. It happened thus:

Captain George Harris, of the Royal Navy, who was related to Thomas Harris of Covent Garden, and with whom Grimaldi was slightly acquainted, had recently returned to England after a long voyage. The crew being paid off, many of the men followed their commander to London, and proceeded to enjoy themselves after the usual fashion of sailors. Sadler's Wells was at that time a famous place of resort with the blue-jackets, the gallery being sometimes almost solely occupied by seamen and their female companions. A large body of Captain Harris's men resorted hither one night, and amongst them a man who was deaf and dumb, and had been so for many years. This man was placed by his shipmates in the front row of the gallery. Grimaldi was in great force that night, and, although the audience were in one roar of laughter, nobody appeared to enjoy his fun and humour more than this poor fellow. His companions good-naturedly took a good deal of notice of him, and one of them, who talked very well with his fingers, inquired how he liked the entertainments; to which the deaf and dumb man replied through the same medium, and with various gestures of great delight, that he had never seen anything half so comical before.

As the scene progressed Grimaldi's tricks and jokes became still more irresistible; and at length, after a violent peal of laughter and applause which quite shook the theatre and in which the dumb man joined most heartily, he suddenly turned to his mate, who sat next to him, and cried out with much glee, "What a damned funny fellow!"

"Why, Jack," shouted the other man, starting back with great surprise, "can you speak?"

"Speak!" replied the other. "Ay, that I can, and hear, too."

Upon this the whole party, of course, gave three vehement cheers, and at the conclusion of the piece adjourned in a great procession to the Sir Hugh Myddleton, hard by, with the recovered man, elevated on the shoulders of half-a-dozen friends, in the centre. A crowd of people quickly assembled round the door, and great excitement and curiosity were occasioned as the intelligence ran from mouth to mouth that a deaf and dumb man had come to speak and hear, all owing to the cleverness of Joey Grimaldi.

The landlady of the tavern, thinking Grimaldi would like to see his patient, told the man that if he would call next morning he should see the actor who had made him laugh so much. Grimaldi, being apprised of the circumstance, repaired to the house at the appointed time, and saw him, accompanied by several of his companions, all of whom still continued to manifest the liveliest interest in the sudden change that had happened to their friend, and kept on cheering, and drinking, and treating everybody in the house, in proof of their gratification. The man, who appeared an intelligent well-behaved fellow, said that in the early part of his life he could both speak and hear very well; and that he had attributed his deprivation of the two senses to the intense heat of the sun in the quarter of the world to which he had been, and from which he had very recently returned. He added that on the previous evening he had for a long time felt a powerful anxiety to express his delight at what was passing on the stage; and that after some feat of Grimaldi's which struck him as being particularly amusing he had made a strong effort to deliver his thoughts, in which, to his own great astonishment, no less than that of his companions, he succeeded. Mr Charles Dibdin, who was present, put several questions to the man; and from his answers it appeared to every one present that he was speaking the truth. Indeed, his story was in some measure confirmed by Captain Harris himself; for one evening, about six months afterwards, as Grimaldi was narrating the circumstance in the green-room at Covent Garden, that gentleman, who chanced to be present, immediately remarked that he had no reason from the man's behaviour while with him to suppose him an imposter, and that he had seen him on that day in full possession of all his senses.

In the month of August, following this circumstance, Grimaldi received a subpoena to attend the trial of Mackintosh, at Stafford. He immediately gave notice to the manager of Sadler's Wells, that he was compelled to absent himself for a few days, and Bradbury, of the Circus, was engaged to supply his place. Mr Harmer and himself went down together; and on the day following their arrival, a true bill having been found against Mackintosh by the grand jury, the trial came on.

Grimaldi forgets the name of the prosecutor's counsel, and regrets the circumstance very much, observing that the lengthy notice which the gentleman bestowed upon Joe ought to have impressed his name on his memory. If this notice were flattering on account of its length, it certainly was not so in any other respect; in as much as the gentleman in question, in the exercise of that licence which many practitioners unaccustomed to briefs assume, was pleased to designate the principal witness for the prisoner, to wit, Mr Joseph Grimaldi, as a common player, a mountebank-stroller, a man reared in and ever accustomed to vice in its most repulsive and degrading forms—a man who was necessarily a systematic liar—and, in fine, a man upon whose word or oath no thinking person could place any reliance.

During this exordium, and pending the logical deductions of the ingenious gentleman whose name is unhappily lost to his country, the prisoner eyed his witness with intense anxiety, fearing, no doubt, that in his examination, either by angry words, or by attempting to retort on the counsel, or by volunteering jokes, or by seeking revenge upon himself, against whom he had such just ground of complaint, he might pass the rope round his neck instead of serving his cause; but his fears were needless. His witness had gone there to discharge what he considered a solemn duty; and, apart from all personal considerations, to give his honest testimony in a case involving a man's life and death. Grimaldi went there, of course, prepared to give his evidence in the manner best befitting himself and the occasion; and, if he wanted any additional incentive to caution and coolness, he would have found it in the taunts of the opposing counsel, which naturally made him desirous to show, by his behaviour, that the same man who could play the clown upon a public stage could conduct himself with perfect propriety as a private individual—in the same way as many young gentlemen, who are offensive in wigs, become harmless and obscure in social life.

No fewer than nine witnesses were examined for the prosecution, all of whom, to Grimaldi's astonishment and horror, swore positively to the identity of the prisoner. The case for the prosecution being closed, he was immediately put into the box for the defence; when, after stating that the prisoner was in his company at Woolwich at the time of the commission of the burglary, he proceeded to detail as briefly as he could all that had happened on the day and night in question. Grimaldi carefully suppressed any extraneous matter that related to himself or his own feelings which might have been injurious to the prisoner, and produced the playbill of the night to prove that there could be no mistake respecting the date. He was then submitted to a very long and vexatious cross-examination, but he never lost his temper for an instant or faltered in his testimony in any way; and at its conclusion he was well rewarded for his good feeling and impartiality by the highly flattering terms in which the presiding judge was pleased to express his opinion of the manner in which he had conducted himself.

His wife was the next witness called, and she fully corroborated his evidence. Two more witnesses were examined on the same side, when the judge interposed, putting it to the jury whether they really deemed it necessary to hear any further evidence, and not hesitating to say that the full conviction on his own mind was that the witnesses for the prosecution were mistaken and that the prisoner at the bar was innocent of the offence laid to his charge. The jury fully coincided in the learned judge's opinion, and immediately returned a verdict of "Not guilty", after a trial which had already lasted for upwards of nine hours.

Previous to his return to town, on the following morning, Grimaldi sought and obtained a few minutes' private conversation with Mackintosh. In this interview, he used his utmost endeavours to awaken Mackintosh's mind to a sense of his situation, to induce him to reflect on the crimes he had committed, and to place before him the inevitable consequences of his career if he held the same course; by all of which remonstrances the man appeared much affected, and for which he expressed himself very grateful. It was scarcely necessary for Grimaldi to add that any communications between them must be discontinued for the future; but, lest his true repentance might be endangered by the loss of the only friend he seemed to have, he gave Mackintosh permission to write to him if he ever needed his assistance, and assured him that if it were in his power to relieve him, the appeal should never be made in vain. It says something for the honour of human nature and the sincerity of the man's repentance that he never took undue advantage of this permission, and, indeed, was never heard of by Grimaldi again.

Grimaldi returned to town, as he had every reason to do, with a light heart; and as he never heard any further intelligence either of the half-dozen gentlemen or the six Lucretias to whom he had so unwittingly introduced his wife, he experienced no further trouble or disquiet on this score.

CHAPTER TEN

O N HIS RETURN TO TOWN from Stafford, of course Grimaldi went immediately to Sadler's Wells; where, to his great surprise, he was informed by Mr Dibdin that he was not wanted just yet, in as much as Bradbury had been engaged for a fortnight, and had not been there above half the time. He added, too, that Bradbury had made a great hit and had become very popular. This intelligence vexed Grimaldi not a little, as he naturally feared that the sudden popularity of the new favourite might affect that of the old one; but his annoyance was much increased when he was informed that the proprietors were anxious that on the night of Bradbury's benefit they should play in the same pantomime. Grimaldi yielded his consent with a very ill grace, and with the conviction that it would end in his entire loss of favour with the audience. When the proposition was made to Bradbury in Grimaldi's presence it was easy to see that Bradbury liked it as little as himself; which was natural enough. It was not for Joe, however, to oppose the suggestion, as the combination of strength would very likely draw a great house, and he had only taken half of it with the proprietors for that night. It was accordingly arranged that they should appear together on the following Saturday; Bradbury sustaining the part of the Clown for the first three scenes in the pantomime, then Grimaldi taking it for the next three scenes, and Bradbury coming in again to close the piece. Grimaldi was so much dissatisfied with these arrangements that on the morning of the day fixed he told his friend Richard Lawrence that he was certain it was "all up with him", and that Bradbury had thrown him completely out of favour with the public.

The result, however, was not what he anticipated. The moment Grimaldi appeared he was received with the most tremendous applause. Animated by this encouraging reception, he redoubled his exertions, and went through his three scenes amidst the loudest and most enthusiastic plaudits. This reception rather vexed and confused Bradbury, who had to follow, and who, striving to outdo his predecessor, made such a complete failure, that, although it was his own benefit and he might reasonably be supposed to have a good many friends in the house, he was actually hissed, and ran off the stage in great disorder. Grimaldi finished the pantomime for him, and the brilliant manner in which it went off sufficiently testified to him that all the fears and doubts to which he had previously given way were utterly groundless. Indeed, when the performances were over, Bradbury frankly admitted that Grimaldi was the best Clown he had ever seen, and that, if he had been aware of his abilities, he would not have suffered himself to be put in competition with Joe on any account whatever.

This Bradbury was a clever actor in his way, and a very good Clown, but of so different a character from Grimaldi that it was hardly fair to either to attempt instituting a comparison between them. He was a tumbling Clown rather than a humorous one, and would perform many wonderful and dangerous feats. He would jump from the flies—that is, from the curtains above the stage—down on to the stage itself, and do many other things equally surprising. To enable himself to go through these performances without danger, he always occupied a very long time in dressing for the part, and adjusting no fewer than nine strong pads about his person to protect those parts of his frame which were the most liable to injury; wearing one on the head, one round the shoulders, one round the hips, two on the elbows, two on the knees, and two on the heels of his shoes. Thus armed, he would proceed to throw and knock himself about in a manner which, to those unacquainted with his precautions, appeared to indicate an intense anxiety to meet with some severe, if not fatal accident. Grimaldi, on the contrary, never wore any padding in his life; nor did he attempt any of the great exploits which distinguished Bradbury. His Clown was of a much more composed and subdued temperament, although much more comical and amusing. Bradbury was very original withal, and copied no one; for he had struck out a peculiar line for himself, and never departed from it.

After the night at Sadler's Wells Grimaldi heard nothing more of Bradbury for some time; but at length he received a note from the rival Clown, dated, to Joe's excessive surprise, from a private madhouse at Hoxton, requesting him to visit Bradbury there without delay, as he was exceedingly anxious to see him. Joe was much astonished at this request, as little or no intimacy had previously existed between them, and the place where the letter was dated was so very unexpected and startling. Not knowing what to do, he showed the letter to his friend Lawrence, who recommended him by all means to go and volunteered to accompany him. As Joe gladly availed himself of this offer, they went together to Hoxton, and, inquiring at the appointed place, were introduced to Bradbury, who was a patient in the asylum and had submitted to the customary regulations: all his hair being shaved off, and his person being kept under strict restraint. Concluding that he had a maniac to deal with, Grimaldi spoke in a very gentle, quiet manner, which the patient observing, burst into a roar of laughter.

"My dear fellow," said Bradbury, "don't look and speak to me in that way!—for though you find me here, treated as a patient, and with my head shaved, I am no more mad than you are."

Grimaldi rather doubted this assurance, knowing it to be a common one with insane people, and therefore kept at a respectful distance. He was not long in discovering, however, that what Bradbury said was perfectly true. The circumstances which had led to his confinement in the lunatic asylum were briefly these:

Bradbury was a very dashing person, keeping a tandem, and associating with many gentlemen and men of title. Upon one occasion, when he had been playing at Plymouth, a man-of-war sailed from that town to Portsmouth, and several friends among the officers took him on board with them. It was agreed that they should sup together at Portsmouth. A splendid meal having been prepared, they spent the night, or at least the larger portion of it, in great hilarity. As morning approached, Bradbury rose to retire, and then, with considerable surprise, discovered that a magnificent gold snuff-box with a gold chain attached, which he was accustomed to wear in his fob and which he had placed on the table for the use of his friends, had disappeared. He mentioned the circumstance, and a strict search was immediately instituted, but with no other effect than that of proving that the valuable box was gone. When every possible conjecture had been hazarded and inquiry made without success, it was recollected that one of their companions, a young gentleman already writing 'Honourable' before his name and having a coronet in no very remote perspective, had retired from the table almost immediately after supper: it was suggested that he might have taken it in jest, for the purpose of alarming its owner. Bradbury and several others went to this gentleman's room, and communicated to him the loss and their doubts respecting him. The young gentleman positively denied any knowledge of the box, and, after bitterly reproaching them for their suspicions, abruptly closed the door in their faces, leaving Bradbury in a state of violent mortification at his loss.

On the following morning, nothing more having been heard of the missing property, the gentleman, against whom Bradbury now nourished many serious misgivings, sent down word to his friends that he was so much vexed with them for their conduct of the night before in supposing it possible he could have taken anything away even in jest, that he should not join them at breakfast, but, on the contrary, should immediately return to town. This message, instead of allaying, as it was doubtless intended to do, Bradbury's suspicions, caused him to think still worse of the matter: and upon ascertaining that the young man had actually taken a place in the next coach which started for London, he lost no time in obtaining a warrant, by virtue of which he took him prisoner just as he was stepping into the coach. Upon searching his portmanteau, the box was found, together with several articles belonging to his other companions. Bradbury was determined to prosecute, not considering the young man's nobility any palliation of the theft: he was instantly taken before a magistrate, and fully committed for trial.

No sooner did this affair become known to the relatives and connexions of the offender, than, naturally anxious to preserve the good name of the family, they proceeded to offer large sums to Bradbury if he would relinquish the prosecution, all of which proposals he for some time steadily refused. At length they offered him a handsome annuity, firmly secured for the whole of his life: he was not proof against this temptation, and at length signified his readiness to accept the bribe. The next point to be considered was, how Bradbury could accept the money without compounding a felony, and increasing the obloquy already cast upon the thief. Bradbury hit upon and carried into execution a most singular plan: he caused the report to be circulated that he had suddenly become insane, committed many extravagant acts, and in a short time was, apparently against his own will, but in reality by his own contrivance, deprived of his liberty, and conveyed to the asylum where Grimaldi visited him. The consequence of this step was that when the stealer of the snuff-box was placed upon trial, no prosecutor appearing, he was adjudged not guilty and liberated accordingly. Intelligence of this was directly sent to Bradbury, who proceeded to make arrangements for his own release; this was soon effected, and it was on the eve of the day of his departure that Grimaldi saw him in the madhouse. Bradbury's only object in writing—or rather in causing the letter to be written, for he could not write a line himself, nor read either—was to ask Joe to play for his ensuing benefit at the Surrey, which he readily consented to do; then wishing Bradbury a speedy deliverance from his disagreeable abode, Grimaldi took his departure.

The next day Bradbury came out of the asylum, telling everybody that he was perfectly recovered, having got well in as sudden a manner as he fell ill, and in the following week his benefit took place. Grimaldi played and sang for him, and took money at the gallery door, to boot. The house was quite full, and everything went on well until Bradbury made his appearance, when, impelled by some strange and sudden whim, he was guilty of a disgusting piece of irreverence and impertinence. The consequence of this was that the audience very naturally and properly took great offence, and upon a repetition of the conduct, literally hooted him from the stage.

This was the ruin of Bradbury as a pantomimist. He did not appear again in London for many years, and, although he played occasionally in the country theatres, never afterwards regained his former rank and celebrity in the profession. As far as pecuniary matters were concerned, it did not matter much to him, the annuity affording him a handsome independence; but whether he afterwards sold it and dissipated the money, or whether the annuity itself was discontinued in the course of years, this at least is certain, that when he died he was in very indifferent circumstances, if not in actual want.

In October 1807 Covent Garden commenced the new campaign, and brought forward *Mother Goose*, which ran, with the same degree of success as before, until nearly Christmas, and was played altogether twenty-nine times. On the fifteenth of October, a most frightful accident occurred at Sadler's Wells. The pantomime was played first that night, which, joined to his having nothing to do at Covent Garden, enabled Grimaldi to go home early to bed. At midnight he was awakened by a great noise in the street, and loud and repeated knocks at the door of his house. At first he concluded it might be some idle party amusing themselves by knocking and running away; an intellectual pastime not at that time exclusively confined to a few gentlemen of high degree. But, finding that it was repeated, and that the noise without increased, he hastily slipped on a morning-gown and trousers, and hurried to the street door. The people who were clamouring outside were for the most part friends, who exclaimed when Grimaldi appeared that they had merely come to assure themselves of his personal safety, and were rejoiced to find that he had escaped. He now learned, for the first time, that some vagabonds in the pit of the theatre had raised a cry of "Fire!" during the performance of the last piece, *The Ocean Fiend*, and that the audience had risen simultaneously to make their escape: that a violent rush towards the doors had ensued, and that in the confusion and fright a most fearful loss of life had taken place. He waited to hear no more, but instantly ran off to the theatre.

On arriving there, Grimaldi found the crowd of people collected around it so dense as to render approach by the usual path impossible. Filled with anxiety, and determined to ascertain the real state of the case, he ran round to the opposite bank of the New River, plunged in, swam across, and finding the parlour window open and a light at the other end of the room, he threw up the sash and jumped in *à la Harlequin*. What was his horror, on looking round, to discover that there lay stretched in the apartment no fewer than nine dead bodies! Yes! there lay the remains of nine human beings, lifeless, and scarcely yet cold, whom a few hours back he had been himself exciting to shouts of laughter. Paralysed by the sad sight, he stood awhile without the power of motion; then, hurrying to the door, hastily sought to rid himself of the dreadful scene. It was locked without, and he vainly strove to open it, so knocked violently for assistance. At first the family of Mr Hughes were greatly terrified at hearing these sounds issuing from a room tenanted, as they imagined, only by the dead; but at length recognising the voice they unlocked the door, and Grimaldi gladly emerged from the apartment.

It was not known until next day how many lives were lost: but when the actual loss of life could be ascertained, it appeared that twenty-three people, male and female, were killed, not to mention many dangerous and severe accidents. This melancholy catastrophe was mainly attributable to the imprudence of those persons who reached the theatre doors first, and who, upon finding that nothing really was the matter, sought to return to their places. The meeting of the two crowds in the passages caused a complete stoppage; and this leading the people inside to believe that all egress was blocked up, impelled them to make violent efforts to escape, for the most part fatal to the unfortunate persons who tried them. Several people flung themselves from the gallery into the pit, others rushed hopelessly into the densest part of the crowd and were suffocated, others were trodden under foot, and hence the melancholy result.

This accident happening on the last night but four of the season, it was deemed prudent not to reopen the house that year. Such performers as were entitled to benefits, and had not yet taken them, took them at the Circus; and thus terminated the season of 1807—the most melancholy termination of a season which Sadler's Wells Theatre had ever known.

At Covent Garden on the twenty-sixth of December, was produced *Harlequin in his Element* or *Fire, Water, Earth and Air*, in which Bologna and Grimaldi were the Harlequin and Clown. It was highly successful, and in Grimaldi's opinion deservedly so, for he always considered it one of the best pantomimes in which he ever played. During this season, he also performed in

215

an unsuccessful melodrama entitled *Bonifacio and Bridgetino*, and Baptiste in *Raymond and Agnes*, which latter piece went off very well and was repeated several times.

At this time Grimaldi had a cottage at Finchley, to which he used to drive down in his gig after the performances. If there were no rehearsal, he remained there until the following afternoon; if there were, he returned to town immediately after breakfast. His principal reason for taking the house originally was that his young son, of whom he was extremely fond, might have the benefit of country air: but both he and his wife became so much attached to it that when his original term expired he renewed the lease, and retained it altogether for several years.

Grimaldi met with numerous little adventures during these night-drives after the theatre: sometimes he fell asleep as soon as he had turned out of town, and only awoke when he arrived at his own gate. One night he was so fatigued with his performance that he still continued to sleep, when the horse, a very steady one, who could always find his way home without assistance, had stopped at the gate. The best of it was that upon this particular night the manservant, who always sat up for him, had fallen asleep too; so there sat he slumbering on one side of the fence, while on the other side, not six feet off, sat his master in the gig, fast asleep too; and so they both remained, until the violent snorting of the horse, which probably thought it high time to turn in for the night, awoke the man, who roused the master and speedily set all to rights. But as one circumstance which occurred to him during these night journeys will be narrated at greater length in another part of the volume, we will leave the subject for the present.

Grimaldi very grievously offended Mr Fawcett in March 1808,

from a very slight cause, and without the remotest intention of doing so. Fawcett called one afternoon at his cottage at Finchley on the road to town from his own house at Totteridge, which was only two miles distant from Grimaldi's, and asked Grimaldi to play for his benefit, then close at hand: this he most willingly promised to do.

"Ah," said Fawcett, "but understand I don't want you to play Clown or anything of that sort, I want you to do Brocket in *The Son-in-Law.*"

Grimaldi demurred a little to this proposition, considering that as he had made a great hit in one branch of his profession, he could not do better than retain his standing in it, without attempting some new line in which, by failure, he might injure his reputation. Not wishing to disoblige Mr Fawcett if he could possibly help it, he replied that he must decline giving an answer at that moment, but that in the course of a day or two he would write. Having consulted his friends in the meantime, and being strongly advised by them not to appear in the character Mr Fawcett had mentioned, Grimaldi wrote, declining in respectful terms to do so, and stating the grounds of his objection. Odd as it may appear, the little circumstance angered Mr Fawcett much: he never afterwards behaved towards Grimaldi with any cordiality, and for the three years immediately following never so much as spoke to or noticed Grimaldi whenever they chanced to meet.

On March the fourteenth, Grimaldi received permission from Mr Kemble to play for his sister-in-law's benefit at the Birmingham theatre, which was then under the management of Mr Macready, the father of the great tragedian. Immediately upon his arrival, Grimaldi repaired to his hotel, and was welcomed by Mr Macready with much cordiality and politeness, proposing that he should remain in Birmingham two, or, if possible, three nights after the benefit at which he was announced to perform, and offering terms of the most liberal description. Anticipating a proposal of this nature, Grimaldi had, before he left town, inquired what the performances were likely to be at Covent Garden for some days to come. Finding that if the existing arrangements were adhered to, he could not be wanted for at least a week, he had resolved to accept any good offer that might be made to him at Birmingham, and therefore closed with Mr Macready without hesitation. After breakfast they walked together to the theatre to rehearse; and here Grimaldi discovered a great lack of those adjuncts of stage effects technically known as 'properties': there were no tricks, nor indeed was there anything requisite for pantomimic business. After vainly endeavouring to devise some means by which the requisite articles could be dispensed with, he mentioned his embarrassment to the manager.

"What! properties?" exclaimed that gentleman. "Wonderful! You London stars require a hundred things, where we country people are content with one: however, whatever you want you shall have. Here, Will, go down to the market and buy a small pig, a goose, and two ducks. Mr Grimaldi wants some properties, and must have them."

The man grinned, took the money, and went away. After some reflection Grimaldi decided in his own mind that the manager's directions had been couched in some peculiar phrases common to the theatre, and at once went about arranging six pantomimic scenes, with which the evening's entertainments were to conclude. While he was thus engaged, a violent uproar and loud shouts of laughter hailed the return of the messenger, who, having fulfilled his commission to the very letter, presented him with a small pig, a goose, and two ducks, all alive, and furthermore, with Mr Macready's compliments, and he deeply regretted to say that those were all the properties in the house.

Grimaldi accepted them with many thanks, and arranged a little business accordingly. He caused the old man in the pantomime and his daughter to enter, immediately after the rising of the curtain, as though they had just come back from market, while he himself, as Clown and their servant, followed carrying their purchases. He dressed himself in an old livery coat with immense pockets, and a huge cocked hat; both were, of course, over his Clown's costume. At his back he carried a basket laden with carrots and turnips; stuffed a duck into each pocket, leaving their heads hanging out; carried the pig under one arm, and the goose under the other. Thus fitted and attired, he presented himself to the audience, and was received with roars of laughter. His songs were all encored—*Tippitywitchit* three times—and the hit was most decided. The house was full to the ceiling, and it was equally full on the following night, when Grimaldi played Scaramouch; the third night was as good as any of the preceding; and the fourth, which terminated his engagement, was as successful as the rest. Just as he was going on the stage on this last evening, and had even taken up his 'properties' for that purpose, a note was put into his hands, which was dated that morning, and had just arrived from London, whence it had been dispatched with all possible speed. He opened it hastily, and read, in the hand of an intimate friend:

"Dear Joe, They have announced you to play tomorrow night

at Covent Garden; and as they know you have not returned from Birmingham, I fear it is done to injure you. Lose not a moment, but start immediately on the receipt of this."

Grimaldi instantly ran to Mr Macready, and showing him the letter, told him that although he was very sorry to disappoint his Birmingham friends, he could not stop to play.

"Not stop to play!" echoed the manager. "Why, my good fellow, they will pull the house down. You must stop to play, and post up to London afterwards. I'll take care that a chaise and four are waiting for you at the stage door, and that everything shall be ready for you to start, the moment you have finished your business."

Grimaldi played with the same success to a brilliant house, received two hundred and ninety-four pounds from the manager as his remuneration for three nights, threw himself into the chaise, and at twelve o'clock, within a few minutes after he had quitted the stage, was on his road to London. The weather was tempestuous, the roads in a most desperate condition, and, to make matters worse, he treated the postboys so liberally in the hope of accelerating their speed that they became so drunk as to be scarcely able to sit at their horses. After various escapes and perils, they discovered at the end of an unusually long stage that they had come fourteen miles out of the road, "all in consequence," as one of the boys said, with many hiccups, and much drunken gravity, "all in consequence of only taking one wrong turn."

The result of this combination of mischances was that Grimaldi did not reach Salt Hill until seven o'clock on the following evening; having been nineteen hours on the road. Here he jumped into another chaise which fortunately stood ready at the door, and hurried up to London, without venturing to stay for any refreshment whatever. He drove straight to the theatre, where he found his friend waiting his arrival with great trepidation. Hearing that the overture to the piece in which he was to perform was then playing, he gave his friend the two hundred and ninety-four pounds to take care of, ran to his dressing-room, dressed for his part, which Farley had already made preparations for performing himself, and went on the stage the moment he got his cue, much to the astonishment of his friends and greatly to the surprise of some individuals connected with the management of the theatre, who had anticipated a very different result from his visit to Birmingham.

Of course some unforeseen circumstance was to happen, and some unexpected demand to be made on the money so easily earned. A short time before Grimaldi went to Birmingham, being short of cash, he had commissioned a friend on whom he placed great reliance to get his bill at one month for one hundred and fifty pounds discounted. The friend put the bill into his pocket-book, and promised to bring the money at night. Night came, but the money did not: it had not arrived when he returned from Birmingham: the friend was nowhere to be found, and Grimaldi had soon afterwards the satisfaction of paying the whole sum, without having received a sixpence of the money.

The Covent Garden season recommenced on the twelfth of September. Seven days afterwards the theatre was burned to the ground, after the performance of *Pizarro* and the *Portrait of Cervantes*. The company removed to the Italian Opera House, and subsequently to the Haymarket; but as Grimaldi was not wanted, he availed himself of an offer to visit the Manchester theatre, then managed by Messrs Ward, Lewis and Knight, and left town for that purpose. There was a strong rivalry between the coach proprietors on the road at that time, but for the safety of the passengers, it was expressly understood between them that the coaches should never be allowed to pass each other but that the coach which took the lead at starting should retain it all the way through, unless any temporary stoppage of the first vehicle enabled the second to assume the post of honour. Grimaldi's coach was the last, and just as they were going into Macclesfield, the 'Defiance' (which was the name of the other coach) stopping to change horses and to allow the passengers to take tea, became entangled with the wheels of the second vehicle in the darkness of the evening; and when the second coach overset, which it did immediately, the empty 'Defiance' fell upon the top of it so neatly and dexterously that the passengers had to be dragged through the two coaches before they could be extricated. Fortunately nobody was much hurt, although Grimaldi was the worst off, for he was the undermost, and five stout men (they carried six inside at that time) fell on top of him. The only disagreeable part of the matter was that they were delayed upwards of four hours, and that the unfortunate 'Defiance' was left both literally and figuratively *on* the road for a much longer time.

During this provincial trip Grimaldi played six nights at Manchester and one at Liverpool, for which he received in all two hundred and fifty-one pounds. The only drawback upon the expedition was that he sustained two accidents, the effects of which were quite bad enough but might have been much more serious. He arranged and got up a very pretty little pantomime called *Castles in the Air*, in which he of course played Clown.

His first appearance was to be from a large bowl, placed in the centre of the stage and labelled Gooseberry Fool; and to pass through this, it was necessary for him to ascend from beneath the stage, through a trap-door which the bowl concealed. On the first night he ascended from below at the proper time; but when he gained the level of the stage, the ropes which were attached to the trap broke, and he fell back into the cellar. He was terribly shaken and stunned by the fall, but quickly recovering himself, he ascended the stairs, went on the stage, and played as though nothing had happened to discompose him. In spite of his assumed calm, however, Grimaldi was in agony during the whole of the first scene; but the pain wholly left him as he went on, in the excitement of the part; and by the time he had finished the pantomime he was as well as he had been before its commencement.

This was at Manchester. The Liverpool theatre belonging to the same managers, and being resorted to by the same company, they all travelled thither for one night for the purpose of playing *Castles in the Air* as the afterpiece, having the same Master-Carpenter with them as they had at Manchester. Grimaldi sought the man out, and explaining to him the nature of the accident which had happened through his negligence on the previous night, entreated him to render all secure for that evening and to prevent a repetition of the occurrence. This the carpenter promised, but failed to do notwithstanding, for a precisely similar accident took place at Liverpool. Grimaldi had ascended to the stage and got his head through the bowl, when, as a shout of laughter and welcome broke from the audience, the ropes gave way and he was left struggling in the trap. For a second or two he did not fall; for, having passed through the trap nearly to his waist, he strove to support himself by his arms. All his endeavours, however, were vain; the weight of his body pulled him downwards, and the trap being small his elbows were caught by the edges and forced together above his head, thereby straining his shoulders to such an extent that he thought his arms were wrested from their sockets. Joe fell a considerable distance, and when he rose from the ground he was in excessive pain. He managed with great difficulty to crawl through his first scene, and then warming with his exertions and kindling with the great applause he received, he rallied successfully and got through the part with flying colours. When he reached his inn, which, now that the excitement of acting was over, was a task of considerable difficulty, he was well rubbed with the infallible embrocation and put to bed in a very helpless state. On the following morning, scarcely able to crawl, he was assisted into the coach, and returned home.

Grimaldi acted very little at the Haymarket with the Covent Garden company till after Christmas, when *Mother Goose* was re-revived with a new last scene, representing the ruins of Covent Garden Theatre transformed by a touch of Harlequin's wand into a new and splendid building. In March he sustained for the first time the character of Kanko in *La Perouse*. He took his benefit on the twenty-third of May. The season terminated a few nights afterwards; and with it, it may be incidentally observed, terminated the theatrical career of the celebrated Lewis, who retired from the stage at this period.

CHAPTER ELEVEN

THE PANTOMIME WAS USUALLY PLAYED first at Sadler's Wells. When this was the case Grimaldi was at liberty by about half-past eight: he would sometimes call at the Sir Hugh Myddleton, take a glass of wine and water with some friends who frequented the house, and then start off in his gig to Finchley. He had several times met at this tavern a young man of the name of George Hamilton, a working jeweller, residing somewhere in Clerkenwell, a sociable, good-tempered merry fellow enough, but rather too much addicted to drinking and squandering his money. This man was very sensitive about the subject of trade, being, as the phrase goes, above his business, having an ambition to be a gentleman, and resenting any allusion to his occupation as a personal affront. Hamilton was a very ingenious and skilful man at his business, and could earn a great deal of money; but his companions suspected that these absurdities led him into spending more than he could well afford. Grimaldi was so strongly impressed with this opinion that, with a good-hearted impulse, he frequently felt tempted to remonstrate with him upon his folly. Their slight intimacy, however, restrained him, and the man continued to take his own course.

These were Hamilton's mental peculiarities: he had a remarkable physical peculiarity besides, wanting, either from an accident or a natural defect, the third finger of his left hand. Whether he wished to conceal this imperfection, or had some other defect in the same hand, is uncertain; but he invariably kept his little finger in a bent position beneath the palm of it; so that when he sat or walked, as he usually did, with his left hand half-hidden in his pocket, the defect was not observable; but when he suddenly changed his position, or drew forth his hand in discourse, it had always the appearance of having only two fingers upon it.

Grimaldi's first acquaintance with this person was in 1808, when he was very frequently at Sadler's Wells and the Sir Hugh Myddleton. At the termination of the summer season he lost sight of Hamilton in consequence of his engagements taking him elsewhere; but in Easter, 1809, when Sadler's Wells reopened, and Grimaldi resumed his habit of calling at the tavern for half-an-hour or so before driving out to Finchley, he again encountered Hamilton. He had been married in the interval, and frequently took his wife, a pretty young creature, to the tavern with him, as at that time many tradesmen in the neighbourhood were accustomed to do.

Grimaldi paid little attention to these circumstances at first; but a change had come over the man which irresistibly attracted Joe's attention. Hamilton had become very violent and irritable, had acquired a nervous restlessness of manner, an occasional incoherence of speech, a wildness of look, and betrayed many other indications of a mind somewhat disordered. He dressed differently, too: formerly he had been neatly attired, and looked like a respectable, well-doing man; but now he was showy and gaudy, wore a number of large rings and other articles of cheap jewellery, and his desire to be thought a great man had increased greatly, so much so, indeed, that his declamations against trade and all concerned in it deeply affronted the worthies who were wont to assemble at the Sir Hugh, and occasioned many disputes and altercations. All these things evidently made the wife very unhappy. Although he usually abstained from drinking to his customary excess in her presence, he said and did enough to make her wretched, and frequently, when she thought she was unobserved, she would sit in a remote corner and weep bitterly.

One night Hamilton brought with him a new friend, a man of very sinister appearance and marvellously ill-favoured countenance. They were, or affected to be, both greatly intoxicated. The strange man was introduced by his friend to Grimaldi, and began entering into conversation with him; but as there was something remarkably repulsive in his appearance, Joe rose and left the room. The two men came together very often. Nobody knew who or what the stranger was; nobody liked or even spoke to him; and it was constantly observed that whenever Hamilton was in a state of gross intoxication he was in this person's company. The old visitors of the Sir Hugh shook their heads mysteriously, and hoped he had not fallen into bad company; although, truth to tell, they could not help thinking that appearances were greatly against him.

One night Grimaldi was sitting alone in the room reading the newspaper, when Hamilton, the stranger, and the poor wife came in together. The former was in a state of intoxication, so much so that he could scarcely stand. The wife had evidently been crying and seemed truly wretched; but the strange man wore an air of dogged triumph that made him look perfectly hideous. Curious to see what passed, Grimaldi held the paper before his face and watched them closely. They did not recognise him, but walked to the other end of the room. Hamilton hiccoughed forth an order for something to drink, stammering in reply to the earnest entreaties of his wife that he would go home directly he had taken "this one glass more". It was brought but not tasted, for his head had fallen upon the table and he was fast asleep before the liquor came.

The man whom Hamilton had a minute before named for the first time—Archer, he called him—regarded his sleeping companion in silence for some minutes, and then leaning behind him to reach the wife, who was on the other side, touched her lightly on the shoulder. She looked up, and he, pointing with a contemptuous air to the sleeping drunkard, took her hand and pressed it in a manner which it was impossible to misunderstand. She started indignantly from her seat, and darted at the man a look which completely quelled him. He sat with his arms folded and his eyes fixed on the ground for above a quarter-of-an-hour, and then, suddenly rousing himself, tendered his assistance in attempting to awaken the husband. His harsh voice and rough gestures accomplished what the whispered persuasion of the wife had been unable to effect: Hamilton awoke, emptied his glass, and they all left the apartment together; she studiously avoiding any contact with the man called Archer.

This little scene interested Grimaldi much. He sat thinking upon what had passed so long that he was upwards of an hour later than usual in reaching home. He felt a strong inclination to speak to Hamilton, and kindly but firmly to tell him what he had seen and what he thought. On consideration, however, he determined not to interfere, deeming it more prudent to leave the issue to the good sense and proper feeling of his wife, who evidently knew what danger threatened her and how to avert it. The situation of these persons occupied so much of Grimaldi's thoughts, that when he called as usual at the tavern next night he felt a strong anxiety to meet them there again. He was disappointed, for Hamilton was seated in the room alone. He nodded as Grimaldi entered, and said, "Are you going to Finchley, tonight?"

"No," was the reply, "I wish I was: I have an engagement at my house here in town which will prevent my doing so."

"I thought you always went there on summer evenings," said Hamilton, glancing over the paper as he spoke, and speaking in an uninterested and careless style.

"No, not always," said Grimaldi. "Pretty nearly though—five nights out of six."

"Then you'll go tomorrow?" asked Hamilton.

"Oh, certainly! tomorrow, and every night this week except tonight."

They exchanged a "Good evening!" and parted.

It so happened that Grimaldi was reluctantly obliged to remain in town not only the next night but the night after also, in consequence of the arrival in town of some country friends. On the third night, the ninth of July, he called at the tavern to take his usual glass before mounting his gig, and, his mind being still occupied with the thoughts of the poor young woman and her dissipated husband, he inquired whether Hamilton had been there that night. The reply was, he had not: he had not been there for three evenings, or, in other words, since Grimaldi had seen and spoken to him. When Grimaldi produced his purse to pay for the wine and water he had drunk, he found he had nothing but two five-pound notes. He gave the waiter one, requesting change, and put the other in his waistcoat pocket. He usually carried notes in a pocket-book, but upon this evening he did not happen to have it about him; in fact, he had received the notes very unexpectedly while he was in the theatre, from a person who owed him money. He put the change in his purse, got into the gig, and drove homeward.

On that particular evening Grimaldi had a call to make in Tottenham Court Road, which delayed him for some little time. As he was passing through Kentish Town, a friend, who was standing at his door, the weather being sultry, insisted upon his coming in and taking a glass of wine: this detained Joe again, as they stood chatting for half-an-hour or so; and by the time he had resumed his journey homewards it was near the middle of the night.

It was a fine, clear night; there was no moon, but the stars were shining brightly; the air was soft and fresh, and very pleasant after the heat of the day. Grimaldi drove on at a quicker pace than usual, fearing that they might be alarmed at home by his being so late, and having just heard some distant clock strike the three-quarters after eleven. Suddenly the horse stopped. Near the spot was a ridge across the road for the purpose of draining the fields on the higher side, forming a little hollow, which in the summer was dry and in the winter generally full of mud. The horse knew it well, being accustomed to pause there for a minute, to cross the ditch slowly, and then to resume his usual trot. Bending forward to assure himself that he had arrived at this part of the road, Grimaldi heard a low whistle and immediately afterwards three men darted out of a hedge. One seized the horse's bridle, and the two others rushed up, one to each side of the gig, then, presenting pistols, they demanded his money.

Grimaldi sat for a moment quite incapable of speaking, the surprise had come so suddenly upon him; but hearing the cocking of a pistol close beside him, he roused himself, and seeing that he had no chance against three armed men, cried, "Mercy, gentlemen, mercy!"

"You won't be hurt," said the man on his left, "so long as you give your money directly."

"No, no," said the man at the horse's head, "you won't be hurt, Your money is what we want."

"You shall have it," Grimaldi answered, "but I expect you not to injure me." He fumbled at his pocket for his purse, and while doing so looked narrowly at the persons by whom he was attacked. They all wore black crêpe over their faces, so that not a feature was discernible, and were clad in very large black frocks. The disguises were complete: it was impossible to make out anything of their appearance.

"Look sharp!" said the left-hand man. "The money!—come, we can't stay here."

Grimaldi extricated the purse, and handed it to the speaker. The man at the horse's head looked sharply on, and cried:

"Tom, what has he given you?"

"His purse," was the reply.

"That won't do," said the man. "You have more money about you; I know you have: come, hand over, will ye?"

"I have not indeed," replied Grimaldi. "Sometimes I carry a little in my pocket-book; but tonight I forgot to bring it with me."

"You have more money with you, and you know it," said the man who held the bridle. "You have got a bank-note in your lefthand waistcoat pocket."

The circumstance had really escaped Grimaldi's memory; but, being reminded of it, he drew forth the note, and delivered it to the man to whom he had resigned his purse.

"It's all right, Tom," said the man on his right. "We had better be off now."

As he spoke, he moved round the back of the gig, as if with the intention of going away. It was the first time he had uttered a note, and his voice struck Grimaldi as being a familiar one, though he could not, in his confusion, recollect where or when he had heard it. He had no time to reflect on the matter, for the man at the horse's head demanded of the man on his left whether he had got his watch.

"No," said the fellow, "I forgot his watch. Give it here!" With these words he again raised his pistol, which was all this time on full cock.

Grimaldi gave it up, but not without a sigh, for it was the very watch which had been presented to him with his own portrait on the dial-plate. As he put it into the man's hand, he said:

"If you knew who I am, you would not treat me in this manner."

"Oh, we know you well enough, Mr Grimaldi," said the man at the reins. "We have been waiting for you these three nights, and began to think you would not come tonight."

The other men laughed, and the man whose voice had struck him recommended his companion to give the watch back again.

"Oh, yes, I dare say!" said with a sneer the man who held the horse.

"Well, I don't know," said the fellow who had been addressed as Tom. "I don't think it's worth a couple of pounds."

"No, no, it is not; and besides, I say he shall have it again," cried the man, whose voice, familiar at first, now seemed perfectly well known to Grimaldi. "Here!" He snatched the watch from his comrade's hand, who made no effort to retain it, and handed it into the gig. Grimaldi gladly received it back; but in the act of doing so he saw that the hand from which he took it had, or appeared to have, *but two fingers upon it.*

The watch was no sooner returned than the robbers made off with great rapidity, and Grimaldi was once again alone, in a far greater state of alarm and trepidation than when the robbers surrounded him. The revulsion of feeling was so great that he felt as if his existence depended upon instant flight, and that his flight would be far more speedy if he ran than if he rode. Acting upon the impulse of his disordered nerves, he sprang at once out of the gig, but, not jumping sufficiently high to clear it, was thrown into the road head foremost with great force, and struck his temple heavily against a flint. The blow and the previous fright quite bewildered him, but did not render him insensible; he was up again directly and found himself, at the expiration of some ten minutes, stopped by the patrol, to whom he was well known. He had no recollection of running, but he had run for a long distance, and the first thing he was conscious of was being half-supported by this man, and receiving many eager inquiries what had befallen him.

Grimaldi spoke as plainly as his agitation would permit, and related what had passed.

"Just what I have expected to happen to somebody for these many nights past," said the patrol. "Sir, I have watched those three men repeatedly; it was only last night I warned 'em that I did not like to see them loitering about my beat, and that if anything wrong happened I should suspect them. Make your mind easy, sir; I know where they are to be found, and I'll lay my life that in less than two hours I have them safe."

"And what am I to do?" Grimaldi inquired.

"Nothing tonight, sir," was the patrol's reply. "I would only recommend you to get home as fast as you can. At twelve o'clock tomorrow, you attend at Bow Street; and if I don't show you the men, I shall be as much surprised as you have been tonight."

The horse came up just then, having trotted on very composedly, with the gig at his heels: taking the patrol's advice, Grimaldi got in, and having promised to meet him next morning, made the best of his way home, which he reached without further hindrance or interruption.

Grimaldi found his wife, as he had expected, very much terrified at his being so late; nor were her fears allayed by his wild demeanour and the appearance of the blow on his temple. To her hurried inquiries he gave the best answers that occurred to him, and being unwilling to give her any unnecessary alarm, merely remarked that he had a fall from his gig, which had made him giddy and uncomfortable. The pains he afterwards took to keep the real truth from coming to her knowledge were infinite. Every newspaper that came into the house he carefully searched to ascertain that it contained no paragraph relative to the robbery; and so successful were his precautions that she had not the least inkling of the circumstance until more than two years afterwards, upon their giving up the cottage at Finchley and returning to town; when her first exclamation was, "Oh, Joe, if I had only known this at the time, I never could have slept another night in Finchley!" This was exactly what Grimaldi had supposed, and he was not a little delighted to find that he had been enabled to remain during the whole of that time in a place to which he was very much attached, and where, in the society of his wife and child, he had spent some of the happiest hours of his existence.

Grimaldi got very little sleep after the robbery, his thoughts turning all night upon the distressing consequence it seemed likely to involve. That Hamilton was one of the men, he felt pretty well sure: the voice and defect in the left hand were strong proofs against him. Added to this there was other evidence, circumstantial, it is true, but still very weighty. It was plain, from the knowledge which one of the thieves possessed relative to the note, that he or someone connected with him had been in the tavern in the earlier part of the night, and had there closely watched Grimaldi's actions. The doubtful character of Archer and his suspicious looks and manner had struck Joe often; the thieves had been waiting three nights, and for three nights Hamilton had been absent from his usual place of resort. The more Grimaldi thought of these things, the more sure he felt that Hamilton was a highwayman: then came the reflection, that if, upon Joe's evidence, Hamilton was sentenced to death, it would most probably involve the fate of his young wife, of whose meekness and gentleness Joe had seen so many tokens. He tossed and tumbled through the night, meditating upon these things over and over again; he rose the following morning feverish and dejected, trusting the thieves might escape rather than that he should be the means of bringing any of his fellow-creatures to a violent death, or dooming others to living and hopeless wretchedness.

Pleading an early call to rehearsal as the reason for his going so early to town, Grimaldi left Finchley immediately after breakfast and drove to Bow Street, where he found the patrol already waiting. The moment he caught sight of the man and observed the air with which he approached to receive him, all the hopes which he had involuntarily nourished evaporated,

235

and he felt terrified at the thought that a capital prosecution at the Old Bailey was certainly reserved for him.

"Well, sir," said the man, as he helped him out of the gig, "it's all right. I have got three men, and I have no doubt they are the fellows."

Grimaldi's distress was redoubled, and he inquired, trembling, whether any of the stolen property had been found upon them. The man replied with evident chagrin that he had not succeeded so far, and therefore supposed they had got rid of the booty before he found them; but if they were sworn to, they would be committed at once; and that when it was known among their companions, he had little doubt but that he should be able to trace out some evidence relative to the note. With this brief preparation he led Grimaldi at once into the presence of the magistrate, to whom Joe recounted the particulars of the robbery, hinting that as he had not been personally injured by the thieves, he had no wish to prosecute if it could be avoided; an intimation to which the patrol listened in high dudgeon, and which the magistrate appeared to regard with some doubt, merely observing that the circumstances might possibly be taken into consideration with a view to the mitigation of punishment, but could not be urged or recognised at all in that stage of the proceedings.

The patrol was then examined, and, after stating in effect what he had stated to Grimaldi on the previous night, deposed that he had taken the prisoners into custody at a place which he named. The magistrate inquired whether any of the stolen property had been found upon them or traced, whether any such disguises as Mr Grimaldi had described were discovered in their possession, and whether any suspicious implements, offensive or defensive, had been found upon them. To all these questions, the patrol answered in the negative, and the magistrate then ordered that Grimaldi should be taken to view the prisoners. He also inquired if Grimaldi thought he should recognise them; who replied that he had no doubt that he should know one of the men.

Grimaldi was taken into another room, and the first person he saw was, as he expected, George Hamilton himself; the other two prisoners were perfect strangers to him. They had described themselves to the magistrate as gentlemen; but he might have exclaimed, with young Mirabell, "For gentlemen they have the most cut-throat appearance I ever saw."

Hamilton behaved himself with great coolness and self-possession. He advanced without the least appearance of agitation, and said:

"How do you do, Mr Grimaldi? It is an odd circumstance, is it not, that I should be charged with robbing an old friend like you? But strange coincidences happen to all of us."

Composed as the man's manner was, if Grimaldi had entered the room with any doubt of his guilt, it was at once and entirely dispelled. The practised eye of an actor was not so easily deceived. Hamilton had evidently made a desperate effort to assume an easy confidence of manner, knowing that upon the success with which he did so depended his only chance of escaping from the gallows.

"Why, what's this!" said the jailer, or turnkey, or whoever had accompanied them, to the room. "Do you know him, sir?"

"Yes," said Grimaldi, looking hard at Hamilton, "I know him very well."

"Well, then, sir, of course you can tell whether he is one of the men who robbed you?"

The pause which ensued was of not more than two or three seconds duration, but it was a trying one to two of the parties present. Hamilton looked as if he awaited the reply without fear, and acted the innocent man boldly. The turnkey and constable turned away for an instant to speak to each other; and as they did so Grimaldi held up his left hand, turning down two of the fingers in imitation of Hamilton's, and shook his head gravely. The man instantly understood his meaning, and saw that he was known. All his assumed fortitude forsook him; his face became ashy pale, and his whole frame trembled with inward agitation. It appeared as if he would have fallen on the floor, but he rallied a little; and after bestowing a look of intense supplication upon Grimaldi, laid his finger on his lip and fixed his eyes on the ground.

"Well, sir," said the patrol, "there they are; can you swear to them all, or to any of them?"

A thousand thoughts crowded through Grimaldi's brain, but one was uppermost—the desire to save this young man, whom he strongly suspected to be but a beginner in crime. After a moment's pause, he replied that he could not swear to any one of them.

"Then," said the turnkey to the patrol, with a meaning look, "either you have gone upon a wrong scent altogether, or these chaps have had a very narrow escape."

After informing the magistrate that it was not in his power to identify the prisoners, Grimaldi hurried away. The men were discharged in the course of the afternoon, and thus terminated the interview at the police-office. A day or two afterwards Hamilton called at Grimaldi's house, and humbly acknowledged that he was one of the men who had robbed him; that he had been incited to the act, partly by an anxiety to acquire money faster than he could make it in trade, and partly by the persuasions of his friend Archer; but that it was his first attempt at crime, and should be his last. He thanked his benefactor in the warmest and most grateful manner for his clemency; and Grimaldi then acquainted him with the designs of Archer upon his wife, severely reprobating the vicious habits which had led him to abandon one by whose means he might have been rendered happy and respectable, and saved from his guilty career, and leaving her exposed to the insults of men inured to every species of villainy and crime. Hamilton assured him that neither his information nor his advice was ill-bestowed, and after a long interview they parted, he pouring forth his thanks and promises of reformation and Grimaldi repeating his forgiveness and his admonitions.

Grimaldi had reason to hope that Hamilton kept his promise and shrunk from his old associates, for he resided nearly twenty years after that period in Clerkenwell, carrying on a good business and bearing the reputation of an honest man.

At this time Grimaldi was in the habit of taking three benefits every year: that is to say, two at Sadler's Wells, and one at Covent Garden. Regularly on the morning of each of these occasions, for very many years, some person called at his house for ten box-tickets always paying for them at the time in exactly the amount required, and leaving the house immediately as if anxious to avoid notice. Grimaldi was in the constant habit of receiving anonymous remittances for tickets and therefore did not attach much importance to this circumstance, although it struck him as being singular in one respect, in as much as the greater part of his friends who took tickets for his Sadler's Wells benefits did not take them on his Covent Garden nights, and vice versa. The family became at last so used to it that when they were sorting tickets on the night before one of his benefits, his wife would say, "Don't forget to put ten on the mantelpiece for the gentleman who calls early in the morning." This continued for perhaps twelve years or more, when one day, as Grimaldi's servant was giving him the money paid as usual by the unknown person for his admissions, he casually inquired of the girl what kind of person in appearance this gentleman was.

"Oh, I really don't know, sir", she replied. "There is nothing particular about him, except … "

"Well, except what?"

"Except, sir, that he has only got two fingers on his left hand."

The mystery was explained.

The fate of this man was truly pitiable. A neighbour's house having taken fire, and being in imminent hazard of destruction, Hamilton rushed in with several others to save some children who were in danger of perishing in the flames. He darted upstairs through the smoke and reached the second storey. The instant he set his feet upon it, the whole flooring gave way, and sank with him into the mass of glowing fire below, from which his body, burnt to a cinder, was dug out some days afterwards.

CHAPTER TWELVE

O N THE EIGHTEENTH OF SEPTEMBER 1809 the new theatre in Covent Garden opened with *Macbeth* and the musical afterpiece of *The Quaker*. It was at this period that the great O P (Old Price) Row began, of which so much has been said, and sung, and written, that little of novelty or interest could accompany the description of it here. Everybody knows that the O P Row originated in the indignation with which the play-going public regarded an increase in the prices of admission of one shilling each person to the boxes, and sixpence to the pit, with which was coupled a considerable increase in the number of private boxes; and everybody knows, moreover, that the public expressed their dissatisfaction night after night in scenes of the most extraordinary and unparalleled nature. The noises made by the audience utterly overwhelmed every attempt that the actors could make to render themselves audible. Not a word that was said on the stage could be distinguished even in the front row of the pit, and the O P rioters, fearful that the exercise of their voices would not create sufficient uproar, were in the habit of bringing the most extraordinary variety of curious and ill-toned instruments with them to add to the noise and discordance of the scene. One gentleman who constantly seated himself in the boxes regaled himself and the company with a watchman's rattle, which he sprang vigorously at short intervals through the performances; another took his seat regularly every night in the centre of the pit armed with a large dustman's bell, which he rang with a perseverance and strength of arm quite astounding to all beholders; and a party of three or four pleasant fellows brought live pigs, which were pinched at the proper times and added considerably to the effect of the performances.

But rattles, bells, pigs, trumpets, French horns, sticks, umbrellas, catcalls, and bugles, were not the only vocal weapons used upon these occasions: Kemble was constantly called for, constantly came on, and constantly went off again without being able to obtain a hearing. Numbers of Bow Street officers were in regular attendance: whenever they endeavoured to seize the ringleaders these were defended by their partisans, and numerous fights (in one of which a man was nearly killed) resulted. Scarce an evening passed without flaming speeches being made from the pit, boxes, and gallery; and sometimes half-a-dozen speeches would be in course of delivery at the same time. The greater portion of the time the magistrates were occupied in investigations connected with the disturbances, and this state of things continued for nearly seventy nights. Placards were exhibited in every part of the house, principally from the pit; of the quality of which effusions the following may be taken as specimens:

Notice to the Public—This house and furniture to be sold, Messrs John Kemble & Co declining business.

Notice to the Public—The workhouse in Covent Garden has been repaired, and greatly enlarged for the use of the Public.

Cause of Justice—John Bull versus John Kemble—verdict for the plaintiff.

A large coffin with the inscription:

Here lies the body of New Prices, who died of the whooping-cough, Sept twenty-third, 1809, aged six days.

The instant the performances began the audience, who had been previously sitting with their faces to the stage, as audiences generally do, wheeled round to a man and turned their backs upon it. When they concluded, which, in consequence of the fearful uproar, was frequently as early as half-past nine, they united in singing a parody on *God Save the King*, of which the first verse ran thus:

God save great Johnny Bull,
Long live our noble Bull,
God save John Bull.
Send him victorious,
Loud and Uproarious
With lungs like Boreas;
God save John Bull!

Then followed the O P dance and a variety of speeches, and then the rioters would quietly disperse.

The opinions of the Press being, as a matter of course, divided on every question, were necessarily divided upon this. The *Times* and *Post* supported the new system; in consequence of which a placard was exhibited from the pit every evening for at least a week with the inscription:

The Times *and* Post *are bought and sold,*
By Kemble's pride and Kemble's gold.

The *Chronicle*, on the other hand, took up the opposite side of the question, and supported the O P rioters with great fervour and constancy. In its columns one of the most popular of the numerous squibs on the subject appeared, which is here inserted. It may be necessary to premise that 'Jack' was John Kemble; that the 'Cat' was Madame Catalani, then engaged at Covent Garden and much opposed at that time, in consequence of her being a foreigner; and that the 'boxes' were the new private boxes, among the great objects of popular execration.

THE HOUSE THAT JACK BUILT

This is the House that Jack built.

These are the boxes, let to the great, that visit the house that Jack built.

These are the pigeon-holes, over the boxes, let to the great, that visit the house that Jack built.

This is the Cat, engaged to squall, to the poor in the pigeonholes, over the boxes, let to the great, that visit the house that Jack built.

This is John Bull, with a bugle-horn, that hissed the Cat, engaged to squall, to the poor in the pigeon-holes, over the boxes, let to the great, that visit the house that Jack built.

This is the thief-taker, shaven and shorn,

That took up John Bull, with his bugle-horn, who hissed the Cat, engaged to squall, to the poor in the pigeon-holes, over the boxes, let to the great, that visit the house that Jack built.

That is the manager, full of scorn,

WHO RAISED THE PRICES to the people forlorn.

And directed the thief-taker, shaven and shorn,

244

To take up John Bull, with his bugle-horn, who hissed the Cat, engaged to squall, to the poor in the pigeon-holes, over the boxes, let to the great, that visit the house that Jack built.

When this had gone on for several nights Kemble sent for Grimaldi, and said that as the people would not hear dialogue they would try pantomime, which might perhaps suit their tastes better. Accordingly *Don Juan* was put up for the next night, Grimaldi sustaining his old part of Scaramouch. He was received on his entrance with great applause, and it happened oddly enough that on that night there was little or no disturbance. This circumstance which he naturally attributed in some degree to himself, pleased him amazingly, as indeed it did Kemble also, who, shaking him cordially by the hand when he came off, said, "Bravo, Joe! we have got them now: we'll act this again tomorrow night." And so they did; but it appeared that they had not "got them" either, for the uproar recommenced with, if possible, greater fury than before, all the performers agreeing that until that moment they had never heard such a mighty and indescribable din.

Eventually, on December the fifteenth, the row terminated, on the proprietors of the theatre lowering the charge of admission to the pit, removing the obnoxious private boxes, rescinding Madame Catalani's engagement, discharging Mr James Brandon, house and box book-keeper, who had rendered himself greatly offensive to the O P people, abandoning all prosecutions against those who had been required to answer for their misconduct at the sessions, and offering a public apology.

The ungracious task of making it fell upon Mr Kemble, who delivered what it was deemed necessary to say with remarkable self-possession and dignity. It was received by the audience with great applause, and a placard was immediately hoisted in the pit, bearing the words, '*We are satisfied*'; it was speedily followed by a similar announcement in the boxes; and thus terminated the famous O P war.

At Christmas, 1810, Grimaldi appeared, as usual, in the Covent Garden pantomime, which was called *Harlequin Asmodeus* or *Cupid on Crutches*. It was acted for forty-six nights, and was played occasionally until May 1811. During this month he had to play Clown at both theatres, the pantomime being acted as the first piece at Sadler's Wells and as the last piece at Covent Garden. Not having time to change his dress, and indeed having no reason for doing so, in consequence of his playing the same character at both houses, he was accustomed to have a coach in waiting, into which he threw himself the moment he had finished at Sadler's Wells, and was straightway carried to Covent Garden to begin again.

One night it so happened that by some forgetfulness or mistake on the part of the driver, the coach which usually came for Grimaldi failed to make its appearance. It was a very wet night, and not having a moment to lose, he sent for another. After a considerable interval, during which Grimaldi was in an agony of fear lest the Covent Garden stage should be kept waiting, the messenger returned in a breathless state with the information that there was not a coach to be got. There was only one desperate alternative, and that was to run through the streets. Knowing that his appearance at Covent Garden must by this time be necessary, he made up his mind to do

246

it, and started off at once. The night being very dark, he got on pretty well at first; but when he came into the streets of Clerkenwell, where the lights of the shops showed him in his Clown's dress running along at full speed, people began to grow rather astonished. First, a few people turned round to look after him, and then a few more, and so on until there were a great many, and at last one man who met him at a street corner, recognising the favourite, gave a loud shout of, "Here's Joe Grimaldi!"

This was enough. Off set Grimaldi faster than ever, and on came the mob, shouting, huzzaing, screaming out his name, throwing up their caps and hats, and exhibiting every manifestation of delight. He ran into Holborn with several hundred people at his heels, and being lucky enough to find a coach there, jumped in. But this only increased the pressure of the crowd, who followed the vehicle with great speed and perseverance; when, suddenly poking his head out of the window, he gave one of his famous and well-known laughs. Upon this the crowd raised many roars of laughter and applause, and hastily agreed, as with one accord, that they would see him safe and sound to Covent Garden. So, the coach went on surrounded by the dirtiest bodyguard that was ever beheld, not one of whom deserted his post until Grimaldi had been safely deposited at the stage door; when, after raising a vociferous cheer, such of them as had money rushed round to the gallery doors, and, making their appearance in the front just as he came on the stage, set up a boisterous shout of, "Here he is again!" and cheered him enthusiastically, to the infinite amusement of every person in the theatre who had got wind of the story.

One of Grimaldi's earlier appearances in the regular drama occurred in the following June (1812) when, for his own benefit, he played Acres in *The Rivals*. The house was a very good one, and he cleared upwards of two hundred pounds by it.

This year was rendered remarkable to Grimaldi by some temporary embarrassment into which he was plunged, partly, he says, by the great expense consequent upon keeping a country as well as a town house, and partly by the great extravagance of his wife, who, although an excellent woman, had like everybody else some fault; hers was a love of dress which almost amounted to a mania. Finding that retrenchment must be the order of the day, he gave up his house at Finchley, discharged his groom, sold his horse and gig, and placed his affairs in the hands of Mr Harmer, the solicitor, to whom circumstances had so oddly introduced him a few years before. Seven or eight months served to bring affairs into the right train again; by the end of that time every one of his creditors had been paid to the last penny of their demands.

In 1812, there was nothing particularly worthy of notice at Sadler's Wells. Grimaldi's second benefit, which took place in October, was a great one, the receipts being two hundred and twenty-five pounds. It was supposed the theatre would not hold more than two hundred pounds; but no benefit of his ever brought him less than two hundred and ten pounds; and indeed one, which we shall presently have occasion to mention, produced nearly two hundred and seventy pounds.

In the latter end of this month, Grimaldi entered into an engagement to perform for two nights with Mr Watson of the Cheltenham Theatre, who arranged to give him a clear half of whatever the receipts might be. Previously to leaving town, Joe consulted with Mr Hughes about this speculation, who told him

248

that Cheltenham was a bad theatrical town, on account of its having many other amusements; but still he fancied he might clear his expenses, and perhaps forty or fifty pounds besides. At the appointed time he left London, having received a species of half-notice from Mr Harris that he would not be wanted at Covent Garden; and on the next night he played Scaramouch and sang *Tippitywitchit* with great éclat at Cheltenham. The following evening he played Clown in a little pantomime of his own concoction. The house was full on each occasion, the performances gave perfect satisfaction, and Grimaldi was induced by the manager to stay in that part of the country two days longer, and to go to Gloucester, nine miles off, at which place Mr Watson likewise had a theatre. Thither they started early on the following morning, played the same pieces as at Cheltenham, and met with an equal degree of success.

After the performances were over, Mr Watson and Grimaldi supped together; and when the cloth was removed, the former said:

"Now, Joe, I can only allow you to take one glass of punch, time is so very precious."

"I do not understand you," replied Grimaldi.

"Why, what I mean is, that it is now twelve o'clock, and time to go to bed," he answered.

"Oh! with all my heart," said Grimaldi. "But this is something new, I suspect, with you. Last night, I remember it was three hours later than this, before you suffered me to retire; and the night previous it was even later than that."

"Ay, ay," replied Watson, "but tonight we had perhaps better get to bed soon, as tomorrow I want you to go out rather early with me."

"What do you call rather early?" inquired Grimaldi.

"Why, let me see, we must start before three," answered the manager.

"Indeed!" said Grimaldi, "then I shall wish you good night at once"—and so saying, without any loss of time, he went to his chamber. After they had stepped into a chaise next day, he found that their destination was Berkeley Castle, to which its host had sent them a special invitation, and that their morning's amusement was to consist of coursing.

He had the honour of an acquaintance with Colonel Berkeley (now Lord Segrave), at whose table he was occasionally in the habit of dining, and upon their arrival at the castle was most hospitably received. The castle was full of company. Several noblemen were there, as well as distinguished commoners: among the former was Lord Byron, whom Grimaldi had frequently seen and who always patronised his benefits at Covent Garden, but with whom he had never conversed. Colonel Berkeley introduced Joe to such of the company as he was unacquainted with, and, in common with the rest, to Lord Byron, who instantly advanced towards Grimaldi, and, making several low bows, expressed in very hyperbolical terms his "great and unbounded satisfaction in becoming acquainted with a man of such rare and profound talents", etc.

Perceiving that his lordship was disposed to be facetious at his expense, Grimaldi felt half inclined to reply in a similar strain; but, reflecting that he might give offence by doing so, abstained—resolving, however, not to go entirely unrevenged for the joke which he was evidently playing him: he returned all the bows and congees three-fold, and as soon as the ceremonious introduction was over, made a face at Colonel

Berkeley, expressive of mingled gratification and suspicion, which threw those around into a roar of laughter; while Byron, who did not see it, looked around for the cause of merriment in a manner which redoubled it at once.

"Grimaldi," said the Colonel, "after breakfast, at which meal we expect your company and that of Mr Watson, you shall have a course with the greyhounds yonder; then you must return and dine with us. We will have dinner early, so that you can reach the theatre in time to perform."

To this, Grimaldi had no further reply to make, than to express his gratitude for such consideration and kindness. After they had taken a plentiful meal, they went out with the dogs and had some famous sport. Hares were so plentiful that they started twenty-seven in one field; and the day being fine, and the novelty great, Grimaldi was highly delighted with the proceedings. Upon their return to the castle they found most of the party with whom they had breakfasted assembled together, and shortly afterwards they sat down to dinner. Lord Byron sat on Grimaldi's left, and a young nobleman whom he knew very well, from his being constantly behind the scenes at Covent Garden, but whose name he could not recollect, sat on his right.

"Grimaldi," whispered this young nobleman, just as dinner commenced, "did you ever meet Byron before?"

"Never, my lord," answered Grimaldi. "That is, never to converse with him."

"Then, of course, you have not met him at a dinner-party?"

"Never, my lord."

"Well, then," continued the young gentleman, who, as anybody but Grimaldi would have seen, was playing on his simplicity in conjunction with Lord Byron, "I will tell you why

251

I asked these questions: I was anxious, if you should chance not to know his lordship's peculiarities, to point out to you one trifling but still distinguishing one, to which if you happen to oppose yourself, he will infallibly take a dislike to you; and I need not assure you that it is always best for a public character to be on good terms rather than bad with such men."

Grimaldi bowed his thanks, and really did feel very grateful.

"What I allude to is simply this," added his noble friend. "Byron is very courteous at the dinner-table, but does not like to have his courtesy thrown away, or slighted; I would recommend you, if he asks you to take anything, as he is almost sure to do, no matter whether it be to eat or drink, not to refuse."

"I am very much obliged to you, my lord," was Grimaldi's reply. "In fact, I look upon your kindness as a great personal favour, and I shall carefully act upon your recommendation."

And so he did, and so indeed he had plenty of opportunity of doing, for Lord Byron asked him to partake of so many things, none of which he liked to decline, that at last he was quite gorged, and was almost fearful that if it lasted much longer, he should be unable to perform that night at Gloucester.

Towards the end of the repast his lordship invited him to eat a little apple-tart, which he thought he could manage and more especially as he was very fond of it; he therefore acquiesced, with many thanks; and the tart being placed before him, commenced operations. Byron looked at him for a moment, and then said, with much seeming surprise:

"Why, Mr Grimaldi, do you not take soy with your tart?"

"Soy, my lord?"

"Yes, soy: it is very good with salmon, and therefore it must be nice with apple-pie."

Poor Grimaldi did not see the analogy, and was upon the point of saying so; but his friend on his right touched his elbow, when, recollecting what he had previously communicated, he bowed assent to Byron's proposal, and proceeded to pour some of the fish-sauce over the tart. After one or two vain attempts to swallow a mouthful of the vile mess, he addressed Lord Byron with considerable formality, begging him to observe, "that no one could do more justice than himself to his kindness, but that he really trusted he would forgive his declining to eat the mixture he had recommended; as, however much the confession might savour of bad taste, he really did not relish soy with apple-tart."

He was much relieved by Byron's taking the apology in very good part, and by the rest of the company laughing most heartily, at what, he says, he cannot possibly tell, *unless* it had been determined to put a joke upon him. We should imagine that it had been; but, in any case, should be strongly disposed to say that a great deal more of innate politeness was displayed on the side of simplicity than on that of nobility.

Shortly afterwards they took their leave and returned to Gloucester, where they found the theatre crowded as before. The performances went off as well as possible; and after all was over, Watson presented Grimaldi with one hundred and ninety-five pounds as his share. At seven o'clock next morning he was on his road to London, where he arrived that night. Early on the following morning, Grimaldi waited upon his friend, Mr Hughes; and having reminded him that "Cheltenham was a very bad theatrical town, on account of its spas and other amusements, but that it was possible forty or fifty pounds might be made there," triumphantly exhibited his one hundred and ninety-five pounds. In the evening he called at Covent Garden, and saw Mr H Harris, who informed him that Mr Dimond, of the Bath and Bristol theatres, wished to engage him for five weeks—that his terms were twenty-five pounds per week, with half a clear benefit at each of the places named; and that if he liked to go, he was at perfect liberty to do so, the proprietors of Covent Garden not needing his services until Christmas. His salary was to be paid, however, just as though he were performing. Of this liberality Grimaldi gladly availed himself; and after expressing his gratitude, wrote to Dimond, accepting the proposal. A week after he had returned from Gloucester, he left town for Bath.

Two days after his arrival in Bath he appeared at the theatre, where he was fortunate enough to elicit the warmest applause and approbation from a crowded audience: nor was he less successful at Bristol, the theatre being completely filled every night he performed. Grimaldi remained in this part of the country during five weeks, playing four nights in every week at Bath, and the remaining two at Bristol. By this trip he realised two hundred and eighty-seven pounds and one hundred and twenty-five pounds for salary, and one hundred and sixty-two pounds for benefits; but although it was a lucrative expedition it was by no means a pleasant one, the weather being exceedingly inclement, and he being compelled to return to Bath every evening after the performances at Bristol were over. The nightly rides at that season of the year were by no means agreeable; he suffered very much from colds, and, upon the whole, was very far from sorry when his engagement terminated.

During Grimaldi's stay at Bath, a little incident happened, developing, in a striking point of view, a very repulsive trait of discourtesy and bad breeding in a quarter where, least of any, such an exhibition might have been looked for. Higman, the bass-singer, who was then in great repute and was afterwards the original Gabriel in *Guy Mannering*, was invited with Grimaldi to dine with a reverend gentleman of that city. They accepted the invitation, and upon their arrival found a pretty large party of gentlemen assembled, the clerical host of course presiding. The very instant the cloth was removed, this gentleman commanded, rather than asked, Higman to sing a song. Not wishing to appear desirous of enhancing the merit of the song by frivolous objections, he at once consented, although he had scarcely swallowed his meal. It was deservedly much applauded and complimented, and the moment the applause had ceased, the reverend doctor turned to Grimaldi and in the same peremptory manner requested a song from him. Grimaldi begged leave to decline for the present, urging—what was indeed the truth—that he had scarcely swallowed his dinner. The observation made by the host in reply rather astonished him.

"What, Mr Grimaldi!" he exclaimed, hastily, "not sing, sir! Why, I asked you here, sir, today expressly to sing."

"Indeed, sir!" said Grimaldi, rising from the table. "Then I heartily wish you had said so when you gave me the invitation; in which case you would have saved me the inconvenience of coming here today, and prevented my wishing you, as I now beg to do, a very unceremonious good night."

With these words he left the apartment, and very soon afterwards the house. It may appear to a great many persons a remarkable circumstance that a pantomime Clown should have been called upon to read a lesson of politeness and common decency to a reverend divine. The circumstance, however, happened literally as it is here narrated.

Having now none of those amusements which in former years had served to employ his idle hours—having lost his butterflies, given up his pigeons, removed from Finchley, sold his house, and resigned his garden—Grimaldi devoted the whole of his leisure time to the society and improvement of his son. As he could not bear to part with Young Joe, and was wholly unable to make up his mind to send him to any great boarding-school, the boy was partly educated at the same school at which his father had been a pupil, and partly by masters who attended him at home. The father appears to have bestowed great and praiseworthy care upon his education. Although at this time he was only twelve years old he had not only quite mastered the common rudiments of learning, but had become well acquainted with French literature and wrote the language with ease and propriety. He had at a very early age manifested a great fondness for music, especially the violin, and had acquired great proficiency on that instrument, under the tuition of one of the first masters in the country. As Young Joe was a very clever boy, was an excellent dancer, and displayed a great fondness and aptitude for the stage, his father finding that his inclinations lay irrevocably that way, determined to encourage them, and accordingly proceeded to instruct him in melodrama and pantomime. Grimaldi fancied that in his old age, when his own heyday of fame and profit was over, he should gather new life from the boy's success, and that old times would be called up vividly before him when he witnessed his popularity in characters which had first brought his father before the public, and enabled him gradually, after the loss of his property, to acquire an independent and respectable station in society. The wish was a natural one, and the old man cherished it dearly for many years. It was decreed otherwise; and although in his better days the blight of this hope caused him great grief and misery, he endeavoured to bear it with humility and resignation.

On the twenty-sixth of April 1814 Grimaldi resumed his labours at Sadler's Wells. He acted in a drama called *The Slave Pirate*, which was successful. His first benefit brought him two hundred and sixteen pounds, and his second two hundred and sixty-three pounds and ten shillings; the last named being the best he ever had at that house. The great attraction of this benefit was the first appearance on any stage of his son, who performed 'Friday' in *Robinson Crusoe*, Grimaldi playing the latter part himself, and thus introducing his son to the public in the same piece in which his father had brought him forward, thirty-three years before. For six weeks previous to the début, the pains Grimaldi had taken to render him master of the character and the drillings he gave him were innumerable, although they rather arose from the nervousness of the father than from any lack of intelligence on the part of the son, who not only rapidly acquired the instructions communicated to him but in many instances improved upon them considerably. His intended appearance was kept a profound secret until within a week of the night on which he was to perform; and when the announcement was at length made, the demand for tickets and places was immense. The result was that the benefit not only turned out the best Grimaldi ever had, but the reception of the son was enthusiastic, and his exertions were both applauded by the public and commended in the newspapers. It may appear a mere matter of course to say that the father considered the performance the best that he had ever seen; but long afterwards, when the boy was dead, and censure or praise was alike powerless to assist or harm him, Grimaldi expressed in the same strong terms his high opinion of his son's abilities, and his conviction that had Young Joe been only moderate and temperate in the commonest degree, he must in a few years have equalled, if not greatly excelled, anything which Grimaldi himself had achieved in his very best days.

On the twentieth of December following Grimaldi sustained a severe loss in the death of his constant and sincere friend, Mr Richard Hughes, who had been his well-wisher and adviser from infancy, and whose relationship to his first wife gave him a strong and lasting claim on his regard. As another instance of the severe and mental trials which an actor has to undergo, it may be mentioned that during the time his friend was lying dead Grimaldi was engaged for many hours each day in rehearsing broadly humorous pantomime, and that, as if to render the contrast more striking, the burial being fixed for the twenty-sixth of the month, he was compelled to rehearse part of his Clown's character on the stage, to run to the funeral, to get back from the churchyard to the theatre to finish the rehearsal, and to exert all his comic powers at night to set the audience in a roar.

This pantomime was founded upon the story of Whittington and his Cat, and had a very extended run. On the night of its production Grimaldi's spirits were so affected by the calamity he had sustained that it was with only great difficulty that he could go through his part, in which he very nearly failed. Although his health paid very dearly for this and other efforts of the same nature the constant bustle and excitement of his professional duties aided in recovering him and enabling him to act with his accustomed vivacity.

The harlequinade of *The Talking Bird* was produced at Sadler's Wells this season, in which Grimaldi first enacted the Bird and afterwards the Clown. During the run he performed the remarkable feat of playing three very heavy parts (two of them Clowns) at three different theatres on the same night. He was intimately acquainted with a Mr Hayward, who, being married to a clever actress at the Surrey, one Miss Dely, begged him as a great favour to act for her at that theatre on her benefit night. Grimaldi asked and obtained permission from the proprietors of Sadler's Wells, but could not do the same at Covent Garden, as Mr Harris was absent from town. He did not think it a point of any great importance, however, in as much as he had not been called upon to act for some time, and nothing was then announced in which it was at all likely he would be wanted. Unfortunately, on the very night of the benefit *La Perouse*, in which Grimaldi acted, was advertised at Covent Garden. In this dilemma, he hurried over the water, explained the circumstances, and pointed out the impossibility of his performing at the Surrey. But the Surrey people who had advertised Grimaldi, stoutly contending that there was no impossibility in the case, assured him that all would be right; that he should play there first, then go to Sadler's Wells, and then to Covent Garden, to finish the evening. To the end that he should be in good time at each house it was proposed that a chaise with the best horses that could be procured should be provided, and held in readiness to carry him at the greatest possible speed from place to place.

Not having the heart to disappoint the parties interested, Grimaldi consented to this arrangement. At the Surrey he played with Bologna in the pantomime; the moment it was over he jumped into a chaise and four that was waiting at the door, and started for Sadler's Wells. Bologna accompanied him to see the issue of the proceeding, and, by dashing through the streets at a most extraordinary pace, they reached Sadler's Wells just at the commencement of the overture for the pantomime. Hurrying to repaint his face, which had been very much bedaubed by the rain, which poured upon it as he looked out of the chaise-window entreating the post-boys to drive a little slower, and thrusting himself into the dress of *The Talking Bird*, he was ready at the instant when the call-boy told him he was wanted. There still remained Covent Garden, and towards the close of the pantomime Grimaldi grew very anxious, looking constantly towards the sides of the stage to see if Bologna was still there; for as he was the Perouse of the night, and was wanted a full half-hour before Grimaldi, Joe felt something like security so long as Bologna remained. At length the pantomime was over, and once more taking their seats in the same chaise, they drove at the same furious pace to Covent Garden, and were ready dressed and in the green-room before the first bars of the overture had been played. This change of dress assisted greatly in recovering Grimaldi from his fatigue, and he went through the third part as well as the first, feeling no greater exhaustion at the close of the performances than was usual with him on an ordinary night. The only refreshment which he took during the whole evening was one glass of warm ale and a biscuit. He plumed himself very much on this feat; for although he had played Clown at two theatres for twenty-eight nights successively, he considered it something out of the common way, and triumphed in it greatly.

Grimaldi had a specimen next day of the spirit which Fawcett still cherished towards him, and which, but for the kindness of Mr Harris, might have injured him severely on many occasions. Applying as usual at the treasury for his weekly salary of ten pounds, he was informed by the treasurer, with great politeness and apparent regret, that he had received orders from Mr Fawcett to stop it for that week. He instantly posted off in search of that gentleman, and upon finding him, requested to know why his salary was not to be paid.

"Because, sir," replied Mr Fawcett, "because you have thought fit to play at the Surrey Theatre without mentioning the matter to *us*, or asking *our* permission."

Grimaldi whistled a little to express his total unconcern, and, turning away, muttered, "For *us* and for *our* tragedy, thus stooping to your clemency, we beg your hearing patiently." In crossing the stage to the door, he met Mr Harris, who had that instant entered the theatre, having arrived in town not ten minutes before. He shook Joe kindly by the hand, and inquired how he was.

"Why, sir," said Grimaldi, "I am as well as can be expected, considering that my salary has been stopped."

"Why, what have you been about, Joe?"

"Played for Mrs Hayward's benefit at the Surrey, sir."

"Oh! without leave, I suppose?"

"Why, sir," answered Grimaldi, "there was no one in the theatre who was, in my opinion, entitled actually to give or refuse leave; you were out of town: with Mr Fawcett I have nothing to do—he has neither connexion with nor influence over my line of business, nor do I wish him to have any; Mr Farley is the only gentleman under yourself whom I consider myself obliged to acknowledge as a superior here—and to him I did name it, and he told me to go, for I should not be wanted."

"Joe," said Mr Harris, after a moment's pause, "go to Brandon, and tell him to give you your money. And, mind, I've entered into an arrangement for you to go and see Dimond again in October, upon the same terms as before: so mind you go, and I'll take care you are neither fined nor wanted."

For this double liberality he expressed his best thanks, and returning to the treasury, with the manager's message, received his salary, and departed.

On the fifteenth of the next month, Grimaldi's first benefit for that season took place at Sadler's Wells. He sustained the part of Don Juan again; and his son, J S Grimaldi, played Scaramouch, this being his second appearance. He acted the part capitally, and had a great reception, so that his father now in good earnest began to hope he would not only support the name of Grimaldi but confer upon it increased popularity. The receipts of this night were two hundred and thirty-one pounds and fourteen shillings. Three months afterwards his second benefit occurred: Monday, the ninth of October, was the day fixed for it, but on the preceding Saturday Grimaldi was suddenly seized with severe illness, originating in a most distressing impediment in his breathing. Medical assistance was immediately called in, and he was bled until nigh fainting. This slightly relieved him; but shortly afterwards he had a relapse, and four weeks passed before he recovered sufficiently to leave the house. There is no doubt but that some radical change had occurred in his constitution, for previously to this attack he had never been visited with a single day's illness, while after its occurrence he never had a single day of perfect health.

On the Monday, finding it would be impossible for him to play, Grimaldi procured a substitute and immediately had bills printed and posted outside the theatre. His absence made a difference of about fifty pounds in the receipts; but as his son played Scaramouch and played it well, he sustained no greater pecuniary loss, and had the satisfaction of hearing from all quarters that his son was rapidly improving. After the lapse of a month Grimaldi became tolerably well and as it was now time for him to keep his engagement with Dimond, he went to Bath in November, and remained there until the middle of December, occasionally acting at Bristol. The profits of this trip were two hundred and ninety-four pounds.

It was either during this provincial trip, or about this time, that Grimaldi first became acquainted with Mr Davidge, the late lessee of the Surrey Theatre. He was then the Harlequin at Bath and Bristol, and although he afterwards became a round and magisterial figure, was then a very light and active pantomimist. In the pantomimes Davidge was the Harlequin, and Grimaldi of course the Clown. They were accustomed to call the Pantaloon, who was a very indifferent actor, by the name of 'Billy Coombes'—why, they best knew, but it seems not to have been his real name. This worthy had given both Davidge and Grimaldi mighty offence upon several occasions, possibly by making his appearance on the stage in a state of intoxication. Grimaldi forgot the precise cause of the affront, but, whatever it was, they deemed it a very great one; and Davidge, upon several occasions, took opportunities of hinting, in speeches fraught with determination and replete with a peculiar variety of expletives, that he was resolved some time or other to be revenged upon that Billy Coombes.

One evening while the pantomime was in progress, and the two friends were exciting much mirth and applause, Davidge pointed to a chest which was used in the piece, and whispering that there was a lock upon it with a key, remarked that Billy had to get into it directly, and asked whether it would not be a good joke to turn the key upon him. Grimaldi readily concurred, and no sooner was Billy Coombes beneath the lid of the chest than he was locked in, amidst the plaudits of the audience, who thought it a capital trick. There were but two more scenes in the pantomime, which Davidge had to commence. Just as he was going on the stage, Grimaldi inquired whether he had let out the Pantaloon.

"No," he replied hastily, "I have not, but I will directly I come off." So saying, he danced upon the stage, followed by Grimaldi, and the usual buffeting ensued with the accustomed effect. The pantomime was over a few minutes afterwards, and Grimaldi, who felt very tired when he had gone through his part, in consequence of his recent illness, went straight home and was in bed a very short time after the curtain fell.

There was a call the next morning for the rehearsal of a few new pantomime scenes, which Grimaldi had prepared to vary the entertainments. However, as the Pantaloon was not forthcoming, they could not be gone through with any useful effect. When Davidge arrived, Grimaldi mentioned the circumstance.

"I suppose," he said, "our victim has taken our conduct in high dudgeon, and doesn't mean to come this morning. We shall be in a pretty mess at night if he does not!"

"What do you mean?" said Davidge, with a look of surprise.

"This Billy Coombes, he is not come to the theatre today, and is not to be found at his lodgings, for we have sent a man there."

"By G— ," said Davidge, "I never let him out of the box!"

On reflection, they had certainly finished the pantomime without him although it did not strike them at the time, because, as he was no great actor, the business of the last two scenes had been arranged entirely between Davidge and Grimaldi. They lost no time in inquiring after the chest, and it was at length discovered in a cellar below the stage. On raising the lid the Pantaloon was discovered, and a truly pitiable object he looked, although they were both not a little relieved to find he was alive, for, not knowing that the chest was perforated in various places, they had entertained some serious fears that when he did turn up he might be found suffocated. Every necessary assistance was afforded him, and he never suffered in the slightest degree from his temporary confinement. He said that he had shouted as loud as he could, and had knocked and kicked against the sides of his prison, but that nobody had taken the least notice of him, which he attributed to the incessant noise and bustle behind the scenes. With the view of keeping the stage as clear as possible, everything used in a pantomime is put away at once; the chest was lowered by a trap into the cellar, notwithstanding the shouts from the Pantaloon, who, knowing that he would be released next day, went to sleep very quietly.

This was the version of the story given by the ingenious Mr Coombes and in this version Grimaldi was an implicit believer. We are rather disposed to think that Mr Coombes might have thrown an additional light upon the matter by explaining that he had got into the chest that morning to turn the tables upon his assailants, the more so, as he received various little presents in the way of compensation for his imprisonment, with which he expressed himself perfectly satisfied.

At this time Grimaldi repeatedly met with Lord Byron, not only at Covent Garden but at various private parties to which he was invited; and eventually they became very good friends. Lord Byron was, as all the world knows, an eccentric man, and he loses nothing of the character in Grimaldi's hands. "Sometimes," he says, "his lordship appeared lost in deep melancholy, and when that was the case, really looked the picture of despair, for his face was highly capable of expressing profound grief; at other times he was very lively, chatting with great spirit and vivacity; and then occasionally he would be a complete fop, exhibiting his white hands and teeth with an almost ludicrous degree of affectation. But whether 'grave or gay, lively or severe', his bitter, biting sarcasm never was omitted or forgotten."

It never fell to Grimaldi's lot to hear any person say such severe things as Byron accustomed himself to utter, and they tended not a little to increase the awe with which, upon their first interview, he had been predisposed to regard him. As to Grimaldi himself, Byron invariably acted towards him with much condescension and good humour, frequently conversing with him for hours together; and when the business of the evening called him away, he would wait at the 'wings' for him, and as soon as he came off the stage, recommence the conversation where it had been broken off. Grimaldi rarely contradicted him, fearing to draw down upon himself the sarcasms which he constantly heard fulminated against others; and when they spoke on subjects with Byron's opinions upon which he was unacquainted, he cautiously endeavoured to ascertain them before he ventured to give his own, fearing, as Byron felt so very warmly upon most questions, that Joe might chance to dissent from him upon one in which he took great interest.

Before Lord Byron left England upon the expedition whence he was destined to return no more, he presented Grimaldi, as a token, he said, of his regard, with a valuable silver snuff-box, around which was the inscription, *The gift of Lord Byron to Joseph Grimaldi*. It was of course preserved with the most scrupulous care, and valued more highly than any article in his possession. It is but an act of justice to both parties to say, that Lord Byron always treated Grimaldi with the greatest liberality. In 1808, when he saw Grimaldi for the first time, Byron sent a message to his residence requesting that he would always forward to him one box ticket whenever he took a benefit. This Grimaldi regularly did, and in return invariably received on the following day a five-pound note.

CHAPTER THIRTEEN

During a period of thirty-eight years, that is to say from 1782 to 1820, inclusive, Grimaldi was never absent for any season from Sadler's Wells, except for the season of 1817. The cause of his non-engagement was this. His former articles expiring a few days before the close of the previous season, he received a note from Mr Charles Dibdin, requesting to know upon what terms he would be disposed to renew them. Grimaldi replied that they had only to make the pounds guineas, and he would be content. There was no objection to this proposition, but he was informed that the proprietors had arrived at the resolution of no longer allowing him two benefits in each year, and of permitting him in future to take only one. Grimaldi considered this a very arbitrary and unjust proceeding. As he had never under any circumstances cleared less than one hundred and fifty pounds from a benefit, this reduction necessarily involved the diminution of his yearly income by a large sum; and as he paid sixty pounds for the house on every such occasion, which was probably more than it would otherwise have had in it, he did not think that the proprietors could urge any just reason for proposing the alteration. After considering these points he wrote to Mr Charles Dibdin, at that time a proprietor himself, that he could on no consideration give up either of his accustomed benefits. To this note Grimaldi received no reply, but he confidently expected that they would not attempt a season without him, he being at that time unquestionably the lion of the theatre, and certainly drawing money to the house. He was, however, deceived, for he heard no more from Mr Charles Dibdin, and eventually learned that Paulo was engaged in his place.

On the fourteenth of April Sadler's Wells commenced its season, upon which occasion the unexpected absence of Grimaldi occasioned quite a commotion among the audience. He had said nothing about it himself, nor was the circumstance known to the public until the bills were put forth, when the announcement of Paulo's engagement and Grimaldi's secession occasioned much surprise and some manifestations of feeling. Grimaldi had been spending a few days at Egham; and upon his return to town, towards the latter end of March, was not a little amazed to see the walls in the neighbourhood of his house in Spa Fields completely covered with placards emanating from the rival parties, some bearing the words '*Joey for ever!*' others displaying '*No Paulo!*' and others, again, '*No Grimaldi!*' It was supposed by some that Grimaldi himself had a hand in the distribution of these bills; but he solemnly denied it, declaring that he never saw or heard anything of them until they were paraded upon the walls on his return to town.

The theatre opened with *Philip and his Dog,* and a new harlequinade, called *April Fools,* or *Months and Mummery.* Being informed that it was Dibdin's intention, if any disturbance occurred in consequence of his absence, to address the house and state that it had resulted from Grimaldi's express wish, Grimaldi went to the boxes on the opening night, determined, if any such statement were made, to address the audience from his place and explain the circumstances under which he had left the theatre. He was spared this very disagreeable task, however, no other expression of public feeling taking place except that which is of all others most sensibly and acutely felt by a manager—the people stayed away. Instead of every seat being taken and standing-places eagerly secured, as had been formerly the case, the theatre was not a quarter filled. There were only forty persons, and these principally friends of the proprietors, in the boxes; not more than a hundred in the pit, and the gallery was not half full. Grimaldi stayed only the first act of the first piece, and then, seeing no probability of being called for, walked away to Covent Garden. The next morning the newspapers, one and all, made known Grimaldi's absence, and regretted it as a circumstance which could not fail to prove very injurious to the interests of the theatre. They did this without decrying the merits of Paulo, who was really a very good Clown, but who laboured under the double disadvantage of not being known at Sadler's Wells and of following in the wake of one who had been a great favourite there for so many years.

Grimaldi's non-engagement at Sadler's Wells was no sooner made known than the provincial managers vied with each other in their endeavours to secure him. Mr W Murray, the manager of the Edinburgh and Glasgow theatres, offered him an engagement at each for six nights when Covent Garden closed, which he immediately accepted. The terms were these: Grimaldi was to have the best night's receipts out of each six, Murray the second best, and the other four nights to be equally divided between them, deducting forty pounds for expenses. Grimaldi had no sooner closed with this proprietor than he was waited upon by Mr Knight, of the Manchester and Liverpool theatres, who offered him an engagement for three weeks, into which he also entered. There then followed such a long list of offers, that if he had had twelve months at his disposal instead of six weeks, they would have occupied the whole time. Many of these offers were of the most handsome and liberal nature; and it was with great regret that he was compelled to decline them.

As there was nothing for Grimaldi to do at Covent Garden, in consequence of the early decease of *Puss in Boots*, he accepted an overture from Mr Brunton, who was the lessee of the Birmingham theatre, for himself and his son to act there for seven nights. It was Young Joe's first provincial excursion, and the profits were somewhere about two hundred pounds. Grimaldi took Worcester in his way on his return, and agreed, at the presiding request of Mr Crisp, the manager, to stop and play there one night. He offered forty pounds down, or a fair division of the receipts. Grimaldi chose the former terms, acted Scaramouch to a very crowded house, sang several songs, and finished with a little pantomime in which he and his son were Clowns. He supped with the manager, who, at the conclusion of the meal, presented him with a fifty pound note, saying, if Grimaldi would accept that sum in lieu of the one agreed upon, it was heartily at his service, and he (the manager) would still be a great gainer by the transaction. This liberal treatment gave Grimaldi a very favourable impression of the Worcester manager, whom he assured that should he ever be in that part of the country again, he would not fail to communicate with him. The next day father and son both returned to town, when the former had the satisfaction of hearing that he had not been wanted at Covent Garden. He found several letters from provincial managers offering great terms; but as he was obliged to be in London at the opening of Covent Garden, he had no option but to decline these proposals.

Grimaldi appeared but seldom during the remainder of the season at Covent Garden, which closed on the second of July. On the following day he left London for Scotland. When he reached Edinburgh, he heard from Mr Murray that in consequence of Emery being engaged to play at Glasgow, he should be obliged to limit Grimaldi's nights there to three instead of six, as agreed upon. This very much surprised Joe; but as there was no help for it, he acquiesced with a good grace, and left Edinburgh immediately for Glasgow, where he was to act on the following night. *Whittington, Don Juan, Valentine and Orson*, and *The Rivals* were the pieces acted at Glasgow. In the first three his son performed with Grimaldi; in the latter Grimaldi played Acres, and was very well received. He played this part throughout his provincial trips, and always to the perfect satisfaction and amusement of the audience. He never played Richard III in the provinces, but limited his performance of characters out of pantomime or melodrama to Acres, Moll Flaggon, and one other part. When Grimaldi had finished at Glasgow, he joined the company at Edinburgh, where he played Acres twice. The song of *Tippitywitchit* took amazingly with the gude folks of Auld Reekie, and both he and his son were received with great kindness and favour. On the day after the completion of the engagement, Mr Murray called at Grimaldi's lodgings, and wrote him a cheque for four hundred and seventeen pounds, as his share, concluding by inviting him to pay a similar visit during the following summer.

On the twenty-second Grimaldi left Edinburgh for Berwick, where he had promised to play for two nights, and where he came out the following evening. He was greatly amazed when he saw the theatre at this town: it was situated up a stable yard in a loft, to reach which it was necessary to climb two flights of stairs, the whole entrance being mean and dirty, and, to ladies especially, particularly disagreeable. But his surprise was far from being confined to the exterior of the theatre: on the contrary, when he surveyed its interior and found it neat and complete, perfect in its appointments, and even stylish in its decorations, his amazement was increased. It was still further augmented by the appearance and manner of the audience to which he played in the evening, for he had never by any chance acted (taking the size of the building into consideration) to a more fashionable and brilliant box-company.

The second night was as good as the first, and he received for his exertions ninety-two pounds and seven shillings. On this evening he supped with the manager, and during their meal the servant brought in a letter directed to Grimaldi, which had just been left at the door by a footman in livery, who, after delivering it, had immediately walked away. He broke the seal, and read as follows:

Sir, Accept the enclosed as a reward of your merit, and the entertainment we have received from you this evening.

A FRIEND

Thursday, July 24th, 1817

The 'enclosed' was a bank-note for fifty pounds.

Next day Grimaldi bade adieu to Berwick and went direct to Liverpool, where he made his first appearance on the thirtieth; and here, according to previous arrangements, he remained three weeks. His salary was to be twelve pounds per week, with half a clear benefit, or the whole house for forty pounds, which he chose. As the night fixed upon for his benefit (which was the last of his engagement) drew nigh, Grimaldi began anxiously to deliberate whether he should speculate in the 'whole house' or not. He had no friends or acquaintances in Liverpool to assist him, but, on the other hand, he had made a tremendous hit; so, not being able to decide himself, he called in the aid of his friends, Emery, Blanchard and Jack Johnstone, who chanced to be there at the time, and requested their advice how he should proceed. With one accord they advised him to venture upon taking the house, which he, adopting their advice, forthwith did, paying down his forty pounds, but with many doubts as to the result. He lost no time in making out his bill, and getting it printed. The play was *The Rivals*, in which he acted Acres, and the afterpiece the pantomime of *Harlequin's Olio*, in which his son was to appear as Flipflap, a kind of attendant upon Harlequin, and he as the Clown.

Several days elapsed, but nothing betokening a good benefit presented itself, and Grimaldi began to suspect it would turn out a complete failure. On the morning of the very day he had sold only fourteen tickets, and walked to the theatre with rather downcast spirits. At the box door he met Mr Banks, one of the managers, who addressed him with:

"Well, Joe, a precious benefit you will have!"

"So I expect," he answered with a sigh.

"Have you looked at the box-book?" inquired the manager, with a slight degree of surprise in his manner.

"No," said Grimaldi. "I really am afraid to do so."

"Afraid!" echoed the manager. "Upon my word, Mr Grimaldi, I don't know what you would have, or what you are afraid of. Every seat in the boxes is taken: and if there had been more, they would have been let."

Hastening to the box-office, Grimaldi found that this good news was perfectly correct. His benefit, which took place on the twentieth of August, produced the greatest receipts ever known in that theatre: the sum taken was three hundred and twenty-eight pounds and fourteen shillings, being eleven pounds more than was received at Miss O'Neill's benefit (who was a wonderful favourite in the town), and beating John Emery's by five pounds. He cleared upwards of two hundred and eighty pounds by following the advice of his friends; upon the strength of which they all dined together next day, and made very merry.

Many offers from other theatres came pouring in, but Grimaldi only accepted two: one to act at Preston, and the other to play four nights at Hereford for Mr Crisp, for whom he naturally entertained very friendly feelings, remembering the courteous and handsome manner in which he had treated him at Worcester. Two days after his great benefit Grimaldi travelled over to Preston to fulfil his engagement with Mr Howard, the manager, but was very much dispirited by the number of Quakers whom he saw walking about the streets. The manager, however, was more sanguine, and, as it afterwards appeared, with good reason. Grimaldi played Acres and Scaramouch to full houses, the receipts on the first night being eighty-four pounds, and on the second, eighty-seven pounds and sixteen shillings. His share of the joint receipts was eighty-six pounds, with which sum, as it far exceeded his expectations, he was well contented.

On the second day after Grimaldi's arrival in Preston a little circumstance occurred which amused him so much that he intended to have introduced it in one of his pantomimic scenes, although he never did so. He was walking along the street by the market-place, when, observing a barber's pole projecting over the pavement, and recollecting that he wanted shaving, he opened the shop-door, and looking in saw a pretty little girl, about sixteen years of age, who was sitting at needlework. She rose to receive him, and he inquired if the master was within.

"No, sir," said the girl, "but I expect him directly."

"Very good," replied Grimaldi. "I want to look about me a little, I'll call again."

After strolling through the market-place a little while, he called again, but the barber had not come home. Grimaldi was walking down the street after this second unsuccessful call, when he encountered Mr Howard, the manager, with whom he fell into conversation, and they walked up and down the street talking together As he was going to the theatre and wished Grimaldi to accompany him, they turned in that direction, and passing the barber's shop, again looked in. The girl was still sitting at work; but she laid it aside when the visitors entered, and said she really was very sorry, but her father had not come in yet.

"That's very provoking," said Grimaldi, "considering that I have called here three times already."

The girl agreed that it was, and, stepping to the door, looked anxiously up the street and down the street, but there was no barber in sight.

"Do you want to see him on any particular business?" inquired Howard.

"Bless my heart! no, not I," said Grimaldi. "I only want to be shaved."

"Shaved, sir!" cried the girl. "Oh, dear me! what a pity it is you did not say so before! for I do most of the shaving for father when he's at home, and all when he's out."

"To be sure she does," said Howard. "I have been shaved by her fifty times."

"You have!" said Grimaldi. "Oh, I'm sure I have no objection. I am quite ready, my dear."

Grimaldi sat himself down in a chair, and the girl commenced the task in a very business-like manner, Grimaldi feeling an irresistible tendency to laugh at the oddity of the operation, but smothering it by dint of great efforts while the girl was shaving his chin. At length, when she got to his upper lip, and took his nose between her fingers with a piece of brown paper, he could stand it no longer, but burst into a tremendous roar of laughter, and made a face at Howard, which the girl no sooner saw than she dropped the razor and laughed immoderately also; whereat Howard began to laugh too, which only set Grimaldi laughing more; when just at this moment in came the barber, who, seeing three people in convulsions of mirth, one of them with a soapy face and a gigantic mouth making the most extravagant faces over a white towel, threw himself into a chair without ceremony, and dashing his hat on the ground, laughed louder than any of them, declaring in broken words as he could find breath to utter them, that "that gentleman as was being shaved, was out of sight the funniest gentleman he had ever seen", and entreating him to "stop them faces, or he knew he should die". When they were all perfectly exhausted, the barber finished what his daughter had begun; and rewarding the girl with a shilling, Grimaldi and the manger took their leaves.

Having settled at the theatre, received his money, and made several purchases in the town (for he always spent a percentage in every place where he had been successful), Grimaldi returned to Liverpool on the twenty-fourth of August. After two days he went to Hereford, and having waited on Mr Crisp, the manager, went to look at the theatre. To his great astonishment and concern he found this nothing more than a common square room, with a stage four yards wide and about as many high, the head of the statue in *Don Juan* being obscured by the flies and thus rendered wholly invisible to the audience. What made this circumstance the more annoying was that on the statue being seen to nod its head depended the effect of one of the very best scenes of Scaramouch. As Grimaldi did not hesitate to express his great mortification and annoyance, and his decided indisposition to act in such a place for four nights, which was the term originally proposed, a fresh arrangement was entered into, by which he engaged to play two nights at Hereford and two at Worcester, where he knew there was a better theatre.

Having now concluded his provincial engagements Grimaldi repaired to Cheltenham for rest and relaxation, and remained there until the second week in September, when he returned to London. While at Cheltenham, he stumbled upon his old friend, Richer, the rope-dancer, who had retired from the profession, and was now married to the widow of a clergyman who had died extremely rich. They were living in great style, and to all appearances very happy.

The following account of Grimaldi's gains during this short excursion will afford some idea of the immense sums he was in the habit of receiving about this time. The amount was so much more than he had supposed that on going over the calculation he could scarcely believe he was correct. It was as follows:

	£	s	d
Brighton, four nights	100	0	0
Birmingham, six	210	0	0
Worcester, one	50	0	0
Glasgow and Edinburgh, nine	417	0	0
Berwick, two	102	7	0
Liverpool, sixteen	324	14	0
Preston, two	86	0	0
Hereford, two	43	10	0
Worcester (2nd visit), two	90	8	0
Total	£1,423	19	0

The accounts which Grimaldi received at Sadler's Wells on his return were unusually bad. They were fully corroborated by Mr Hughes, who informed him it had been the very worst season the theatre had ever known. Having nothing to do at Covent Garden, and entertaining a very pleasant and lively recollection of the profits of his last trip, Grimaldi determined on making another excursion, and accepted an offer from Elliston to play four nights at Birmingham, by which he cleared one hundred and fifty pounds. From Birmingham he went to Leicester, where Elliston also had a theatre, and where he played for two nights, being accompanied by Mr Brunton, who was Elliston's stage manager. They were very successful, Grimaldi's share of the receipts being seventy pounds.

The morning after his last performance here, Grimaldi took a post-chaise and started for Chester, where he had undertaken to act for one week. As the chaise drove up to the White Lion the London coach drove up too, and, seated on the outside, Grimaldi saw to his great surprise his old friend Bologna, who, it appeared, had been engaged expressly to perform with him in *Mother Goose*. The unexpected meeting afforded great pleasure to both, and having ordered a private sitting-room and a good dinner they sat down together and fell into conversation; in the course of which Bologna, by various hints and other slight remarks, gave his friend to understand that his old characteristic of never being able, without a strong effort, to make up his mind to spend a penny was by no means impaired by time. The room was handsomely fitted up; and the dinner, which was speedily placed before them, consisted of a great variety of expensive delicacies, the sight of which awakened in Bologna's mind a great many misgivings concerning the bill, which were not at all lessened by the landlady's informing them, with a low curtsey, as she placed the first dish on the table, that she knew who they were, and that she would answer for their being provided with every luxury and comfort the house would afford. They were no sooner left alone than Bologna, with a very dissatisfied air, informed his friend that he saw it would never do to stay in that house.

"Why not?" inquired Grimaldi.

"Because of the expense," he answered. "Bless me! look at the accommodation: what do you suppose they'll charge for all this? It won't suit me, Joe; I shall be off."

"You can do as you please," rejoined his friend, "but if you'll take my advice, you'll remain where you are: for I have found from experience that if there is a choice between a first-rate and a second-rate house, one should always go to the former. There you have the best articles at a fair price; while at the other you have bad things, worse served up, and enormously dear."

Bologna was ultimately prevailed upon not to leave the house, contenting himself with various economical resolutions, which he commenced putting in practice when the waiter appeared to know if they would order supper.

"Supper!" exclaimed Bologna. "Certainly not; not on any account. Suppers are extremely unhealthy; I never take them by any chance."

"You may get some supper for *me*," said Grimaldi, "and have it ready at half-past eleven."

"What will you like to order, sir?"

"I'll leave it to the landlady. Anything nice will do."

"Good Heavens?" said Bologna, as the waiter went out of the room. "What a bill you'll have to pay here!"

They strolled about the town; arranged with the manager to commence next night with *Mother Goose*, and having beguiled the time till supper, repaired to the inn, where a fine brace of partridges, done to a turn, were placed before Grimaldi. His companion eyed them with very hungry looks, congratulating himself aloud, however, upon having saved himself that expense, at all events.

There was a silence for some minutes, broken only by the clatter of the knives and forks; and then Bologna, who had been walking up and down the room in a restless manner, stopped short, and inquired if the birds were nice?

"Very," replied Grimaldi, helping himself again. "They are delicious."

Bologna walked up and down the room faster after this, and then rang the bell with great vehemence. The waiter appeared, and Bologna, after long consideration, hesitatingly ordered a Welsh rarebit.

"Certainly, sir," said the man; and by the time Grimaldi had finished his supper, the Welsh rarebit appeared.

"Stop a minute, waiter," said Bologna. "Grimaldi, do you mean to take supper every night?"

"Certainly. Every night."

"Well, then, waiter, remember to bring me a Welsh rarebit every evening when Mr Grimaldi takes his supper. I don't want it; but it has so rude an appearance to sit looking on while another man is eating, that I must do it as a matter of form and comfort. You'll not forget?"

"I'll be sure to remember, sir," was the reply.

The moment he was gone Grimaldi burst into a great roar of laughter, which his friend took in high dudgeon, muttering various observations regarding extravagance, which were responded to by divers remarks relative to shabbiness. Neither of them gave way, and the supper arrangement was regularly acted upon; Grimaldi always having some warm dish of game or poultry, and Bologna solacing himself with a Welsh rarebit and the reflection of having saved money while his companion spent it. They stayed at Chester nine days in all, and when the bills were brought at last, found, as Grimaldi had anticipated, that the charges were moderate, and well merited by the manner in which they had been accommodated.

"Well, Bologna," said Grimaldi, with a triumphant air, "are you satisfied?"

"Pretty well," he replied. "I must acknowledge that the bills are not so heavy as I feared they would have been; but there is one terrible mistake in mine. Look here! they have charged me for supper every night just as they have charged you. That must be wrong, you know: I have had nothing but Welsh rarebits!"

"Certainly," said Grimaldi, looking over the bill. "You had

better ring for the waiter; I have no doubt he can explain the matter."

The bell was rung, and the waiter came.

"Oh! here's a mistake, waiter," said Bologna, handing him the bill. "You have charged me for supper every night here, and you'll remember I only had a Welsh rarebit. Just get it altered, will you?"

"I beg your pardon, sir," replied the waiter, glancing from the bill to the customer. "It's quite right, sir."

"Quite right?"

"Quite sir: it's the rule of the house, sir—the rule of every house on the road—to charge in that way. Half-a-crown for supper, sir; cold beef, fowl, game, or bread and cheese: always half a crown, sir. There were a great many other dishes that you might have had; but you recollect giving a particular order for a Welsh rarebit, sir?"

The saving man said not another word, but paid the nine half-crowns for the nine Welsh rarebits, to his own great wrath and his friend's unspeakable amusement.

The next morning they returned to London, and on the road Grimaldi had another instance of his companion's parsimony, which determined him never to travel in his company again. When the coach came to the door, he was perfectly amazed to find that the economical Harlequin was going to travel outside, but not surprised to hear him whisper, when Joe expressed his astonishment, that he should save a pound by it, or more.

"Yes," answered Grimaldi, "and catch a cold by sitting outside all night, after your exertions at the theatre, which will cost you twenty pounds at least."

"You know nothing about it," replied Bologna, with a wink. "I shall be safe inside as well as you."

"What! and pay outside fare?"

"Just so," replied he. "I'll tell you how it is. I've ascertained that there's one place vacant inside, and that the coach belongs to our landlady. Now, I mean to remind her what a deal of money we have spent in the house; to tell her that I shall be soon coming here again; and to put it to her, whether she won't let me ride at least part of the way inside."

Grimaldi was not a little offended and vexed by this communication, feeling that, as they had been stopping at the house as companions and friends, he was rather involved in the shabbiness of his fellow-traveller. His angry remonstrances, however, produced not the slightest effect. Bologna acted precisely as he had threatened, and received permission from the good lady of the house, who was evidently much surprised at the application, to occupy the vacant inside place; it being stipulated and understood on both sides, that if anywhere on the road a passenger were found requiring an inside place, Bologna should either give up his, or pay the regular fare on to London.

As Grimaldi could not prevent this arrangement, he was compelled to listen to it with a good grace. The manager, who came to see them off, brought one hundred pounds for Grimaldi, all in three-shilling pieces, packed up in a large brown-paper parcel; and this part of the luggage being stowed in the coach-pocket, away they went, Bologna congratulating himself on his diplomacy, and Grimaldi consoling himself with the reflection that he should know how to avoid him in future, and that he was now, at least, safe from any further exhibition of Bologna's parsimony during the journey. The former resolution he kept, but in the latter conclusion he was desperately wrong.

It was evening when they started, and at four o'clock in the morning, when they stopped to change horses, a customer for an inside place presented himself; whereupon the driver, opening the coach door, civilly reminded Bologna of the conditions upon which he held his seat. Bologna was fast asleep the first time the man spoke, and having been roused, had the matter explained to him once more; upon which he sat bolt upright in the coach, and repeating all the man had said, inquired with great distinction whether he understood it to be put to him that he must either pay the inside fare or get out.

"That's it, sir," said the coachman.

"Very well," said Bologna, without the slightest alteration of tone or manner. "Then I shall do neither the one nor the other."

The coachman, falling back a space or two from the door, and recovering from a brief trance of astonishment, addressed the passengers, the would-be passengers, the ostlers and stable-boys, who were standing around, upon the mean and shabby conduct of the individual inside. Upon this the passengers remonstrated, the would-be passengers stormed, the coachman and guard bellowed, the ostlers hooted, the stable-boys grinned, Grimaldi worked himself into a state of intense vexation, and the cause of all the tumult sat quite immovable.

"Now, I'll tell you what it is," said the coachman, when his eloquence was quite exhausted, "one word's as good as a thousand. Will you get out?"

"No, I will not," answered the sleepy Harlequin.

"Very well," said the man. "Then off goes my benjamin, and out you come like a sack of sawdust."

As the man was of that portly form and stout build which is the badge of all his tribe, and as, stimulated by the approving murmurs of the onlookers, he began suiting the action to the words without delay, Bologna thought it best to come to terms; so he turned out into the cold air and took his seat on the coach-top, amidst several expressions of very undisguised contempt from his fellow-passengers. They performed the rest of the journey in this way, and Grimaldi, alighting at the Angel at Islington, left Bologna to go on to the coach-office in Holborn, previously giving both the guard and coachman something beyond their usual fee, as an intelligible hint that he was not of the same caste as his companion.

Two or three days afterwards, meeting Bologna in the street, he inquired how he had got on at the coach-office.

"Oh, very well," said Bologna. "They abused me finely."

"Just what I expected."

"Yes, and very glad I was of it, too."

"What do you mean?"

"Saved my money, Joe; that's what I mean. If they had been civil, of course I must have given something, not only to the coachman but the guard besides; but as they were not civil, of course I did not give either of them a penny, and so saved something handsome by it."

Bologna had many good qualities, and he and Grimaldi always remained on good terms; but as he was not upon the whole the most entertaining travelling companion that could be found, they never afterwards encountered each other in that capacity.

Sadler's Wells had closed when Grimaldi reached London, after a season which had entailed a very severe loss on the proprietors; the balance against whom was so heavy, as to cause it to be rumoured that one more such season would throw a few of the shares into new hands, which in reality shortly afterwards occurred. In a pecuniary point of view, it was an extremely fortunate thing for Grimaldi that he had remained absent from Sadler's Wells during the summer of 1817, his gain in the provinces being considerably more than it would have been if he had remained in town; while, on the other hand, the degree of exertion he had to encounter in the provinces was greatly inferior to that which he must have sustained at Sadler's Wells. In addition to the one thousand four hundred and twenty-three pounds and nineteen shillings of which an account is given earlier, he received for four nights at Birmingham one hundred and fifty pounds, for two nights at Leicester seventy pounds, and for six at Chester one hundred pounds, making a clear gain of one thousand seven hundred and forty-three pounds and nineteen shillings for fifty-six nights' performances; whereas, if he had remained at Sadler's Wells, he would have merely received thirty weeks' salary at twelve pounds each and two benefits of one hundred and fifty pounds each, making a total of six hundred and sixty pounds for 180 nights' performances. He was therefore a gainer not only in the saving of bodily exertion, but in the sum of one thousand and seventy-three pounds and nineteen shillings by his fortunate and unlooked-for expulsion from Sadler's Wells.

In February 1818 Grimaldi received several intimations that if he chose to make application to the proprietors of Sadler's Wells, he might return almost upon his own terms; but he declined doing so, partly from feeling rather annoyed at the manner in which he had been treated, and partly from discovering how well provincial excursions answered in a pecuniary point of view, and how much more conducive they were to his health than remaining in town. Nevertheless, when Mrs Hughes, the widower of his friend, waited upon him and entreated him herself to return, he scarcely knew how to refuse, and at last told her that if he returned at all to that establishment it must be as a part proprietor. Grimaldi said this thinking that it would either release him from any further requests to go back to Sadler's Wells, or enable him to share in the profits which had been for many years accruing to the proprietors. But in this idea, as in many others, he was totally mistaken. After some little preliminaries, in the shape of meetings, discussions, waiving of objections, etc, the proposal was accepted, and he became the purchaser of a certain number of shares in Sadler's Wells from Mrs Hughes herself. This being arranged, Grimaldi accepted an engagement for the ensuing season upon his old terms, merely bargaining that he should be permitted to leave town about the end of July for six weeks in each year, to fulfil provincial engagements.

The Covent Garden season terminated on July the seventeenth (sixteenth), and his benefit at Sadler's Wells, which occurred two nights afterwards, being over (the receipts were two hundred and forty-three pounds and nineteen shillings) Grimaldi left town to fulfil the engagements he had entered into with country managers. He went first to Liverpool, where he acted from July the twenty-seventh until August the nineteenth; his profits amounted to three hundred and twenty-seven pounds, being two pounds and a few shillings more than the result of his previous visit. Thence he went to Lancaster, the theatre of which town, like the one at Berwick, he found up a stable-yard, but very neat and commodious. Here he played two nights, for which he received one hundred and eleven pounds and sixteen shillings. From there he went to Newcastle-upon-Tyne, where he performed five nights, realising two hundred and forty-three pounds and fourteen shillings as his share of the profits.

During Grimaldi's stay at Newcastle, he recollected that the best pickled salmon sold in London was called by that name and came from thence, and he resolved to have a feast of it, naturally concluding that he should procure it in high perfection in the place whence it was brought for sale. Accordingly, one evening he ordered some to be got ready for supper upon his return from the theatre. The waiter of the hotel he was staying at promised this should be done, but in so curious a manner that Grimaldi could not help fancying that he did not understand his meaning. He therefore asked the waiter if he had heard what he said.

"Oh dear, yes, sir!" was the reply. "I'll take care it shall be ready, sir."

This appeared to settle the point, and as soon as the play was over, Grimaldi returned to the inn, anticipating how much better the salmon would be than the London pickle. The cloth was duly spread, and a covered dish placed before him.

"Supper, sir—quite ready, sir," said the waiter, whisking away the cover, and presenting to Grimaldi's sight a mutton cutlet. "You'll find this excellent, sir."

"No doubt; but I ordered pickled salmon!"

"I beg your pardon, sir—did you, sir?" (with a slight appearance of confusion).

"Did I! Yes, to be sure I did. Do you mean to say you do not recollect it?"

"I may have forgotten it, sir; I suppose I *have* forgotten it, sir."

"Well, it does not matter much; I can make a supper of this. But don't forget to let me have some pickled salmon tomorrow evening."

"Certainly not, sir," was the waiter's answer; and so the matter ended for the night.

On the following evening, Grimaldi invited the manager, at the close of the performances, to go home and sup with him, which he willingly did. As on the preceding evening, the meal was prepared and awaiting their arrival. Down they sat, and upon the removal of the cover a rump-steak presented itself. A good deal surprised, Grimaldi said to the waiter:

"What's this! Have you forgotten the pickled salmon again?"

"Why, really, sir, dear me!" hesitated the man, "I believe I have—I really fancied you said you would have beef tonight, sir. Tomorrow night, sir, I'll take care that you have some."

"Now, mind that you *do* remember it, for tomorrow is the last day I shall be here, and I have a particular wish to taste some before I leave the town."

"Depend upon me, sir. You shall certainly have some tomorrow, sir," said the waiter. The manager preferred meat, so it was no great matter, and they took their hot supper very comfortably.

There was a crowded audience next night, which was Grimaldi's benefit, and the last of his performances. He played Acres and Clown, received the cash, bade farewell to the manager, and hurried to his inn, greatly fatigued by his performances, and looking forward with much pleasure to the pickled salmon.

"All right tonight, waiter?" he inquired.

"*All* right tonight, sir", said the waiter, rubbing his hands. "Supper is quite ready, sir."

"Good! Let me have my bill tonight, because I start early in the morning."

Grimaldi turned to the supper-table; there was a dish, with a cover: the waiter removed it with a flourish, and presented to his astonished eyes—not the long-expected pickled salmon, but a veal cutlet. These repeated disappointments were rather too much, so he pulled the bell with great vehemence and called for the landlord. Grimaldi having stated his grievance, he appeared to understand as little about the matter as his waiter; but at length, after many explanations, Grimaldi learned to his great surprise that pickled salmon was an article unknown in Newcastle, all of it being sent to London for sale. The brilliant waiter not having the remotest conception of what was wanted, and determined not to confess his ignorance, had resolved to try all the dishes in the most general request until he came to the right one.

Grimaldi saw a coal-mine on this expedition, his curiosity having been roused by the manager's glowing description. We should rather say that he went down into one, for his survey was brief enough. He descended some two or three hundred feet in a basket, and was met at the bottom of the shaft by a guide, who had not conducted him for when a piece of coal weighing about three tons fell with a loud noise upon a spot over which they had just passed.

"Hollo!" exclaimed Grimaldi, greatly terrified. "What's that?"

"Hech!" said the guide, "it's only a wee bit of cool fallen doon: we ha'e that two or three times a day."

"Have you?" replied Grimaldi, running back to the shaft. "Then I'll thank you to ring for my basket, or call out for it, for I'll stop here no longer."

The basket was lowered, and he ascended to the light without delay, having no wish whatever to take his chance again among the "wee bits of cool".

While upon this last expedition he received a letter from Mr Harris, in which that gentleman informed him that it would be necessary for him to be in London by the seventh of September to attend the opening of Covent Garden. In consequence of this Grimaldi was obliged to forego his Edinburgh engagement with Mr Murray, which annoyed him greatly, for he had calculated upon clearing pretty nigh five hundred pounds by that portion of his trip; besides, being at Newcastle, he was within one day's journey of Edinburgh. However, he was obliged to attend to the summons and so returned to London, where a few days afterwards he encountered Mr Harris, with whom he had the following vexatious colloquy.

"Ah, Joe!" Mr Harris exclaimed, with evident surprise, "why, I did not expect to see you for three weeks to come!"

"You did not, sir!" exclaimed Grimaldi, with at least an equal degree of astonishment.

"Certainly not; I thought you were going into Scotland."

"So I was; but I received a letter from you, recalling me to town by today; which summons I have obeyed, by sacrificing my Edinburgh excursion, and with it about five hundred pounds."

"Ah!" said Mr Harris, "I see now how all this is. I suppose you left Newcastle the same day as you received my letter?"

"I did, sir."

"That was unfortunate; for I changed my mind after writing that letter, and wrote again on the following day, giving you permission to stay away until the first week of October. Never

293

mind; as you *are* here, we'll find you something to do; we'll try *Mother Goose* for a night or two next week."

To this obliging promise Grimaldi made no reply, not deriving the smallest degree of comfort from it. Mr Harris, observing that his offer had failed in producing the intended effect, added, "And as to the loss of your Edinburgh engagement, that I must endeavour to make up to you in some way or other at a future time."

Joe thanked him for this kindness, and Mr Harris did not forget his promise.

The result of Grimaldi's first season's proprietorship at the Wells was far from propitious. At first all went on very well; but after he left (as previously stipulated) in July, the houses fell to nothing and when he arrived in town again in September, he was informed that there would be a clear loss instead of any profit. This both surprised and vexed him; for Sadler's Wells had always been considered a very good property, and he had fully expected that he should, merely upon becoming a proprietor, have to receive a sum of money yearly, in addition to his regular salary. The first proprietors' meeting which he attended occurred a few days after the close of the season; and when all the books and papers connected with the business of the theatre were produced it was found that a heavy loss was really attendant upon the year's campaign.

"And pray what may be the amount?" Grimaldi inquired, rather dolefully, for he now began to repent of his purchase, and to fancy that he saw all his recently acquired wealth fading away.

Mr Richard Hughes shook his head when he heard this question, and said, "Ah, Joe, the loss is three hundred and thirty-three pounds and thirteen shillings."

"Oh, come!" cried Grimaldi, "it's not so bad as I thought—three hundred and thirty-three pounds and thirteen shillings is not so much among six persons!" which was the number of proprietors at that time.

"Joe," said Mr Hughes, gravely, "is this the first meeting you have attended?"

"Yes."

"Ah, then I do not wonder that you have misunderstood me. What I meant was, that the loss to each person is three hundred and thirty-three pounds and thirteen shillings. The gross loss is six times that sum."

This communication was a very unexpected blow to all Grimaldi's hopes; but as there was nothing better to be done he paid his share of the money at once with as good a grace as he could assume, having thus gratified his wish to become a proprietor of Sadler's Wells by the expenditure, first, of a large sum of money for his shares, and secondly, of another sum of upwards of three hundred and thirty pounds at the end of the first season. Grimaldi anticipated other heavy demands upon his provincial gains of 1817 and 1818, and bitterly regretted having connected himself with the establishment in any other way than as a salaried actor.

The Christmas pantomime at Covent Garden was entitled *Baron Munchausen*, and proved as successful as its predecessors had done for some years. One night a fellow engaged as a carpenter, and whose business it likewise was to assist in holding a carpet in which the pantomime characters are caught when they jump through the scenes, went to Ellar who was the Harlequin, and holding up the carpet, said that it was very dry, thereby intimating in the cant phrase that he required something to drink. Ellar, from some cause or other, either because he had already fee'd the men liberally, or was engaged at the moment in conversation, returned some slight answer, unaccompanied by the required gratuity, and the fellow went away grumbling. On the following evening Ellar was informed that the man had been heard to talk about being revenged upon him; he only laughed at the threat, however, and all went on as usual until the third night afterwards, when, as he and Grimaldi were on the stage together, in the scene where he used to jump through the 'moon', Grimaldi was surprised to observe that Ellar hesitated, and still more so when, drawing close to him, Ellar said, in a whisper, "I am afraid they don't mean to catch me. I have knocked three times against the scene, and asked if they were ready; but nobody has said a word in reply."

"It's impossible," whispered Grimaldi. "I don't believe there is a man in the theatre who would dream of such a thing. Jump, man, jump."

Ellar still paused and Grimaldi, fancying that symptoms of impatience were beginning to appear among the audience, told him so, and again urged him not to stop the business of the scene, but to jump at once.

"Well, well," cried Ellar, "here goes!—but Heaven knows how it will end!" And in a complete state of uncertainty whether any men were there to catch him, or he was left to break his neck, he went through the scene. His fears were not without good reason; for the fellows whose business it was to hold the carpet were holding it, as they well knew, in a position where he could never reach it, and down he fell. Suspecting his danger while in the very act of going through the panel, he endeavoured to save his head by sacrificing his hand. In this he fortunately succeeded, as he sustained no other injury than breaking the hand upon which he fell. The accident occasioned him great pain and inconvenience, but he insisted on going through the part, and the audience were quite ignorant of the occurrence.

The circumstance was not long in reaching the ears of Mr Harris and Mr Fawcett, who were made acquainted not only with Ellar's accident but with the man's threat, and the occasion which had given rise to it. Fawcett immediately caused all the carpenters to assemble on the stage and told them that if Mr Ellar would undertake to say he believed the accident had been brought about wilfully, they should every one be discharged on the spot. Ellar being sent for, and informed that this was the proprietor's deliberate intention, replied without hesitation that he could not believe it was intentional, and whispered to Grimaldi as he left the house that the fellow had got a wife and half-a-dozen children dependent upon him. This praiseworthy resolution, which prevented several men from being thrown out of employment, was rendered all the more praiseworthy by Ellar's having no earthly doubt that the mistake was intentional, and by his knowing perfectly well that if he had fallen on his head in lieu of his hand he would most probably have been killed on the spot.

While upon the subject of stage accidents, we may remark that very few of these mischances befell Grimaldi, considering the risks to which a pantomime actor is exposed and the serious injuries he is constantly encountering. The hazards were not so great in Grimaldi's case as they would have been to any other man similarly situated, in as much as his Clown was a very quiet personage, so far as the use or abuse of his limbs was concerned, and by no means addicted to those violent contortions of body which are painful alike to actor and spectator. His Clown was an embodied conception of his own, whose humour was in his looks and not in his tumbles, and who excited the laughter of an audience while standing upon his heels and not upon his head.

While playing in *Baron Munchausen* at Covent Garden one evening very shortly after Ellar's accident, Grimaldi observed his Highness the Duke of York, accompanied by Sir Godfrey Webster and another gentleman, sitting in his Royal Highness's private box, and laughing very heartily at the piece. Upon his coming off the stage about the middle of the pantomime, he found Sir Godfrey waiting for him.

"Hard work, Grimaldi!"

"Hard and hot, Sir Godfrey!"

"Have a pinch of snuff, Grimaldi," said Sir Godfrey, "it will refresh you." With this he produced from behind him, where he had been holding it, the largest snuff-box Grimaldi had ever beheld. The sight of it amused him much. Sir Godfrey laughed and said, "Take it to that gentleman," pointing to the Pantaloon, who was on the stage, "and see if he would like a pinch."

Grimaldi willingly complied, and having shortly afterwards to enact a foppish scene, swaggered about the stage, ostentatiously displaying this huge box, which from its enormous size really looked like a caricature made expressly for the purpose, and offered a pinch to the Pantaloon with all that affection of politeness in which he was so ludicrous. The audience laughed at its gigantic size, and the Pantaloon, looking suspiciously at him, demanded:

"Where did you get this box?"

To this, affecting modest reserve and diffidence, the Clown made no answer but turned away his head.

"You've stolen it!" continued Pantaloon.

This the injured Clown strongly denied upon his honour, with many bows and slides, and averred it was a gift.

"Given to you!" cried the Pantaloon, "and, pray, who gave it to you?"

In answer to this, he pointed significantly to the box, whither Sir Godfrey had retired, and the merriment which this occasioned was great indeed. The Duke, to whom, as he discovered afterwards, the box belonged, was convulsed with laughter, nor were the gentlemen with him less merry, while the audience, either suspecting that some joke was afloat, or being amused at the scene, joined in the hearty laughter emanating from the royal box.

"Where are you going to take the box?" asked Pantaloon, as he turned to go off.

"Where it has often been before," cried Grimaldi, pointing upwards. "To my uncle's!" And so saying, he ran off the stage amid a fresh burst of merriment.

Sir Godfrey was with him in two minutes. Whether he thought the box was really in danger of being so disposed of, is uncertain, but he popped round behind the scenes as quickly as possible.

"Capital, Grimaldi!" he cried, still laughing; "you have won me a wager—so you ought to go smacks in it," and he slipped five guineas into his hand.

"So, so," said the Duke of York, who, unperceived by Grimaldi, had followed his friend. "This is the way stakes are divided, eh?—I'll tell you what, Sir Godfrey, although Mr Grimaldi is not a porter, I entertain no doubt that he would carry your box for you every evening upon such terms as these."

Having vented this joke, his Royal Highness returned to his box. As he was not often behind the scenes at the theatre, this was, with one exception, the only time Grimaldi encountered him.

CHAPTER FOURTEEN

B Y HIS SIX WEEKS' EXCURSION IN 1818 Grimaldi cleared six hundred and eighty-two pounds and twelve shillings but the disastrous result of the Sadler's Wells season and the expenditure of ready money in the purchase of his shares swallowed up nearly the whole of his gains in the provinces—so that notwithstanding his great success and the enormous sums he had so recently acquired, the autumn of 1818 found him still poor, and entirely dependent on his salary for support. He looked forward, however, to the next season in the hope that some success might repay a portion of the money he had already lost.

The opening of Sadler's Wells (in April 1819) was attended by many difficulties and embarrassments. Only ten days before the commencement of the season Mr Charles Dibdin suddenly relinquished his post of acting stage manager, and was with great difficulty prevailed upon to make the necessary arrangements for the first week. As he left the theatre at Whitsuntide and nobody could be found to supply his place Grimaldi was obliged to fill it himself and to relinquish, though with great unwillingness, his summer excursion, with all its advantages. He produced a new pantomime of his own invention, called *The Fates*, which ran the whole of the season and drew very good houses. The result was that when the books were made up at the end of the season each of the proprietors had something to receive; which was a very agreeable improvement on the untoward prospects with which the preceding year had opened.

Gradually, but surely, during the whole of this year Grimaldi felt his health sinking, and heavy and painful infirmities creeping upon him. He learnt when it was too late that if at this time he had retired from the profession and devoted one or two years to relaxation and quiet, his constitution would in all probability have rallied, and he would have been enabled to resume his usual occupations with every hope of being long able to perform them, instead of being compelled, as he eventually was, to quit the stage when he was little more than forty years old.

The Christmas pantomime at Covent Garden was *Harlequin Don Quixote*, which was not quite so successful as the pantomimes at that house usually had been, although Grimaldi played Sancho Panza in the opening, and afterwards Clown. Its success was so equivocal that another pantomime called *Harlequin and Cinderella* was produced in April; but this had no greater success than its predecessor. Having a few nights to spare in March he accepted a theatrical invitation from Lynn in Norfolk, where he acted four nights and received one hundred and sixty pounds.

At Sadler's Wells a new system had been acted upon. The authorities being greatly puzzled in the choice of a stage manager, and having received an offer from Mr Howard Payne to take the theatre for one season at a certain rental, agreed to let it. Mr Payne commenced his campaign at Easter, and a most unprofitable one it proved, for he lost a considerable sum of money, as did the proprietors also, and Grimaldi not unnaturally began to be weary of the speculation. As both his benefits, however, were bumpers, he left the theatre in good spirits in the month of September to fulfil an engagement at Dublin, little dreaming at the time that, with the exception of his farewell night, he was destined never again to act upon the Sadler's Wells stage.

Grimaldi's travelling companions were Ellar and his son, all three being engaged by Mr (Henry) Harris to act at his theatre in Dublin, and receiving permission to absent themselves from Covent Garden for that express purpose. Since Grimaldi's last journey to the Irish capital in 1805 roads and coaches had improved and steam-packets had supplied the place of the old sailing-boats, so that they reached their destination in half the time which the same journey had occupied before.

The theatre in which they were to act was called the Pavilion, and had formerly been an assembly-room. It was perfectly round, and very ill adapted for dramatic representations; the stage room, too, was so inconvenient, and they were so pressed for want of space, that when *Harlequin Gulliver* was in preparation, they were at a loss where to put the Brobdignagians. These figures were so very cumbersome and so much in the way, that the men who sustained the parts were at last obliged to be dressed and put away in an obscure corner before the curtain was raised, whence they were brought forward when wanted upon the stage, and into which they were obliged to retreat when they had no more to do, and to remain there as quietly as they could until the pantomime was over, there being no room to get them out of their cases. The dresses and makings-up were very cumbrous and inconvenient; but as no other mode of proceeding presented itself the unfortunate giants were obliged to make the best of a bad bargain, and to remain in a great state of perspiration and fatigue until they could be reduced to the level of ordinary men. Grimaldi pitied the poor fellows so much that after the first night's performance was over he thought right to represent to them that no relief could be afforded, and to ask whether they could make up their minds to endure so much labour for the future.

"Well, then," said the spokesman of the party, "we have talked it over together, and we have agreed to do it every night, if your honour—long life to you!—will only promise to do one thing for us; and that is, just to let us have a leetle noggin of whisky after the green rag comes down." This moderate request was readily complied with, and the giants behaved themselves exceedingly well, and never got drunk. The party stayed seven weeks at Dublin. Grimaldi made a great deal of money by the trip, and realised two hundred pounds by his benefit alone.

Between September 1820, when Covent Garden reopened, and Christmas, when the new pantomime was brought forward, Grimaldi frequently appeared as Kasrac in *Aladdin*, nor did his increasing infirmities render his performance more painful or wearisome than usual. The pantomime was called *Harlequin and Friar Bacon*, and was exceedingly successful, as it was received with great approbation, and was repeated for fifty-two nights. This season his son was for the first time regularly engaged at Covent Garden. He played Fribble in the opening, and afterwards the Lover, and bade fair to become a great public favourite.

Sadler's Wells was let at Easter, 1821, for the ensuing three seasons to Mr Egerton, well known to the public as a performer at Covent Garden. He and Grimaldi had been very good friends for many years; but some clauses were introduced into his agreement for hiring the theatre which Grimaldi as a proprietor so strongly disapproved that he refused to affix his signature to the document, and a coolness took place between them which was never afterwards removed. Notwithstanding this difference, he always continued to entertain a high respect for Egerton, who was greatly liked by his friends and the profession generally, and who had been at one period of his career a much better actor than the playgoers of the present day remember him. This gentleman was afterwards connected with Mr Abbott in the management of the Victoria Theatre (the Old Vic), in which speculation they both sustained considerable losses. Both are since dead.

On April the twenty-third Farley produced his melodrama of *Undine*, or *The Spirit of the Waters*, in which Grimaldi sustained a new character. In the autumn, Ellar, Grimaldi and his son again repaired to Dublin. *Friar Bacon* was played twenty-nine nights out of the thirty-two for which Grimaldi and his party were engaged, and the pieces were so successful that it would have been the interest of all parties to prolong their engagements if the arrangements at Covent Garden had admitted of their doing so. It was at this period, that, with an agony of mind perfectly indescribable, Grimaldi found his health giving way by alarming degrees beneath the ravages of premature old age. On the eighteenth night of their performance in Dublin he became so ill that he was obliged to throw up his part at a very short notice and to send immediately for medical aid. He was attended by one of the most eminent physicians in Dublin, and under his treatment recovered sufficiently to be enabled to resume his character in about a week. But he felt, although he could not bear to acknowledge it even to himself, that his restoration to health was only temporary, that his strength was rapidly failing him, that his limbs grew weaker, and his frame became more shaken every succeeding day, and that utter decrepitude, with its long train of miseries and privations, was coming upon him. His presentiments were but too fully realised, but the realisation of his worst fears came upon him with a rapidity which even he, conscious as he was of all the symptoms, had never deemed possible. The successful sojourn of the party at Dublin at length drew to a close, as it was necessary that they should return to London to be in readiness for the pantomime. On the sixth of December 1821 they bade farewell to Ireland, and after a most boisterous voyage landed at Holyhead, whence they posted in haste to town, and the day after their arrival began the rehearsals for Christmas. Grimaldi was terribly shaken by the journey home and the sea-sickness, and felt worse in point of general health than he had yet done.

The pantomime was *The Yellow Dwarf.* Although the performers began to rehearse at an unusually late period, its success was perfect; but, notwithstanding it ran forty-four nights, Grimaldi never thought it a favourite with the public. He himself played the Yellow Dwarf, and his son played a part called 'Guinea Pig'. *Cherry and Fair Star* was revived at Easter, in consequence of its great success in the previous season, and answered the purpose extremely well.

During the whole of this summer Grimaldi's health gradually but steadily declined. Sometimes there were slight fluctuations for the better, in which he felt so much improved as to fancy that his strength was beginning to return; and although the next day's decay and lassitude showed but too clearly that they were but brief intervals of strength, he fondly regarded these red-letter days as tokens of a real and permanent change for the better. Perhaps even now, as he had nothing to do at Sadler's Wells and was too unwell to accept country engagements, if he had remained quiet during the Covent Garden recess, lived with great regularity, and acted upon the best medical advice, he might have retained for many years longer some portion of his health and spirits. But Mr Glossop, who was then the lessee of the Coburg Theatre (now the Victoria), made him an offer which he could not resist, and he acted there for six weeks, at a considerable sum per week and a free benefit. The engagement turned out so profitable a one for the management that he might have renewed it for the same space of time if he had not become too ill to appear upon the stage.

At this crisis of his disorder Grimaldi was advised to try the Cheltenham waters. He went to Cheltenham in August, and being somewhat recovered by the change of air, consented to act for Farley and Abbott, who had taken the theatre on speculation, for twelve nights. He cleared one hundred and fifty pounds and whether this sum of money, or the waters, or the change of scene revived him is uncertain, but he felt greatly improved in health when he returned to London for the opening of Covent Garden, to commence what ultimately proved to be his last season at that theatre.

Harlequin and the Ogress, or *The Sleeping Beauty*, was the pantomime of the season (1822–3). The rehearsals went off very briskly, and the piece met with the success which generally attended the production of pantomimes at that house. Nothing, indeed, could exceed the liberality displayed by Mr Harris in getting up this species of entertainment; to which circumstance, in a great measure, the almost uniform success of the pantomimes may be attributed. This spirit was not confined to the stage and its appointments, but was also extended in an unusual degree to the actors. Every suggestion was readily listened to, and as readily acted upon, if it appeared at all reasonable: every article of dress was provided at the expense of the management; the principal actors were allowed a pint of wine each, every night the pantomime was played, and on the evening of its first representation they were invited to a handsome dinner at the Piazza coffee-house, whither they all repaired directly the rehearsal was over. At these dinners Farley took the chair, while Brandon acted as vice; and there is no doubt that they materially contributed to the success of the pantomimes. There can be no better means of securing the hearty good-will and co-operation of the parties employed in undertakings of this or any other description than treating them in a spirit of generosity and courtesy.

In this pantomime Grimaldi played a part (in the opening) with the very pantomimic name of 'Grimgribber'—and that sustained by his son (in the harlequinade) was expressively described in the bills as 'Whirligig'. It ran until nearly the following Easter, when a new melodrama by Farley appeared, called *The Vision of the Sun* or *The Orphan of Peru*. In this piece, which came out on the twenty-third of March 1823, Grimaldi played a prominent character (Tycobrac, slave to an enchanter), but even during the earlier nights of its very successful representation he could scarcely struggle through his part. His frame was weak and debilitated, his joints stiff, and his muscles relaxed; every effort he made was followed by cramps and spasms of the most agonizing nature. Men were obliged to be kept waiting at the side-scenes, who caught him in their arms when he staggered from the stage and supported him while others chafed his limbs—which was obliged to be incessantly done until he was called for the next scene, or he could not have appeared again. Every time he came off his sinews were gathered up into huge knots by the cramps that followed his exertions, which could only be reduced by violent rubbing, and even that frequently failed to produce the desired effect. The spectators, who were convulsed with laughter while he was on the stage, little thought that while their applause was resounding through the house he was suffering the most excruciating and horrible pains. But so it was until the twenty-fourth night of the piece, when Grimaldi had no alternative, in consequence of his intense sufferings, but to throw up the part.

On the preceding night, although every possible remedy was tried, Grimaldi could scarcely drag himself through the piece; and on this occasion it was only with the most extreme difficulty and by dint of extraordinary physical exertion and agony that he could conclude the performance, when he was carried to his dressing-room exhausted and powerless. Here, when his bodily anguish had in some measure subsided, he began to reflect seriously on his sad condition. And when he remembered how long this illness had been hovering about him, how gradually it had crept over his frame, and subdued his energies, with what obstinacy it had baffled the skill of the most eminent medical professors, and how utterly his powers had wasted away beneath it, he came to the painful conviction that his professional existence was over. Enduring from this terrible certainty a degree of anguish, to which all his bodily sufferings were as nothing, he covered his face with his hands and wept like a child. The next morning he sent word to the theatre that he was disabled by illness from performing. His son studied the part in one day, and played it that night with considerable success. The piece was performed forty-four nights during the season; but although Grimaldi afterwards rallied a little, he never attempted to resume the part.

In spite of all his sufferings, which were great, and a settled foreboding that his course was run, it was some years before hope deserted him: and for a long time, from day to day he encouraged hopes of being at some future period able to resume the avocations in which he had spent his life.

Grimaldi repaired again, in the month of August, to Cheltenham, recollecting that it had had some beneficial effect on his health in the previous year. During his stay he so far recovered as to be enabled to play a few nights at the theatre, then under the management of Mr Farley. Here he encountered Mr Bunn, who informed him that Mr Charles Kemble was then starring at Birmingham, and that Colonel Berkeley having promised to act for his benefit, he had come over to Cheltenham to ascertain what part the Colonel would wish to play. Mr Bunn added that he was there as much for the purpose of seeing Grimaldi as with any other object, as he wanted him to put a little money into both their purses, by playing a few nights at Birmingham. Grimaldi declined at first, but being pressed, and tempted by Mr Bunn's offer, consented to act for two nights only, the receipts to be divided between them.

It was Mr Charles Kemble's benefit night when Grimaldi and his son arrived at Birmingham; and as that gentleman was a great favourite there, as indeed he was everywhere throughout his brilliant career, Grimaldi entertained some fears that the circumstance would prove prejudicial to his interests. He sought a few moments conversation with Mr Kemble in the course of the evening, and informed him that his son had received an offer of eight pounds per week from the Drury Lane management, but that rather than he should leave Covent Garden, with which his father had now been connected so long and where he had experienced so much liberality, young Joe was ready to accept an engagement there at six pounds per week, if agreeable to the proprietors.

"Joe," said Mr Charles Kemble, "your offer is a very handsome one, and I agree to it at once. Your son is now engaged with us on the terms you have mentioned."

They shook hands and parted. Grimaldi strolled into the greenroom and there met Colonel Berkeley, who, after a short conversation, said that he very much wished to play Valentine to his Orson: to which Grimaldi replied that it would give him great pleasure to afford him the opportunity whenever he felt disposed.

"Very well," said Colonel Berkeley, "then we will consider the matter settled. As soon as you have done here, you must come to Cheltenham for one night. I will make all necessary arrangements with Farley—your son shall play the Green Knight, and I will give you one hundred pounds as a remuneration. We will try what we can do together, Joe, to amuse the people."

Grimaldi had not intended to act again after his Birmingham engagement, until the production of the Christmas pantomime at Covent Garden; but seeing that Colonel Berkeley was anxious to effect the arrangements, and feeling grateful for the liberality of his offer, he pledged himself without hesitation to accept his terms. The play was never done, however, by these three performers, for Grimaldi's theatrical career was over.

The night after Mr Charles Kemble's benefit Grimaldi produced a little pantomime of his own, called *Puck and the Puddings*. The hit was so complete and the sensation he excited so great that he felt infinitely better than he had done for a long time, and was, indeed, so greatly restored that he was induced to accept an engagement for one additional night, the success of which equalled—it could not excel—that of the two previous evenings. When the curtain fell on the third night, Mr Bunn presented him with one hundred and eighty-six pounds and twelve shillings as his share of the profits, accompanied with many wishes for his speedy and perfect restoration to health, which Grimaldi himself, judging from his unwonted spirit and vigour, cheerfully hoped might be yet in store for him. These hopes were never to be realised: the enthusiastic receptions he had met with—unusually enthusiastic even for him—had roused him for a brief period, and called forth all his former energies only to hasten their final prostration. With the exception of his two farewell benefits, this was his last appearance, his final exit from the boards he had trodden from a child, the last occasion of his calling forth those peals of merriment and approbation which, cheerfully as they sounded to him, had been surely ringing his death-knell for many years.

Grimaldi slept at Birmingham the night after his closing performance, and on the following morning returned to Cheltenham, where he was attacked by a severe and alarming illness, which for more than a month confined him to his bed, whence he rose at last a cripple for life.

From the period at which we have now arrived, down to within a year or so of his death, Grimaldi experienced little or nothing but one constant succession of afflictions and calamities, the pressure of which nearly bowed him to the earth; afflictions which it is painful to contemplate, and a detailed account of which would be neither instructive nor entertaining. A tale of unmitigated suffering, even when that suffering be mental, possesses but few attractions for the reader; but when, as in this case, a large portion of it is physical, it loses even the few attractions which the former would possess and grows absolutely distasteful. Bearing these circumstances in mind, we shall follow Grimaldi's example in this particular, and study in the remaining pages of his life to touch as lightly as we can upon the heavy catalogue of his calamities, and to lay no unnecessary stress upon this cheerless portion of his existence.

Independent of his sufferings of the body, he had to encounter mental afflictions of no ordinary kind. He was devotedly attached to his son, who was his only child, for whom he had always entertained the most anxious solicitude, whom he had educated at a great expense, and upon whom a considerable portion of the earnings of his best days had been most liberally bestowed. Up to this time young Grimaldi had well repaid all the care and solicitude of his parents: he had risen gradually in the estimation of the public, had increased every year in prosperity, and still remained at home his father's friend and companion. It is a matter of pretty general notoriety that the young man ran a reckless and vicious course, and in no time so shocked and disgusted even those who were merely brought into contact with him at the theatre for a few hours in a night, that it was found impossible to continue his engagements.

The first notification his father received of his folly and extravagance was during their stay at Cheltenham, when one morning, shortly after Grimaldi had risen from his sick-bed, he was waited upon by one of the town authorities, who informed him that his son was then locked up for some drunken freaks committed overnight. Grimaldi instantly paid everything that was demanded, and procured his son's release; but in some skirmish with the constables, Young Joe had received a severe blow on the head from a staff, which, crushing his hat, alighted on the skull and inflicted a desperate wound. It is supposed that this unfortunate event disordered his intellects, as from that time, instead of the kind and affectionate son he had previously been, he became a wild and furious savage; he was frequently attacked with dreadful fits of epilepsy, and continually committed actions which nothing but madness could prompt. In 1828 he had a decided attack of insanity, and was confined in a strait-jacket in his father's house for some time. As no disorder of mind had appeared in him before, and as his miserable career may be dated from this time, it is not unreasonable to suppose that the wound he received at Cheltenham was among the chief causes of his short-lived delirium.

They returned to London together in 1823, and for the next three months Grimaldi consulted the most eminent medical men in the hope of recovering some portion of his lost health and strength. During that time he suffered an intensity of anxiety which it is difficult to conceive, as their final decision upon the remotest probability of his recovery was postponed from day to day. All their efforts were in vain, however. Towards the end of October (1823) Grimaldi received a final intimation that it was useless for him to nourish any hope of recovering the use of his limbs, and that although nature, assisted by great care on his part and the watchfulness of his medical attendants, might certainly alleviate some of his severe pain, his final recovery was next to impossible, and he must make up his mind to relinquish every thought of resuming the exercise of his profession. Among the gentlemen to whose kindness and attention he was greatly indebted in this stage of his trials, were, Sir Astley Cooper, Sir Matthew Tierney, Mr Abernethy, Dr Farr, Dr Temple, Dr Uwins, Dr Mitchell, Mr Thomas and Mr James Wilson. To all these gentlemen he was personally unknown; but they all attended him gratuitously, and earnestly requested him to apply to them without reserve upon every occasion when it was at all likely that they could be of the slightest assistance.

It was with no slight despair that Grimaldi received the announcement that for the rest of his days he was a cripple, possibly the constant inmate of a sick-room, and that he had not even a distant prospect of resuming the occupations to which he had been attached from his cradle, and from which he was enabled up to this time to realise an annual income of one thousand five hundred pounds: and all this without any private fortune of resources, with the exception of his shares in Sadler's Wells Theatre, which had hitherto proved a dead loss. For some hours after this opinion of his medical men had been communicated to him he sat stupefied with the heaviness of the calamity, and fell into a state of extreme mental distress, from which it was a long time before he was thoroughly roused. As soon as he could begin to exercise his reason he recollected that it was a duty he owed to his employers to inform them of his inability to retain his situation at Covent Garden, the more especially as it was time they made some arrangements for the ensuing Christmas pantomime. Accordingly, he sent a note to the theatre, acquainting them with his melancholy condition, and the impossibility of his fulfilling his articles (which had only been entered into the preceding January, and were for three years,) and recommending them to engage without loss of time some other individual to supply his place.

The communication was received with much kindness and many good wishes for Grimaldi's recovery. After several interviews and much consideration it was resolved that his son should be brought out as principal Clown in the ensuing Christmas pantomime. J S Grimaldi appeared for the first time on the twenty-sixth of December 1823 in that character in the pantomime of *Harlequin and Poor Robin*, or *The House That Jack Built*, and his success was complete. His father sat in the front of the house on his first night, and was no less gratified by his reception in public than by the congratulations which poured upon him when he went round behind the stage and found everybody delighted with the result of the trial. The pantomime proved very successful: it had an extended run, and the proprietors of the theatre, highly satisfied with the young man's success, with much liberality cancelled his existing articles, which were for six pounds per week, and entered into a new agreement by which they raised his salary to eight pounds. To Grimaldi, also, they behaved in a most handsome manner; for although his regular salary was, as a matter of course, stopped from the day on which he communicated his inability to perform, they continued to allow him five pounds a week for the remainder of the season; an act of much consideration and kindness on their part, and a far greater token of their recollection of his services than he had ever expected to receive.

The three years for which Egerton had taken Sadler's Wells having now expired, he was requested by the proprietors to state what views he entertained as to retaining or giving up the property. It being found impossible to comply with his terms, and a Mr Williams, who at that time had the Surrey, having made an offer for the theatre, they agreed to let it to him for one season. Soon after this agreement was entered into, Williams called upon Grimaldi one morning upon business, and in the course of the interview the latter inquired by what plan he proposed to make both theatres answer.

"Why, Mr Grimaldi," replied Williams, "if two theatres could be kept open at the same expense as one, and the company equally—mind, I say *equally*—good, don't you think it very likely that the speculation would succeed?"

"Yes, I think it would," rejoined Grimaldi, doubtfully, for as yet he understood nothing of the manager's drift. "I think it would."

"And so do I," said the other, "and that's the way I mean to manage. I mean to work the two theatres with one and the same company: I mean to employ one-half of the company in the earlier part of the evening at Sadler's Wells, and then to transfer them to the Surrey, to finish there; at that theatre I shall do precisely the same: and I am now having carriages built expressly to convey them backwards and forwards."

This system, which has since been tried (without the carriages) at the two great houses, was actually put in practice. On Easter Monday, 1824, the carriages began to run, and the two seasons commenced. The speculation turned out as Grimaldi had anticipated—a dead failure: the lessee lost some money himself, and got greatly into debt with the proprietors; upon which, fearing to increase their losses, they took measures to recover possession of the theatre. When they obtained it, they were obliged to finish the season themselves; by which, as they had never contemplated such a proceeding and had made no preparations for it, they sustained a very considerable loss.

It was in this year of 1824 that Grimaldi had the other opportunity, referred to in a previous chapter, of conversing with the Duke of York. His Royal Highness took the chair at the Theatrical Fund dinner, and kindly inquiring after Joe's health of someone who sat near him, desired to see him. Grimaldi was officiating as one of the stewards, but was of course surprised at the Duke's wish, and immediately presented himself. The Duke received him with great kindness, and hearing from his own lips that his infirmities had compelled him to relinquish the exercise of his profession, said he was extremely sorry to hear Grimaldi say so, but heartily trusted, notwithstanding, that he might recover yet, for his loss would be a "national calamity". He added, when Grimaldi expressed his acknowledgements, "I remember your father well: he was a funny man, and taught me and some of my sisters to dance. If ever I can be of any service to you, Grimaldi, call upon me freely."

In this year Grimaldi was much troubled by pecuniary matters and the conduct of his son. He was living on the few hundred pounds he had put by, selling out his stock, spending the proceeds, and consequently rising every morning a poorer man. His son, who had now a good salary and was rising in his profession, suddenly left his home, and, to the heart-rending grief of his father and mother, abandoned himself to every species of wild debauchery and riot. His father wrote to him, imploring him to return, and offering to make every arrangement that could conduce to his comfort, but Young Joe never answered the letter and kept on his headlong course.

This shock was a heavy one indeed, and in Grimaldi's weak and debilitated state it almost broke his heart.

For four years Grimaldi never saw any more of his son, save occasionally on the stage of Sadler's Wells, where he was engaged at a salary of five pounds per week; or when he met him in the street, when the son would cross over the road to get out of the way. Nor during all this time did he receive a single line from him, except in 1825. He had written to the young man, describing the situation to which he was reduced and the poverty with which he was threatened, reminding him that between the two theatres Young Joe was now earning thirteen pounds per week, and requesting his assistance with some pecuniary aid. To this application his son at first returned no reply; but several of Grimaldi's friends having expressed a very strong opinion to him on the subject, he at length returned the following note:

Dear Father, At present I am in difficulties; but as long as I have a shilling, you shall have half.

This assurance looked well enough upon paper, but had no other merit; for he never sent his father a farthing, nor did he again see him (save that he volunteered his services at two farewell benefits) until he came to Grimaldi's door one night in 1828, and hardily claimed shelter and food.

In 1825 the proprietors of Sadler's Wells resolved to open the theatre on their joint account, with which view they secured the services of Mr T Dibdin as acting-manager. It was determined at a meeting of proprietors that it would be advantageous to the property if one of their number were resident on the premises to assist Mr Dibdin and regulate the expenditure. As Grimaldi had nothing to do, it was proposed in the kindest manner by Mr Jones, one of the shareholders, that he should fill the situation, at a salary of four pounds per week. It need scarcely be said that he accepted this proposal with great gratitude. They commenced the season with much spirit, turning the old dwelling-house partly into wine-rooms according to the old fashion, and partly into a saloon, box-office, and passages. The dresses of the opening piece were of a gorgeous description, and every new play was got up with the same magnificence. They also determined to take half-price, which had never before been done at that house, and to play the twelve months through, instead of confining the season to six; this last resolution originating in the immense growth of the neighbourhood round the theatre, which in Grimaldi's time had gradually been transformed from a pretty suburban spot into the maze of streets and squares and closely-clustered houses which it now presents. These arrangements were all very extensive and speculative; but they overstepped the bounds of moderation in point of expense, and the season ended with a loss of fourteen hundred pounds.

Next year they pursued a different plan, and reduced their expenditure in every department. This reduction was superintended by Grimaldi, and the very first salary he cut down was his own, from which he struck off at once two pounds per week. They tried pony-races, too, in the area attached to the theatre, and, so variable is theatrical property, cleared a sum equal to their losses of the preceding year between Easter and Whitsuntide alone. The following season was also a successful one, and at length he began to think he should gain something by the proprietorship.

It was about this time, or rather before, that Grimaldi was sub-poenaed as a witness in an action between two theatrical gentlemen, of whom Mr Glossop was one, when his smart parrying of a remark from a counsel engaged in the case occasioned much laughter in court. On his name being called, and his appearing in the witness-box, there was some movement in the court, which was very crowded, the people being anxious to catch a sight of a witness whose name was so familiar. Sir James Scarlett, who was to examine him, rose as he made his appearance, and, looking at him with great real or apparent interest, said, "Dear me! Pray, sir, are you the great Mr Grimaldi, formerly of Covent Garden Theatre?"

The witness felt greatly confused at this inquiry, especially as it seemed to excite to a still higher pitch the curiosity of the spectators. He reddened slightly, and replied, "I used to be a pantomime actor, sir, at Covent Garden Theatre."

"Yes," said Sir James Scarlett, "I recollect you well. You are a very clever man, sir." He paused for a few seconds, and, looking up in his face, said, "And so you really are Grimaldi, are you?"

This was more embarrassing than the other question, and Grimaldi feeling it so, fidgeted about in the box, and grew redder and redder.

"Don't blush, Mr Grimaldi, pray don't blush; there is not the least occasion for blushing," said Sir James Scarlett.

"I don't blush, sir," rejoined the witness.

"I assure you, you need not blush so."

"I beg your pardon, sir, I really am not blushing," repeated the witness, who beginning to grow angry, repeated it with so red a face, that the spectators tittered aloud.

"I assure you, Mr Grimaldi," said Sir James Scarlett, smiling, "that you *are* blushing violently."

"I beg your pardon, sir," replied Grimaldi, "but you are really quite mistaken. The flush which you observe on my face is a *Scarlet* one, I admit; but I assure you that it is nothing more than a reflection from your own."

The people in the court shouted with laughter, and Sir James Scarlett, joining in their mirth, proceeded without further remark with the business of the case.

CHAPTER FIFTEEN

IN FEBRUARY 1828 a very highly-esteemed and kind friend to Grimaldi, and an actress of deserved popularity, whose wonderful talents have gained for her universal praise and an ample fortune, and whose performances have been for many years the delight and admiration of the public—Miss Kelly—called at his house to inquire after his health, and to ascertain whether it was probable that he would ever again be enabled to appear upon the stage. Grimaldi replied, with natural emotion, that he could no longer dare even to hope that he should ever act more.

"Then," asked Miss Kelly, "why not take a farewell benefit? I dare say you are not so rich as to despise the proceeds of such an undertaking."

Grimaldi shook his head, and replying that he was much poorer than anybody supposed, proceeded to lay before her his exact position, not omitting to point out that whenever Sadler's Wells was again let by the proprietors he would certainly lose his situation, and thus be deprived of his sole dependence. As to taking a benefit, he said, he felt so ill and depressed that he could not venture to undergo the labour of getting one up. Far less would his pecuniary means warrant his incurring the chance of a loss.

"Leave it all to me," said Miss Kelly. "and I'll arrange pretty nearly everything for you without a moment's loss of time. There must be two benefits, one at Sadler's Wells and the other at Covent Garden. The former benefit must take place first, so you go and consult the proprietors upon the subject at once, and I'll lose no time in furthering your interests elsewhere."

The promptitude and decision which Miss Kelly so kindly evinced infused something of a similar spirit into the invalid. He promised that he would see the proprietors immediately; and, in spite of a severe attack of spasms, which almost deprived him of speech, went that same night to Sadler's Wells and stated his intention to take a farewell benefit. He was received with the greatest friendship and liberality: they at once entered into his views, and gave an unanswerable proof of the sincerity with which they did so, by offering him the use of the house gratuitously. Monday, the seventeenth of March was fixed for the occasion; and no sooner was it known decidedly when the benefit was to take place than Mr T Dibdin, assembling the company, acquainted them with the circumstance and suggested that their offering to play gratuitously would be both a well-timed compliment and a real assistance. The hint was no sooner given than it was most cheerfully responded to—the performers immediately proffered their services, the band did the same, and every person in the theatre was anxious and eager to render every assistance in his or her power, and to "put their shoulders to the wheel, in behalf of poor Old Joe".

The following is a copy of the bill of performance put forth on this occasion:

SADLER'S WELLS,
Mr Grimaldi's Night,
And Last Appearance at this Theatre,
Monday, March 17th, 1828

It is most respectfully announced that Mr Grimaldi, from severe and incessant indisposition, which has oppressed him upwards of four years, and continues without any hope of amelioration, finds himself compelled to quit the profession in which, from almost infancy, he has been honoured with as great a share of patronage and indulgence as ever fell to the lot of any candidate for public favour. Nor can he quit a theatre where his labours commenced, and were for so many years sanctioned, without attempting the honour of personally expressing his gratitude; and however inadequate he may prove to paint the sincerity of his feelings, it is his intention to offer an address of thanks to his friends and patrons, and conclude his services with the painful duty of bidding them

FAREWELL

The entertainments will commence with the successful romance of Sixes, or The Fiend; *Hock (a drunken prisoner) by Mr Grimaldi. After which, the favourite burletta of* Humphrey Clinker; *to which will be added the popular farce of* Wives and Partners; *and the whole to conclude with a grand Masquerade on the stage, in the course of which several novelties will be presented—Mr Blackmore on the corde volante; Mr Walbourn's dance as 'Dusty Bob'; Mr Campbell's song of* Bound 'Prentice to a Waterman; *Mrs Searle's skipping-rope dance; Mr Payne's juggling evolutions; and the celebrated dance between Mr J S Grimaldi and Mr Ellar. After which, Mr Grimaldi will deliver his farewell address: and the whole will conclude with a brilliant display of fireworks, expressive of*

GRIMALDI'S THANKS

The house was crowded to suffocation on the night. He performed the trifling part for which he had been announced in the first piece with considerable difficulty but immense approbation, and in the stage of the performance in which it was announced in the bills of the day, came forward to deliver his farewell address, which ran thus:

"Ladies and Gentlemen—I appear before you this evening for the last time at this theatre. Doubtless, there are many persons present who think that I am a very aged man: I have now an opportunity of convincing them to the contrary. I was born on the 18th of December 1779, and consequently, on the 18th of last December attained the age of forty-eight.

"At a very early age—before that of three years, I was introduced to the public by my father at this theatre; and ever since that period have I held a situation in this establishment. Yes, ladies and gentlemen, I have been engaged at this theatre for five-and-forty years. By strict attention, perseverance, and exertion did I arrive at the height of my profession, and, proud I am to acknowledge, have oftimes been honoured with your smiles, approbation, and support. It is now three years since I have taken a regular engagement, owing to extreme and dangerous indisposition: with patience have I waited in hopes that my health might once more be re-established, and I again meet your smiles as before; but, I regret to say, there is little, or, in fact, no improvement perceivable, and it would therefore now be folly in me ever to think of again returning to my professional duties.

"I could not, however, leave this theatre without returning my grateful thanks to my friends and patrons, and the public; and now do I venture to offer them, secure in the conviction that they will not be slighted or deemed utterly unworthy of acceptance.

"To the proprietors of this theatre, the performers, the gentlemen of the band—in fact, to every individual connected with it, I likewise owe and offer my sincere thanks for their assistance this evening. And now, ladies and gentlemen, it only remains for me to utter one dreadful word, ere I depart— Farewell!—God bless you all! May you and your families ever enjoy the blessings of health and happiness!—Farewell!"

Grimaldi was received and listened to in the kindest and most encouraging manner; but his spirits met with so severe a shock in bidding a formal farewell to his friends, that he did not entirely recover from the effects of it for some days, and so completely dreaded going through a similar ordeal at Covent Garden, that, had not Miss Kelly kept him firm to the task he would have abandoned his intention with regard to the latter place altogether.

The receipts of his benefit were two hundred and thirty pounds; but Grimaldi received a great number of anonymous letters containing remittances, which amounted in the whole to eighty-five pounds more; so that he cleared by the night's performance a total of three hundred and fifteen pounds, which was a well-timed and most fortunate assistance to him.

On the twenty-fifth of March, being a little recovered and having at last made up his mind to take the second benefit, Grimaldi walked to Covent Garden, and having been warmly welcomed by the performers, went to Mr Charles Kemble's room and was received by him in the most friendly manner.

"Well, Joe," said Mr Kemble, "I hope you have come to say that you feel able to be with us again?"

"Indeed, my dear sir, it is unfortunately quite the reverse; for I am come to tell you that I never shall act more."

"I am very sorry to hear you say so, Joe; I have been in hopes it would be otherwise," returned Mr Kemble.

"We have known each other a good many years, sir," said Grimaldi.

"We have indeed, Joe—many years!"

"And I think, sir," continued Grimaldi, "that if it were in your power, you would willingly serve me?"

"Try me, Joe, try me!"

He then stated his intention of taking a farewell benefit at Covent Garden, and requested Mr Kemble's assistance in obtaining the use of the house; if possible at a low price but if not, then upon the usual terms. Mr Kemble listened until he had finished, and said, "My dear Joe, I perfectly understand you; and if the theatre were solely mine, I should say, 'Take it—'tis yours, and without charge at all': but, unfortunately, our theatre is in Chancery, and nothing can be done without the consent of others. However, Joe, the proprietors meet every Tuesday, and I will mention it to them. So after Tuesday you shall hear from me."

Grimaldi thanked Mr Kemble, and they parted. He awaited the arrival of the day fixed in great anxiety; but it came and passed, and so did another Tuesday, and several more days, without any intelligence arriving to relieve his suspense. Seeing it announced in the papers that Mr Kemble was about to proceed to Edinburgh, to act there, Grimaldi wrote a note to him, reminding him of what had passed between them, and requesting a reply. This was on April the thirteenth. In the evening of the same day he received an answer, not from Mr Kemble himself but from Mr Robertson, the respected treasurer of the theatre, which ran thus:

Dear Sir,

I am directed by the proprietors of this theatre to acquaint you, in reply to your application relative to a benefit, that they much regret that the present situation of the theatre with regard to Chancery proceedings will prevent the possibility of their accommodating your wishes.

The contents of this letter, of course, greatly disappointed and vexed Grimaldi, who, remembering the number of years he had been connected with the theatre and the great favourite he had been with the public, could not help deeming it somewhat harsh and unkind conduct on the part of the proprietors to refuse him the house for one night, for which, of course, he would have paid. Mr Price was the lessee of Drury Lane at this time, and once or twice Grimaldi thought of applying to him, but fearing it would be useless he dismissed the idea. In this state of indecision two or three weeks passed away, when one day he received a note from Mr Dunn, the Drury Lane treasurer, requesting him to attend at the theatre at twelve o'clock the next day, as Mr Price wished to see him. On complying with this very unexpected request, he was informed by Mr Dunn that the lessee had been compelled to meet another party on business and therefore could not wait to see him; but that he was deputed to say that he had been apprised of Grimaldi's wish to take a benefit, and that the theatre was at his service for the evening of Friday, the twenty-seventh of June 1828, the last night but one of the season. "That," added Mr Dunn, "is unfortunately the only evening we can offer you. Had Mr Price known earlier of your wishes, he would have had an extended choice of nights, and he would have felt happy in obliging so distinguished a veteran." Much delighted with this politeness and consideration Grimaldi gratefully accepted the theatre for the night mentioned. He was much puzzled at the time to think who could have mentioned the circumstance to Mr Price, and befriended him so greatly; on mature consideration, however, he had little doubt that it was Lord Segrave to whom he was obliged, for when he told Miss Kelly that he had been offered Drury Lane, she remembered Lord Segrave having expressed great surprise when she told him Grimaldi had been refused Covent Garden, and his having added that "he should see Price shortly".

Every assistance that could be afforded Grimaldi in arranging his benefit was cheerfully rendered. To three gentlemen in particular, for the valuable and cordial aid they rendered to the indefatigable exertions of Miss Kelly, he was under deep and lasting obligations. These were, Mr James Wallack, Mr W Barrymore, and Mr Peake, scarcely less a favourite with the public than with the members of the profession, to the literature of which his abilities and humour have long been successfully devoted.

About the middle of June, hearing that Mr Charles Kemble had returned from the north, Grimaldi resolved to call upon him and to thank him for the exertions which Grimaldi felt assured Mr Kemble had made relative to his benefit. He had another object in view—which was to apprise Mr Kemble that he had entered into engagements of a satisfactory nature at Drury Lane; which intelligence Grimaldi hoped would afford him unmitigated satisfaction, after the strong desire he had always expressed for his prosperity.

Mr Kemble was evidently surprised to hear this, and instead of manifesting the gratification which Grimaldi had expected, evinced feelings of a directly opposite nature. At length he exclaimed, "Take a benefit at Drury Lane!"

"Yes, sir," replied Grimaldi, "and knowing that you feel a great interest in my success, I have called upon you to thank you for all your past kindnesses, and to inform you what I intend doing on my farewell night."

With these words, he placed in Mr Kemble's hands an announce-bill, of which we subjoin a copy. These bills were afterwards recalled, for reasons which will presently appear.

THEATRE ROYAL, DRURY LANE
Mr GRIMALDI'S LAST APPEARANCE IN PUBLIC
On Friday, June 27th, 1828

It is respectfully announced, that Mr Grimaldi, after more than four years of severe and unremitting indisposition, which continues without hope of alleviation, is compelled, finally to relinquish a profession in which, from infancy, he has been honoured with as liberal a share of public patronage as ever has been accorded to candidates of much higher pretensions.

Numerous patrons having expressed surprise that Mr Grimaldi's benefit did not take place at the Theatre Royal, Covent Garden, he takes the liberty of stating, that after bidding farewell to his friends and supporters at Sadler's Wells (the scene of his favoured exertions from the early age of three years), he applied to the present directors of Covent Garden Theatre, who, in the kindest manner, expressed their regret that the well-known situation of the theatre precluded the possibility of indulging their strong inclination to comply with the request he had ventured to prefer. On transferring the application to Mr Price, the lessee of the Theatre Royal, Drury Lane, Mr Grimaldi has the pleasure to say, that it was acceded to with a celerity which enhanced the obligation, and demands his most sincere acknowledgement.

Mr Grimaldi made his first appearance at the Theatre Royal, Drury Lane, where he continued twenty-four years, and, but for a very trifling misunderstanding, might have retained his engagement to the present time: it is, however, most grateful to his feelings to finish his public labours on the spot where they commenced, and where for nearly a quarter-of-a-century his exertions were fostered by public indulgence, and stimulated by public applause.

To many anxious friends who, from a genuine spirit of goodwill, have inquired the cause why, during so long a period of professional exertion, Mr Grimaldi has not been able to realise a competency that might have precluded the necessity of this appeal, he can only plead the expenses attendant on infirmities, produced by exhausting and laborious duties, the destructive burthen of which were felt some years before he finally yielded to their pressure, and which at length compelled him to relax his exertions at the period when ability to continue them would have insured him a comfortable independence. However inadequate he may prove to the painful yet pleasing endeavour to express personally his gratitude on the night of his retreat, it is his intention to offer an address of thanks, in which, though mere words may not be equal to paint the depth and sincerity of his feelings, he will hope to gain credit for the heartfelt sensation of dutiful respect which accompanies his last farewell.

Mr Kemble read the bill through very attentively and laid it gently upon the table without saying a word, but still looking very much displeased. Grimaldi, not knowing very well what to say, remained silent, and nothing was said for a minute or two, when Fawcett entered the room.

"Here, Fawcett," said Mr Kemble. "Here's a bill for you—read that."

Fawcett read it in profound silence, and when he had done so, looked as if he could not at all understand what was going forward or what he ought to do. At length he asked what he was to infer from it, and Mr Kemble was about to reply when Grimaldi interrupted him.

"I beg your pardon, sir," he said, "but if Mr Fawcett is to be appealed to in this business, it is but just that before he expresses any opinion upon it he should understand all the circumstances."

With this, he proceeded to detail them as briefly as he could. When he had finished, Mr Kemble said, with an air of great vexation, "Why did you not say, that if you could not take a benefit here, you would do so at the other house! I declare you should have had a night for nothing, sooner than you should have gone there."

Although this remark was very unexpected, Grimaldi made no further reply than that he had never thought of applying to Mr Price, but that that gentleman, he presumed at the solicitude of some unknown friend, had made an offer to him; he then begged Mr Fawcett, as he now knew all, to express his opinion upon the matter.

"Why, really," said that gentleman, "had I been situated as Grimaldi has been, I should certainly have acted as he has done. If one theatre could not accommodate me and another could, I should feel no hesitation in accepting an offer from the latter. However," added Mr Fawcett, after this very manly and straightforward avowal, "I think it would be best, Grimaldi, and I hope you will take my advice, not to send out this bill. It might be deemed offensive, and cannot, as I see, be productive of any good whatever."

Grimaldi thanked him, and expressed his intention of acting upon his opinion. Addressing Mr Kemble, he said that from what had just before fallen from him it appeared that if Mr Kemble had thought proper, he (Grimaldi) might have had Covent Garden for his benefit, even gratuitously; but that presuming Grimaldi had not the power of taking a benefit at Drury Lane, he had refused him, which was not the conduct of a friend, and was very unlike the treatment he had expected to receive. Grimaldi then left the room, and never saw either gentleman again. Upon cool reflection he was inclined to consider that Mr Kemble had some private and very good reasons arising out of the management of the theatre for acting as he had done, which there is little doubt was the case, as he could have neither had the intention nor the wish to injure a man whom he invariably treated with kindness and courtesy.

The three gentlemen who were mentioned in conjunction with Miss Kelly exerted themselves with so much energy that Grimaldi's benefit far exceeded his most sanguine expectations. In addition to the most effective company of the theatre were secured the services of Miss Kelly, Madam Fearon, Miss Fanny Ayton, Miss Love, Mathews, Keeley and Bartley, besides an immense number of pantomime performers who crowded to offer their aid, and among whom were Barnes, Southby, Ridgway and his two sons, and young Grimaldi. Mr James Wallack arranged everything, and exerted himself as much as he could have done if the night had been his own. The bill ran thus:

Mr GRIMALDI'S FAREWELL BENEFIT

On Friday, June 27th, 1828,
will be performed
JONATHAN IN ENGLAND
after which
A MUSICAL MELANGE
To be succeeded by
THE ADOPTED CHILD,
and concluded with
HARLEQUIN HOAX,
In which Mr Grimaldi will act clown in one scene,
sing a song, and speak his
FAREWELL ADDRESS

It was greatly in favour of the benefit that Covent Garden had closed the night before; the pit and galleries were completely filled in less than half-an-hour after opening the doors, the boxes were very good from the first, and at half-price were as crowded as the other parts of the house. In the last piece Grimaldi acted one scene, but being wholly unable to stand, went through it seated upon a chair. Even in this distressing condition he retained enough of his old humour to succeed in calling down repeated shouts of merriment and laughter. The song, too, in theatrical language, 'went' as well as ever; and at length, when the pantomime approached its termination, he made his appearance before the audience in his private dress, amidst thunders of applause. As soon as silence could be obtained and he could muster up sufficient courage to speak he advanced to the foot-lights, and delivered, as well as his emotions would permit, the following farewell address:

Ladies and Gentlemen: In putting off the Clown's garment, allow me to drop also the Clown's taciturnity, and address you in a few particular sentences. I entered early on this course of life, and leave it prematurely. Eight-and-forty years only have passed over my head—but I am going as fast down the hill of life as that older Joe—John Anderson. Like vaulting ambition, I have overleaped myself, and pay the penalty in an advanced old age. If I have now any aptitude for tumbling, it is through bodily infirmity, for I am worse on my feet than I used to be on my head. It is four years since I jumped my last jump—filched my last oyster—boiled my last sausage—and set in for retirement. Not quite so well provided for, I must acknowledge, as in the days of my Clownship, for then, I dare say, some of you remember, I used to have a fowl in one pocket and sauce for it in the other.

Tonight has seen me assume the motley for a short time—it clung to my skin as I took it off, and the old cap and bells rang mournfully as I quitted them forever.

With the same respectful feelings as ever do I find myself in your presence—in the presence of my last audience—this kindly assemblage so happily contradicting the adage that a favourite has no friends. For the benevolence that brought you hither—accept, ladies and gentlemen, my warmest and most grateful thanks, and believe, that of one and all, Joseph Grimaldi takes a double leave, with a farewell on his lips, and a tear in his eyes.

Farewell! That you and yours may ever enjoy that greatest earthly good—health, is the sincere wish of your faithful and obliged servant. God bless you all!

It was with no trifling difficulty that Grimaldi reached the conclusion of this little speech, although the audience cheered loudly and gave him every possible expression of encouragement and sympathy. When he had finished, he still stood in the same place, bewildered and motionless, his feelings being so greatly excited that the little power illness had left him wholly deserted him In this condition he stood for a minute or two, when Mr Harley, who was at the side scene, kindly advanced and led him off the stage, assisted by his son. As a token of his respect and gratitude Grimaldi took off a new wig which he wore on the occasion and presented it to Mr Harley, together with the original address, which he held in his hand.

Having been led into a private room, and strengthened with a couple of glasses of Madeira, Grimaldi had to sustain another and a scarcely less severe trial in receiving the farewells and good wishes of his old associates. The street was thronged with people who were waiting to see him come out, and as he entered the coach which stood at the stage door they gave him three hearty cheers, amid which he drove off. But all was not over yet, for hundreds followed the vehicle until it reached his house, and upon getting out he was again hailed with a similar overwhelming shout of approbation and regard ; nor could the crowd be prevailed upon to disperse until he had appeared on the top of the steps, and made his farewell bow.

Grimaldi was too exhausted and nervous after the trying scenes through which he had just passed to make any calculation that night of what the benefit had produced ; but the next day, being somewhat recovered, he found the result to be as follows. The house cost him two hundred and ten pounds, the printing seventy pounds more, making the expense two hundred and eighty pounds. The money taken at the doors amounted to rather more than four hundred pounds, besides which he sold one hundred and fifty pounds worth of tickets, making a total of five hundred and fifty pounds. Deducting the expenses, the clear profits of the benefit amounted to two hundred and seventy pounds. There was another source of great profit, which must not be forgotten, namely, the number of anonymous communications Grimaldi received, enclosing sums of money and wishing him a happy retirement. He received six letters each containing twenty pounds, eleven containing ten pounds, and sixteen containing one pound each. Thus, the amount forwarded by unknown hands was no less than three hundred pounds which, added to the amount of profits just mentioned, makes the gross sum realised by this last benefit five hundred and eighty pounds, besides the three hundred and fifteen pounds which he had cleared at Sadler's Wells.

The highest tribute that can be paid to those who in secret forwarded their munificent donations, or to those who rendered him their valuable professional assistance, or to that large number who came forward to cheer the last public moments of a man who had so often, and so successfully, beguiled their leisure hours, is, that they smoothed the hard bed of premature and crippled old age, and rendered the slow decline of a life, scarcely in years past its prime, peaceful and contented. This benefit closed Grimaldi's theatrical existence, and filled his heart with deep and lasting emotions of gratitude.

CHAPTER SIXTEEN

ONLY ONE MORE CIRCUMSTANCE connected with Grimaldi's theatrical existence remains to be told, and to that one we most anxiously and emphatically invite the attention of all who admire the drama—and what man of thought or feeling does not?—of all those who devote themselves to the cause of real charity and of all those who now, reaping large gains from the exercise of a glittering and dazzling profession, forget that youth and strength will not last for ever, and that the more intoxicating their triumphs now, the more probable is the advent of a time of adversity and decay.

Counting over his gains, and dwelling upon his helpless state, Grimaldi was not long in finding that even now, whenever his little salary at Sadler's Wells should cease, he would not have adequate means of support. There was only one source to which he could apply for relief, and to that source he at once turned. It is well known to all our readers that two charitable societies exist in London, called the Drury Lane and Covent Garden Theatrical Funds. They are distinct bodies, but were established with the same great and benevolent object. Every actor who, throughout his engagement at either of the large theatres, contributes a certain portion of his earnings to one of these funds, is entitled, if he should ever be reduced to the necessity of seeking it, to an annuity in proportion to the time for which he has contributed. To one of these most excellent institutions—the Drury Lane Theatrical Fund—Grimaldi had belonged for more than thirty years, promoting its interests not merely by his subscriptions but by every means in his power. Feeling that in his hour of need and distress he had some claim upon its funds, he addressed the secretary and stated the situation to which he was reduced. Early on the following morning Grimaldi was visited by the gentleman to whom he had applied, who informed him that he was awarded a pension of one hundred pounds a year for the remainder of his life, and that the secretary was deputed to pay him immediately the amount of one quarter in advance. Grimaldi's fears vanished at once, and he felt that want at all events could never be his portion.

The unfortunate young man to whom allusion has been frequently made in the course of the last few pages was, as may easily be imagined, one of the chief sources of Grimaldi's care and trouble in his latter days. After remaining in his father's house for two months (in 1828) in a state of madness, he grew better, left one night to attend Sadler's Wells, where he was engaged, and was seen no more until the middle of the following year, when he again presented himself in a state of insanity and was conveyed to his own lodgings and carefully attended. The next year Young Grimaldi was dismissed from Sadler's Wells on account of his dissolute conduct; engaged at Drury Lane with a salary of eight pounds per week, most favourably received, and discharged at the end of the first season for his profligacy and drunkenness. After this, he obtained an engagement for a month at the Pavilion in Whitechapel Road, but left that theatre also in disgrace, and fell into the lowest state of wretchedness and poverty. His dress had fallen to rags, his feet were thrust into two worn out slippers, his face was pale with disease and squalid with dirt and want, and he was steeped in degradation. The man who might have earned with ease, with comfort, and respectability, from six to seven hundred pounds a year, and have raised himself to far greater gains by common providence and care, was reduced to such a dreadful state of destitution and filth that even his own parents could scarcely recognise him.

Young Grimaldi was again received, and again found a home with his sick father. At Christmas, 1829, he obtained a situation at the Coburg through the kindness of Davidge, and there he remained until Easter, 1830, when he took the benefit of the Insolvent Debtors' Act to relieve himself from the creditors who were hunting him down. His support in prison and contingent expenses, amounting to forty pounds, were all paid by his father. He next accepted an engagement at Edinburgh, which turned out a failure; and another at Manchester, at Christmas, 1830, by which he gained a few pounds. He then returned to the Coburg, where he might have almost permanently remained but for his own misconduct, which once again cast him on the world.

In the following autumn, the son again presented himself at his father's door, reduced to a state of beggary and want not to be described. His mother, who had suffered greatly from his misdeeds, outrageous conduct, and gross and violent abuse, besought his father not to receive him or aid him again, remembering how much he had already wasted the small remnant of his means only to minister to his extravagance and folly. But Grimaldi could not witness his son's helpless and miserable state without compassion, and he was once more forgiven, once more became an inmate of the house, and remained there in a state of utter dependence.

In 1832 Sadler's Wells was let out for one season to Mrs Fitzwilliam and Mr W H Williams. They retained Grimaldi for some little time, but finding that he must be dismissed very shortly, he made preparations for meeting the consequent reduction of his income by giving up the house in which he had lived for several years and taking a cottage at Woolwich, whither he had an additional inducement to retire, in the hope that change of air might prove beneficial to his wife, who had already been ill for some time. They repaired to their new house in the latter end of September, and in the beginning of November the son received a letter from a brother actor, entreating him to perform for a benefit at Sadler's Wells. His reception was so cordial and his acting so good, that on the very same evening, notwithstanding all that had previously passed, he was offered an engagement for the ensuing Christmas at the Coburg, and the next day on his return to Woolwich he communicated the intelligence to his parents. The following day was Young Joe's birthday; he completed his thirtieth year that morning; and before it had passed over, the then lessee of the Queen's Theatre waited upon him and offered him an engagement for a short time at a weekly salary of four pounds. He agreed to take it and arranged to begin on the following Monday, November, twenty-fifth, in a part called Black Caesar.

It was sorely against his father's will that Young Joe went to fulfil this engagement, for his health had been waning for some time, and Grimaldi was fearful that he might relapse into his old habits. However, Young Joe was determined to go, and borrowing some money from his father, as was his usual wont, he left Woolwich on the Sunday morning. On the Wednesday Grimaldi had occasion to go to town, and eagerly embraced it as an opportunity for seeing his son, to whom, despite all the anxiety and losses Young Joe had caused him, he was still most tenderly attached. He wrote to him, naming the friend's house at which he would be found, and the young man came. He looked in excellent health, was in high spirits, and boasted of his success in terms which were justified by its extent. Shortly after dinner he left, observing that as he had to appear in the first scene of the first piece he had no time to lose. His father never saw him more.

Grimaldi returned to Woolwich next day, and anxiously hoped on Sunday to see the misguided man at dinner, as he had promised. The day passed away, but Young Joe did not come; a few more days elapsed, and then Grimaldi received an intimation from a stranger that his son was ill. He immediately wrote to a friend (Mr Glendenning, the printer) requesting him to ascertain the nature of his indisposition, which he feared was only the effect of some new intemperance, and if it should appear necessary, to procure Young Joe medical assistance. For two days Grimaldi heard nothing; but this did not alarm him, for he entertained no doubt that his son's illness would disappear when the fumes of the liquor he had drunk had evaporated.

On December the eleventh a friend came to Grimaldi's house as he was sitting by his wife's bed, to which she was confined by illness, and when, with much difficulty, he had descended to the parlour, he was told with great care and delicacy that his son was dead. In one instant every feeling of decrepitude or bodily weakness left him; his limbs recovered their original vigour; all his lassitude and debility vanished; a difficulty of breathing under which he had long laboured disappeared, and starting from his seat he rushed to his wife's chamber, tearing without the least difficulty up a flight of stairs, which, a quarter-of-an-hour before, it had taken him ten minutes to climb. He hurried to her bedside, told her that her son was dead, heard her first passionate exclamation of grief, and, falling into a chair, was once again an enfeebled and crippled old man.

The remains of the young man were interred a few days afterwards in the burial-ground of Whitfield's Tabernacle in Tottenham Court Road; but some circumstances apparently of a suspicious nature being afterwards rumoured about, and it being whispered that marks of blows had been seen upon his head by those who laid him out, an inquest was held upon the young man's body. Grimaldi states that the body was exhumed: from some passages in the newspapers of the day, it would appear that the body was not disinterred. Be this as it may, it was proved before the coroner that Young Grimaldi's death had arisen from the natural consequences of a mis-spent life; that his body was covered with a fearful inflammation; and that he had died in a state of wild and furious madness, rising from his bed and dressing himself in stage costume to act snatches of the parts to which he had been most accustomed, and requiring to be held down to die, by strong manual force. This closing scene of his life took place at a public house in Pitt Street, Tottenham Court Road, and here the dismal tragedy ended. It was long before Grimaldi in any degree recovered from this great shock; his wife never did. She lingered on in a state of great suffering for two years afterwards, until death happily relieved her.

Grimaldi was now left alone in the world. He had always been a domesticated man, delighting in nothing more than in the society of his relations and friends; and the condition of solitary desolation in which he was now left nearly drove him into a state of melancholy madness. His crippled limbs and broken bodily health rendered it necessary to his existence that he should have an attentive nurse, and, occasionally at least, cheerful society; finding his situation wholly insupportable, he resolved to return to town and wrote to a friend whose wife was his only remaining relative, to procure a small house for him in his own neighbourhood, where he too had lived so long and happily. A neat little dwelling next door to this friend's house in Southampton Street, Pentonville, was taken and furnished for Grimaldi, and thither he removed without more delay. Many of his old friends came from time to time to cheer him with a few minutes' conversation, and he experienced the warmest and kindest treatment from his neighbours and from Mr Richard Hughes, who bore in mind his promise to his dying sister to the last moment of Grimaldi's life.

Grimaldi concludes his *Memoirs* by taking a more cheerful view of his condition than could well have been expected of a man suffering so much, and ends in these words:

My histrionic acquaintance frequently favour me with their company, when we together review past scenes, and contrast them with those of the present time. My esteemed friend, Alfred Bunn, has been with me this very day, and I expect to see my amiable patroness, if she will permit me to call her so, Miss Kelly, tomorrow.

In my solitary hours—and in spite of all the kindness of my friends I have many of them—my thoughts often dwell upon the past; and there is one circumstance which always affords me unmitigated satisfaction; it is simply that I cannot recollect one single instance in which I have intentionally wronged man, woman, or child, and this gives me great satisfaction and comfort.

This is the eighteenth of December, 1836. I was born on the eighteenth of December, 1779, and consequently have completed my fifty-seventh year.

Life is a game we are bound to play—
The wise enjoy it, fools grow sick of it;
Losers, we find, have the stakes to pay,
The winners may laugh, for that's the trick of it.

J GRIMALDI

Grimaldi died on the thirty-first of May 1837, having survived the completion of the last chapter of his biography by just five months, during which his health had considerably improved, although his bodily energies and physical powers had remained in the same state of hopeless prostration. Having gradually recovered from the effects of the severe mental shocks which had crowded upon him in his decline, he had regained his habitual serenity and cheerfulness, and appeared likely to live and even to enjoy life—incompatible with all enjoyment as his condition would seem to have been—for many years. Grimaldi had no other wish than to be happy in the society of his old friends; and uttered no other complaint than that, in their absence, he sometimes found his solitude heavy and irksome. He looked forward to the publication of his manuscript with an anxiety which it is impossible to describe, and imagined that the day on which he exhibited it in a complete form to his friends would be the proudest of his life. He was destined never to experience this harmless gratification; the sudden dissolution which deprived him of it mercifully released him from all the pains and suffering which could not fail to have been, sooner or later, the attendants upon that state of death in life to which he had been untimely reduced.

It had been Grimaldi's habit for some time previous to his death to spend a portion of each evening at a tavern hard by, where the society of a few respectable persons, resident in the neighbourhood, in some measure compensated him for the many long hours he spent by his lonely fireside. Utterly bereft of the use of his limbs, he used to be carried backwards and forwards (he had only a few doors to go) on the shoulders of a man. On the night of his death, he was carried home in the usual manner and, cheerfully bidding his companion good night, observed that he should be ready for him on the morrow at the customary time. Grimaldi had not long been in bed, when his housekeeper, fancying she heard a noise in the room, hurried down, but all was quiet: she went in again later in the night, and found him dead. The body was cold, for he had been dead some hours. A coroner's inquest was held on the following day. The testimony of the medical gentlemen who had been promptly called in fully established the fact that Grimaldi's death had arisen from causes purely natural; and the jury at once returned a verdict that he had died by the visitation of God. Grimaldi was buried on the ensuing Monday, June the sixth, in the burying-ground of St James's Chapel, on Pentonville Hill. In the next grave lie the bones of his friend, Mr Charles Dibdin, so frequently mentioned in these volumes; the author of many of the pieces in which he shone in his best day's and of many of the songs with which he was wont to set his audience in a roar.

Any attempted summary of Grimaldi's peculiarities in this place would be an impertinence. There are many who remember him, and they need not be told how rich his humour was—to those who do not recollect him in his great days, it would be impossible to convey any adequate idea of his extraordinary performances. There are no standards to compare him with or models to judge him by—all his excellences were his own, and there are none resembling them among the pantomime actors of the present day. It is no disparagement to all or any, to say, that the genuine droll, the grimacing, filching, irresistible Clown left the stage with Grimaldi, and though often heard of, has never since been seen.

In private, Grimaldi was a general favourite, not only among his equals but with his superiors and inferiors. That he was a man of the kindest heart and the most child-like simplicity, nobody who has read the foregoing pages can for a moment doubt. He was innocent of all caution in worldly matters, and has been known, on the seller's warranty, to give forty guineas for a gold watch, which, as it subsequently turned out, would have been dear at ten. Among many acts of private goodness may be mentioned—although he shrunk from the slightest allusion to the story—his release of a brother actor from Lancaster jail, under circumstances which showed a pure benevolence of heart and delicacy of feeling that would have done honour to a prince.

With far more temptations to indulge in the pleasures of the table than most men encounter, Grimaldi was through life remarkably temperate, never having been seen, indeed, in a state of intoxication. But he was a great eater, as most pantomime actors are who enjoy good health and abstain from dram-drinking; and it was supposed at the time of his disease that an attack of indigestion consequent upon too hearty a supper at too late an hour materially hastened, if it did not actually occasion, his death.

Many readers will ridicule the idea of a Clown being a man of great feeling and sensibility: Grimaldi was so, notwithstanding, and suffered most severely from the afflictions which befell him. The loss of his first wife, to whom he had been long and devotedly attached, preyed upon his mind to a greater or less extent for many years. The reckless career and dreadful death of his only son bowed him down with grief. The young man's notorious conduct had embittered the best portion of Grimaldi's existence: and his sudden death, when a better course seemed opening before him, had well-nigh terminated his unhappy father's days. But although, in the weakened state in which he then was, the sad event preying alike upon his mind and body, changed Grimaldi's appearance in a few weeks to that of a shrunken imbecile old man; and although, when he had in some measure recovered from this heavy blow, he had to mourn the loss of his wife, with whom he had lived happily for more than thirty years; he survived the trials to which he had been exposed, and lived to recover his cheerfulness and peace. Deprived of all power of motion; doomed to bear, at a time of life when he might reasonably have looked forward to many years of activity and exertion, the worst bodily evils of the most helpless old age; condemned to drag out the remainder of his days in a solitary chamber, when all those who make up the sum of home were cold in death, his existence would seem to have been a weary one indeed; but he was patient and resigned under all these trials, and in time grew contented, and even happy.

This strong endurance of griefs so keen and reverses so poignant may perhaps teach more strongly than a hundred homilies, that there are no afflictions which time will not soften and fortitude overcome. Let those who smile at the deduction of so trite a moral from the biography of a Clown reflect that the fewer the resources of a man's own mind, the greater his merit in rising superior to misfortune. Let them remember, too, that in this case the light and life of a brilliant theatre were exchanged in an instant for the gloom and sadness of a dull sick-room.

AFTERWORD

In 1836 JOSEPH GRIMALDI completed about four hundred pages of autobiographical notes—largely dictated—on his fifty-eighth birthday. He came to realise that his bulky, garrulous manuscript—"exceedingly voluminous", says Dickens—could not be published as it stood; he was apparently recommended to find a collaborator; and three months later he made a contract with a prolific but obscure journalist and hack playwright, Thomas Egerton Wilks (1812–54), to "rewrite, revise and correct" his *Memoirs*. This Grub Street journeyman undertook to have the book ready for publication by the 1st of December, in return for half the proceeds, but within two months Grimaldi was dead and Wilks had to finish the job on his own. Not only did he cut it heavily and condense it, but he interpolated anecdotes 'gleaned' from the Clown's conversation, without being able to verify them and without indicating what Grimaldi wrote and what Wilks remembered. He also, lamentably, transposed the whole narrative into reported speech, so that the Clown was scarcely ever permitted to speak in the first person singular.

Wilks finished his version of the *Memoirs* in September, and offered them to Richard Bentley (1794–1871) for publication. Although the manuscript was badly edited and still much too long, Bentley bought it, secured the copyright from Grimaldi's executor, Richard Hughes, and asked Charles Dickens to re-edit it. Dickens, then twenty-five, had moved out of Wilks's class by the success in the previous year of his volume of collected pseudonymous pieces, *Sketches by Boz*, and the serialisation of *The Posthumous Papers of the Pickwick Club*; and when Bentley approached him over the Wilks-Grimaldi manuscript, *Oliver Twist* was still appearing in monthly instalments in *Bentley's Miscellany*, which Dickens edited and which Bentley had launched that year.

Dickens was at first reluctant to embark on the job. He wrote to Bentley on the 30th of October 1837 that:

I have thought the matter over, and looked it over, too. It is very badly done, and is so redolent of twaddle that I fear I cannot take it up on any conditions to which you would be disposed to accede. I should require to be assured three hundred pounds in the first instance without any reference to the sale—and as I should be bound to stipulate in addition that the book should not be published in numbers I think it would scarcely serve your purpose.

Bentley, however, was undeterred; he agreed to Dickens' terms, advancing him three hundred pounds on one half of the profits, minus production costs; and Dickens signed a contract at the end of November, undertaking to deliver a new version *within two months*—as long as it made two post octavo volumes. (Bentley also undertook to pay eighty-five pounds to Richard Hughes for the use of the original material.)

Dickens went at it in a rush, to meet his deadline. A week after the contract was signed, he said that: "I think I am bringing the points out as well as it is possible to do from Mr Wilks's dreary twaddle." Two days later: "The Grimaldi grows under the alterations much better than I supposed possible."

By the 5th of January, he had actually finished the text, except for his introductory and concluding chapters—by which "I had set great store". Like the original author, Dickens apparently dictated most of it: John Forster, Dickens' biographer, says that he often found Dickens' father "in exalted enjoyment of the office of amanuensis". Although Forster may be right in saying that Dickens "did not write a line of this biography", this does *not* mean that it was mainly the work of his father—a common error which I repeated in my biography of Grimaldi. Readers will notice, as the first reviewers did, the Dickensian touches in the narrative. The novelist explained his method in a letter to Dr J A Wilson (1795–1882), senior physician at St George's, and among the doctors who had treated Grimaldi. Dr Wilson had, it seems, written to Dickens, offering his own memories of the clown; but his letter came just before the review copies were dispatched. Dickens replied:

I am very happy to find that I had not formed a wrong estimate of the poor fellow's character, I have merely been editing another account, and telling some of the stories in my own way, but I was much struck by the many traits of kindheartedness scattered through the book, and have given it that colouring throughout.

The *Memoirs of Joseph Grimaldi* was published a few weeks later in February 1838, under the editorship of 'Boz', without notes. In 1846 a new edition was published with notes complied by Charles Whitehead (1804–62). He was forty-two when the *Memoirs* were first published. A novelist, dramatist and poet of early promise, he won a short-lived reputation as a humorist by his anonymous *Autobiography of Jack Ketch* (1834); and his novel

Richard Savage (1842) won some acclaim. He was also a close friend of Dickens, and recommended him for the job which turned into *The Pickwick Papers*. Whitehead wrecked his career through alcoholism, emigrated to Australia in 1857 and died there in destitution.

It seems that neither Dickens nor Whitehead ever referred to the original Grimaldi manuscript, which remained in the hands of Richard Hughes, but merely worked on Wilks's truncated and rewritten version. Dickens' 'perfect fever' of enthusiasm was apparently not strong enough to make him consult the source, or attempt to describe Grimaldi's clownship and the pantomimes in which he played. Not surprisingly, at least one reviewer suggested that Dickens did not appear to have seen Grimaldi. The novelist was, indeed, only ten when Joe retired; yet he took pains to point out defensively—in a letter to *Bentley's Miscellany* which remained unpublished—that he had been brought up from the country in 1819 or 1820 to see Grimaldi, "in whose honour I am informed I clapped my hands with great preciosity"; and he claimed that he had seen Grimaldi act in 1823, although this must have been in some isolated performance at a benefit show, for the Clown made only a few fleeting appearances after his retirement in 1822.

The original manuscript disappeared from sight after it was put up for sale in London in 1874, at a hundred guineas—a price partly accounted for by the addition of over sixty portraits plus many playbills, drawings, views of theatres, etc, all bound in red morocco. It was puffed in the catalogue as "perhaps as genuine and faithful an autobiography as ever was written, full, frank and delightfully clownish, childlike and simple—the cream of all which last-named recommendations the two able editors who edited *and* polished it for the press, thirty-five years ago, neglected to skim off. The clown was as true to his pen as he was to his calling."

RICHARD FINDLATER